# Praise for Some Of Us Are Brave

This is an outstanding, excellent, informative compilation of interviews. Yes, "Some of Us are Brave," but after finishing this inspiring book, you will also agree that "Some of Us are Brilliant", "Some of Us are Revolutionary...."

> – Gerald Horne, author, *Race Woman: The Lives of Shirley Graham Du Bois*

Radio tends to be such an ephemeral medium. That is why this collection of interviews and conversations conducted with fascinating women by Thandisizwe Chimurenga over many years is important for preserving that historical record.

> – Firoze Manji, Adjunct Professor, Institute of African Studies, Carleton University, Ottawa, Canada

Step into a world of unyielding strength and unwavering resilience as *Some of Us Are Brave: Interviews and Conversations with Sistas in Life and Struggle* takes you on an extraordinary journey through nearly a decade of insightful interviews from the groundbreaking Black women's radio program of the same name. From 2003 to 2011, renowned journalist and commentator Thandisizwe Chimurenga captivated audiences with her engaging conversations and deep resonant voice, shining a powerful spotlight on the lives of exceptional Black women activists, writers, and educators.

Through Chimurenga's skillful interviews and her genius in excavating and bringing powerful stories told by her contemporaries to the forefront, luminaries such as Ella Baker, Ida B. Wells, Pearl Cleage, Paula Giddings, Ava DuVernay, Alice Walker, Assata Shakur, Elaine Brown and many others fiercely reveal their truths while flooding their humanity onto these pages. These women are not mere storytellers; they are architects of change, guardians of truth, and beacons of hope. Each of them share not only the struggles of the past, but the determination of the present and the hope for Black futures. Their stories highlight the intersections of race, gender, and class, shedding light on the common threads that tie together communities across continents. They expose the systems of power and oppression that perpetuate inequality worldwide. By exploring our interconnectedness, they inspire readers to reflect on their own roles in dismantling these systems and forging a more just and equitable future for all.

Like her mentor Ida B Wells before her, Chimurenga's voice – the intentionality of the interviews she conducted, her power in curating the stories being told, the dissemination of these Black women's voices, her own unique and authoritative perspective, and her love for Black people – dismantles the very disinformation that would seek to destroy us. This book of interviews brings Truth home, settling it in the pit of our bellies to digest, nurture and heal.

At a time when teaching the purview of being Black in America is being criminalized, SOUAB pierces through the veil of rhetoric and propaganda, delivering profound and unfiltered Truth. As an invaluable resource for educators and students alike, this collection offers a sanctuary for critical thinking and transformative learning.

The tapestry of voices woven within these pages celebrates the unique journeys and perspectives of Black women, presenting an unwavering testament to our indomitable spirit.

> – Shaunelle Curry, Founder, Media Done Responsibly; Author, *Shairi's Journey*; Adjunct Professor, California State University, Los Angeles Departments of TV, Film, Media and Pan-African Studies

This latest offering from journalist Thandi Chimurenga is something that Florida Governor Ron DiSantis would ban in a heartbeat and try and create a law banning Thandi and the powerful women she features in this book. To put it simply, this book is fiya and will cause a lot of discomfort to those who hate Black women and want to see Black history and Black liberation be erased. This won't happen on Sister Thandi's watch. She's the Ida B Wells of our time who carries keen insight, unapologetic love for our people and lots of receipts to chin check haters and institutional racists.

> – David "Davey D" Cook, Professor, Africana Studies, San Francisco State University and Host, Hard Knock Radio, KPFA, Pacifica-Berkeley

# SOME OF US ARE BRAVE

*Interviews and Conversations
with Sistas on Life, Art and Struggle*
2003–2016

Volume 1:
The Shoulders on Which We Stand
Art for Our Sake

*Thandisizwe Chimurenga*

Daraja Press

Published by
Daraja Press
https://darajapress.com
Wakefield, Quebec, Canada

Second printing: January 2024

ISBN: 9781990263118

Cover and interior design: Kate McDonnell

Library and Archives Canada Cataloguing in Publication

Title: Some of us are brave : interviews and conversations with sistas on life, art and struggle, 2003-2016 / Thandisizwe Chimurenga.

Names: Chimurenga, Thandisizwe, editor.

Description: Includes bibliographical references. | Contents: Volume 1: The shoulders on which we stand art for our sake.

Identifiers: Canadiana 20230482341 | ISBN 9781990263118 (v. 1 ; softcover)

Subjects: LCSH: Women, Black—United States—Interviews. | LCGFT: Interviews.

Classification: LCC HQ1163 .C45 2023 | DDC 305.48/896073—dc23

"'Tis woman's strongest vindication for speaking that the world needs to hear her voice. It would be subversive of every human interest that the cry of one-half the human family be stifled. ... The world has had to limp along with the wobbling gait and one-sided hesitancy of a man with one eye. Suddenly the bandage is removed from the other eye and the whole body is filled with light. It sees a circle where before it saw a segment. The darkened eye restored, every member rejoices with it."

– Anna Julia Cooper,
*A Voice From the South, by a Black Woman of the South*

It is the mission of SOUAB *(Some of Us Are Brave)* to provide an empowering space for women of Afrikan descent – to assist them in finding their voices and speaking their truths, their experiences and their perspectives to the world; to be a resource for the communities from which we come; and to make a contribution to the global movement for racial, economic, political and social justice and peace.

– Mission Statement, *Some of Us Are Brave*

# Table of contents

## The Shoulders on Which We Stand

## Art for Our Sake

# INTRODUCTION
Thandisizwe Chimurenga

**Volume One**
*The Shoulders on Which We Stand*
*Art for Our Sake*

*"Cuando una mujer negra habla, prest'atencion"*

One day in late 2003 I was talking with Armando Gudino, then-program director of radio station KPFK (Pacifica-Los Angeles), in North Hollywood. A tall, heavyset Chicano with glasses, mustache and goatee, "Mando" would occasionally shave his head bald giving the appearance of the stereotypical, intimidating 'East Los Vato'. At some point in the conversation Mando said to me, *"Cuando una mujer negra habla, presta atencion,"* which he then translated as: "When a Black woman speaks, pay attention."

I remember the way he said it: with this matter-of-factness. It seemed, to me, he was saying it with the conviction and the seriousness that you repeat old folk wisdom that has been handed down thru the generations.

*Now, it could very well be that he was NOT saying it that way, and that I am only imagining he said it that way.* But that is what I remember of it. That is how I remember it. And I have remembered those words ever since: "When a Black woman speaks, pay attention."

I probably remember it because we know for a fact that the world does not pay enough attention to what Black women say.

It's why Cooperation Jackson, a Black self-determination and economic democracy experiment in Jackson, Mississippi, stresses human rights budgeting. "What would the budgets of municipal governments look like if Black women came up with them? Not "had a say in them," but actually created them?" They might provide a vision of what our communities truly need for safety and security.

It's why #TrustBlackWomen was initiated; to affirm the autonomy, respect, integrity, and dignity of Black women and their reproductive health decisions.

It's why #BlackLivesMatter, social media hashtag and movement in the streets, resonated and still resonates with Black people the world over: Stop killing our people. We keep us safe. We must love and protect one another.

*"Cuando una mujer negra habla, presta'tencion."*

Since we knew our purpose was to center the voices of Black women, I suggested to the group *When and Where We Enter*, from Paula Giddings' book on Black women's history here in the U.S., or *Some Of Us Are Brave* after the groundbreaking anthology on Black Women's Studies edited by Akasha Gloria Hull, Patricia Bell-Scott and Barbara Smith. The group chose the latter and we debuted on the airwaves of KPFK 90.7 FM-Los Angeles as *Some Of Us Are Brave: A Black Womens' Radio Program* (SOUAB) on June 10, 2003. It was founded by Black women, many of us activists, who understood that our voices, views and experiences had been marginalized – 'disappeared' in the words of journalist Jill Nelson – from both mainstream and alternative media. For eight years, SOUAB "provided an empowering space for women of Afrikan descent" on the airwaves of Southern California. We took Mother Anna Julia Cooper's words to heart.

*Some of Us Are Brave: A Black Womens' Radio Program* (SOUAB) went on the airwaves of 90.7 FM in Los Angeles on June 10, 2003. It was founded by Black women, many of us activists, who understood that our voices, views and experiences had been marginalized – 'disappeared' in the words of journalist Jill Nelson – from both mainstream and alternative media. For eight years, SOUAB "provided an empowering space for women of Afrikan descent" on the airwaves of Southern California. We took Mother Anna Julia Cooper's words to heart.

The voices of Black women on a variety of subjects, some widely known some not, will be found within these pages. These volumes exist as part of an effort to place intellectual production into our own Black hands and out of the hands of foundationally anti-Black institutions. It is but a small contribution to the literature on Black women's lives and thought primarily here in the United States. This documenting and preserving is a historical record and is proof that not only have we been here, we matter: to ourselves, our families, the communities from whence we come and the diaspora.

SOUAB ignited something in me. I'm so glad I heeded LaTrice Dixon's call for a group of Black women to approach KPFK-Pacifica about being on air. Once I learned how to do audio production I invested in equipment and kept it on me wherever I went, ever-ready to "capture some sound." It's probably not hard to tell which interviews/presentations herein come from my first time venturing out into the world of radio, as evidenced by some of my questions and responses to the guests.

The majority of transcribed interviews/presentations contained here (Volume 1: The Shoulders on Which We Stand and Art for Our Sake, 2003-2016) were conducted and recorded by myself. They primarily aired on *Some of Us Are Brave* between 2003 and 2011. A few of the interviews and presentations transcribed here were recorded by me and aired elsewhere such as on *Beneath The Surface* or other programming on KPFK; the *Women's Magazine* on KPFA, the Pacifica sister station in Berkeley, California; WRFG community radio in Atlanta, Georgia; and one or two were planned to air and ended up gathering dust.

One presentation – that of Elaine Brown – was recorded by an anarchist radio collective that made it freely available and was used as part of a KPFK radio program that I produced. Another presentation, that of Ramona Africa of the MOVE Organization, was given to a South Los Angeles audience and transcribed by white allies. It was never aired on *SOUAB* but since I had a hand in organizing it I've included it here.

Both the SPearl Sharp conversation with Ruby Dee and Nora Davis Day and Ellene Miles speaking with Tina Mabry were in my possession, and both SPearl and Ellene graciously gave their permission to print the transcripts here.

We tried to keep copies of every *SOUAB* program at the time that it aired. Sometimes we were successful or were able to get a copy at a later date, however, as a group, we never set up a centralized system or location for those copies. We never set up a de facto archive for *SOUAB*. Thus, this volume is made up of primarily of my own work.

*SOUAB* started out as a one-hour show. Internal radio station chaos eventually cut the show to 30 minutes. This explains why some interviews are longer than others. There are also instances where I was simply getting "sound bites" from individuals and may or may not have interviewed them at a later date.

Despite the absence of other Black women producers' work in this volume, trust me when I say that ALL who took the mic under the name of *Some of Us Are Brave* made a unique and great contribution to our world by amplifying the voices of Black women. *Asé!*

**Thandisizwe Chimurenga**
Los Angeles, CA
January 31, 2023

# ACKNOWLEDGMENTS

The founders of *Some of Us Are Brave* are Ayanna Canada; Crystal Blackcreek Carlisle; J. Evan Dunlap; Iyatunde Folayan (Latrice Dixon); Grayce Gadsen; Sister Charlene Muhammad; Sherri Ross; Nancy Webb and myself; *Some of Us Are Brave* team members and supporters, at different times, were the following: Iyanifa Fayomi Falade Aworeni; Kali Sampson Alexander; Angela Birdsong; Laini Coffee; Rhonda Dixon; Jan Robinson Flint; Haleemah Henderson; Zakiya Kyle; Ellene Miles; Kaia Niambi Shivers, S. Pearl Sharp, and Oya Kali. All of you, every last one of you, made an invaluable contribution. I salute you.

To former KPFK management Eva Georgia (General Manager) Armando Gudino (Program Director) and Nate Scott (Operations Manager): Thank You for cracking that door open.

*Many, Many Thanks and Tons of Love* to Dave Adelson, Kwazi Nkrumah and my late but great compañero, Fernando Velasquez.

A *"Good Bruthas Lookin' Out For The Sistas"* Award goes to sound engineers Mark Maxwell and Teddy Robinson; Extra dap to Teddy for hookin' up such a dope theme; and ABSOLUTELY POSITIVELY NOTHING BUT LOVE to all KPFK Listeners and Guests for rocking with us for all those years. You are greatly appreciated.

To Christabel Nsiah-Buadi and Joanne Griffith: I should've taken your advice way, way earlier. Thank You.

Tatyanna Wilkinson and Angie Birdsong: y'all some hardcore MVPs. Love You! Thank You!

To Nana Gyamfi and Dr. Karin L. Stanford, my sistas from other misters: Medase for your SistaShip;

*Huge Thanks* to the initial funders to get transcripts for this book:
Baba Kofi Opantiri (Rest In Eternal Peace)| Maryanne | Carlos | Merna | Michael | Dez | Frieda and Katherine | Sheba | Baye | Dorothy | Casey | Pamela | Ginna | Charles | Kali | Mama Geri | Zenzele | Jennifer | Lorelei | Lynn | Chris | Shawn | Yvette | and Makani

*Big, Huge, Ginormous Thanks* to Jesse Strauss, Frieda Werden and Makani Themba: your assistance with transcription has to be really, really shouted out. Like, REALLY.

To Firoze Manji and the staff and comrades of Daraja Press: thank you for your enthusiasm, your support and most of all your patience. *Nakupenda!*

Lastly, but most importantly, I thank Almighty Mother-Father God, my Ancestors and the Orishas/Obosum who continue to hold me up, and my brother Darryl and sister-in-law Miriam for their material support of my work. Love You! Thank You!

Inevitably, unfortunately, someone is always left out of an acknowledgment. Please charge it to my head and not my heart.

**Thandi**

# The Shoulders
# on Which We Stand

# Aminata Umoja:
# Revolution Without Women Ain't Happening

*This recording aired sometime in 2008 on "The Liberation Hour" on KPFK, a temporary Wednesday evening program that would eventually move to Saturdays under the name of "Freedom Now," hosted by Dedon Kamathi.*

• • •

**Thandisizwe Chimurenga:** We'll take a look at the future of our movements for self-determination and liberation by taking a look back, a look back to 1993 where tonight we will hear ... a presentation by Aminata Umoja of the New Afrikan People's Organization.

Aminata Umoja, founding member of the New Afrikan People's Organization currently resides in Atlanta, Georgia, where she is recognized as a Master Teacher in the Atlanta public schools system. Her high-spirited presentation entitled "Revolution Without Women Ain't Happening" was delivered at a conference entitled "New Afrikan Women in the Field: Cultivating Our Legacy of Struggle," held in Birmingham, Alabama in July 1993.

The spirit of Sankofa[1] says that in order to move forward, we must look back. There's no shame in going back and taking care of business being critical, analytical, looking at things with new and fresh eyes in order to

---

1 Sankofa is a word from the Akan language of Ghana that means "go back and get it." It is often used to refer to a cultural concept and practice that encourages people to look back to their cultural heritage in order to move forward and build a better future. Sankofa is often used as a symbol of African-American cultural heritage and is used in a wide range of contexts, from art and fashion to education and activism.

step with a sure footing into the future. Our movements for freedom, for reparations, for liberation, for independence, for social justice, do not have any place in them for homophobia, or for sexism. Homophobia and sexism are the twin sons of patriarchy. In the Black community, we have yet to have discussions on these topics in an honest and frank manner in which everyone can say what's on their mind.

**Aminata Umoja:** Free The Land! Free The Land! Free The Land!

We in the New Afrikan People's Organization say "Free the Land" because We recognize that you can't have freedom, you cannot have liberation, you cannot have independence unless you have a land base. So We talk about "Free The Land." Because that's what We plan to do. We're struggling for a free, independent New Afrika. Where Black people are in control; where self-determination is practiced in its highest form.

People know about "Free the Land." People in Algeria certainly know about "Free the Land," because they wanted to free their land from the French. And they were successful in freeing the land. The women participated on every level of struggle. And now Algeria is free, but its women are not.

In Zimbabwe, they understood that land had to be free. Again the sisters were right there – every level of struggle. Zimbabwe is free, but its women are still oppressed.

Even in Cuba, the progressive country of Cuba, they talked about "Free the Land." And again, they were able to win freedom. The Cuban revolution was successful. But the women of Cuba still have to fight against sexist oppression.

Participating in struggle is not enough. Sisters, We will not be free if We don't also fight against sexist oppression every step of the way. Now, i don't know about you, I love the Black man, but I don't love the Black man so much – and myself so little – that I'm willing to help him get his freedom at the expense of my own. I'm in this movement because I want to be free! I want my children to be free. My male child and my female child. And that's not going to happen unless We fight against sexist oppression. Unless We fight for revolution.

Now, revolution is a scary word to some people, but it simply means complete change. And all of us in this room should understand clearly that amerikkka has to be completely changed! We know that every time We see our people on the streets. We know that when We hear about our young men shooting each other down. We know it when We see our young women pregnant. We know it when We see our people addicted and hung up on crack and alcoholism. We know that when you get sick in amerikkka, the sicker you get, the more money you have to pay – what a sick country!

So, if you love your people – whether you be a revolutionary or a progressive – you have to talk about complete change. And complete change is revolution! And in the New Afrikan People's Organization that's the kind of change We're talkin' about. We're not talking about just land and independence. We're talkin' about a place where all people can live in freedom. Where the men and women of our nation, and the children can live in freedom. And in order to do this, We have to talk about sexist oppression. Or what We'll experience will be a political revolution. You see, a political revolution is when power changes hands.

But, nothing really changes for the people themselves. No, We can't just have a political revolution; We must have a political revolution and a social revolution. You see, We're not just struggling for land and independence, We're also struggling for liberation! We're not gonna follow the same mistakes as Zimbabwe and Cuba and Algeria. Oh no! Our people are too precious to us for that. No, so We understand in the New Afrikan People's Organization that We have to fight against sexist oppression.

Well, what is sexist oppression? Well, the sisters in the New Afrikan Women's Task force define sexist oppression – as it is practiced currently (and has been practiced historically) – as the subjugation of women by men. It's male supremacy. It's the belief that men are superior to women physically, culturally, mentally, economically --- on every level. It's male patriarchy. It's the belief that men are inherently superior, based solely on biology. That they're the natural leaders. Well, certainly many people believe that. i mean, the bible says "women be subservient to your husbands." The Qur'an says something similar. And how you gon' argue with God? How you gon' argue with Allah? This is sexist oppression.

You see, We have an intimate, intimate relationship with sexist oppression; because it is the first form of oppression We learn. We learn it from our mommas and daddies. We learn it at home. We learn it before We even find out about racism. We learn it before We even find out about classism. We learn that "the father is the head of the household," then come momma, then come the children. Some of you might be sayin' "Huh, she's only talking about two-parent households." Even in a single-parent household, you hear women talkin' 'bout, "You wait 'til i tell your Uncle Joe! You wait 'til i tell you grandfather – he's gonna deal with you!" You even hear sisters who are heading their households say to their male children, "You are the man of the house." Indicating that in some way, he is more special – more unique. And he is special and unique, but so is his sister!

We have an intimate relationship with sexist oppression. And because of that, it is difficult for us to get rid of it. Because it requires us to reject a part of our culture. But isn't that what We do? As revolutionaries? Isn't that why you're here today? Because you're trying to find out how you can promote the liberation of our people? Isn't that why many sisters stop pressing their hair? Isn't that why many of us drop 'Joy' and 'Van' and 'Bob', and take on 'Aminata' and 'Safiya' and 'Chokwe' and 'Akinyele'? Isn't that why We practice Kwanzaa? Because We're trying to rid ourselves of the negative aspects of our culture. As We struggle toward freedom. We're trying to develop a culture that's a liberating culture. A culture that will bring hope to the hopelessness. A culture that will push us forward. To Freedom! Not one that will maintain our oppression. That's what We're supposed to do – as revolutionaries.

Well, this requires a new perception of the world, doesn't it? Not the perception that you were taught, and i was taught in the amerikkkan system, but a new perception. One that's based on afrocentrism. One that's based on a history of resistance. One that's based on the fact that We are oppressed. You see, once you get this new perception, you start gettin' excited. Because then you can figure things out! You start beginning to realize that our people are not inherently ignorant. That our people are not inherently lazy. You're able to combat some of the discussions you hear in our community.

From my understanding, there's been a lot of talk about mass work - about dealing with the masses. When We talk to our people, what kinds of things do We hear? We hear things like, "Niggers ain't gon' ever do anything." We hear things like, "You know the Koreans can come over here, the Japanese can come over here, these other folks come over here and they develop their own businesses – Black people ain't never gon' get it together! Why can't We do that?" But once you understand what your place is in the world, once you understand that you have been oppressed, and there is an oppressor; once you understand that you have been raped and We are trying to be healed of that victimization, then you start seeing things more clearly. And you understand that We have a self-hatred thing going on. The sister talked earlier about the competitiveness at the business place – that ain't nothin' but self-hatred! When We talk about, "She's too light; She's too dark," that ain't nothin' but self-hatred.

We're able to identify those things, and you know – once you can identify a problem, then you can go about solving the problem. Our perception of the world has to be different – and with that difference, you study. With that difference, you continuously analyze your life – every aspect – from the way you worship God, to what you call yourself, to the way you dress.

Well, as nationalists, We've been pretty successful with that – oh yeah. We're into studying; We are into analyzing; We're into re-evaluating our positions. And We've grown. We've grown tremendously. But when it comes to the area of sexist oppression, We've failed. We haven't studied that much. We just started having the kind of dialogue that you've experienced today on a serious level.

Well, why is that? Why is it that We've failed when it came to sexist oppression? Well, i believe that there are a couple of reasons, and of course i'm gonna share them with you. One is that We've been taught to think in terms of things as a hierarchy. This is a western way of thinking. We're taught to think in terms of things as "what comes first? what comes second? what comes third?" And then, We were taught (as young Black women growing up in the struggle) that the race, that "the nation must come first." Well see that's a joke, 'cause really what they talkin' about is the Black man, right? Because if you talkin' about the nation, then certainly it fits that We should fight against sexism, because We're half of the nation! We're more than half of the nation! But naw, We bought into that. We bought into supporting "the Black man"; to our own detriment, We bought into that.

I think another reason why We failed – in terms of really dealing with sexist oppression – is We were taught that "that was the white woman's thang;

sistas don't deal with that. That's the white woman's thang!" And see, that was easy to buy into. Because white women were doing it (for white women!) they weren't doing it for us. Certainly We were turned off by white women, because they were middle class white women, struggling to be a part of our oppression. Struggling for "equal rights"; not struggling for a revolution, not struggling for a total difference in society. They were just struggling to put their foot on our necks too!

So, We couldn't deal with white women.

We also didn't trust white women because We know that they grew from our disasters. When the COINTELPRO[2] was attacking us, when the government was attacking Black organizations, white women continued to grow. So We had a mistrust for them – a mistrust that was based in history. They have always been very clear: that Black people don't really mean anything to them. Unless it's to expedite their own cause. And We were clear about that.

The third reason why i think that We didn't deal with white women, or feminism at that particular time (and even now), is because many of them have an extreme dislike for men. And that turned us off – that they would actually resent men – at least that's what We were taught in the sixties.

And if none of that worked – if you didn't go for the hierarchy and you didn't go for the white woman's position (feminism) – well there was always name calling, wasn't there? There was always name calling, and that would get you, right? "You're a ballbreaker," "you a castrator," "you must be a lesbian." So, what did We do, sisters? What did We do? We kinda put our own needs to the side. But the truth is that white women don't have any hold on fighting against sexism! Black women have been fighting against sexism for at least one hundred years (and that's just based on my narrow base of knowledge)! From my few studies, I know We've been practicing anti-sexism for at least one hundred years.

Sister Mary Chad, in 1880, organized the Colored Women's Progressive Association. Its job was not just to work for race; its job was also to push forth women's issues. "Consistent with the Black women's concerns, the

---

2 COINTELPRO (Counter Intelligence Program, 1956-1971) was a series of covert and illegal projects actively conducted by the FBI aimed at surveilling, infiltrating, discrediting, and disrupting domestic American political organizations.

clubs were not organized for race work alone," Josephine St. Pierre Ruffin said, "but for work along the lines that make for women's progress." This was a hundred years ago! Sisters were talkin' about "We have to fight for our people, but We must also fight for our rights" – one hundred years ago. I wanna tell you a little about how the clubs grew strong. Sister Ida B. Wells[3] is partly responsible for that. You know, Ida B. Wells was a famous journalist during that time, and she did a lot of anti-lynching work. She would write down whenever people were lynched. During this period in 1893, a brother named Henry Smith was accused of raping a five-year-old little white girl. As you can imagine, the white community was in a rage. So they decided to close the schools and have a picnic. The men and women and children all came to see Henry Smith first tortured with hot irons and then burned to death. And then, after the brother was burned, they scrambled to the site of the fire to pick his bones, his buttons, and his teeth off the ground – to take them home for souvenirs.

Well, Britain heard about this incident, and they could not believe how inhumane it was. So, they asked Sister Ida B. Wells – this is a hundred years ago – to come to Britain, and talk about the tragedy. And Ida B. Wells did. And Britain couldn't believe it! They couldn't believe that kind of thing went on in the United States. So they said, "What about your liberal white people?!? What about people like Frances Willard?"[4] You see, Frances Willard was supposed to be progressive – she was the president of the Women's Temperance Union (temperance means that she was fighting to stop alcohol). Ida B. Wells said, "Frances has been kind of quiet on the issue. As a matter of fact, Frances has kind of added fuel to the fire. She's saying that 'Black people hang out at the bars all the time. Black men are getting plenty drunk; and white women and children are in danger!' " Frances Willard just happened to be in England at the time. And was very upset that Ida B. Wells was saying these things; and basically called her out and said, "You lying on me Ida B. Wells!" And Ida B. Wells said, "Well, if I'm lying, name one Black woman that's in your organization of women!"

3 Ida B. Wells (1862-1931) was an investigative journalist, educator, and early leader in the American civil rights movement. She was one of the founders of the National Association for the Advancement of Colored People (NAACP). Wells dedicated her life to the struggle for African-American equality, especially that of women.
4 Frances Willard (1839-1898) was an educator, temperance reformer, and women's suffragist. Willard became the national president of Woman's Christian Temperance Union (WCTU) in 1879 and her influence led to Prohibition in the United States.

Frances couldn't say a thing. So, what happened? Well, you know amerika was very concerned about how she looked to England. So Ida B. Wells was actually successful in stopping some of those lynchings – they didn't stop altogether, but they decreased tremendously.

That pissed the press off. They wrote an open letter to the women of England. They said, "Look, now y'all are nice – you got a good heart – but you don't know the nigger woman. The nigger woman has no morality. She will lie. She will do whatever is necessary."

That response pissed Sisters off! And they decided to have a woman's club here, and a women's club there – wasn't enough. So they united and became one large national organization: The National Association of Colored Women (NACW). The president of that association was Mary Church Terrell.[5] Now at this founding meeting many sisters were there, very impressive guests. You had Ida B. Wells, you had the daughter of Frederick Douglass,[6] you had the daughter of Ellen Craft,[7] you had Frances Ellen Harper;[8] but the most impressive guest, a sister who is a known freedom fighter, a sister who risked her life over and over and over again for our people, and a sister who by her presence was obviously conscious of women's rights – Harriet Tubman[9] attended this meeting. Oh, Sisters, white women ain't got nothin' on us! Fighting for our rights is a part of who We are!

So, what happened?

We continued to work. We worked on every level. We were in SNCC; We were in SCLC; We were in the House of Umoja; We were in the A-APRP;

5  Mary Church Terrell (1863-1954) was one of the first African-American women to earn a degree, and became known as a national activist for civil rights and suffrage. She helped found the National Association of Colored Women (1896) and served as its first national president.

6  Frederick Douglass (1817-1895) was a social reformer, abolitionist, orator, writer, and statesman. After escaping from slavery, he became a leader of the American abolitionist movemen, becoming famous for his oratory and antislavery writings. After the American Civil War, Douglass campaigned for the rights of freed slaves.

7  Ellen Craft (1826–1891) was born into slavery in Georgia. In a daring escape to the northern states, she posed as a white male planter with her husband posing as her servant. The couple spent 19 years in England and only returned to the United States after the end of the American Civil War and the emancipation of the slaves.

8  Frances Ellen Watkins Harper (1825-1911) was an abolitionist, suffragist, poet, temperance activist, teacher, public speaker, and writer. She was one of the first African-American women to be published in the United States. In 1896 she helped found the National Association of Colored Women and served as its vice president.

9  Harriet Tubman (1822-1913) was an abolitionist and social activist. Born into slavery, Tubman escaped, then helped dozens of her people out of slavery via the Underground Railroad. During the American Civil War, she served as a scout and spy for the Union Army. In her later years, Tubman was an activist in the movement for women's suffrage.

We were in the Provisional Government-Republic of New Afrika. We're in NAPO now. We worked on every level, so what happened? If We didn't want to deal with white women, why didn't We come together and start fighting for our own issues? Because of the hierarchy. Because We deeply believed that, "We should struggle for the nation first." Because We were so afraid of homosexuality and homophobia – that someone would call us 'lesbian' and We'd run.

*I'll tell you one thing: I don't care what you call me, I'm fighting for my rights. I am fighting for my rights as a woman, and I am fighting for my rights as a New Afrikan. I will not struggle and dedicate my life to free only half of our nation – it does not make sense.*

And I want you to know that I am pissed off today! And one of the reasons why i am pissed is because We remain invisible. And it makes me angry. We hear over and over again about how We have to focus on 'the Black male', 'the Black boy'. In the sixties, it was "the Black man" - "Sisters Support Your Black Man!" "Black Men Are In Danger!"

And now in the nineties, it's the Black boys. "Black Boys Are Killing Themselves!" YES, the Black Man is in danger. YES, Black Boys are in danger. AND SO ARE BLACK GIRLS. AND SO ARE BLACK WOMEN. OUR NATION IS IN DANGER. *How dare you continue to ignore our cry!*

We have to leave this meeting feeling empowered. We have to leave this meeting going out and speaking against sexist oppression. To the masses of our people. No, to them it may not matter whether We call it "womanism" or "feminism". To them it may not matter what We talk about in theoretical discussions. But We cannot disregard the necessity for intellectual debate; that's how We get our theory so We can move forward. If We were to discard that, We'd be discarding W.E.B. Du Bois,[10] Amilcar

---

10 W.E.B. Du Bois (1868-1963) was a sociologist, historian, civil rights activist, and writer. He was the first African-American to earn a PhD from Harvard University. Du Bois co-founded the National Association for the Advancement of Colored People (NAACP) and authored many works, including *The Souls of Black Folk* and *Black Reconstruction in America*. He died in Ghana after the United States refused to renew his passport.

Cabral,[11] Malcolm X[12] – We cannot do that. We cannot afford to do that. So, when you leave here and you go to the barbershop to get your haircut; and you go to the hairdresser and get your hair done; and you sit in your living room with your family; and you're sitting in your church prayer group, or your bible study – you must fight against sexist oppression. Not only because it will benefit our nation, but because it is your human right to be free. It is your God-given right to be free! Don't let anyone take it from us. Don't let anyone take it from my daughter and her daughter.

Free The Land, Brothers and Sisters.

11  Amilcar Cabral (1924-1973) was a political leader and revolutionary who fought for the independence of Guinea-Bissau and Cape Verde from Portuguese colonial rule in the 1950s and 1960s. He was a gifted orator and writer, and his speeches and writings on the need for African unity and liberation continue to be influential. He is remembered as a key figure in the struggle against colonialism and imperialism in Africa and a pioneer in the development of revolutionary theory and practice. He was assassinated months before Guinea-Bissau and Cape Verde gained their independence.

12  Malcolm X (1925-1965) (born Malcolm Little, later el-Hajj Malik el-Shabazz) was an African-American civil rights leader and Muslim minister who advocated for Black self-determination, separatism, and self-defense. He was assassinated on February 21, 1965, in New York City. *The Autobiography of Malcolm X* is considered a classic of African-American literature and an important work on the African-American experience in the 20th century.

# Ayana Jamieson:
## Octavia Estelle Butler (OEB) Legacy Society

*Ayana Jamieson is the founder of Octavia E Butler legacy network. Her work revolves around the intersections of critical depth psychology, race, culture, and mythology. As an interdisciplinary scholar, Ayana's dissertation "Certainty of the Flesh: a Biomythographical reading of Octavia E. Butler's Fictions," explores Butler's biographical origins and the mythic aspects of her literary work. Recorded January 27, 2016.*

• • •

**Thandisizwe Chimurenga:** With me now is Ayana Jamieson. She is the founder of the Octavia E. Butler Legacy Network. Ayana, thank you so much for being on the show today! Welcome to Uprising: the Rootwork Edition here on KPFK.

**Ayana Jamieson:** Thank you very much for having me.

**TC:** So to let our listeners know: KPFK has got about 100,000 watts, it is the largest radio signal west of the Mississippi; somewhere out there in radio land is somebody who has absolutely no clue who Octavia Butler was and is. Could you give us a brief rundown on who she was and is, and why the need to create the Octavia Butler Legacy Network?

**AJ:** Octavia Butler was born in 1947, she was a native of Pasadena. Her mother was a domestic worker, a maid, and she ended up being one of the most famous science fiction writers of all time. She was the first science fiction writer to win the MacArthur Genius fellowship. And she wrote some very LA-centric and California-centric books and short stories that lots of people have kind of grabbed on to and are really inspired by her work. She's taught in universities and high schools, and people use her work for the foundations for their social justice work. And she put LA on the map. One of her most famous books, which she was on Democracy Now talking with Amy Goodman about, was called *Parable of the Sower*. It's a version of Los Angeles where the middle class services that we love, that we take for granted, like garbage collection and police and fire and public education, those things are no longer available to us, water and gasoline are scarce. And folks have to figure out what they're going to do to survive. So they start walking the LA highways. It's one of the books published right after the LA riots that people enjoyed and admired. And it's sort of taken off from there.

Butler's first book was published in the 1970s. All of her work was written in my lifetime. And that's one of the things I love about her work, and that she's from around the corner from where I grew up. She's buried up in Pasadena, and I founded the Legacy Network when I went to visit her grave and found it, or what I thought at the time was her grave; I found it overgrown next to a cinderblock wall in the August heat. I mean crabgrass totally grown over, you wouldn't have known it was there, right? Except that another fan had taken a photograph of the location and posted on the internet. So I started to wonder: well, if this person is such a meaningful figure, a cultural figure for us in California and the United States and the Black Diaspora at large and science fiction fans, why isn't her ...what is her legacy? Why don't folks know where she's buried? Why isn't her grave taken care of? How can I raise awareness about this issue? And things sort of snowballed from there. And that was 2011, and now it's 2016, so five years later, a lot has happened with Octavia Butler Legacy Network.

**TC:** So, this year marks the 10th anniversary of her death, of what we call her transition. Adrienne Maree Brown, one of her children, one of "Octavia's Brood," the author, also says it's like the "tenth year of her birth as an ancestor." You all have got some special things planned for this year around Octavia Butler; please tell us about them.

**AJ:** The first thing that's coming up in about a month is a launch event that's open to the public. We're partnering with some LA folks, it's a nonprofit arts organization called Clock Shop, and they have commissioned some new works based on the archives at the Huntington Library, where I do research on Octavia Butler's papers. All of the things that she collected over her more than four decades career is there at the Huntington Library. They commissioned new works and we collaborated with them on an event to kick off this entire year's worth of programming. We're raising funds to provide entertainment for that evening, and to make sure that we have funds on hand to support folks that want to come and see the different commissioned pieces throughout the year, and to come visit the exhibition. That's one thing that's happening this year. We've got some things coming up in 2017 and we're hoping to partner with more organizations and institutions to highlight Octavia's work. I'm not sure if you are aware of this but we partnered with Princeton University and we produced a symposium called "Ferguson Is the Future"[1] and it was well received and folks asked us like, "you know we couldn't attend we watched the livestream, what's coming up next what can we do and how can we be involved?"

So Moya Bailey,[2] my collaborator, and I have been working with folks ... my "digital alchemist", the person that runs all the social media aspects of OEBLegacy ... Moya Bailey and I partnered with Ruha Benjamin of Princeton University to produce the "Ferguson Is the Future" symposium. And that symposium, people touted it as being like this AfroFuturist Black Renaissance, like a revival and a coming home, like a home going for us. Octavia's name came up several times. We had her contemporaries there, folks that she mentored and inspired, activists, artists, filmmakers, science fiction writers. They're together to gather to talk about how we can envision a future, right? For all of us here in this country, how we can dream about something different, regardless of the circumstances that we're enduring right now.

**TC:** You mentioned partnerships and Moya Bailey, an alumnus of Spelman College;[3] I know that there's an event coming up at the end of February. It's going to be simultaneous with something happening here in

1 On August 9, 2014, 18-year-old Michael Brown was shot and killed by police officer Darren Wilson in Ferguson, Missouri, a suburb of St. Louis. This was followed by several waves of protests.
2 Moya Bailey is an Associate Professor in the Department of Communication Studies at Northwestern University. She first coined the term "misogynoir" in 2008, which is the "unique type of discrimination experienced by Black women, specifically the anti-Black racist misogyny that Black women experience, particularly in US visual and digital culture."
3 Spelman College is a private, historically Black, women's liberal arts college in Atlanta, Georgia.

Los Angeles, and something happening in Atlanta, Georgia, on Spelman's campus, please tell our audience about that.

**AJ:** My understanding is that there's going to be a commemoration on the Spelman campus. They haven't shared too many details with us but I know that, like us, they want to honor Octavia Butler and lift her up and provide an opportunity for people to gather. I know there's going to be some academic papers and there may be some artists involved. She passed away on February 24, 2006. And so February 24, 2016 will be the ten-year anniversary of her transition to being our ancestor. They're doing some things in Spelman and up in the Bay Area. A gentleman, I believe named Channing Joseph, is doing some programming and they contacted us, and there's the Clock Shop launch that's happening that weekend. In New Orleans, the Wild Seed Collective – that's Desirée Evans, and Soroya, G. Louise McElroy – they're doing something and we hope to be able to connect with all of them and turn up the volume and amplify and magnify all of the wonderful things that are being inspired by her work. The mission of Octavia Butler Legacy Network, is to highlight what's going on already and connect people and form a network and those are some of the folks that we've really enjoyed witnessing over the past few years. Although we will be here in Los Angeles, we're excited about all of the things that are happening at Spelman and in the Bay and New Orleans and elsewhere.

**TC:** So you not gon' give me no specifics on what y'all doing in LA?

**AJ:** [Laughter] In LA, the launch event is going to take place at the Clock Shop headquarters and there's going to be music there. We're going to do a like a call-and-response Earthseed ritual and folks are going to be invited to talk about how Octavia inspired them, and just gather together to honor her life and legacy and that's February 27, coming up next month. We'll put up a link to all of that information in our GoFundMe[4] where we're raising money for that event so that we can support the entertainment and transportation for some folks to get there, and those kinds of things.

**TC:** It's going to be at the Clock Shop headquarters.

**AJ:** Yes, that's right. And Clock Shop is located at 2806 Clearwater Street LA, that's 90039. And their website is clockshop.org. And they will have

4 https://www.gofundme.com/f/oeblegacy

lots of information posted, when you look there, and details about what we're doing. We're going to have music by DJ Lynnee Denise.

**TC:** Nice!

**AJ:** We'll have some hors d'oeuvres, and we're going to be serving cocktails and having some salutes from writers and artists. And we, Moya and I, collaborated with Clock Shop on developing the programming for that event and we hope that people will come and we hope that folks will come to the different things that we have scheduled throughout the year. And we hope to meet the rest of our fundraising goal by the end of February so that we can partner and contribute more to the event and events that are taking place throughout the year.

**TC:** It seems that there are an awful lot of people out there who love and appreciate Octavia Butler's work, who are turning to it now. And who feel that it speaks to what is going on right now. Why do you think that is?

**AJ:** Folks have called some of the things that Octavia wrote "critical dystopias," right? So not just taking whatever conventions of science fiction exists, but using the California landscape and the the historically rooted nature of being Black or a person of color, or an immigrant or a differently-abled person or a person with variable non-conforming sexuality, right? So all of these places on the margins, Octavia wrote from those perspectives. So all of those intersections at the margins, Octavia wrote from those perspectives. So women of color, folks that we would read or would identify as queer, or folks with disabilities, or hybrid people, people that don't quite fit into the dominant culture and are trying to just survive, and some crazy apocalyptic circumstances. Those are the people that Octavia featured in her writing.

And so when we look at her writing, and we see the struggles that we are going through now. I mean, we've got there's ... an epidemic in South America where people are being infected by something that makes their baby's heads small, right?[5] Gives them a genetic defect from a mosquito bite, that's an epidemic we're battling. We have the water in Flint that's polluted with lead, you know, environmental degradation, or people call it environmental racism. We have people being gunned down, unarmed folks and kids and

---

5  Zika virus is spread by mosquitoes within a narrow equatorial belt from Africa to Asia. Zika can spread from a pregnant woman to her baby, which can result in birth defects.

women or people just seeking help being gunned down by police officers and other citizens, and there being no recourse right? There being nothing to back us up. And you know, in Octavia Butler's books, people figure it out. People solve problems and come together as in different community circumstances. And so we're looking at her writing going, what next? And how, and how do we survive this and what what tools can we have internally and externally and with each other to live through this time, right, that that feels like the apocalypse, right? Not just us being snatched from the place that we're from, right, originally? And being forced to work for free. But how do we navigate this universe that we're in? Right? How do we survive when, in science fiction,television and film, and lots of books, there are no people of color? There are no women with personalities. There's only space for us being pathologized or playing stereotypical roles.

And Octavia wrote us out of that nonsense, and showed us a way to look at our history and honor it and honor difference without feeling ashamed about it. I mean, her mother was not just a maid, right? Some of her earliest memories are living in a house, what I call plantation style, right? Where she remembers the white family that her family worked for, like Dick and Jane, and Spot their dog, right? She writes about this in *O Magazine*, where she's remembering their dog and how there were people but her mother was a maid, her grandmother was the cook, her uncle was like, a gardener or something. Right. So she knows what it was like to grow up in Jim Crow, California. And of course, California had more Jim Crow laws on the books than any other state.

California, most people don't know, had more Jim Crow laws on the books than any other state in the union. Actually, people in state prisons were being forcibly sterilized up until the 1990s or afterward, right? Without permission, so, you know, we're living in this science fictional world, right? And what Walidah Imarisha says, and that's Adrienne Maree Brown's co-editor on *Octavia's Brood*, she says that all social justice organizing is science fiction, because if we're going to imagine a world without poverty, or imagine a world without prisons or imagine a world without starvation or racism or whatever it is, that world doesn't exist yet, right? Just like my PhD did not exist for my grandmother or my great grandmother, those are things that my ancestors had to dream into existence as if they were literature, right? As if they were not yet written. And so, you know, we all stand here as a testament to their dreaming, right? We are that manifestation, right? The things that you are doing ... I mean, even just, you know, the choice to use your own name and to be your own person, right? Without having to have somebody with papers to vouch for you as you travel. So those are the things that appealed to people in Octavia's writing.

**TC:** Ayana, if KPFK listeners want more information on the work that you are doing throughout the year, more information on this upcoming celebration of our ancestor Octavia E. Butler, how can they get that info?

**AJ:** We're going to be using our GoFundMe campaign to post updates for people that have supported the campaign already. So that's www.gofundme. com/OEBLegacy, that's one place; you can also go to ClockShop, clockshop. org, and they're going to have all of the events listed by the time our time together is on the air. And we also have our social media @OEBLegacy on Twitter, @OEBLegacy for Tumblr, and OctaviaButlerLegacy.com, you can always find us there. We've got a Facebook page that is a nexus for information, so if you look up Octavia Butler and Ayana Jamieson, you'll see all of the different collaborations and things that I've done and the things that are upcoming.

I would love to come back and talk to you when we have some other things going on – other conferences and things – to keep your list eners informed because it's important. Octavia was on KPFK and I know that she believed in the work that's being done. And even if she didn't know all of us and all of us didn't get to see her speak, because she left her papers to the Huntington Library, I feel like she knew that we would be there researching and trying to do some work that had not been done before, right? I mean, her collection is the largest, most complicated collection of any literary manuscripts at the Huntington Library. And so I'm just excited to be able to share some of that research with people coming up in the next year, and to have more opportunities for people to gather and get together and honor her legacy on the anniversary of her passing, but also forever, right? That's why I founded the network and I'm so happy to talk about it to given the opportunity.

**TC:** Thank you so much, Ayana, for being with us today. We appreciate all that you do.

**AJ:** Thank you so much. Have a good day.

# Barbara Ransby on Ella Baker

*Dr. Barbara Ransby is the John D. MacArthur Chair, and Distinguished Professor in the Departments of Black Studies, Gender and Women's Studies, and History at the University of Illinois, Chicago. An award-winning author, she spoke on her book* Ella Baker and the Black Freedom Movement *at the Auburn Avenue Research Library in Atlanta, Georgia, at the invitation of Project South: Institute for the Elimination of Genocide in 2006.*

•  •  •

One question as a biographer – and I must say sort of parenthetically, I was but a reluctant biographer – my approach to history is one that's more from the ground up. I'm more interested in what large groups of people do together in mass action and collective struggle than I am what any single individual does, so I wouldn't be – on the surface – a very good candidate to be someone's biographer, right? But the reason I took up the task of telling Ella Baker's[1] story is the uniqueness of that story and how embedded that story is in a larger story of struggle.

So why is Ella Baker's story so important?

Ella Baker takes us to places as historians and activists that we might not go otherwise. Ella Baker's story takes us down from King's mountaintop into the valleys and back alleys of the Black Freedom Movement. She introduces

---

1 Ella Josephine Baker (1903-1986) was an African-American civil rights activist whose career spanned more than five decades. She worked alongside some of the most noted civil rights leaders of the 20th century.

us to people with dust on their boots and dirt under their fingernails. While Dr. King[2] and Roy Wilkins[3] and A. Philip Randolph[4] went to Washington to meet with the president of the United States, Ella Baker went to Fayette County, Tennessee, and met with armed sharecroppers who were militantly fighting against plantation owners who were trying to evict them because of their civil rights activity.

Who was Ella Baker? There are a lot of different ways that I could describe Ella Baker, but I think what I want to hold forth for you tonight is that Ella Baker was both a dreamer and a doer. And those are two important descriptors because they're often things that are juxtaposed against one another. We think there are the people who act, and there are the people who think. And Ella Baker understood the importance of both of those – that is, she understood the importance of this thing called praxis: Thinking, analyzing, taking ideas seriously, but not for some abstract reason; to apply those ideas in the real world.

Ella Baker was a radical democrat. She was a tireless crusader for racial justice and human rights as well as economic justice. Ella Baker – I'll give you a little synopsis for those of you who said you didn't know anything about Ella Baker – I'll tell you some of the highlights of her political career, and then I want to step back and say a little bit about why I think that career is important, and what lessons we can extract form it.

Ella Baker was born on December 13, 1903, and she died exactly 83 years later on her birthday, in Harlem. She was pretty much busy the whole time in between. She was asked by one interviewer: What did she do most in her career, and she said, "I was a troublemaker." And she was a troublemaker. She was involved in every phase of the Black freedom struggle – the struggle for jobs and housing in Harlem in the 1930s, the struggle against fascism abroad and racism at home in the 1940s. She even made trouble in the movement. She fought sexism, elitism and egomania within the

---

2  Martin Luther King Jr. (1929-1968) hardly needs any introduction. He was an American Baptist minister and activist who was one of the most prominent leaders in the civil rights movement from 1955 until his assassination in 1968.

3  Roy Wilkins (1901-1981) was a prominent activist in the Civil Rights Movement in the United States. His most notable role was his leadership of the National Association for the Advancement of Colored People (NAACP). Wilkins was a central figure in many notable marches of the civil rights movement.

4  Asa Philip Randolph (1889-1979) was an American labor unionist and civil rights activist. In 1925, he organized and led the Brotherhood of Sleeping Car Porters, the first successful African-American led labor union.

organizations that she worked in. She organized co-ops in New York City during the depression. She worked as a field secretary and later as a director of branches for the NAACP. And then she came to Atlanta in 1957 to work alongside Martin Luther King in the founding of the Southern Christian Leadership Conference.

Now I should say also that Ella Baker was a comrade, an ally, a supporter of Dr. King, but she was also a critic of Dr. King. She had a very different notion of leadership. She didn't believe in saviors. She didn't believe in charismatic leaders. She had a very famous saying that strong people don't need strong leaders. And in that, what she meant was that there is a real disempowering effect if we place too much confidence in a single individual, however great, however brave, however smart they may be; and relinquish the power we have within ourselves – particularly ourselves acting as a collective. So Ella Baker challenged and criticized that style of leadership, and she pushed King on this question.

I often like to juxtapose – King made this comment once about leadership in which he said: "leadership often flows from the pulpit to the pews." Ella Baker had exactly the opposite view. For Ella Baker it was, in her words: "the movement that made King rather than King who made the movement."

But I tell this story about King to make a point. The point is not simply that she had an alternative view, but the point is that she worked with him anyway. The point is that she understood the importance of coalition, and she understood the importance of struggle not just in the larger arena of society, but in the political families that we inhabit.

And so I actually saw a book by John Henrik Clark out in the exhibit hall out there. John Henrik Clark was one of the people that I was able to interview in my research on Ella Baker. He knew her in the 1930s in Harlem. He said that one of the things that was so profound about Ella Baker is that she would have a loud, throw down, serious fight with you one day about a political issue – a principled issue; and he said she'd see you on the street the next day and she'd cross the street to give you a hug. And it was not in spite of the fight, it was because of the fight, that she was very clear if somebody was on the right side, they were her comrade, her brother, her sister. But she wasn't afraid to struggle. And I think that's a very important lesson. It's an example of her humanism. It's also an example of the way in which she was able to sustain herself as a long-distance runner in the struggle for social change.

Ella Baker is probably best known not for her work in the 1930s, '40s and '50s, but her instrumental role in the founding of the Student Nonviolent Coordinating Committee, or SNCC, in 1960. And SNCC in some ways was really the homecoming for Ella Baker. SNCC embodied many of the values and ideals that Ella Baker had fought for, for nearly 30 years. She did not instill these ideas in the young people in SNCC, but she teased them out. In other words, she identified people who had like-minded views. She amplified, deepened and strengthened those views in the process of mentoring them as an intellectual.

Now, I want to say something about this idea of her being an intellectual, because that's important too. Often times we're comfortable seeing women in the struggle as foot soldiers, as help, maids, as widows, as wives; but we don't often talk about them as strategists, as tacticians, as intellectuals. Ella Baker was all of those things. She was also nurturing, and there was no contradiction.

One of the things she inspired in SNCC, and I think one of SNCC's critical contributions, is that SNCC represented a critical shift in the way in which Black politics worked on the ground. SNCC abandoned uplift ideology – that is that notion that college-trained, middle class skilled professionals ought to go into poor communities and teach people how to act, how to live, how to fight for their lives, etc. Rather, Ella Baker said to the young people in SNCC: "Go humbly, go as an act of solidarity, and go prepared to learn." So SNCC people were taught by Ella Baker not to go into poor communities in the South and assume that they had the answers, but rather to go into those communities and to tap the wisdom that was already there.

I talk about Ella Baker as a part of a larger tradition of popular education, some of which Project South certainly embodies in its work, and many other people doing this work around the country, in the tradition of Paulo Freire and others. Ella Baker began working in education in the 1930s but then brought that with her into the 1960s. She had the notion that the insights, the information, the analyses, were in the students, and it was the role of the teacher to tease that out.

Now I want to highlight a few things about Ella Baker's legacy. What is it that we should take away from, or what can we take away from, this long laundry list of activity over some 50 years in which Ella Baker was involved – and she was involved in over three dozen organizations, various kinds of organizations fighting against, as I said before, fascism, fighting for housing; she was in solidarity with the struggle for Puerto Rican independence, in opposition to Apartheid, very involved in the Free Angela movement – the campaign to free then-political prisoner Angela Davis[5] in the 1970s; she joined a socialist organization called the Mass Party Organizing Committee. So really, a vast array of activities. But what are the things that stand out?

First and foremost, Ella Baker was a radical. Now, that's something that I make a point of saying because, today, when one deploys that language we do so on a very volatile political landscape – you're sort of looking over your shoulder to see if the NSA is listening or fearful of being sent off to Guantanamo. But Ella Baker's story allows us to really reclaim the integrity of that term: radical, meaning *getting to the root*. Radical, meaning trying to identify the fundamental cause, the root cause, of injustice, and to attack that injustice at the root. And this is what Ella Baker spent her entire life trying to do.

The second thing that Ella Baker did was to stretch the boundaries of Black politics in this country to encompass a global perspective. To encompass a global perspective. She didn't travel very much. She didn't go very far. But she understood the connection between Black sharecroppers in Mississippi and Vietnamese peasants. She understood the connection between Black parents fighting for decent schools in Harlem and Puerto Rican parents in a different language down the block fighting for the same thing. And in her organizational affiliations and in her personal relationships she built international ties that allowed the young people that she worked with and other people that she worked with to have a global vision of the struggle for social justice and the struggle for Black freedom.

---

5 Angela Davis (born 1944) is an American scholar, activist, and author who is known for her work in ocial justice movements, particularly in the areas of race, gender, and prison abolition. She became a professor of philosophy at the University of California, Los Angeles (UCLA), but was dismissed in 1970 due to her political activism and affiliation with the Communist Party USA. Throughout her career, Davis has been an outspoken advocate for the rights of oppressed and marginalized communities.

Ella Baker also had the idea that class was a critical component of any struggle for social change. She struggled nonstop with organizations like the NAACP, like SCLC and others, to reject elitism as a modus operandi within their organizations; and when she went down to organize for NAACP in the south in the 1940s, she made a point of going into pool halls and beer gardens and other places – she actually got chastised for doing this. There was also a funny exchange, because also these were male spaces, and there were scenes where she would go in and get up on a bar stool and call on people to join the NAACP, and many people would, just as a result of the guts that she was displaying. But she gets one letter at one point from Roy Wilkins, who was then in charge in New York. He says: "You know, I'm really worried about your reputation, Ella. You can't do this sort of thing." And she writes in the back and says: "I am worried about our reputation. That's why I'm doing these things." So she sort of flipped it on its head.

Ella Baker was an internationalist, a radical, a teacher; and a critical component of her teaching and her organizing is that she understood the power of listening and the power of silence. And sometimes, those of us who are academics don't know the power of that, or the power to know when to shut up. But that important component of communication, which means really listening to people that you're working with; meaning, listening to people in communities that you're trying to organize; listening to people with whom you disagree. And she was a role model for, I think, a lot of young people in SNCC in that regard. She was notorious for sitting very, very patiently through very long meetings. And that was an act of – that was a political gesture. That was a political principle – to actually listen.

One thing I haven't said very much about – and don't have time to talk very much about, but I think I would be remiss not to say something – is the question of gender. It is significant that Ella Baker is a woman. She's not a feminist. She doesn't claim that label, but in many ways in her practice, in fighting for larger democratic space in the organizations that she worked in and in the movement, she made a way for women to give leadership, to speak out, to assert themselves; and not only that she encouraged and mentored young men in the movement to think of being a political man in that context – in a very different way than society would have encouraged them to do so. A number of men that I interviewed that worked with her in the 1960s – having her as a role model transformed how they thought about their own masculinity. In other words, being a warrior in the struggle was not just defending a sister, but was sometimes stepping back and allowing a sister to defend herself. This kind of message, this kind of style of work, emanated from Ella Baker.

So, where does that leave us? Ella Baker was – I said at the outset – both a dreamer and a doer. That's very important, I think, for us to remember today because the power of dreams and imagination and creativity in a movement cannot be understated.

Ella Baker always reminded people in her speeches and in her workshops, to think of something larger than the here and now. There was a very famous speech she gave in 1960, Bigger Than a Hamburger. She was telling young people sitting in at lunch counters: "this is not just about the demand we have right here. This is about something bigger." She was very much known for doing that.

So I think as we remember Ella Baker tonight, we have to remember her in her rightful context, and we have to remember her in her full complexity, as both a dreamer and a doer, as someone who worked alongside Septima Clark and Fanny Lou Hamer and Ann Braden and Annie Devine and Johnny Tilman, Conny Curry and many others. And we have to also infuse our memory with new dreams. Langston Hughes has a very famous poem that talks about – If dreams die, life is a broken-winged bird that cannot fly. A movement without dreams is also broken.

So as we look into the next period of organizing, and as we come face-to-face with a contestation over memory and history – and I have to say this: I realize this is a very important week in Atlanta, and Atlanta was in the national spotlight because of the death of Coretta Scott King, and I think if anyone was in doubt about history as a battlefield, that what happened at the funeral really brought that home. It was almost a scene to me of these conservative white men as kind-of vultures circling the casket. What was happening there was a serious fight about how she and that phase of the movement will be remembered, what words will be used to define and describe and summarize, and who will claim that legacy. That is a very, very important battle, and that's why such an array of faces were in that room.

But back to the question of dreams. In tribute to Ella, let's dream together of a nation without a prison industrial complex and an insatiable appetite for Black bodies. Let us dream about a nation in which it would be impossible to have a trillion-dollar budget and still not be able to rescue poor people from flooded cities. Let's have a dream where we imagine a world without poverty at all – where there are no poor people's days. Let's imagine a world where we have a creative and radical popular culture where it would be unthinkable to commodify Black women's bodies as a form of entertainment, and the best way we can pay tribute to Ella Baker is to collectively have that dream and to collectively work to make it real.

Thank you.

# Carole Boyce-Davies on Claudia Jones

*Dr. Carole Boyce-Davies is a professor and leading authority on Black women writing cross-culturally and Caribbean women writers. She is the author or editor of several works including* Claudia Jones: Beyond Containment; Moving Beyond Boundaries: International Dimensions of Black Women's Writing *and* Black Women Writing and Identity: Migrations of the Subject. *This interview was conducted for SOUAB on December 20, 2009 and was aired on December 24, 2009.*

• • •

**Thandisizwe Chimurenga:** On the line with me now is Dr. Carole Boyce Davies. She is a professor of Africana Studies at Cornell University and she is the author of the book *Left of Marx.* It is a biography of Claudia Jones. Welcome to *Some of Us Are Brave*, Dr. Boyce Davies.

**Carole Boyce-Davies:** What a great name for a show. I'm really pleased to be on any show named that, given the history of that concept.

**TC:** Yes, ma'am. Thank you again. We greatly appreciate your time to speak with us today. December 24 is the anniversary of Claudia Jones' death in London, England. It is the 24th, correct? Not the 25th?

**CBD:** Yes, it is. Well, people are not sure, because she is imagined to have died on Christmas Eve night or early in the morning of Christmas day, because she was scheduled to go to lunch at a friend's home on Christmas day and never showed up. This is how they know. We have to assume that that's the date, somewhere in the middle there. She was found in her bed asleep with her glasses on and reading, so she had a peaceful exit from the world doing the thing she liked.

**TC:** Exactly, doing the thing she liked. Can you please tell our audience why you titled this book *Left of Karl Marx*; my understanding is that it's a literal and figurative reason behind that title is that correct?

**CBD:** Absolutely. Well, my landmark to finding Claudia Jones when I went in search of her gravesite was that she was buried next to Karl Marx. I went on a tour of Highgate Cemetery in London, and I would encourage people who go to London to go and see it, because there are many historic figures buried there. I went looking for the grave of Karl Marx and found this huge bust with flowers freshly strewn at the foot of the bust of Marx. And then next to it, a flat stone on the ground was Claudia Jones's site.

So she was really left of Marx when you stand and confront the bust of Marx, so that gave me the idea – actually, Sylvia Winter, who is pretty famous on the West Coast as well, was at a conference and when I explained what I just told you she said, "Wow, that's a title there." She has some role in making sure I grabbed it as a title, as a conceptual way of understanding her.

So I moved from that looking at how she is placed for eternity technically, left of Marx, to suggest as well that there's a whole body of activism and scholarship that is informed by Marxism, but actually is much more practical, much more activist-oriented, much more able to take the concepts that Karl Marx put forward and advance them. And for Claudia Jones being able to do that linking – class, race, gender and of course working class issues as far as Black women are concerned – was definitely left of Marx in terms of the ideological positioning.

So I'm not saying more radical than, I'm saying "left of" in terms of the ability to take race and gender and move it in a much more practical analytical way.

**TC:** Not necessarily more radical, just taking it further?

**CBD:** Absolutely. Taking it beyond Marx and moving it out into an interesting bit. Actually, on the same bust of Marx there's an inscription which says that "the philosophers of the world have studied the world, but now it's time for us to change it." Now, it's time for us, people who now read these materials and understand what he was trying to do conceptually, theoretically, now it's time for us to change it.

I think that's what she tried to do – to be a major change agent by taking the philosophical positions and making them hers. I think this is what she does and contributes, I think, to our way of understanding Black women's identities and Black women's positioning politically and in an activist way as well.

**TC:** Claudia Jones was born in 1915 in Trinidad and came to the United States at a young age, came to New York and ended up in Harlem.

**CBD:** Absolutely.

**TC:** She's coming of age around the time of the Harlem Renaissance.

**CBD:** Absolutely

**TC:** She becomes involved in political activism and joins with the Communist Party, which leads her to writing for the *Workers' World*, is that correct?

**CBD:** Yes, and the *Young Communist Review* and several other left newspapers. She for a while was editor of the *Daily Worker*, associate editor of the *Daily Worker*. She also had many other positions through the years with the *Weekly Review* and several other journals and newspapers of the Communist Party. So she begins her life as a journalist and ends her life as a journalist.

**TC:** Let's talk about that briefly in the time that we have. I knew she was a journalist. I thought she was only affiliated with one paper. Through the course of her relationship with the Young Communist League, she is associated with several journalistic ventures, several newspapers. Talk about that.

**CBD:** Well, the point is that, as she moves through her affiliation with the Communist Party – and she joins the Communist Party when she is a very young woman, she's around age 18 and joins the Young Communist League. The Young Communist League had an organ called the *Young Communists' Review*, so she works with that one. Then, throughout her life, as she moves through the ranks of the Communist Party, she works as a journalist with several of its other organs.

So my argument is that she develops an amazing set of credentials as far as journalistic skill is concerned. This is what allows her when she gets to

London to found her own newspaper, *The West Indian Gazette and Afro-Asian Caribbean News*. So to me, she puts together all this knowledge that she acquires and then puts it into service of the Afro-Caribbean community in London which is of course developing rapidly at that time. And it becomes the first major newspaper for Black people in London.

**TC:** In the 1950s during the height of McCarthyism and also during the "burgeoning civil rights movement," Claudia Jones gets deported. They couldn't do it with Robeson[1] and Du Bois[2], but they did wreck their careers. Claudia Jones gets deported and gets to England and there she founds that Black newspaper.

**CBD:** Absolutely, she founds *The West Indian Gazette* which is then later named *The West Indian Gazette and Afro-Asian Caribbean News*. And I see this as her attempt to bring together the Black community in an extended way. In other words, not just African peoples but also Asian. This is why the subtitling "Afro-Asian Caribbean News" is really important to understand what she was trying to do.

**TC:** Why did you feel it was important to do a biography of this woman? What is it about Claudia Jones' life and her work, what she was attempting to do, what she did accomplish – what is it that we need to know about Claudia Jones in the 21st century?

**CBD:** Well, we need to know first of all that there was a Black woman who was, probably, the leading theoretician in the Communist Party in the period that she was involved with the CPUSA. This would be the end of the 1940s and into the 1950s up to her deportation. That's really important.

Then, secondly, that she is part of a group, and I think the scholarship is beginning to come out now. That she is not a singular figure at all. That Angela Davis[3] is not an aberration at all. That there actually was a cohort of Black women who were in the Communist Party, and who operated in political ways that allowed us to bridge some of the earlier kinds of activities

1 Paul Robeson (1898-1976) was an American singer, actor, and civil rights activist. Robeson was an outspoken advocate for civil rights and a supporter of many progressive causes, including labor rights and anti-colonialism. He faced persecution during the McCarthy era for his political beliefs and was blacklisted in the United States. Despite this, he continued to perform and speak out for his beliefs until his death in 1976.
2 See footnote on W.E.B, Du Bois, page 10
3 See footnote on Angela Davis, page 23

that Black women had been engaged in. With what you see appearing then in the Civil Rights period, in the Black Power period and, of course, in what becomes the Black feminist movement in the 1980s.

Before that, though, she had contributed to a number of discussions that always brought together the questions of Black women as far as race, class, gender are concerned. And I think she therefore is like the missing figure in a lot of the considerations of Black women's history that need to be put back on the table. To me, that is the central thrust of what I was trying to do.

Of course, we know about C.L.R. James[4] and we know about the men who would be parallel figures at the time. People like Claudia get erased substantially, because of the kinds of political activities and also, because I think of gender and ways in which we privilege male discourses often over that which women contribute.

**TC:** I am speaking with Dr. Carole Boyce Davies. She is professor of Africana Studies at Cornell University, and she is the author of the wonderful work *Left of Karl Marx*. It is a biography of Claudia Jones.

Dr. Carole Boyce Davies, thank you so much for the work you have done. Thank you for giving us of your time today on *Some of Us Are Brave*, we greatly appreciate it.

**CBD:** It is my pleasure and happy holidays.

---

4 C.L.R. James (1901-1989) was a Trinidadian writer, historian, and political activist. He is known for his contributions to Marxist theory, as well as for his work in the anti-colonial and Pan-Africanist movements. James was a member of the Trotskyist movement for much of his life, and was involved in the Socialist Workers Party in the United States. He was a supporter of workers' struggles and was involved in various labor movements in both the United States and the United Kingdom.

# Deadria Farmer-Paellmann: Queen Mother Dr. Delois Blakely and Reparations

*Deadria Farmer-Paellmann is a legal strategist, adjunct law professor, human rights activist, and the Executive Director of the Restitution Study Group, a human rights research and advocacy institute founded in 2000. She has been credited for popularizing the slavery reparations movement through her groundbreaking research exposing corporate complicity in slavery and in 2002 she filed a landmark class action lawsuit for slavery reparations against blue-chip corporations. Aired December 10, 2009*

• • •

**Thandisizwe Chimurenga:** On the line with me now is Deadria Farmer-Paellmann. Deadria is a legal strategist in the New York area. I first became aware of Deadria Farmer-Paellmann around the issue of reparations and a lawsuit that was filed. Did I get that part correct?

**Deadria Farmer-Paellmann:** Absolutely.

**TC:** Okay, now Deadria, why don't you, first of all, let me thank you so much for your time. Welcome to *Some of Us Are Brave*.

**DFP:** Thank you, thank you for having me.

**TC:** Can you tell our audience a bit about this lawsuit that was filed around the issue of reparations?

**DFP:** Sure. There are major corporations in the United States that played a role in slavery. And what I did as a law student was to begin researching who they were, and I pursued them, asking them to apologize and pay restitution to the descendants of enslaved Africans. And so some of them actually did make payments. And in total, after, I'd say about five years of fighting in court, and outside of court, a total of about $120 million was paid out to various organizations in various different formats. And about $1 billion in loan funds were made available to Black businesses from one of the institutions, but these are primarily banks and insurance companies that either financed slavery or in one way or another through insurance policies, or through giving loans to people who used slave labor.

**TC:** Okay, so giving loans to build a bigger boat to go on an expedition or giving a loan so a person could go on an expedition to the west coast of Africa and bring back cargo, our ancestors

**DFP:** That was one thing, or business loans may have came with enslaved Africans as collateral on the loans. And sometimes, you know, people defaulted and the banks ended up owning enslaved Africans. One example is the bank JP Morgan Chase, you know, they ended up, one of their predecessor banks ended up owning enslaved Africans. Then one of the big insurance companies, Aetna Incorporated, wrote life insurance policies on the lives of enslaved Africans. And that's essentially what that work is. And the effort is continuing, because people have got this passion to do this research all over the world. And now there are institutes and various universities where they do the research that I started doing right out of my kitchen.

**TC:** So now tell me about this, how is it that you came to this issue of reparations?

**DFP:** It started when I was a kid, to be honest with you, my grandfather talking about the "40 acres and a mule" that were owed us. And when I got older, I decided to go to law school to sort of figure out, you know, what is this and how do we get it? And initially, I thought it would be pursuing the government. And while doing my research, I realized that, strategically, we might be better off pursuing corporations, because they were certainly much more vulnerable than the government. The government, you have to get permission from the government to sue it. And what I realized is major corporations don't have the same kinds of legal protections. And so that's the direction that I headed in.

**TC:** So as you grew older and began to seriously look into this work, you came across a woman by the name of Queen Mother Moore, is that correct?

**DFP:** Well, you know, it's interesting, absolutely. Queen Mother Moore, the "Mother of the Reparations Movement." In fact, she had just passed away at the very time that I began doing the work as a law student. And when working with her was the woman with ...

**TC:** So this was around 1998?

**DFP:** 1997. She passed away maybe two weeks before I went to my first slavery reparations conference, you know, where I could get my major education on the issue. Exactly, okay? I never actually got to meet her.

**TC:** But you got to meet a woman who worked side by side along with Queen Mother Moore?

**DFP:** I feel blessed that I was able to meet her. Queen Mother Dr. Delois Blakely was her assistant, main partner in doing work around reparations for I would say at least 30 years. They traveled around the world working together and Dr. Blakely shared a little story about her own life with me. And this fascinated me as much as the stories about slavery fascinated me, that the elders would tell me that got me very interested in certain aspects of slavery reparation, and I can tell you a little bit about this story.

**TC:** We need to talk with you more in depth about that reparations work and we're going to have you back but for now, tell our listeners the story of Dr. Delois Blakely who is still here. She is 67 years old now.

**DFP:** Dr. Blakely was a nun before becoming a community activist and involved with grassroots activism. She left the sisterhood, when she was about 26 years old. She served about 10 years. And at that time, there was great interest in her because she was called the "Harlem Street Nun" when she was a nun, and when she left she continued the same kind of work that she did on the street, which was primarily working with gangsters, trying to get them to live a more righteous life; with prostitutes, trying to get them off the streets, and with children, drug addicts; these were the people that she was drawn to serve as a nun. And she worked with them after she left the convent. And there was great interest in her when she left the convent. In fact, there was even a book that was being developed. And she engaged in talks to do a movie. In 1989 she sat down with Columbia-

TriStar and told them her story. And they were very anxious to make a film out of her story, they wanted to option the contract to tell her story, but somehow things never happened. However, one year later, a story was being developed into a movie that looked remarkably like hers. It was about a Black nun, not named Delois, but named Delores, and that nun was played by Whoopi Goldberg in the film *Sister Act*. It was carried to Disney and Disney made like half a billion dollars off this story, that clearly is the story of Dr. Delois Blakely.

**TC:** Now when you say "clearly is the story of Dr. Delois Blakely" you have, in addition to the nun, the similarity of the names, what other similarities of this character?

**DFP:** The kind of work she did: working with children and being a very close friend of a gangster. In *Sister Act* Whoopi Goldberg's character is dating a gangster, and in the documentation that Dr. Blakely shared with Columbia-TriStar she talked about her close relationship with a gangster. Now she wasn't dating him, she was someone who advised him and someone that he protected because this particular gangster, a very well known gangster in Harlem, essentially protected his community. He was someone who was looked up to – he was loved and he was hated – this gangster, Bumpy Johnson. In any case, this is another similarity.

The nun in this Disney story was a singer. Delois Blakely was a singer, as a nun she was called Sister Marie, but in *Sister Act* the character was called Sister Mary. So there's a lot of similarities in addition to the fact that they're both dark-skinned women. Both have the same bubbly personalities. In fact, Dr. Blakely recommended that Whoopi Goldberg play her in the movie. There's just a lot of similarities but, of course, you know, the challenge is proving the connection. And both stories came out of the same studio. A lot of people think that *Sister Act* started at Disney but it was at Columbia-TriStar first. The executive producer that carried *Sister Nun* to Disney had it originally at Columbia Tristar, a year after negotiations stopped with Dr. Blakely. So that, clearly, there's a connection. It took a long time to figure out how the story ended up with Disney. But we found the documentation. My specialty is doing hardcore research and it took extensive research and very, very expensive legal databases to find the evidence that the story was originally at Columbia-TriStar. And so we know now that that's how it ended up at Disney, came from where she was to Disney.

**TC:** And so shall I make the assumption that since legal research has been involved, a legal action may be forthcoming?

**DFP:** We're not going to rule out a legal action but, at this point, Dr. Blakely has made a decision that there's a lot that's not in that story about her life. And at this point, she's just basically decided to tell her story. And, so at this time, we're in post-production, we've already shot a film that we call *Sister Nun*. And Dr. Blakely's character shows you some of the work that she does as a Harlem street nun, some of the things that she's done, as Community Mayor of Harlem. For example, one of the things that she's well known for is consoling the families of the various African nationals who are killed, particularly by police officers. She's one of those people that's always escorting these bodies home to the family's home and consoling them. I think most people know that the Church does not support the death penalty. She's been an advocate against the death penalty and she's gone to support demonstrations against the execution of Stanley "Tookie" Williams[1] in San Francisco. And that was a major part of her work as an advocate, demonstrating against that, both before and after he was executed. But there's a lot that we have prepared in this story so that the world can know who the real woman is. And so that she can inspire other women and other people to tell their stories and to try to keep a little bit more of the truth in the story about the work. Disney does a great job of giving you Dr. Blakely but Disney does not give you the issues that Dr. Blakely dealt with, and that's what *Sister Nun,* Dr. Blakely's film, gives you.

**TC:** Right, right. I'm speaking with Deadria Farmer-Paellmann. She is a legal strategist based in the New York area. She is responsible for the major litigation that has come about regarding reparations and corporations, the role that corporations have played in the enslavement of African people in this country. She is also the executive producer of the film *Sister Nun*, which is based on the life of Dr. Delois Blakely, a confidant and comrade-in-arms of Queen Mother Moore. Dr. Delois Blakely's film *Sister Nun* was the basis for the well-known film *Sister Act* with Whoopi Goldberg. Deadria, give us an

---

1 Stanley "Tookie" Williams III (1953-2005) was an American gangster who co-founded and led the Crips gang in Los Angeles.

idea, now the film is currently in production, is that correct?

**DFP:** Right. We've actually shot the film. We have about two more weeks left in post-production. It is we call it a mockumentary because it is humorous although it deals with very serious issues. We have a special twist to our story. Dr. Blakely, well, you know what? You have to come and see the film to see what happened.

**TC:** I was going to say no, don't give it up just yet.

**DFP:** She's not very passive I'll tell you that much. We won't give you the punch line. But she's tough. She's a tough woman in this film.

**TC:** And the film is being directed by a sister by the name of Renee Alberta?

**DFP:** Right. Renee Alberta is a Sundance Film Festival director. She's directed several films from Sundance and has worked on their board. And needless to say we're applying to participate in the Sundance Film Festival in the next few weeks. Also, the lead actress in the film is Yolonda Ross,[2] and you've seen Yolonda in the films *Stranger Inside, Antwone Fisher* and many others. She's out there doing wonderful, wonderful projects.

**TC:** And she will be playing the part of Sister Nun.

**DFP:** She is actually playing Sister Nun.

**TC:** Okay, okay. So if people want more information on this film, where can they get it from?

**DFP:** Well, they can reach out to my organization, Dry Bones Productions, the number is 917-365-3007, or they can visit us online at sisternun.com.

**TC:** And if people want information regarding that research that you did that led to those court cases regarding reparations and the corporations, where can they get that information?

**DFP:** They can go to my other organization. That's restitutionstudygroup. com

**TC:** Restitution Study Group dot com. I've been speaking with Deadria Farmer- Paellmann today. Thank you so much for your time. We greatly appreciate it. We appreciate all the work you have done, the work you are currently doing and the work you're going to do in the future.

**DFP:** My pleasure to serve, thank you.

**TC:** Thank you so much.

---

2 Currently starring in Showtime's *The Chi.*

# LisaGay Hamilton
## *Beah: A Black Woman Speaks*

*LisaGay Hamilton is an accomplished actor of the stage and screen. She is known for her roles on television's* The Practice *and* Men of a Certain Age *as well as the young Sethe in the film adaptation of Toni Morrison's* Beloved. *She is also the writer, director and producer of the 2005 Peabody Award-winning film* Beah: A Black Woman Speaks. *This interview was broadcast on August 27, 2003, on the drive-time public affairs show* Beneath the Surface *on KPFK.*

• • •

**Thandisizwe Chimurenga:** Good afternoon. Hey, how are you all doing? This is Thandisizwe Chimurenga and I'm filling in for vacationing Jon Wiener, who wanted to be here tonight but could not get away. This is a special edition of *Beneath the Surface* right here on Fiercely Independent KPFK. And I am in the studio today with a very special guest: LisaGay Hamilton.

LisaGay Hamilton is an actress and a director, a documentarian, a chronicler of our history. And we're going to be talking with Lisa about a very special film that is in the beginning stages now of distribution. The International Documentary Association is in Los Angeles screening films for Academy Award consideration. The film that LisaGay Hamilton has directed and produced in association with others is called *Beah: A Black Woman Speaks,* talking about Beah Richards the actress who was also from Mississippi as Nina Simone talks about in her song.

We're gonna be talking with LisaGay Hamilton about Beah Richards, her work, her life, her meaning and a lot of other things today on Beneath The Surface. So please sit back, relax and enjoy.

• • •

How are you today?

**LisaGay Hamilton:** I am doing well. Thank you for having me.

**TC:** Thank you so much for coming on the show. I'm trying not to babble so much. I saw the film opening night last Friday and I immediately went home and started typing, started emailing and you were one of those emails that I sent. I was like, "This film is – it's magnificent, it's brilliant, it's awe-inspiring." I was just like, "Oh my God. I got to tell people about this show. I got to do something." And I said I was gonna come [to the next showing] because you were supposed to be there for discussion. I said, "I'm going to find a way to get this woman's contact info and have her on the show."

**LGH:** And where do we meet?

**TC:** And where do we meet? I was going in the bathroom, you were coming out. And I was like, "Hey, it's you!" You're like, "Yeah." "How much time do we have? Okay. Can you come on the show?" "Okay. All right." And here we are today now with LisaGay Hamilton.

Now you were formerly of *The Practice* which aired on ABC. And you've done a number of other works with Isaiah Washington[1] and ... *True Crime*?

**LGH:** Correct.

**TC:** Of course now, if you don't remember that you ought to remember the young Sethe in *Beloved*. LisaGay Hamilton played that part and I want to talk to you about that at some point during the show. But the reason we're here today is because of Beah Richards. *Beah: A Black Woman Speaks.* Beah Richards played Baby Suggs in *Beloved*. She played the mother of Sidney Poitier[2] in *Guess Who's Coming to Dinner.* She played the mother of James Earl Jones[3] in *Great White Hope* and she's done a number of roles

---

1 Isaiah Washington (born 1964) is an American actor and film producer who came to prominence for portraying Dr. Preston Burke in the first three seasons of the series *Grey's Anatomy* from 2005 to 2007.

2 Sidney Poitier (1927-2022) was a Bahamian-American actor, film director, and diplomat. In 1964, he was the first Black actor and first Bahamian to win the Academy Award for Best Actor.

3 James Earl Jones (born 1931) is an American actor. Jones gained international fame for his voice role as Darth Vader in *Star Wars* (1977). He has received three Tony Awards, two Emmy Awards and a Grammy Award.

both on stage and on screen. But I did not know the depths of this woman. I did not know the activism that she was involved in.

I didn't know she was hanging out at kitchen tables with Paul Robeson[4] and W.E.B Du Bois[5] and William Patterson[6] and ...

**LGH:** Louise Patterson.[7]

**TC:** Louise Patterson. I did not know the depths of this woman and her activism and her commitment, not only to her art but to her people and so please talk to us about that. First of all, tell me, you stated at Indie Film that during the filming of *Beloved* you barely spoke to her because you were intimidated by her. And so we go from you barely speaking to her to you spending all this time, all these hours with her chronicling her, up to her death in the year 2000. Talk to me about what was it that you – Why did you need to do this film? What was it that brought you to this?

**LGH:** First of all, I think Beah Richards represents in our community a sense of royalty. I think we all have seen her on television and in film and we're always in awe of her work. I can't think of one person who didn't say how amazing they thought that she was in her work as an actor. So certainly I carried that with me, and similar to you and probably a lot of other people I knew nothing about her activism and who she was.

After the filming of *Beloved* some years passed and I happen to bump into a friend of hers that was on the street and said, "Beah isn't feeling well." She suffered from emphysema and was relatively home-bound at that point and enjoyed having visitors. So I called and went and visited her once. And I distinctly remember when I left the house walking down her stoop, I was vibrating. I was shaking, I was vibrating. Something was going on. And I remember actually being a little intimidated by that again.

And then I didn't call her for a week, because it just scared me. And then she called me. And she's saying, "Where have you been?" It's like, "What

4  See footnote on Paul Robeson, page 30
5  See footnote on W.E.B. Du Bois, page 10
6  William Patterson (1891-1980) was an African-American leader in the American Communist Party and head of the International Labor Defense, a group that offered legal representation to communists, trade unionists, and African-Americans in cases involving issues of political or racial persecution.
7  Louise Thompson Patterson (1901-1999) was an American social activist and college professor. She spent most of her life involved in civil rights and was one of the first Black women to be enrolled into the University of California at Berkeley.

do you want with me?" She said, "Well, come back over." And just sort of began this friendship. And each time I would walk up her stoop and then walk down those steps I left a different person.

And I thought to myself, "You know, I should tape-record these sessions. I should ..." Because I can't remember everything that she's telling me and sharing with me until finally it just so happened that Jonathan Demme, who was the director of *Beloved*, had asked me what was I interested in doing, what new projects was I interested in. And I said, "Well, I don't know but perhaps we should think about doing something on Beah Richards." And the rest is just sort of history.

And so I did not know the depth and breadth of Beah's life. And so it was an evolutionary process of discovery just as the film went on I also learned about her as well.

**TC:** The film is currently playing at the ArcLight Cinema on 6360 Sunset Boulevard. And it's being screened through the International Documentary Association. A film needs to screen for approximately seven days for paying audience in order to qualify for Academy Award consideration. It's been screening since last Friday and it will screen again tomorrow, which is the last day at 10 am.

**LGH:** Correct.

**TC:** We want to encourage all of our KPFK listeners, especially those of you who have like 8,000 hours of sick leave saved up or 5,000 hours of annual leave. You need to go and see this film. It is airing at 10 am at the ArcLight Cinema at 6360 Sunset Boulevard, Sunset at Vine. And towards the end of the show it's possible that we will be able to facilitate some of our KPFK listeners going to see this show, but we're going to see about that. But I wanted to talk with you some more about Beah Richards and her activism. I found out that she was a co-founder of an organization called Sojourners for Truth and Justice. Can you talk about that?

**LGH:** Yes. We're sort of jumping in the middle of Beah's life. She lived –

**TC:** I'm still babbling so I'm jumping around. Just forgive me and ...

**LGH:** No. I'm working with you here. Let's see. In 1951 Beah moved to New York City. And having very little money and not knowing very many people she went to New York on the invitation of William Patterson and Louise Patterson who were members of the leading party, or members of the founding of the leadership of the Communist Party; a very influential couple. They were responsible for fighting for the free – to free those Blacks, particularly men who were being illegally and legally lynched for whatever the various crimes were.

And so Beah moved in with this family. And she ended up living with them over a fifteen-year period. And this was a family who had been wiretapped and Mr. Patterson had been arrested and gone to jail. So here was Beah from Mississippi, 1920 in Vicksburg, and here she finds herself in this household in New York City. Louise Patterson and Beah become very, very close friends.

There is about a ten-plus age difference between the two women and there was a mentor-student relationship but eventually on equal par, becoming very close. The white women of the Communist Party at that time were, as a lot of Americans who were of progressive mind, were fighting to stop lynching and in particular stop Black men from being lynched.

Louise and Beah found it challenging, perhaps comical, that white women were fighting for their own men. And so as a result of that Louise and Beah along with extraordinary women like Shirley Graham Du Bois[8], Charlotta Bass[9] ... Dorothy Burnham[10], the list goes on and on – Lorraine Hansberry[11], Alice Childress[12], just an extraordinary group of women, founded at the Sojourners for Truth and Justice.

And this organization was to rally Black women, women of color in United States, globally; in Africa, in Asia to rally to support those women who were fighting for their sons and their brothers and their husbands.

8  Shirley Graham Du Bois (1896-1977), playwright, composer, conductor, director, and author, and wife of W.E.B. Du Bois.

9  Charlotta Bass (1874-1979), educator, newspaper publisher-editor, and civil rights activist. Bass is believed to be the first African-American woman to own and operate a newspaper in the U.S.: she published the *California Eagle* from 1912 until 1951.

10  Dorothy Burnham (born 1915) is a journalist and civil rights campaigner. At time of publication Burnham is still alive at 108.

11  Lorraine Hansberry (1930-1965) was a playwright, writer, and activist. She is best known for *A Raisin in the Sun* which was the first play written by an African-American woman to be produced on Broadway.

12  Alice Childress (1916-1994) was an American novelist, playwright, and actress, acknowledged as the only African-American woman to have written, produced, and published plays for four decades. Childress became involved in social causes, and formed an off-Broadway union for actors.

**TC:** And just reminding our listeners that I'm speaking with LisaGay Hamilton; actress, also a director and documentarian regarding the film that is playing this week, *Beah: A Black Woman Speaks;* chronicling the life and activism of actress Beah Richards. This is a part of our *Black August Resistance, Sisters in Struggle* series. We are concluding *Black August* and we started with – *Some of Us Are Brave*: the Black Women's Radio Program here on KPFK and filling in for Jon Wiener today on Beneath the Surface.

We brought LisaGay Hamilton in to talk about this film and activism in art. You talked about Beah Richards going to New York and linking with Louise Patterson and incidentally around the work of Willie McGee[13] and the whole issue of mentioning and Beah Richards being from Mississippi, knew firsthand what that was about, of course hearing from her family and also just being there she understood what that was about. We have a clip from Beah Richards from a monologue she did. I believe – is it the monologue or the play?

**LGH:** Actually this is a poem.

**TC:** The poem that she wrote called *A Black Woman Speaks*.

**LGH:** Correct.

**TC:** And if I remember correctly from the film it was this poem that she recited in New York City.

**LGH:** She recited this poem at a peace conference in Chicago. This is a poem that Beah wrote right out of the first meeting of Louise Patterson and Rosalie McGee[14] at the house, you may remember a wonderful ... actress here in LA by the name of Frances Williams[15] and in that kitchen Beah went to her room and, believe it or not, in 1951 wrote this poem and what we're going to be hearing is excerpts from *A Black Woman Speaks*.

**TC:** Okay. I got that wrong. And after reciting that poem she then went on to New York City.

13  Willie McGee (1916-1951), an African-American man sentenced to death in 1945 and executed on May 8, 1951, after being controversially convicted for the rape of a white woman. McGee's plight became a *cause célèbre* that attracted worldwide attention, as it was widely decried as a miscarriage of justice.
14  Rosalie McGee, wife of Willie McGee, who campaigned for his release.
15  Frances E. Williams (1905-1995), actress, activist, theatre producer, organizer, and community worker. Williams was the first Black woman to run for the California State Assembly and served on the boards of the Screen Actors Guild, Actors' Lab, and Actors Equity. She represented the World Peace Council at the first Angola Independence Celebration in 1975, and co-founded the Art Against Apartheid Movement in Los Angeles in the 1980s.

**LGH:** Correct. And I should correctly say that it's called "A Black Woman Speaks of White Womanhood and of White Supremacy and of Peace." That's really the name of the poem and eventually just became *A Black Woman Speaks*.

**TC:** Okay. So let's go to that clip now.

**Beah Richards:** It is right that I a woman, Black, should speak of white womanhood. My husbands, my fathers, my brothers, my sons die for it. They said, the white supremacist said, that you were better than me, that your fair brow should never know the sweat of slavery. They lied. White womanhood too is enslaved, the difference is degree.

They brought me here in chains. They brought you here, willing slaves to man. You bore him sons. I bore him sons. No, not willingly. He purchased you. He raped me. You were afraid to nurse your young. Lest fallen breast offend your master's sight and he should flee to firmer loveliness. And so you passed them, your children on to me. Flesh that was your flesh, blood that was your blood drank the sustenance of life from me. And as I gave suck I knew I nursed my own child's enemy.

I could have lied, told you your child was fed till it was dead of hunger. But I could not find the heart to kill orphaned innocence. For as it fed, it smiled and burped and gurgled with content and as for color knew no difference. Yes, in that first while I kept your sons and daughters alive. But when they grew strong in blood and bone that was of my milk you taught them to hate me. You gave them the words mommy and nigger so that strength that was of myself turned and spat upon me, despoiled my daughters, and killed my sons.

**Beah Richards:** And when I finish it all of a sudden they scream. It's a scream of 500 women screaming. I mean, not screaming, they're crying, they're screaming, they have their arms around each other. At this convention, people hear them and they think we are being attacked by the police. They come running. "Okay, what is the matter? What is happening? What happened?" They said, "That woman read a poem." "You did what?" "She read a poem."

**TC:** That was a clip from the film *Beah: A Black Woman Speaks*. And that was Beah talking about the reaction to the poem that she did, *A Black Woman Speaks of White Womanhood, of White Supremacy and Peace*.

**LGH:** Yes. Actually that particular clip is a live performance Beah did. It used to be a show in the 1970s here in LA on KCET called *Inner Visions.* And an entire show was dedicated to Beah. And the side note is that she won a local Emmy for that segment she did on *Inner Visions.*

What's wonderful about that poem is that she wrote it in 1951 and it remained with her through her entire career and it evolved through the years. I have a number of different versions of the poem and it took on different historical connotations here and there, different ending, than it did when she first wrote it. It's probably the hallmark of her work as a poet. Beah was a poet. She was a teacher, she was an activist, she was a dancer, she was a philosopher. I got to learn a little bit about Asa Hilliard, who is a professor at Atlanta, and he speaks about African teachers, and Beah was in fact truly that, an African teacher.

**TC:** And she was born and reared in Vicksburg, Mississippi. Went away to Dillard in New Orleans for a while, but had to drop out, said she couldn't stand it.

**LGH:** Right. Right. I think like some African-Americans who were of a more progressive mind, probably a more evolved mind and a sense of identity and it's really what the film is about, as well as it about how a Black artist survives in this country given the context of racism and sexism and the like. But for Beah, who was born in 1920 as we said, her father was a preacher and he started his own church in Vicksburg and while he – it was a Baptist Church - and while he did speak about Christianity, he also spoke about Africa and Africans and Beah tells a story of her father calling people in the community Black, that the family was Black and that for many Black people in the country they were either colored or negro, but never Black. And that I think is the foundation for Beah.

**TC:** Okay. Well, you know, I'd like to explore more of Beah's beginnings with you and we need to take a short break. We're gonna talk more about Beah's beginnings in Mississippi and we'll be right back.

**TC:** Just before the break we started talking about Beah's background and her beginnings and what gave rise to her and you were talking about the fact that she stated that most of the people around and neighbors, what have you, referred to themselves as maybe negro or colored – at that time. She was born in 1920.

**LGH:** Well, typically.

**TC:** But her family considered themselves to be Black.

**LGH:** Correct. And that came from her father. She speaks of ... and that's what I found inspirational about Beah is the inner voice that her father remembered something of their ancestry. And that is, I think, a profound thought that in fact we all have that capacity to remember, to hear our ancestors speak through us. But because we have been forced to assimilate, because we have been to a certain extent taught by those who hate us the most, we cannot hear clearly, we cannot see clearly and thus our own vision of ourselves is already warped in. We're not quite sure what that vision is like.

And so I was always amazed by Beah. She didn't really want to talk about her beginnings because she had all these things she wanted to say to the community. And I said, "No, no, no. We must hear." And she, we don't have this in the film, but she was a premature baby and she was expected to die. And she speaks about how her father laid her, she was the size of his hand she said, and laid her infant body on his bible and would feed her – would feed Beah with his finger, with ... water and sugar mixture with his finger, and she would suck on it.

And those are her beginnings. I mean, just the image of Beah and words coming through her and words coming on top of her with her father who was a preacher. And of course she survived and she sat at her father's feet and listened to him practice his sermons. So here was this man that Beah constantly heard speak of Africa and of our ancestry and of our accomplishments as Black people.

So as a result of that and I think that's what Beah was also trying to instil in us is that our community as a whole has moved away from family, has moved away from the nucleus, has moved away from that which is really the most important thing and that is nurturing our children.

Beah spoke about there were at least ten, 15, 20 eyes that watched her as she walked past the white school to get to her school, who were always – you could talk to a child and say, "Don't do that. You should stop." And now we don't because we're fearful. We're fearful of our own children who are going to hurt us and retaliate when in fact our children are basically screaming to be loved, screaming to be acknowledged and screaming to be accepted and to help them to identify who they are.

So this is how Beah came up and by the time she attended Dillard University she found that the "Bourgeois Black" of New Orleans and the caste system and those Blacks were fortunate enough to get a college education where they were being taught nothing that was about them. So many would call it the miseducation of Black people and that's what Beah called it and she left Dillard after a year and went home to Vicksburg where she continued to make a living as best she could and continued writing.

**TC:** I was just thinking. You're right, that part was not in the film and I'm just sitting here blown away by you relating that story to me. The whole film blew me away, but what I was thinking was that the depths of this woman. And you know, like I said I'm a OG couch potato. I was like most Black kids, you know, watching TV from yay big or what have you.

When we watch TV a lot it seems always like you think you know a – you think you know the person. So I remember thinking that, "Beah Richards has passed," like I knew her. And I think part of that – part of the problem that arises in a situation like that is if you see, even though she was a dignified actress, when you see people playing maids or the mother in *Guess Who's Coming to Dinner*, the way you talked about in the film this interracial couple or what have you, you tend to write people off sometimes.

"Well, you know, that's the role that they picked. You know why they picked that role." They didn't have to pick that role. And so you begin to think, "Well, that's how that person is." I mean, after all why would they pick that role, right? And so I'm seeing all of these different sides of Beah Richards, even though this was a woman I respected, I knew better than to cast her aside.

**LGH:** Well, let me interrupt there. It's not that they picked that role. I certainly find it daunting as an unemployed Black actor right now – how am I going to make a living as an actor given the roles that are out there for me, do I in fact want to be a part of that material? And the answer to that is most likely no, and that's what most Black actors are faced with today and certainly it was even worse when Beah was at the height of her career. So she even says that's what she'd play. She said, "I was everybody's mother." And that is what she was pigeonholed as, and this is someone who would rather than be pigeonholed complete 100 percent artistically, this is someone who said, "Okay, I'm going to try to make a living, try to pay my bills rather," as Beah would say freedom is living. So I must correct myself on that.

And at the same time try to be a teacher, at the same time I will try to be a poet, I will try to be a playwright, I will try to be a director and that's what Beah was able to do at C. Bernard Jackson's Inner City Culture Center. Hopefully many of our audience members will remember that this was an amazing institution that provided many of the Latina, Asian and African-American artists of this community an opportunity to do Shakespeare, an opportunity to choreograph, an opportunity to be the artist, to be in a community that nurtured them and more importantly to be a part of a institution that was concerned about this community of color that was a diverse community.

And C. Bernard Jackson unfortunately passed and I didn't get an opportunity to know him at all, but would suppose he would have been just an amazing human being. And so Beah was very active within the Inner City Culture Center community.

**TC:** Similar to the works she did with Frank Silvera, and I believe the American Theatre of Being.

**LGH:** Correct. Correct. You were listening. Very good

**TC:** I'm babbling. It's like ...

**LGH:** Not at all.

**TC:** Okay, mention that. Okay, go back to the – Okay, so –

**LGH:** No, there's so much information –

**TC:** There's so much.

**LGH:** You are right. Frank Silvera was an amazing character actor. He was of Jewish and Jamaican descent. And he was probably one of the few Black actors of his generation who could play Asian, who could play Mexican, who could also play Black American. So he was very much a chameleon and probably had more opportunities than most Black actors of his day. This was someone though who was very, very progressive. And it was his story as we've been speaking about today that Black Americans that are of color needed to redefine who they were.

For those who were students of Beah, they would of course know the mantra of the definition of "being." And that is "mortal existence in a complete and perfect state, lacking no essential characteristic, perfect," perhaps even God. And so for Beah, to hear this definition of a being, of a human being lifted a weight and a burden off of her that is so easy if you even just think about it. I mean, it's so basic. But we have lost even that concept of who we are, especially as young Black people and especially in our generation today I think.

We have lost the sense of who we are simply as human beings. And Frank Silvera attempted to do that in his Theatre of Being. He tried to reshape some wonderful members of Theater of Being: Esther Rolle,[16] Whitman Mayo,[17] Lynn Hamilton,[18] just wonderful actors of our day who were a part of that institution. But unfortunately Frank passed away tragically three years after the theater was started. But within that theater their most successful production was *Amen Corner*, which was performed here in LA as well as on Broadway and Beah starred in that play.

And for those who saw her, I've had people who come up to me, even last night someone said, "I saw Beah do Sister Margaret in *Amen Corner*, and it was the most riveting thing I had ever seen," and as a result came back every night to see that production.

**TC:** To see it over and over again. Now even though she got that definition of "being" from Frank Silvera there was still something that she had prior to that. In the film it talks about the fact that she had to have something within her to even associate with the activism that she associated with, going back to Louise and William Patterson. William Patterson along with Paul Robeson and others were the leaders of the movement to charge the United States of America with genocide against the Negro people and this was late 1940s.

**LGH:** Yes, they presented a paper about that doctrine to the UN.

**TC:** And they were under tremendous surveillance at that time. And Beah willingly associated with them. She had an FBI file also.

16 Esther Rolle (1920-1998) was an American actress best known for her role as Florida Evans, on the TV sitcom *Maude*, for two seasons (1972-1974), and its spin-off series *Good Times*, for five seasons (1974-77, 1978-79), for which she was nominated for a Golden Globe Award in 1976.

17 Whitman Mayo (1930-2001) was best known for his role as Grady Wilson on the 1970s TV sitcom *Sanford and Son*.

18 Lynn Hamilton (born 1930) is a retired actress best known for her recurring roles as Donna Harris on *Sanford and Son* (1972-1977) and as Verdie Foster on *The Waltons* (1972-1981).

**LGH:** Yes. It spanned from 1951 to 1972. We sent away for it in the hopes that we would get it to – perhaps it would shed some light. And what's amazing is they really did watch her. And actually there is a lot of wonderful history about Beah and who she associated with and you say, "Wow, she was there? Wow, she was with this person."

**TC:** They wrote the history for us.

**LGH:** They wrote the history for us. But the sad part about it is that for those who've never seen an FBI file, of course I hadn't, is that blocks are whited out and those are the names of the people who are the informants and you could see that that was someone in her house, or a friend. Actually we have a transcript from out of Ohio where this woman who was a Sojourner for Truth member, and is sitting for the House Un-American Activities Committee – Did I say that right?

**TC:** House Un-American Activities Committee. So, McCarthy.

**LGH:** Who just names Beah but is a communist. I mean, just rattles, just rattles off all the names and it's just astonishing that those things happened, but I guess they still are happening now. But in – I lost my train of thought. What were we talking about?

**TC:** Oh, her FBI file.

**LGH:** Oh, right. And so what's listed is she was at, you know, 339 Crenshaw Boulevard and she read a poem. She was at such-and-such, she read a poem. I mean, this is from 1951 and 1972. I mean, that's all that Beah did was read poetry and there you go. My taxes paid for following Beah Richards for 20 years. And she read a poem.

**TC:** Well spent. Well spent. So yes. And as you stated in the film she was obviously feared that – It was obviously feared that she was gonna overthrow the US by reading her poetry.

**LGH:** Exactly. But as Beah said, she had been on a list her whole life. So a blacklist did not scare her and certainly fascism didn't, because she lived with that in Mississippi, but certainly communism didn't scare her.

**TC:** And, you know, that's something that happened on a daily basis in the 1960s after McCarthyism came in terms of the rise of the movement for Civil Rights. It was always said to be something that was happening from outside of us. It couldn't be Black people fed up with their existence. It had to be a communist plot, you know.

I wanted to talk to you about you also ... I know that you are on a mission.

**LGH:** Boring.

**TC:** No, no, no, no.

**LGH:** Let's talk about Beah.

**TC:** I know that you're on a mission and you want to talk about Beah, but because the – I mean, there's obviously a spiritual connection there between you and Beah and doing this work. But what I wanted to talk to you about is that I had read a book or should I say I glanced through a book ... let me not lie ... a couple of years ago. And it was talking about the making of *Beloved*, and this is where you said that you first worked with Beah. And it was talking about, I believe, Oprah had hired a historian or someone to that effect to make sure that everything was accurate and it talked about she was given a run-through, she was going to – for six hours she was supposed to be in character as an escaped slave and she was gonna be dropped in this area and she didn't know who to trust, you know.

Not necessarily all Black people are gonna help you out and not necessarily all the white people are gonna turn you in and she just – and so it was supposed to be for six hours and I think she collapsed after two? She had a breakdown pretty much under the stress and the strain. And a lot of times when we go back and deal with the history of what our ancestors have gone through, you know, we make the connections like, "Okay, I see now. I understand."

And she talked about – Beah Richards talked about some of the things that she felt in the movie in her character of Baby Suggs. I wanted to talk with you also about your experience of Beloved, certainly for me watching the film. I did not read the book. I was intimidated because I remember when it first came out it was like [the size of] a phone book. I said, "I'm not reading that." But I saw the film and I loved the movie. My spirit loved the movie and your portrayal of the young Sethe in that film, I want to talk with you about your experiences on *Beloved*.

**LGH:** Well, hopefully the book *Beloved* has no longer intimidated you. And if in fact you have not read the book –

**TC:** It's a lot thinner now, yeah.

**LGH:** I think the having seen the movie and for the viewers who have not read the book, if you have seen the movie you must, must read.

**TC:** Must read the book.

**LGH:** *Beloved* is, you know, is our great ... it is our classic. And I think what is extraordinary about that text is that as Toni Morrison states so many times when we hear about slavery it is from a white perspective, it is from a male perspective and it is in mass. And here was someone who very wisely took the story of one woman and how slavery had an impact on this one woman. I mean, ultimately it was about all of us but it was about this one woman.

I remember at the first read-through, at the table read-through of *Beloved* and throughout the entire read-through Beah would moan out loud, scream sometimes. And that's why I was intimidated by her. And so – And the room would just go silent and she would just, you know, let out a wail of you know – wouldn't ... try to imitate her but – and just a moan and weeping. And at the end of it she was just exhausted at the end of this read-through.

And she said to us, "What an extraordinary moment in history we were –" I think so tragic why *Beloved* didn't fare well and that Black people didn't go out and support it. This was truly the first time that a great African-American classic was being put to the screen. And whether anyone likes the movie or not this was an attempt to tell our history, and it was a wonderful attempt I think.

And that set the tone for me as Beah and that read-through spoke about our ancestors she said are here. They are in this room right now and the room was silent. I mean, just dead silent. And she said "They're here." She said, "You can't just – They're here. They're in the room." And she was right. I mean, not only were they in the room, they're in this room now with you and me. They're with us all the time.

And if we were to once again revisit the definition of "being," and if we were to be quiet for a while the spirit of the ancestors are so strong. It's extraordinary the spirit and the strength Beah often spoke about, can you imagine the fear, as Oprah perhaps suggested, of not knowing when your next breath is, your next move, when you're going to lose your child, when you're going to ...

And so as an actor this was an extraordinary opportunity to be one with those who suffered so greatly during slavery and having the opportunity to play the younger version of Sethe in this film and the version that I played had more of the physical trauma that came literally with this character. So I was giving ... I was raped, I gave birth, I was trying to kill my children, and you know it was like, "Go act this."

And so there was a zone that, however frightening, I felt an obligation to portray with the greatest sense of awe and respect and truth and certainly acting opposite Beah and being in her vicinity, I think for all of us who were ever on the set with Beah, it was a grounding place for us just to turn and look at her. I mean, anytime I just looked at her, I didn't have to work very hard. And if I just thought about her I didn't have to work very hard.

**TC:** I want to go to a break real quick. We have another clip from this film *Beah: A Black Woman Speaks* that we want people to hear. But we're going to take a quick break, but before we do that have I been calling you an actress? I just realized. Have I been saying *actress* all night long?

**LGH:** Versus?

**TC:** Actor?

**LGH:** I mean, it doesn't really matter. Both are the same. It's just fine.

**TC:** I'm still – I'm in awe. I'm babbling. So you will have to forgive me for giving really ...

**LGH:** Someone call and then tell her she's not babbling. Okay? Let's tell her.

**TC:** We are going to go to another clip from this wonderful film that LisaGay has in concert with others brought to us. It's called *Beah: A Black Woman Speaks*. But before we do that we're going to take a very short break. Stay with us.

**TC:** I would like to thank Beverly for calling in and saying that I was not babbling. I was wondering about that. If anyone else who wanted to call in and say that – I think I'm okay now. Thank you very, very much.

We have a clip from the film. Beah, as you said, was a writer. She was always writing. She was a poet in addition to being an actor. And this clip that we have which appears in the film is from, is it a one-woman play?

**LGH:** It's from another play that she wrote in 1950. Very prolific then, that followed throughout her career as well. And there were a number of productions of a play called *One is a Crowd* at Inner City Cultural Center, so I might remember the production. And this is an excerpt from *One is a Crowd*.

**TC:** Okay. Let's go to that now.

**Female Voice:** "Chained in that slave ship just like you. I stood on that auction block and was inspected and sold just like you. I bought a lash and sustained the pain. I knew the mockery and the shame and picked my bale of cotton just like you. Escaped with the bloodhounds at my heels just like you and did my share of the fighting too. How dare you set a boundary for me? How dare you. I am no male idea of shrinking femininity. I am no clinging vine as Charlie shit. And don't you bring it to me. I have no more fear. I've used it up. Do you hear? I'll have no more of supremacy neither white nor male. Now get out of here. Out. Out. Out! Out!"

**Beah Richards:** I wish you had seen that. And that was really – We call that the "Get Out" scene. Now what did you hear in the get out scene? Get out. And see she's coming out of the East Coast. She's coming out of the West. She's taking off and she's taking the ...

**TC:** That was called the "Get Out" scene in *One Is a Crowd*. And Beah was talking about as she's saying, "Get out," she's taking off her clothes coming out of the west until she's basically naked on stage.

**LGH:** Correct. Correct. Obviously, perhaps in the film Beah starts the monologue and then I take over and that was my voice, not Beah's voice obviously. Doing that monologue and in that excerpt we have a wonderful dancer Jawole from Urban Bush Women,[19] who accompanies that monologue.

Beah was a very, very prolific writer. Not all of her works are in publication. *One Is a Crowd* will be available along with *A Black Woman Speaks*, which

---

19  Founded in 1984 by choreographer Jawole Willa Jo Zollar, Urban Bush Women (UBW) seeks to bring the untold and under-told stories to light through dance.

is the title of not only the poem, but also a collection of poetry by Beah. And we're not quite organized yet with our website, but if people wanted to let us know their email address you can email at beahspeaks@hotmail.com and we'll keep you abreast of the screening schedule around the country as well as when and where you can purchase Beah's publications.

**TC:** And that's B-E-A-H, beahspeaks@hotmail.com.

**LGH:** Correct.

**TC:** Beah was struggling, and we said this is in continuation of *Black August Resistance, Sisters in the Struggle* and Beah, thank you for bringing us this film because it shows us more of Beah Richards who some of us may not have known or thought we knew well. She was a struggler up to the very end and I don't mean that figuratively. I mean, literally she was struggling to the very end and the film captures that. You were a part of that also in terms of her last request. Would you tell us about that?

**LGH:** Actually, I don't want to because I think it's giving something away.

**TC:** Well, but ... We'll revisit that, but that's her last role and you –

**LGH:** You're choosing her last request though and I didn't want to give up the last request. That's too – It's a surprise.

**TC:** But only – The only people who –

**LGH:** It's a surprise.

**TC:** But only the people who get the tickets ...

**LGH:** Here is the point; we are very fortunate enough to be airing on HBO in February and for –

**TC:** Like until February?

**LGH:** Yes, you do. Or you can check out the website www.documentary.org and *Beah: A Black Woman Speaks* along with many other of the wonderful films showing at the IDA, in fact film showcase will be on a tour.

Also, we are aggressively trying to get screenings at the various African-American studies departments and drama schools in LA, be at USC or UCLA, perhaps even up at Berkeley, so you guys just keep a good lookout for *Beah: A Black Woman Speaks* and we'll hopefully get to see what her last request was.

**TC:** Okay. I'm sorry. I won't give it away.

**LGH:** Can I give KPFK a real like boost?

**TC:** Yeah.

**LGH:** It was really cool that we met in the bathroom, because I said to Roz, I'm not joking, I said, "I want to get on 90.7. I want to get on –" And she said, "Okay. I'm working, I'm working, I'm working on it." Somebody didn't call her back from KPFK. I don't know who it was.

**TC:** I don't know either.

**LGH:** But then we saw you in the bathroom, sister. And there you go. And I got on 90.7.

**TC:** Now that's what we call spirit working.

**LGH:** So I'm so honored to be here. And this is my favorite station and this is where I learn all my good stuff. So thank you for having us.

**TC:** We are honored for having you.

**LGH:** Thanks, sis.

# Drs. Regina Freer and Melina Abdullah on Charlotta Bass and Karen Bass

Dr. Regina Freer

Melina Abdullah

Charlotta Bass

Karen Bass

*Dr. Regina Freer, a Professor of Politics at Occidental College, currently engages in research and teaching interests that include race and politics, demographic change, urban politics, and the intersection of all three in Los Angeles. She is working on a political biography of Charlotta Bass and serves on the board of the Southern California Library for Social Studies and Research and the Center for Juvenile Law and Policy at Loyola Law School. Dr. Melina Abdullah is currently a founder and leader of Black Lives Matter–Los Angeles. She is the former chair of the Department of Pan-African Studies at California State University, Los Angeles, is a recognized expert on race, gender, class and social movements, and is one of the leaders of the fight for Ethnic Studies in the K-12 and university systems in the state of California. This interview was broadcast on May 8, 2010.*

• • •

**Thandisizwe Chimurenga:** You're listening to *Some of Us Are Brave, A Black Women's Radio Program* here on KPFK 90.7 FM Los Angeles, 98.7 FM Santa Barbara, and a few other places and worldwide at kpfk.org. *Black Los Angeles: American Dreams and Racial Realities* is due out on May 15 by New York University Press, it is edited by Darnell Hunt and Ana-Christina Ramón, in conjunction with the Ralph J. Bunche Center for African-American Studies at UCLA. This book is a culmination of a groundbreaking research project from the Bunche Center at UCLA, and it represents an in-depth analysis of the historical and contemporary contours of Black life in Los Angeles. In-studio with me now is Dr. Melina Abdullah, she's a Professor of Pan African Studies at Cal State Los Angeles, and Dr. Regina Freer, Professor of Politics at Occidental College. They are just two of the many contributors to this book. Their chapter is entitled "Bass to Bass: Relative Freedom and Womanist[1] Leadership in Black Los Angeles."

Welcome to *Some of Us Are Brave*. Thank you so much for being on the show today.

**Melina Abdullah:** Thank you for having us.

**Regina Freer:** It's a pleasure. Thank you.

**TC:** You title your chapter "Bass to Bass" and you entitled that chapter that way because you started out talking about Charlotta Bass and you went on to Karen Bass. Why is that?

**RF:** I think a lot of people assume there's a connection between the two. Many don't necessarily know Charlotta Bass and so for listeners who aren't familiar with her, she was a political activist. She moved to Los Angeles in the 19-teens and owned and operated and edited the *California Eagle*, one of the preeminent Black newspapers in Los Angeles' history. She was also a candidate for a number of offices and actually ran for Vice President of the United States in the 1950s, most folks don't know that.

People sometimes assume that Karen Bass, who we know much more about as being the first Black woman to lead a California Legislature – or legislature anywhere in the country – has some connection with Charlotta. "They must have been relatives." We found that there wasn't a familial link between the two but we thought that there was a link that was very strong in terms of the politics, the way they approached their politics, and the fact that they both came out of Los Angeles in terms of their activism. We wanted to figure out what the connections were, if they weren't blood.

**TC:** You're saying that the relationship was more political, but what about the tradition of womanist leadership? What is this tradition that you're speaking of?

**MA:** Right. What we really wanted to talk about in the chapter, and we use Charlotta Bass and Karen Bass as case studies for this, is we wanted to think about the kind of leadership that Black women tend to embrace, especially in the Los Angeles context.

---

1 Womanism is a social and political framework that was developed by African-American women in the 1980s, primarily as a response to the perceived limitations of mainstream feminism. Womanism places a strong emphasis on the experiences and struggles of women of color, particularly Black women, and seeks to address issues of race, class, and gender in an intersectional manner. The term "womanist" was coined by author and poet Alice Walker.

We've been writing for a while on womanist leadership and that theory is actually evolved over several writings that we've done, both together and some of the work that we've done by ourselves as well. In thinking about the frame of the book *Black Los Angeles*, what we see is a particular space that allows the rise of womanist leadership in a different way than we see in the rest of the country.

For womanist leadership, there's four core elements of womanist leadership that we explore; this idea of proactivity, so the idea that Black women don't simply respond to crises as they arrive, but we set our own agendas. So it's kind of this idea of visioning that we tend to do, and then the idea that that vision informs a theory, and that theory then informs the way that we act. Those two things work to inform one another becoming practices.

Then what we focus on in this chapter is how Charlotta Bass and Karen Bass embraced the last two elements of womanist leadership most clearly. That's group-centered leadership, so the idea that a collective movement is much more sustainable and has the capacity to be much more transformative than a leader-centered group. Karen Bass, for instance, when she was the Executive Director of Community Coalition, talked about her rejection of celebrity-style leadership.

In the chapter, we talk about how difficult it is for her to put on the clothes literally and figuratively of the Speaker of this State Assembly. Because it requires that she embraces a celebrity-style leadership which she fundamentally rejects in terms of her beliefs.

Then finally this idea of traditional and non-traditional methods. Using everything that the system allows you to use and encourages you to use, like voting, like running for office, but also remembering that the system won't transform itself. The use of non-traditional methods also becomes extremely important. So, this kind of inside-outside relationship, in a section in the chapter, is called "Inside-Outside or in Reference to Karen Bass" because she's in office, but she still thinks of herself as connected to this outside movement.

What we're talking about is how womanist leadership not only unfolds amongst Black women generally but the particular shape that it takes in Black Los Angeles.

**TC:** I noticed also that you briefly hark back to Biddy Mason[2] when you speak of Karen Bass and Charlotta Bass also.

**RF:** I think we were trying to point out that there is this historical trajectory of womanist leadership in the city and that Black women had a particular space to work within Los Angeles. Some of the ironies of Los Angeles are that on the one hand it's Western, it's promising, it has all sorts of hope and possibility that people coming, particularly from the south, were looking forward to that they were going to leave Jim Crow South.

Biddy Mason literally was coming to California as a slave, and was able to fight for her own freedom within the context of this city, and become one of the premier landowners in the city. Really it's a phenomenal story. She helped to start the First AME Church. And so, on the one hand, there's this great possibility for womanist leaders to emerge within the context of Los Angeles, this promising place, but the opportunity for full freedom was consistently denied, and so, you had opportunity for some freedom but not complete freedom and womanist leaders did not stand for that, they fought for full freedom.

They didn't rest on the laurels of the sunshine of the place but rather sought to make this a fully free place for Black people as a whole. We saw Karen Bass picking up Charlotta Bass's mantle in that fight, and Charlotta Bass picking up Biddy Mason's mantle in that fight.

**TC:** Because Karen Bass has shunned that celebrity limelight-type of leadership, not many people know that – Well, of course, some people know that she was a key member of the Free South Africa Movement in the 1970s, in the 80s and early 90s. One of the local organizations that helped to make a national impact regarding the dismantling of apartheid in South Africa.

**RF:** Yes. One of the pleasures of doing this type of historical work is the stories that you unearth that really are empowering to people today and some of the things that we learned about Karen Bass's activism provided that for us. We found out about her activism around the Free South Africa

2 Biddy Mason (1818-1891) was an African-American nurse and a Californian real estate entrepreneur and philanthropist. Enslaved at birth, she acquired knowledge of medicine, child care, and livestock care. The slaveowner moved to California and brought her with him. She sued and a California court granted her and her daughters freedom in 1856.

Movement, but also about things that she was doing as a high school student here in Los Angeles to make the world a better place.

**TC:** Are … are we getting ready to tell some business now?

[Laughter]

**MA:** No, we won't go that far.

[Laughter]

**TC:** Let's just say that she was no stranger to activists.

**RF:** Absolutely. We argue in the chapter that Charlotta Bass created the space for Karen to be able to fight the fights that she did. There really was some literal and figurative connectivity between the two. Charlotta Bass was very active around housing restrictions and trying to dismantle the rigid housing segregation that existed in Los Angeles. One of the things that bumped up against the freedom of this place. "You can have a house, but we're going to tell you where you can have a house here." And Charlotta Bass was very active, one of the most prominent activists in trying to dismantle restrictive covenants. Karen Bass's family was able to move to areas of the city that they wouldn't have prior to that activism opening up that space.

**TC:** Charlotta Bass being a journalist is one of my personal heroines, one of my personal favorites. I just thought it was very interesting that when we talk about womanist leadership, there are those times when we don't give it the respect that it's due mainly because we don't take it seriously. I thought it was interesting in looking at Charlotta Bass's life, the FBI took it seriously. The FBI took it so seriously that … she passed away in 1969. We just had the 41st anniversary of her passing, April 12. About a year or two years before she passed away in 1967, she was in a nursing home where she was recovering from a stroke. She was 91 years old, but the FBI still classified her as potentially dangerous.

**RF:** Absolutely. She has a very thick FBI file.

**TC:** Why is the FBI still wondering about a 91-year-old woman in a nursing home who's recovering from a stroke?

**RF:** She must have still been doing something right.

**TC:** From the hospital bed

**RF:** Exactly.

**TC:** She was still literally kicking.

**RF:** Fighting the fight. That also is something that we learned through exploring these women's lives, is the tenacity. Charlotta Bass owned and operated a newspaper, the major Black newspaper in this city in 1912.

**TC:** Right, and the *California Eagle* actually was started in the 1880s.

**RF:** Absolutely.

**TC:** She came into it in 1912. It's probably the oldest Black paper we know in Los Angeles, but also the oldest ... as it the oldest in California and maybe the West?

**RF:** I can't say for sure if it is in the West, but it was absolutely one of the oldest west of the Mississippi. The fact that ... the tenacity that she had, that she was, in her earliest time here in Los Angeles, she was fighting the fight and was breaking down borders and boundaries and leveling the playing field ...

**TC:** Using the paper.

**RF:** Absolutely, using the paper to do that. The fact that she owned the paper at that point, I think, is exemplary of that. As you bring up, in the very last days of her life, obviously, there are those who were still threatened by the way that she was going to challenge the system.

Charlotta moved from Los Angeles to Lake Elsinore in the last part of her life when she started to get ill. She operated a reading room. We've seen the books that she had in that reading room. She, in fact, was talking about, for example, South Africa. She was talking about apartheid in the late 1960s alerting the world to this travesty at the very sunset of her life. We cannot help but gain some empowerment and strength from the courage that women like Charlotta Bass and Karen Bass picked up on.

**MA:** If I were the FBI, I would see Charlotta Bass as threatening. In fact, womanist leaders are threatening. That's the whole purpose of womanist leadership – to transform the system that is. If we think about what womanism is, it's about pushing for full freedom and not allowing any form of oppression, so challenging oppression wherever we see it. Womanism really is about that challenge. It is a threat. It's building a movement that goes beyond the realm of the individual. Of course, these women are going to be a threat to the existing system. I think it's fitting for her to have, that's a badge of honor that she has a thick FBI file.

**TC:** Thick FBI file. Now, you state womanist leadership as opposed to feminist leadership. Why is that?

**MA:** Well when we talk about womanism, everyone knows the quote by Alice Walker, right? "Womanism is to feminism as purple is to lavender." What does that mean? That womanism is deeper. It's truer. It's richer. Basically, if feminism is a movement to end sexism and sexist oppression as bell hooks calls it, right? I think most of us would say, "Well, if that's what feminism is, then we're feminist, I guess."

We're much more than that because we're Black women. It's not enough for us to be engaged in a fight to end sexism and sexist oppression. We also have to be engaged in the fight to end racism, to end classist oppression, to end heterosexism, and to end all forms of oppression. Womanist leadership is really transformative. Karen Bass, even as the Speaker of the State Assembly, said that she is fundamentally a progressive. What that means to her is that she has to push hard to challenge the existing economic and social structures. I don't think you'll find any leader of a state legislative body ever saying that other than someone like a Karen Bass, who we call a womanist leader.

**TC:** Womanist leadership, activism and organizing in Los Angeles. What are your thoughts about where we go from here? What does the future look like for womanist leadership? We know there's a need for it.

**RF:** Absolutely. I think that there's a lot we can learn from the example of the two Basses, of Charlotta and Karen Bass, that, emergence from collective leadership is going to be really key for our future, that it's not going to come through an individualized leadership model. I think both women are connected in an important way to something that actually, then-candidate Barack Obama indicated for us that we want to see a change, but we are that change.

And so it's going to come from activism. It's going to come from organizing. We can't strictly rely upon those who are inside to do it for us. When Karen Bass says, she's on the inside, but she relies upon connectivity to the outside. We have to lift up and meet that challenge I think as Black

Angelenos. That's going to be really important to our future and our success.

**MA:** I think that we see some of that emerging, that we see both in electoral politics and in grassroots organizing. We see this on the horizon or the possibility of this growing womanist leadership growing. It's a testament to the space that Los Angeles still offers. If we think about electoral politics and we see the congressional race where Karen Bass is now running for Diane Watson's seat, representing an evolution of what Black women's leadership should look like. Offering a more progressive candidate for that district.

Then to succeed Karen Bass, we see [L.A. County Supervisor] Holly Mitchell coming out of an organizing background. A Crystal Stairs organizer, organizing mothers and women, and talking about the importance, of doing the work that we do that's often unrecognized. We see it in the realm of electoral politics, but we also see it in terms of grassroots organizing. And another project that Regina and I have been working on is really about the momentum that we see in communities around the election of Barack Obama that we are going to pick up, eventually, we're going to pick that back up, but this kind of momentum that emerged with his candidacy and ultimate win, is this idea that we are all a part of this movement. In Obama's speech, he said, "What I represent is the possibility of change." Right? What that means is it's not just ... or "The chance for change," I think were the exact words he used. That chance doesn't just rest with President Obama. Many of us are both excited and disappointed by his leadership.

We kind of have this excitement over the fact that he is there. There are things that he's done that are better than it's been done in the past, especially when we think about who the president was before him. But there's also these disappointments, like the healthcare debate wasn't a full debate. The way in which he has responded or not responded to the specific crises that are occurring in Black communities.

I think what that leaves us with is the question, should we totally invest in a single leader, totally invest in inside politics, or is there something else that needs to happen? And womanist leadership is about realizing and recognizing that both need to be invested in, both need to be nurtured, and both need to be developed in order for us to push forward real progress. All of us must pick up the mantle of leadership and all of us must work together to vision and also do the work that is necessary to bring our collective visions to pass.

**RF:** I think a really poignant phrase that came from one of Charlotta Bass's campaigns for office was, "Win or lose, we win by raising the issues." I think that is a testament that if we put all our eggs in the electoral basket, sometimes we lose. But if we raise the issues, we ensure that they're going to be responded to.

**TC:** Dr. Regina Freer of Occidental College, Dr. Melina Abdullah of Cal State Los Angeles. Thank you so much for being on *Some of Us Are Brave* today.

**MA:** Thank you for having us.

**RF:** Thank you. It's a pleasure.

# Paula Giddings on Ida B. Wells

*Paula Giddings is the Elizabeth A. Woodson 1922 Professor Emerita of Africana Studies at Smith College in Northampton, Massachusetts. A former book editor and journalist who has written extensively on international and national issues, she was elected to the American Academy of Arts and Sciences in 2017. Excerpts of this conversation were broadcast on July 19, 2007 on* Some of Us Are Brave: A Black Women's Radio Program *on KPFK.*

• • •

**Thandisizwe Chimurenga:** My name is Thandisizwe Chimurenga. Today, we are speaking with Paula Giddings, author of *When and Where I Enter: The Impact of Black Women on Race and Sex in America.* She's also the author of *In Search of Sisterhood,* which is a biography, if you will, the history of Delta Sigma Theta Sorority. She is the author of numerous scholarly articles …you've edited also several books, is that correct?

**Paula Giddings:** Yes.

**TC:** I don't want to get into all of that today because as most of our listeners know, *When and Where I Enter* is considered by many of us to be one of our Bibles. [Laughter]

**PG:** Thank you.

**TC:** I think I speak for a lot of sisters who feel that way about that book, *When and Where I Enter.*

**PG:** I appreciate that. Thank you.

**TC:** We really appreciate you, Professor Giddings. I know that when the book on Ida B. Wells comes out, that's going to be another one of my many Bibles.

**PG:** Let's hope so.

[Laughter]

**PG:** The book is coming out in March[1] and so I'm at that really nervous, anxious stage. I'm waiting for Collins to come back and take a last look at it and we're ready to go.

**TC:** I believe I mentioned to you once before, we are in possession of a lecture of yours. We believe it occurred around 1993 or so, it was to the Association of Black Women Historians. You were talking about Ida B. Wells. You talked about her beginnings, what it was like for her to experience true Black Power growing up in Holly Springs, in Memphis, at the turn of the century just a few short years after the end of slavery. When you started talking about Ida B. Wells, you said in the writing of your book, *When and Where I Enter*, she walked into the first chapter of *When and Where I Enter* ...

**PG:** And wouldn't leave. [Laughter]

**TC:** And would not leave and you had to promise her a book.

**PG:** That's right.

**TC:** That's what we're anxiously waiting on next March. Tell me about your experience. The experience of writing *When and Where I Enter*, but also that experience of being drawn into the world of Ida B. Wells to the point where you felt that you needed to write a book on her.

**PG:** Of course. As you know, *When and Where I Enter* is really a history of Black women and their impact both on feminist movements and on race movements throughout American history. I remember very distinctly doing a lot of the research and getting a draft done but had problems of figuring out how to begin the book. I tried lots of chapters of introductory chapters.

As you know, the first chapter has to talk about the major themes, and it has to pull the writer in, and it has to talk about the significance of what

1 *Ida: A Sword Among Lions: Ida B. Wells and the Campaign Against Lynching* was published in March 2009.

you're writing about, and I had so much trouble. That's when Ida Wells, really, who I had written about, of course in the book, but she really made her appearance [laughs] and almost said in so many words, "Since you're not going to give me my book right now, you ought to at least know that you have to begin with me." [chuckles]

**TC:** I'll take a chapter now in other words.

**PG:** Of course, the book opens with her. What I intuitively understood then but didn't really intellectually understand for some time, was that her campaign against lynching is really so pivotal to ideas around race, to ideas around gender, to ideas around sexuality, and their interrelationship with one another. That it is so important to the history of African-American men and women in the country.

She, on some level, of course, understood this too, because one of the things I had to think about is why would a woman like Ida B. Wells, she was very petite and she was probably not much over five feet tall. She was a Victorian and very prissy in many ways of growing up.

I said, "What is it that makes a woman latch on to a question, an issue like lynching with all of its horrors, and the madness that's associated with it?" She makes it not just an issue of one among many issues, even though she gets involved with all kinds of ideas, but this is a lifelong campaign of lynching and racial violence, and what it meant to African-American people. I had to answer that question. In trying to answer that question, one really begins to open up a lot of paths of inquiry and understanding, I think, about race and gender in this country.

**TC:** I want to follow that so badly but I also wanted to latch on to something you said about Ida B. Wells being very, very Victorian. I wanted to talk about that for a moment because it seemed like she was also caught in a bind of sorts in that the Victorian image or expectations of what a woman should be did not necessarily click with who she was. I'm thinking that there was some type of internal battle going on with her at the same time.

**PG:** Constantly, a constant battle. One of the things that Black women were faced with and this idea of being a Victorian was not just a question of class, even though class becomes associated with it in some way. One of the ways that Black women had to prove their humanity in so many ways, and their morality after slavery was in terms of their behavior. One of the things that is a great irony in our history is that African-American men and women become free and rush headlong into the Victorian period. [Laughs]

They have to negotiate now ... African-American men and women become free from slavery in the Victorian period. They have to immediately begin to negotiate this issue of Victorian behavior, and gender behavior, the role that they're to play as men and women, which becomes a very important measure of their humanity. Their Victorian behavior being a proper woman, I'm talking about their morality. It's not just a question of imitating white society, but it's also evidence that they have in fact now transcended the slave condition. They have to behave in this Victorian corseted, quite literal way.

Wells herself is a person who has a lot of roiling emotions all the time simmering beneath. She's also a rebel; that's all simmering beneath. She also feels she's had tremendous responsibilities as a young woman that she feels somewhat weighted down by. As you may know, she was orphaned at an early age. At the age of 16, both of her parents were killed in the Yellow Fever epidemic and she was responsible for taking care of five of her younger brothers and sisters from that point on.

She has all these happening in her life and it is political issues, and particularly the lynching issue, which helps her to find a way in the world to act to be able to almost redefine what womanhood should be, and in fact, what manhood should be. One of the things that she understands about lynching, a lot of Blacks assume that it's the ne'er-do-wells who are getting lynched, the roustabouts, the criminals who are getting lynched. Of course, Black men particularly are accused of raping white women and that's the rationale for being lynched.

When Wells begins to investigate lynching, she begins to see there's really many educated people and people with property who are getting lynched. The target is the middle-class. She's saying, "Please don't believe that just because you have behavior that is consonant with what society says behavior should be, of being a gentleman and being a lady, that you will get the rights of citizenship this way, that they will be given to you as a result of your behavior as proven to the world that we have bourgeois values. This is not going to do it. In fact, you'll be targeted." [chuckles]

Protest is really important to get these rights and not just feel that if you do the right thing, if you get educated, and if you behave in a particular way, that the rights of citizenship will be given to you, it will not. This becomes a real cleavage between conservatives and militants in this early period, particularly the late 19th century and early 20th century.

**TC:** I read somewhere that initially, it sounded like Ida B. Wells, we won't say that she condoned lynching. No one condones lynching. I think she bought the myth that had been perpetrated in the beginning regarding the reasons for lynching until her three friends ... Thomas Moss and Calvin McDowell had been lynched? Have you come across that in your research?

**PG:** Yes, and the third person is Henry Stewart. I like to always have their names. One of the things that Wells was very concerned with was how many lynching victims were killed, and no one knew their names., no one talked about them again. They had this ...

**TC:** Right, no name.

**PG:** ... Terrible death. You know, Thandi, it's almost similar to what we're experiencing in some ways today. We talk a lot about the number of Blacks who were in jail who had been put in prisons. I think you would find a lot of people who would say they must have done something wrong [chuckles] if they're in prison. Even if they didn't do exactly what someone said they did, they were doing something they shouldn't have been doing. They weren't living the certain kinds of noble, clean life, and because of that behavior, they're in prison. If their behavior were any different, they were different kinds of people, they wouldn't be in prison.

When Blacks were criminalized, particularly by the 1880s and 1890s – remember, I'll tell you what else is going on is that there are lots of Blacks now who are inundating in the Southern cities. They'll eventually go north as well. There are a lot of former slaves or people coming out of the next generation after slavery and they're unemployed. They're going into the cities, they're beginning to be in segregated neighborhoods. There is crime in lots of those areas. People believe, just as people believe pretty much now [chuckles] that if something's happening, if they're being lynched, if they're being put in jail, they must be doing something wrong because everyone says they are.

Certainly, the propaganda of Southern whites in the period was that these men – there was lots of scientific racism to back this up, to back up the sexual propensities of Blacks and particularly Black men; to back up that they were being criminals and that they were socially maladjusted, et cetera, and inferior in many ways, and that they were raping women. That they were angry, and raping white women; that that was the reason for their being lynched. A lot of people looked in and saw the situation and wondered if it would – I don't think Wells says that she believed some of the worst things being said about African-Americans, but she did say and she was talking also about Frederick Douglass.[2] People wondered what is really going on [chuckles]? People questioned it. They really weren't sure what was going on, until she begins to do her own investigations. Then she begins to understand something, that there's something much deeper going on. That this is a lot of propaganda, but that people believe that Blacks were certainly capable of this. As this was being used, she now begins to understand that this is a political issue, that this charge is being issued because of all kinds of other things, because of political competition, because people want people's property. There are other motives that is really urging this behavior on the part of whites.

**TC:** Then I want to talk about the propaganda. Like most people of the time, she initially believed the propaganda. That's not necessarily a value judgment, I'm just stating. It's almost ironic that she went on to become such a person who was so savvy and understood the importance of media and propaganda, not just writing and publishing a paper, but also speaking about it, traveling, publishing books and pamphlets.

**PG:** Yes. Besides having just incessant energy, she's an excellent writer. She is really one of the early people to understand, which is a really modern idea, that much of this has to do with perception and with writing, with disseminating information. It's an information war, it's a public relations war. It's war that's really going on, that's really a part of what's happening in the society. She is very astute to understand that in particular ways. Before we became so used to the ideas of the importance of public relations, she knew it very early on and took good advantage of it.

What she's writing, it's very vivid. She's one of the first Black journalists

2  See note on Frederick Douglass, page 9

to write narratives about the lynching victims. She's just not editorializing about how terrible lynching is, even though that's part of it. She gives us names, and she gives us the places, and she tells us how these people were lynched. She talks about the evidence of their innocence in many cases.

She really makes us see and feel what is going on. She's one of the earliest investigative reporters who also goes to the sites of these lynchings, she's interviewing witnesses, she's interviewing relatives. Not very many Black journalists particularly are doing this at this point, but she understands how to tell a story, how to be convincing, as well as how to argue her point, and how to use logic, but also to use emotion in vivid characterization. She's very special in that way as well.

**TC:** She certainly is. I remember I think it was *Southern Horrors*. I realized that I love and appreciate Ida B. Wells but I had not read any books she had written. I had read about her. I had read what others had written about her. I'd read maybe some quotes. I realized I had not read a book that she had written. I was reading *Southern Horrors*. I tell people this story all the time. I grew up as a child. I was into horror movies. I know some people into comedy, some people into drama, and some people like horror movies. I used to think the gorier the movie, "Oh, man, I really want to see that one."

I'm reading *Southern Horrors* and her description of this one man who was lynched and I had to put the book down. Let me see how much I can take on film. I couldn't take it. I had to put the book down. When you were talking about the fact that her writing was so evocative, you felt like you were there. You felt the humanity of the people, you also felt the horror of their death. Definitely, she was an excellent writer, a wonderful writer.

**PG:** Yes, indeed.

**TC:** Now I want to go back to this passion you talked about earlier.

**PG:** Can I say something very quickly?

**TC:** Yes, please.

**PG:** Also what's really wonderful about *Southern Horrors*? Most of what was in that pamphlet, *Southern Horrors*, which was the first pamphlet she published in 1892, most of what was in that pamphlet first appeared in *The New York Age,* a very important Black newspaper of the period.

**TC:** That's the one that T. Thomas Fortune was publishing.

**PG:** Editor T. Thomas Fortune, considered the best Black publisher in the country at the time and *The New York Age* was also a Black newspaper that whites read as well. After publishing that long editorial, which makes up much of *Southern Horrors* in *The New York Age*, Black women activists in New York decide to have a testimonial for her to support Wells because of course, she's exiled. She writes that editorial in exile because she has been forced out of Memphis and her newspaper office has been destroyed at that point.

The women hold this amazing, wonderful testimonial for her. One of the purposes of the testimonial was to raise enough funds so that the editorial in *The New York Age* could be published as a pamphlet and distributed. The testimonial indeed was successful. They raised something like more than $500, which was quite a sum at that point, in which other Black women and men came also as well to this testimonial led by women who came from Boston, as well as Philadelphia, as well as Brooklyn and New York City, which were really two separate cities at the time. They'd raised enough money for her to publish that pamphlet. That was a very important moment in her life and in the history of lynching.

**TC:** Yes, it was. Thank you for that. Thank you. I greatly appreciate that. I wanted to ask you about, you were talking about your motivations for writing the book on Wells, what was it that basically drove this perceived Victorian woman to have this lifelong campaign against lynching, if I'm quoting you correctly? What did you find out?

**PG:** She's a complicated person as one could imagine. One, it has a lot to do, I think, with her personal story, and then the connection to how she understands politics and how she begins to understand race and what is happening to Black men and women during her lifetime. As I mentioned before, she is orphaned at an early age. She's not only orphaned, which I won't go into, but there's also an incident in her community in Holly Springs in which her sexual motives, in fact, for wanting to take care of her younger brothers and sisters, rather than have them divided among other families in Holly Springs after the death of her parents. Her morality is really questioned by the community.

You can imagine this young girl, she's 16 years old, she's just lost her parents, she has this responsibility with her younger brothers and sisters.

She's been abandoned by her parents, she's been abandoned in some ways by the community. I think she begins to also live a life where the promise of Blacks attaining freedom is a promise that is also abandoned in so many ways by the society. I think part of it is a connection that she sees lynching as the great symbol of this abandonment, and also of how Blacks are being viewed in such a negative way. Black men are accused of raping white women, and they're accused, therefore, of being monsters.

One reason why they're thought to have the sexual proclivity is because Black women were so immoral. Since Black women were so immoral and didn't control their men, their men were out of control. The entire race is really castigated in a particular way, and she has been castigated in a sense herself. I think she also has a quest of if she can disprove the motives around lynching, if she can disprove these rationales about Blacks that are responsible for or at least people say are responsible for lynching, then she begins to also disprove the inhumanity of Blacks.

If she can disprove that, she's really turning everything upside down, including the social science of the period, including what Southern newspapers, what the press were saying, what others are saying. If she can just turn the world right-side-up again, as Sojourner Truth once said, that a lot of things would change in the society. I know it's a complicated answer to the question. I think she has this sense that lynching is at the heart of the negative ideas around race. That it's also at the heart of that Blacks really have to rise up and defend themselves and defend their integrity and defend the perceptions of the race. If they don't do that, they're lost.

She sees lynching as such a horrible thing. How can you not defend the race against this? This was also a way she's trying to mobilize Blacks to struggle for their rights in a very broad way. Lynching becomes really the mechanism, it becomes a symbol of perceptions of race, and also becomes the issue that she feels can mobilize Blacks to attain their rightful place in society.

**TC:** I know when she talks about the disappointment that she felt from her lawsuit against that railroad being overturned, she talked about wanting to gather up her race in her arms and fly away with them. That feeling of wanting to protect our people, we know she was a very strong race woman. I'm wondering, in the explanation that you just gave, it sounded like also that part of this work in some way, shape, or form would also vindicate her too.

**PG:** Oh, absolutely. I think that's true with most leaders. I think there's a personal aspect that drives as well as a political aspect that drives because something has to make people so assertive and so aggressive to take on an issue like she does and like all leaders do. Not just African-American leaders, but which all leaders do because at the base of leadership is assertion, isn't it? The base of assertion is aggression and at the base of aggression is an anger and dissatisfaction. The idea is that what separates people who do positive things with that aggression versus negative things is this being able to conduct all of that energy into something positive and to transform oneself.

You can see this transformation of Wells. Wells prays about her anger, she's an angry person, she prays. She calls it her besetting sin. It's because she knows it can be destructive if she's not able to transform it into something positive. She works at it. What's interesting about her as I figured to write about is that she's very conscious about all of this. There's a diary that she has that she kept when she was in her 20s. One can see much of this and the struggle. She does struggle to find a positive way to express herself and to commit herself too.

This is there along with her external political commitments with her race love. Not all Black leaders really love Black people. She really did. Also, which you mentioned which is important too, the sense of that Black people needed to be protected. This "race in my arms, I want to embrace them all and fly away with them." To fly away with them in a place where they'll be safe.

There's a theme in much of her writing, and much in also her campaign against lynching, to protect African-Americans, to protect their lives and to protect their bodies and then to protect their well-being. She takes this almost upon herself as a figure to do this. She's a very unrelenting figure until the day she dies. She's very vigorous and never gives up. Also optimistic. Stays optimistic too about the race finding its rightful place in the society.

**TC:** Back to the Victorian part again because this figures so large in her life. I see it's like the remnants and the after-effects of what we're dealing with right now today. This theme of our people need to be protected. "I'm out here doing this work because we need to be protected."

"I'm a defender of the people," but at the same time, we're struggling under the weight of this Victorian puritanical madness which says that women have a particular place and men have a particular place. A woman's place is not to be out advocating for the race. Definitely not advocating for protection, that's a man's job. She's catching flack from men saying, "Move over, let me do it." She says, "You need to come out and do it."

**PG:** Absolutely. She gets flack not just from men too. She's also transgressive of what women should be doing in terms of activism. This was a period in the late 19th century, 20th century. The first, of course, National Association of Colored Women was just the first nationwide organization of Black women is founded in 1896. Women are very active and particularly so in their communities and doing wonderful things around, but most of them, their primary thought was in uplift and education. Within this fear of what women did and not to transgress that into the more political aspects of activism.

Of course, Wells was very political and believed in uplift and helping the community and all that too. She also really wanted to lead the race in other aspects and lynching, of course, is a great example. For a woman to be involved with lynching, it has to do with sexuality and rape. Makes many question her, and she had to learn herself. One of the most surprising things I think in my research on her is how she worked to get beyond those ideas of what's called true womanhood, the ideals of true womanhood.

**TC:** Can you give me an example?

**PG:** She is, in the beginning, very conservative. If you look at her early writing, it's very conservative and did not show political acumen. In fact, she was anti-politics for a very long time, "we shouldn't be concerned with those things. All we should be concerned with is uplifting our community. We shouldn't be worried about what's going on outside of it." She does change and that makes her a very interesting person because you start one way, and really, by the end of her life, she's different.

**TC:** Can you give me an example when you said pushing the boundaries of true womanhood?

**PG:** There's so many ways. One way is in her writing. She was one of the few women who really wrote about national politics and about Black political leaders and men, which she was very critical of. Oh, she had a biting tongue. She had a sting when she was criticizing people. There were a number of women journalists in the period but they were writing about things in the community and about church affairs for the most part and those kinds of issues but not Wells. Wells was writing about politics. That's one thing.

She was the first woman to be elected an officer of the National Press Association. Before she became that active in the press association, women were not certainly in the forefront of the National Black Press Association. She was the first woman to be an officer in something called the Afro-American League which is actually the first nationwide Black organization. It was a civil rights organization that considered, for the most part, the province of men but Wells was right in there with them. Most women were involved with the National Association of Colored Women, the all women's group, but not so much involved with these other political groups.

She's forever transgressing those lines. People talked a lot about her. They wondered about what [kind of] wife she was going to be. When she finally marries Ferdinand Barnett[3] in 1895, people wonder, as another club woman said, if she could be married to a cause as well as to a man [chuckles]. Everyone knew that she was not going to be a typical housewife. What kind of person is she going to be? How are they going to manage this and how was Ferdinand going to deal with her? How was she going to keep up her anti-lynching campaigns while she's married and having children? She has four children in pretty quick succession after she gets married.

She's struggling with lots of those things. Finally, there was a belief in the society at this period of time when she begins having children in the 1900s that women should be at home in the formative years of children when they're growing up. That mothers certainly had to be there. They had to be with the children all the time. They had to shape their wheels at an early stage or otherwise, they'd lose the children forever. Wells believed that too. She's struggling to stay at home with the children but also to continue her activist life.

---

3 Ferdinand Lee Barnett (1852-1936) was a journalist, lawyer, and civil rights activist in Chicago, Illinois, beginning in the late Reconstruction era. In 1895, Barnett married Ida B. Wells. In 1896, Barnett became Illinois' first Black assistant state's attorney.

At some point, she's asked by the women Republicans, she's asked to canvass the state of Illinois and talk to women about voting. She decides to do it but she decides to do it by taking her firstborn with her. That's how she resolved that issue of being with her children and activism. She was nursing at the time. She says at one point, she says, "I think I'm the only woman who ever talked to women about political matters with a nursing baby with me." She's always pushing the envelope all the time.

**TC:** Pushing the envelope. That was something that just seems so unheard of.

**PG:** Sometimes we think that we're just steadily progressing and becoming more modern but we tend to actually go back and forth. There are many aspects of life in the early 20th century called the Progressive Era when women were doing some interesting things. For example, most of the Black women activists like Mary Church Terrell[4] and Fannie Barrier Williams[5], and Margaret Murray Washington[6] who was married to Booker T Washington.[7] Isn't that interesting they all kept their maiden names as well as their married names? They didn't give up their names. They didn't give up their careers.

Women become a little bit more conservative in the 1950s, and then it shifts back again. It's interesting. These women were very, very progressive in this period but Wells was even more progressive than the progressive [chuckles] women in this period. There was very interesting discussions about what the role of women is because roles were changing. We were moving into an industrialized modern period. Black women are becoming more and more educated. They're very much wanting to get into the activist realms. There's really great discussions about the roles of women in this period.

---

4 See note on Mary Church Terrell, p. 9

5 Fannie Barrier Williams (1855-1944) was an African-American educator, civil rights, and women's rights activist, and the first Black woman to gain membership to the Chicago Woman's Club.

6 Margaret Murray Washington (1865-1925) was an American educator, principal of Tuskegee Normal and Industrial Institute which later became Tuskegee University. She was the third wife of Booker T. Washington. After the death of her husband in 1915, Washington worked to improve the educational system for Black Americans.

7 Booker T. Washington (1856-1915) was an American educator, author and orator. Between 1890 and 1915, Washington was the dominant leader in the African-American community. As lynchings in the South reached a peak in 1895, Washington gave a speech, known as the "Atlanta compromise", that called for Black progress through education and entrepreneurship, rather than trying to challenge Jim Crow segregation and disenfranchisement of Black voters in the South. William Monroe Trotter and W. E. B. Du Bois were among Black opponents of Washington's compromise.

**TC:** Let me ask you this, and this will be my last question because I told you 30 minutes and we're a bit over that now. I don't want to take too much more of your time although I am thoroughly enjoying this. In your research on Ida B. Wells, what were you able to find out regarding her home life, her family life? I've always found it so inspiring and wonderful that she was able to do the work that she did while being married with four children. It seemed to me that she had a very supportive and loving spouse that enabled her to do that.

**PG:** Very much so. And Thandi, I was so happy to find a good spouse [laughs] in Ferdinand Barnett. They had a lot of, even though they had their issues, but he was a man ... first of all, he was a lawyer. He also published the first Black newspaper in Chicago. He was as militant in his way even though he was a quiet type of man which Wells was not. He had also had a very militant sensibility so they were very compatible on that level. He obviously liked smart women. He was a widower when he married Ida. His first wife was the first Black woman to graduate from the University of Michigan and also helped him with his newspaper, *The Conservator*; was just a well-known intellectual figure and a musical figure, et cetera.

He liked smart women who were very capable. Ida Wells, of course, also fit this bill. His own father was a cook on the steamboats that plied Lake Michigan. Ferdinand could also cook. He often cooked for the family too. He helped in some of those chores. When it really came to supporting her, he was very supportive of her activism. In some instances urged her to confront some issues because Wells was criticized all the time. I don't know how she survived the criticism.

She must have had a very thick skin even though she could be very emotional about some of the criticism of her activities, and criticism from men as you alluded to earlier of she's taking a man's place and men should be doing this, etc., etc., and she's doing it. Sometimes she'd say, "Okay, let the guys do it. I'm tired." He'd say, "No. You have to do this. This is important. If you don't do it, no one's going to do it."

It was a very good marriage, a very supportive marriage. They were able to compromise with each other in some ways. There's some things that she didn't like but would allow in exchange for some things that he didn't like but would allow. When it came to the big issues, they were very compatible. It seemed to be a very, very good marriage.

**TC:** A very good match. A match made in struggle.

[Laughter]

**TC:** Professor Giddings, we are 45 minutes into this interview, and I told you 30. I knew this was going to happen. I was actually hoping it wouldn't happen. [chuckles]

**PG:** I've enjoyed it too.

**TC:** Thank you. I want to thank you for your time. I greatly appreciate it. In closing, is there an issue or is there anything that you want to get across that I did not ask you about? There's so much when it comes to Ida but is there anything that's really burning that you wanted to mention?

**PG:** I think nothing's really burning. I don't know how to put it in the context. The other thing that's really interesting about her is that she has two lives. She has a life in the South, of course, as this anti-lynching activist and she stays with racial violence as racial violence follows Blacks who migrate to the North. When Blacks migrate to the North, so do the race riots and destructions of Black communities, etc., and she's right there talking about that. It's also very important of what she does once she does get married and settles in Chicago in which she just found the first Black women's suffrage organization.

She creates the Alpha Suffrage Club, which becomes very important in Chicago politics in electing the first Black alderman. She organizes a settlement house for poor Black migrants in Chicago. She's a co-founder of the NAACP which she doesn't get along with particularly well as a whole story but she is there at the beginning of the NAACP. She's also involved in a number of interracial organizations in Chicago. She stays very, very active.

Finally, in the last years of her life, she runs unsuccessfully but she runs for a state Senate seat. The first Black woman to do so in Illinois. She does that the year before her death in 1930. She just is an activist who just ... I say it because some writers have portrayed her as a brave person but who becomes irrelevant in her later years. That's not the case at all. She is just an important factor in national life until her death.

**TC:** I just thought of a question and a half or two other questions.

**PG:** Go ahead.

**TC:** I wanted to ask you about her religion and spirituality, how that was an important part of her life but also her view of spirituality. There's just so many different anecdotes about Ida B. Wells that we can all talk about that we love. One of the ones that I love is when she went to visit the brothers in Arkansas when she snuck back into the South.

After having been run out and threatened with death if she ever set foot in the South again, she snuck back to interview the brothers in Arkansas, the farmers who were accused of shooting up or shooting back. They shot back in defense as they were being attacked and they were put in jail. When they sang her this song, and she said, "If you truly believe God is on your side, why don't you ask God to open up these gates? Don't you believe?"

**PG:** That's right. Stop singing. Get going. Save yourself.

**TC:** You stop singing. Start swinging. Stop singing, start swinging. I was like, "Wow." I wanted to ask you about that but also I know that she had this relationship with Bishop Henry McNeal Turner[8] of the AME Church which was also going to lead into my next question. It was in your book *When and Where I Enter*, where I read and that chapter, it always blows my mind how the precursor to the FBI, I don't know if it was the military. It was in the military intelligence division whatever.

**PG:** That's right.

**TC:** They're keeping tabs on Garvey.[9] One of the reasons why they're saying "see this Garvey is somebody we need to watch is because he's meeting with Ida B. Wells."

**PG:** Exactly.

**TC:** I'm like, "Whoa." The idea of religion and spirituality in her life but also maybe the influence on her but not necessarily the attraction that she has this relationship with Henry McNeal Turner and with Marcus Garvey. If you wanted to comment on those two areas?

---

8 Henry McNeal Turner (1834-1915) was a minister, politician, and the 12th bishop of the African Methodist Episcopal Church (AME). After the American Civil War, Turner began to support Black nationalism and the emigration of Blacks to Liberia.

9 Marcus Garvey (1887-1940) was a Jamaican political activist, publisher, journalist and orator. He was the founder of the Universal Negro Improvement Association (UNIA). Garvey campaigned for an end to European colonial rule across Africa and advocated the political unification of the continent.

**PG:** Spirituality, she's brought up in the Methodist Church but she's catholic with a small c. She attends all churches. She attends Presbyterian churches and Methodists, the AME churches, and Baptist churches. She mobilizes all of them, people knew all of them for her own movement and addresses all of these bodies.

**TC:** In other words, she liked to "church hop" as we say?

**PG:** Yes. She was very involved in church life. In Memphis, she taught Sunday school. The fact she taught Sunday School alongside Thomas Moss, her friend who gets lynched in Memphis. When you look at her diary particularly, you see how often she prays. This is really another key to her activism, I'm really glad you brought this up. She thinks about her life and she thinks about all the travails she's been through particularly with her being orphaned, etc.. She decides that God is doing this, as she says, to fit her for His kingdom. That it's her job to get through this and to get through it being stronger and to get through it.

That there's something that is important that's waiting for her. God must have an objective for her of why he was putting her through all this because she knew she would emerge stronger. She just felt that there was something that she was supposed to be doing. This is another thing that really I think gives her strength to do that kind of thing.

I wish someone would do a really good biography of Bishop Turner, he's one of my favorite people. He's very important. Wells was very, very critical of most clergy and particularly critical of bishops, [laughs] but not Turner.

Bishop Turner was one of the few people who came to her support when others were giving her a very difficult time. He always supported her and thought highly of her. Of course, he wanted Blacks to go back to Liberia. He, like Marcus Garvey, was immigrationist, who believed that Blacks would be better off in Africa. Turner, of his time, was a leading immigrationist just as Garvey was of his time. Wells didn't necessarily believe about going to Africa but she did at one point certainly believe that one should leave the South to really be able to fulfill oneself. They were so oppressive in the South.

At one point, as you might know, in protest of the lynching in 1892 in Memphis, she tells Blacks to go to Oklahoma and leave a city where there's no justice for us as she said.

Thousands of Blacks actually did, into new settlements. This is where some all-Black towns in Oklahoma begin to get settled. She does believe in this movement. There is a religious idea of exodus and finding one's fulfillment in the "Promised Land" that Blacks were searching for. This is a part of her thinking as well. The government is very concerned about Black behavior in World War I. There are rumors that the Germans have influenced Blacks to be anti-American during the war among other issues.

There's a Secret Service file on Ferdinand Barnett as well because he spoke perfect German. He'd learned that in Chicago. They were worried about him. They were particularly worried about Wells because they considered her an agitator. They were trying to keep things so calm during World War I and certainly, to suppress any protest and she just never stopped. She never stopped. At one point, as you might know if you read the autobiography, she was actually confronted by the Secret Service. All these punitive laws had been passed by that point. She really could have found herself in prison or even executed.

When the Secret Service threatened her with this, she said, "You have to do what you have to do and I have to do what I have to do." The files about her, the few that I have found really did say that she's an agitator, we have to watch her and we have to watch this guy Garvey because he's around her. He's going to be influenced by her and this is going to be a problem. She is on some of those, it's not the FBI yet but the pre-FBI most wanted list.

**TC:** Definitely. What a wonderful way to end this conversation.

**PG:** Indeed.

**TC:** I've been speaking with Paula Giddings, author of *When and Where I Enter: The Impact of Black Women on Race and Sex in America* and the author of a forthcoming book on Ida B. Wells Barnett. The title of that book is *Ida: A Sword Amongst Lions?*

**PG:** That's right, Among Lions.

**TC:** A Sword Among Lions. We're waiting with bated breath for that book to come out in March of 2008. Professor Paula Giddings is a professor of African-American Studies at Smith College in Massachusetts. You're also on the board of *Meridians*. What is *Meridians?*

**PG:** *Meridians* is a journal. I'm actually the editor of *Meridians*, which is a journal. The subtitle is Feminism, Race, Transnationalism. It's really the only scholarly journal of its kind in which we publish scholarship by women of color around this issue of transnationalism, it's international as well as race and feminism.

**TC:** You're the editor of *Meridians* and you're on the board of Women's World?

**PG:** That's right.

**TC:** Women's World is?

**PG:** Women's World is a network of women writers in which we really are concerned about the issue of gender-based censorship of women all around the world. Of women not only who are censored over their expressions around feminist issues, around sexuality, around women's roles in the society, etc. We're very concerned about women, because they're women, because they're talking about gender, who are suppressed all around the world.

**TC:** Thank you so much, Professor Giddings, for allowing me to invade your time.

**PG:** Thank you. I enjoyed it.

# Pearl Cleage Speaking with Charlayne Hunter-Gault

*Playwright, author, poet and activist Pearl Cleage is currently the Mellon Playwright in Residence at the Alliance Theatre in Atlanta, Georgia. Her career spans more than forty years and across numerous genres. Charlayne Hunter-Gault and Hamilton Holmes were the first African-Americans to enroll in the University of Georgia in 1961. A former news anchor with the MacNeil/Lehrer Newshour, Hunter-Gault is a multi-award winning journalist and author and her career also spans more than forty years. This event was part of the National Black Arts Festival held in Atlanta, Georgia, July 14-16, 2006.*

**Pearl Cleage:** Thank you very much. I want to thank all of you for being here. I think at this time of major transition and conflict everywhere we turn, it's fitting that the National Black Arts Festival host a conversation about our role as citizens of the world. It's also a time when we need to commit ourselves to thinking deeply about what it means to be active citizens of a country that is at war in so many places all at the same time, for reasons our president seems to find increasingly difficult to articulate or to understand.

The reasons for wars are often presented as complex by those who wage them, but the end result is always the same and it is always very simply explained. War is somebody's child killing somebody else's child. It's time for us to stop it before another drop of blood is shed.

[applause]

**PC:** Thank you. I want to say just a word about how we're going to proceed through the evening and then I will introduce our guest. We're going to be talking for about an hour. Our guest has laryngitis so we're going to try not to work her to death, but we're going to try to get her to talk for about an hour. Then after that, we will be finding books right outside. Any of you who would like to purchase the book, it's a wonderful book. She will be signing right outside.

Now, it's my pleasure to introduce our honored guest, although she truly is someone who needs no introduction. Charlayne Hunter-Gault made civil rights history as the first African-American woman to graduate from the University of Georgia in 1962 and has gone on to establish herself as one of television's premier journalists. She joined *The MacNeil/Lehrer Report* in 1978 as a correspondent and became *The NewsHour*'s national correspondent in 1983.

Beginning her career as the Talk of the Town reporter for *The New Yorker,* she won a Russell Sage Fellowship to Washington University when she joined *Trans-Action* Magazine. In 1967, she joined the investigative news team at WRC-TV in Washington, D.C. and also anchored the local evening news. In 1968, Ms. Hunter-Gault joined *The New York Times* as a metropolitan reporter specializing in coverage of the urban African-American community.

In 1989, she was also a correspondent for MacNeil/Lehrer Productions' five-part series, *Learning in America*. Ms. Hunter-Gault left *The NewsHour* in June 1997 after 20 years at PBS to pursue other projects aimed mainly at addressing what she calls a basic lack of information among Americans about the African continent. Her new book, which we will be talking about today, *New News Out of Africa*,[1] is part of that ongoing work.

Her work was honored with many awards during her ten years at the paper, including the National Urban Coalition Award for Distinguished Urban Reporting. Ms. Hunter-Gault has also being published in *The New York Times Magazine, Saturday Review, The New York Times Book Review, Essence* and *Vogue*. During her association with *The NewsHour*, Ms. Hunter-Gault won additional awards, two Emmys and a Peabody for

---

1  *New News Out of Africa: Uncovering Africa's Renaissance* was published in July 2006.

excellence in broadcast journalism for her work on Apartheid's People, a *NewsHour* series on South Africa.

She also received the 1986 Journalist of the Year Award from the National Association of Black Journalists, the 1990 Sidney Hillman Award, the Good Housekeeping Broadcast Personality of the Year Award, the American Women in Radio and Television Award and two awards from the Corporation for Public Broadcasting for Excellence in Local Reporting. In addition to *New News Out of Africa*, Ms. Hunter-Gault is also the author of *In My Place*, her 1992 memoir about her experiences at the University of Georgia. She currently makes her home in Johannesburg, South Africa. It is an honor to present to you Ms. Charlayne Hunter-Gault.

[applause]

**PC:** You open your book with the words of Countee Cullen's[2] poem *Heritage*. I want to just quote it here.

> *What is Africa to me:*
> *Copper sun or scarlet sea,*
> *Jungle star or jungle track,*
> *Strong bronzed men, or regal black*
> *Women from whose loins I sprang*
> *When the birds of Eden sang?*
> *One three centuries removed*
> *From the scenes his fathers loved,*
> *Spicy grove, cinnamon tree,*
> *What is Africa to me?*

Why did you pick those particular words to open your book?

**Charlayne Hunter-Gault:** I've been scared to death about this tonight, because here I am sitting with Pearl Cleage.

[laughter]

**CHG:** I am just so relieved.

[laughter]

**PC:** I'm honored.

2 Countee Cullen (1903-1946) was a poet, novelist, and essayist associated with the Harlem Renaissance. He was one of the most prominent African-American writers of his time and is known for his lyrical poetry, which often explored themes of race, love, and identity. He was also involved in various civil rights organizations.

**CHG:** Thank you so much. Leave it to a writer to go right to my favorite part of the book. At least one part of my statement. I think that so many Americans are familiar with Countee Cullen, especially African-Americans. I wanted something for this book that resonated throughout for people and I wanted everybody maybe to start with something familiar. I think that many African-Americans have read that poem and I don't know how it has resonated with them, but I thought that it would have resonance for me and for them.

Certainly, it would fit with my theme of trying to describe what Africa was to me as a child growing up in Covington, going to the segregated movie theater on Saturdays, watching the Tarzan movies and not realizing how racist they were. Onto the years where I developed a real consciousness about the continent and about America's involvement in it, about its adventures and misadventures. It just seemed to me to raise the right question that I wanted to keep in my mind as I answered it throughout the pages of the book. It's a wonderful poem.

**PC:** It's a great poem. It was amusing to me to read what you had to say about being a little girl, going to the movies and watching these Tarzan movies, and realizing that I was in Detroit doing the same thing. We all grew up with this terribly incorrect and skewed vision of what Africa was.

**CHG:** Did you know it was incorrect at that time?

**PC:** Well, I certainly didn't when I was just looking at it until I said something to my mother about it. My mother and father talked about how wrong the picture was for about two weeks. Then after that, I understood. You don't realize as a kid, you're going to the movies with your friends. You know that this isn't really what Africa is like even as a child, but I think that we do that thing that Black Americans do, which is we remove what we know is incorrect from the movie.

We just like the story, we like the adventure, we like the love story. We remove ourselves and put those blinders on when it comes time to look at the people who are representing us. I felt that strongly when I read that poem of the book. When I first picked it up, I was really struck by the title, *New News from Africa*. Can you talk a little bit about what you mean by *New News from Africa*?

**CHG:** I just came this afternoon from University of Georgia and I was telling them down there that after all these years, Georgia has evolved for me overtime from the wretched place that it started out to be, to a place I really bonded with. I said, just for example, in my new book I talk about my journalism professor, who came into the journalism class on the first day and asked us, "What are the news?" We all looked at him and then he looked back at us and he said, "Not a single new." I never understood what the point of that was actually.

[laughter]

**CHG:** He didn't explain it. It occurred to me as I was writing this book that it would be the perfect introduction to the book because when we think about the African continent, there isn't a single new image that comes out of it that isn't through the prism of what I called the four Ds: death, disease, disaster and despair. I wanted to talk in my book about what is Africa to me, because I covered and continue to cover those things that do reveal death, disease, disaster and despair, but I cover so much more.

I'm looking for some balance in my report. Also, to present to American audiences in particular, because I think the European audiences do get a little bit more out of the BBC and others but still, there's things that they could do better as well.

The New News is not good news unless it's used in the way that we used it at *MacNeil/Lehrer* which was, good news is news that can be used by people to make intelligent decisions about appropriations for Africa or whether to support the war on terror as it goes to Africa or whatever. The New News is news that I don't think Americans are aware of that may in fact, be having a significant impact on the continent not least, on the death, disease, disaster and despair. Let's do one quick little exercise. How many of you in this room have heard of NEPAD?[3] Raise your hands real high, I want to see.

Well, that's not many. That's less than one handful, or Peer Review on the African continent, or Black Economic Empowerment in South Africa. These are things that are happening on the continent that hold up the

3  The New Partnership for Africa's Development (NEPAD) is an economic development program of the African Union. NEPAD, adopted in July 2001 in Lusaka, Zambia, aims to provide an overarching vision and policy framework for accelerating economic co-operation and integration among African countries.

promise. I didn't say there was a renaissance and I designed this amazing cover. I didn't define the picture cover.

**PC:** I love the cover. It is so stunning.

**CHG:** The sun is rising to indicate that there is a renaissance, a borning, although it's not yet high up in the sky. If these things that I've just mentioned had only five or six people in the audience raise their hands who know about it actually come to pass, you will have on the continent what I like to call the second wind of change.

Harold Macmillan[4] spoke to the South African parliament in 1960 and told them – this was the all-white parliament in Cape Town – that there was a new wind of change blowing across the continent and they should be prepared for it. What he was talking about at that time was the wind of the end of colonialism. Sure enough, it came. As we know, for many reasons, that needs the assistance by the West, of some of the most despotic tyrants in the history of the world, who were propped up because they served as bulwarks against communism during the Cold War.

A lot of things contributed to the independence not realizing the dream that many had hoped, but now there is a second wind of change and its new rules of the road that the African leaders themselves have now put into place. If in fact, they adhere to these new rules of the road like good economic and fiscal management, transparency, empowerment of women, respect for human rights, and these sort of principles.

At the same time on the other hand, with the Peer Review, where they allow prominent Africans like Graça Machel[5] and others not elected, to go into their countries to actually analyze and in a sense, grade them on those areas, and then help them to work towards fixing what is broken, then you will indeed have a new continent or a second wind of change blowing throughout the continent.

Already, not as many as we would like have gone through the process, but some have completed the process, including Rwanda, which just came out of a genocide. Yet Rwanda has come back and is roaring forward. I think

---

4 Harold Macmillan (1894-1986) was a Conservative Prime Minister of the United Kingdom from 1957 to 1963.
5 Graça Machel (born 1945) is a Mozambican politician and humanitarian. She is the widow of former President of Mozambique Samora Machel (1975–1986) and former President of South Africa Nelson Mandela (1998-2013). She is the only woman in modern history to have served as First Lady of two countries.

that's one, if I'm not mistaken, that's gone through it.

The two or three that have gone through it, South Africa has completed it and many more have signed up for it. Which is another reason the West needs the good news, so that the idea of those principles within NEPAD is that okay, Africans say, if we do this, then we will have earned support from the West, which many African countries surely need as they climb out of this period in which, as I said, the West helped them and their awful leaders to fall into. Whatever your question was, that was the answer.

[laughter]

**PC:** That was a good answer. Why do you think it is? I know that many of us complain mightily about the news coverage of almost everything that we get in the American media now, but why do you think specifically that what we still tend to get, the news we get about Africa, is dealing with death and destruction and all of the terrible problems that we know exist? Why is that the only news that we get? Do you think that that's something that we as people can work on? Is the news available and we're just not getting it?

**CHG:** Well yes, the news is available, it's in my book, and you can get it right out there.

[laughter]

**CHG:** That is a complicated question, but I would have expected that from you. Part of it is that the news media in general, whether it's Africa or the Middle East or wherever, has this dictum, "If it bleeds, it leads." They think that that's what you guys and ladies want. That if it's something terrible happening you want to know exactly the minute it happens and everything that happens regardless. Sometimes that's justified and sometimes it isn't, but that's been one of the age-old dictums of the news media, "If it bleeds, it leads."

The second thing is that as it relates to Africa and that particular prism through which news media managers see the continent, if Mozambique has a flood and a baby is born in a tree, well that's so exotic and exciting. It happened that that was a good thing, [clears throat] excuse me, that everybody went and covered it, because it helped to raise awareness and probably stimulate the release of resources. When you have conflict, oh God, that's what African news is made of, conflict. How many of you know that since 1998, the 13 wars that were then waging on the continent have now been reduced to three or less than three?

That in a few days, the Congo, which is still fragile, but how long was that? The conflict of the Congo, 40 years, and they're voting in a democratic election for the first time. It's not going to be perfect but remember, South Africa is the place we all love now as the greatest democracy in Africa but look at how many people, tens of thousands of people, died in the run-up to the South African election in 1994. Look at what happened in the run-up to our independence. I think sometimes, remember 1968 when the cities erupted in flames after the death of Martin Luther King.

Lyndon Johnson[6] put together something called the Kerner Commission, which was to look into the causes of this, whatever people – "conscious" people call it something else, but other people call it riots. Whatever we want to call it. It blew up America, essentially. They concluded that the media were partly to blame. It was such a surprise to America that this happened, and the reason was because the media had no eyes and ears in those communities where the rage was building up, because people didn't have the basic necessities of life and the basic services of life, and so it dried up like a raisin in the sun and exploded.

One of the solutions was to recruit, train and incorporate into the news media more people of color. Sure enough, the texture of the reporting from America's Black communities began to change. I make no apologies, I say in the book that I've always had problems with the term *objective* as it relates to journalists, because we're all products of our environments and our backgrounds. We can make a big effort to be fair, but objective is not possible when you're dealing with something other than your computer, and I'm not my computer.

I bleed when I see people bleed, and so what does it mean? Remember the whole thing about this twoness that we as African-Americans experience, "two warring souls in one dark body." Well, I resolved that a long time ago. I've resolved it as it relates to my perspective on Africa, because it is as an African-American woman I make no apologies for that, because I think

---

6 Lyndon Baines Johnson (1908-1973), often referred to as LBJ, served as the U.S. Vice-President under President John F. Kennedy from 1961 to 1963, and subsequently became President following Kennedy's assassination. Johnson's presidency lasted from 1963 to 1969. He is remembered for his efforts to advance civil rights and combat poverty but his presidency was also marked by controversy over the Vietnam War.

within that I do present a fair and balanced picture of whatever it is I'm covering. What does it do to my coverage that I am an African-American woman? It affects the choices often, that I make.

When there isn't some breaking news like a spark that ignites a war or a flood that ignites whatever, I make choices about people and trying to tell their stories based on what I think is interesting and what I think Americans would be interested in. A white person or an Asian person or some other group might make a different choice. It doesn't mean that any of us have made the wrong choice, it just means that we're all making choices based on our interest, our backgrounds, which argues for diversity.

If you have diversity you'll get Charlayne's report, which is coming from an African-American woman who has more years than we'd like to probably think about, but it's over 40, in the media. We read that and we understand where she's coming from and then we read another report, a different reporter. The viewer and the reader and the listener is able to take all of that information and process it and then come out with good news and therefore, good judgments.

**PC:** Part of that I think is really reflected in the story you tell about a young man who was a member of the Black Panther Party in 1972. You had just started covering Harlem and you were trying to go to a news conference representing the *New York Times*. The young brother, and I'm sure many of you knew radical young brothers like this, asked her what publication, sisters too. Mostly, the brothers were the ones that would get me to do what I'm talking about, which is to ask her what publication she was representing. When she said the *New York Times* the brother said, "You have to leave because we know that we cannot get fair coverage of what's going to happen here in the *New York Times* because the Man (capital M) is not going to let you tell our story in the *New York Times*." Why don't you say what you answered him, because I thought that was such a great answer.

**CHG:** Actually, it was his answer. I said to him, "Okay, it is true. I work for the Man." I said, "Have you ever read anything I've written?" He said, "No." I said, "Let's make a deal. Let me come into this conference." This was when the Panthers were reinventing themselves. They were trying to shed their image of being hell raisers on the West Coast and killing people and killing each other and doing all kinds of evil, and feeding children. Breakfast programs for poor children. I said, "If what you see in the newspaper tomorrow isn't an accurate reflection of what has taken place here, then don't let me come in the next time."

He thought about that for a minute and he said, "Okay, but on one condition," and I said, "Okay, what is that?" He said, "That you come in right." I knew immediately what he meant. I had been the subject of news here at Athens, in Atlanta and I had seen reporters not coming in right when it related to me as the news subject. For years since I left Georgia I had tried at the *New Yorker* and other places I had worked to represent Black people, because this was my interest and focus of coverage, and portray them in ways that were recognizable to themselves.

I knew exactly what the brother meant. I said, "You got a deal." The next time I saw him was sometime after this. He's walking up the street. I see him and he says, "Right on sister." I say, "Power to the people." I knew I was old.

[laughter]

**CHG:** The thing is, I don't even remember what that Panther looked like except he was wearing a black beret and a black jersey and a black pants and black socks and black shoes. I wish I could run into him because it's such a great – What would you call that? You're the English teacher. It's such a great a frame for the expectations. For anything, especially for coming into places like Africa where you get so much exploitation, so much misrepresentation, and so much Afro-pessimism in part perpetuated by our brother who's a wonderful reporter and writer. I think that his own story may have given rise to the term Afro-pessimism.

When I think in fact, he was simply bleeding from what he himself had seen of the blood of Rwanda. As you know, he wrote this book[7] in which he talked about being – After he had seen these bodies floating down the river, where they had been chopped to pieces in the Hutu-Tutsi conflict. He talked about how glad he was that his parents had been on that boat that got out of there all those years ago when the slaves were taken out.

7 Keith Richburg, formerly a reporter for the *Washington Post*; author, *Out of America: A Black Man Confronts Africa* (2009)

People just took that, especially people who had no intention to come in, who had not checked their preconceptions at the door, and wanted to be fed something that would justify their Afro-pessimism. They took that brother's story and then just created this industry of Afro-pessimism and justified it because this brother had written it, and who better could know than a Black man how bad it is?

I just feel really bad because this brother is a righteous brother. I just think that people use what he had written. I say in my book, because I think I even refer to it, but I say somewhere on one of those pages, I said that even when we bleed we have to maintain what it is that we are. We are reporters. Let that blood fuel our passion but not turn us off to the humanity that's out there. Can I tell one quick story?

**PC:** Sure, please.

**CHG:** I covered the floods in Mozambique. Most of you are familiar, because this picture went around the world of the woman having a baby in the tree. I'm sure all of you saw that.

**PC:** I actually put that in a novel. I remember that story very well.

**CHG:** I know how you do things so I'm going to be real careful up here.

[laughter]

**CHG:** Unless you make me the beautiful protagonist. This is an amazing story and it's one of those that helped me appreciate that I am more than my computer. I went sometime after the baby had been born in a tree, but the aftermath of the flood was still horrendous. I found this family in a refugee camp. Actually, it was a church because the father in the family was a minister. There was a refugee camp and he was in the church that was sponsoring this camp, and he and his family were in the church. They told me their story.

The wife, when the waters came rushing, it was in the night and they heard this sound. They realized that the waters were a block away. They came rushing out and they ran and ran ahead of this water and they didn't get to the safety zone. The water was so close now that they just climbed up on the roof of this house where there were some of the neighbors also, and the woman was pregnant. Within hours she gave birth to a baby girl, and the rains are pouring.

As a woman I'm relating to this. I'm the reporter but I'm also remembering childbirth and thinking about what it must have been like doing it, let alone in the hospital with all the help I had, but on a roof with the rain pouring down and all this. This first baby is born a girl but 30 minutes later, another one comes. She has twins. Now, they could not come down from that roof because of the waters and the rain for three days, by which time one of them, I don't remember in which order, one of them had died. They suffered quite a bit.

I turned to the father. I come out of a church, don't we all? My grandfather was a preacher. My grandmother was a saint but my grandfather was a preacher. My father was an army chaplain who later took up a church when he finished his tours of 20 years. I know a little bit about faith, and I know a little bit about doubting faith.

Again, this is perspective because another journalist might have written a story that was as good as mine but might not have asked that question because his daddy wasn't a preacher. I said to him, "What did this do to your faith in God? This terrible ordeal you've just had?" He said quite calmly but convincingly, "It strengthened my faith in God." I said, "Wait a minute, you just told me a story about –" and I repeated the thing. I said, "How could that strengthen your faith in God?" Do you know what he said? He said, "Because God could have taken all of us. He only took one."

Now, to me, that was pretty amazing. I was so moved by this that I – Even all these days after the floods, the waters were still high. We had boots up to here and there were things running through the – I don't even like to think about today. It was some miles out away from the refugee camp to find this house where they had been in, and take the journey that she had described to the roof of where the baby was born.

I almost didn't get through the standup, trying to tell people about this thing. I stood there and I said, "I'm not even going to wipe the tears from my eyes because I am not my computer. I am a journalist, I'm a human being, and how would I be objective about that?" Those are some of the choices that I made, given who I am. I think it's about coming in right. You check your preconceptions at the door. Look, I didn't know I was going to find this family, and everybody's looking for another baby born in a tree. Others are looking for that. Yet, I found a story that is almost more powerful. Certainly, we believe so.

**PC:** You talk a lot about family in the book, when you're talking about the problems that new democracies are facing, and the problems that some of these countries are addressing so aggressively trying to move into the next phase of their existence. One of the things that is such a tremendous threat to the family structure, to the traditional African extended family, is the real terror of HIV and AIDS. You even have a quote in the book from Desmond Tutu[8] talking about how AIDS is the new apartheid because it's so destructive and it is really ripping apart the fabric of what has held all these people together.

Do you have any feeling that the efforts that are being made to work on HIV/AIDS to try to really address this tremendous problem, are they actually making any headway at all or are we going to have to really look at what this will mean for generations to come with all of these orphans with these extended families that are so overwhelmed? I was really moved by one of the things you said, about it used to be when a young parent died that the extended family would gather together. Then they would decide who was going to take the young children.

Now, there are so many young children who need help that when the extended family comes together, everyone looks away when it comes down to what's going to happen to the children. I thought it's the same thing you were saying about the faith question. That one thing, the fact that people could no longer take these children who were their children, their flesh and blood children, is such a terrible thing that it did something I think a lot of your work does, which is to take a question that's so big and so terrifying that we really can't get our minds around it and make it possible for us to look at that. What does that mean?

The question that I'm really asking I guess, is are you hopeful that there is new news about what is happening in the fight against HIV and AIDS in Africa?

**CHG:** Another complicated question. That is a complicated question, because there's some signs of hope and there's some massive signs of despair. I was just talking with a couple of young women from University

8 Desmond Mpilo Tutu (1931-2021) was a South African Anglican bishop and theologian, known for his work as an anti-apartheid and human rights activist. He was Bishop of Johannesburg from 1985 to 1986 then Archbishop of Cape Town from 1986 to 1996, in both cases being the first Black African to hold the position.

of Georgia. They got very excited about this because one of the biggest challenges, AIDS, no question, poverty is overwhelming problem in Africa, but AIDS is certainly right up there with it. One of the biggest challenges is getting people, and Mandela has tried this because his son a couple of years ago passed away from AIDS, getting people to find out their status.

I think I even have this in the book of how people who sneak into public hospitals late at night so that nobody will see because they want to know their status, but they're too embarrassed to come during the day. Even when people like Mandela and his family have stood up, people are still so terrified about this thing. It's not just the confusion that's taken place in South Africa over the issue, but it's the case everywhere on the continent. Now, having said that, I think that the challenge is huge, bigger than anything we've ever had to get our arms around in our lifetimes.

Now, there are variants of hope. For example, even in South Africa, one of the things I talk about is Anglo American's[9] project and I quote a doctor there who's in charge of it, Dr. Brian Brink. A lot of investors are wary about coming into the continent and even South Africa, which is the strongest economy on the continent, because they feel that their workforce is going to be sick and die. Now that there's antiretrovirals which really do work to bring people back to health and gives them many more years of productive work, there's more hope on that front. In Anglo American, although he's still despondent about the fact that the entire workforce has not come forward, a significant number has come forward.

He says that what makes him hopeful about this challenge is the same thing that made him hopeful, ultimately, about apartheid. That the principles had been laid down to end it, and it ended. You know all the reason. The same with AIDS. They know what to do. Of course, there's no cure, but they know what to do to prolong life and have people productive. The big issue is getting people to know their status so that something then can be done about it to prolong their lives.

If they go into denial, they don't get the medical help that they need, and so they just get sicker and sicker and sicker and die. You have countries like Botswana, which is small, which may be partly the reason they are able to

9 Anglo American is a British multinational mining company which owns an 85% share of the De Beers diamond consortium.

take some small steps. They still have a raging problem, but they have the interventions from Bill Gates and other foundations. They're making some progress. Then you have a country like Uganda, which was the model for the continent.

Here's a country with a president that many years ago saw his military dying, and they were engaged in conflict. He saw his cabinet, he saw his other civil servants die, because this is not something that just afflicts the core. They still educated people who want to know better but they didn't. What he did was, he developed a comprehensive program involving every department of his cabinet. He had an AIDS strategy, his private sector, his schools, his young people. I was there, they would do radio programs about AIDS traveling around the country, doing live shows, they had clinics and after-school programs that people could come to and they were user friendly, and they actually began to see a significant decline.

What I'm told now, and I hope I'm not perpetuating erroneous information, but I have read this. There's some conditions to money that they get from the United States. One of them is that you can't counsel abortions, you can't do abortions. There's the emphasis, although there isn't the thing that says you can't use condoms, but it's abstinence and behavior. I think that's the B and then the C is finally condoms.

Somehow the extremely religious people in Uganda, including I'm told the president's wife, are talking about condoms as being evil. The gains that they've made, I'm told, are being aborted. Now, if that's true that's just a sin, if you want to speak in the context of how it's being talked about as an evil. Human nature is what it is. I have a priest, a Catholic archbishop in South Africa, who has gone against the church because his domain is in an area near a mine and he sees the reality of the existence of these people who live and work around the mines, and of the women who are economically deprived.

They come and they have sex workers at the mines. What are you going to tell them? If you don't have any option for them to make money and earn a living and support their families and this is what they do, at least you can keep them protected until you can get an economy that gives them some decent work in which they can support their families but this right now is what the reality is. He has bravely gone against his church and is one of the few in South Africa and on the continent who has done that. He says, "Look, I'm dealing with the reality I'm faced with." He said, "This, to me, is a pro-life stance."

**PC:** Exactly. Mentioning the funds coming from the United States that say that you can't give abortions and you shouldn't be talking that much about condoms and all of that, do you think that that's part of that move away from a more realistic way of looking at things?

**CHG:** I think it's having an impact. I have not myself been in the field in a long time specifically on that story, but I've talked to health workers and health professionals who say the clinics are having to close because in these poor communities, especially in the rural areas where you don't have many clinics anyway, if you have a clinic, it does everything. It's a one stop shop. It's Walmart, if you don't mind.

[laughter]

**CHG:** People go there for everything. They depend on this money for their existence and without it, they go out of business. Somehow, health workers are telling me that a lot of these clinics that are sorely needed in these rural areas in particular are having to close up. Again, let me say, in the interest of fair reporting, this is hearsay that I myself have not reported. I've been told this by healthcare professionals at one of the most prestigious universities in South Africa. I don't have any reason to doubt her and them. This is a troubling thing. This is again, why Americans in particular need new news and good news because you affect politics, you affect decisions.

**PC:** Say it again.

**CHG:** How decisions are made.

[applause]

**CHG:** [coughs] Excuse me. If something is happening, it's your money, folks, and mine. I'm a permanent resident now of South Africa, but I'm also a resident of America. Believe me, I still pay whopping taxes. That's how you affect it. If you don't have the good news – You see now the context I'm using it in, if you don't have the news is somehow flowers growing and blooming and all that good stuff in that sense, which is news that you can use, then all kinds of things can be done in the name of your tax dollars that you don't have a clue about, but when the terrorists come after you –

**PC:** Amen.

**CHG:** – what are you going to say? I didn't know, so don't get me.

[laughter]

**CHG:** That's an extreme thing. I had a conversation with one of the best journalists in South Africa, a talk show host. If you ever come to South Africa with any kind of program or project or talent or whatever, you want to get on this guy's program. He's gotten all kinds of awards for his reconciliation and everybody, the worst racist in the world to the ultra liberals, everybody calls this guy because they trust him, because he's fair.

Right after 9/11, initially he was saying on the air things like our criticism is of a government policy, of American policy, not of Americans. Gradually over time and especially with the Iraq War, that rhetoric has changed. People who used to say, "Our grief is not with Americans, it's with American policy," are now saying, "Our grief is with Americans because they're not affecting the policy."

**PC:** That's right, because we're not doing anything about it.

**CHG:** That's right. Exactly.

[applause]

**PC:** I know that we have a thousand questions that we could ask you, but I also know you're nursing your voice.

**CHG:** It's okay.

**PC:** I'm going to ask one more, because I know people want to get the book and get you to sign it and all of that. I want to ask you one last question, because I know we have some aspiring journalists here. I have a former student here who is a wonderful writer who wants to be a journalist.

I want to ask you what advice you would give to young people who are going into journalism at a time when there's so much bad news, when there's so much cynicism, when there's so much lack of faith in the big institutions that people used to have faith in? What do you say to a young person who wants to be a journalist, who admires the work that you've been able to do? Is that climate still available for them to come in and bring that passion that you have for the work that you do? What would you tell them now?

**CHG:** Well, I would hope so. I had one of the saddest moments that I've had on a lecture tour. I think it was last year and I was in Florida at a university and this young would-be journalist came up to me and said, "I have always wanted to be a journalist, but now I'm reconsidering it." I thought maybe she had decided she wanted to go into law or something else. I said, "Oh no, why?" She said, "Because I'm not sure anymore, living in America, that I could tell the truth." Do you know, tears welled up in my eyes. I just thought, "Oh my," because I saw it coming, but I didn't see it coming this way. I saw the concerns that people were having, and you're having a conversation with somebody and all of a sudden, they start whispering.

**PC:** That's right.

**CHG:** They're throwing whispers. It's interesting because I've lived out of the country now for ten years and I come back and there's a palpable fear here about just – You're in your own house and you ask somebody a question that's political and they start looking up and [crosstalk]

[laughter]

**PC:** Don't you see what y'all molding?

**CHG:** You got these wireless interconnect things that I don't know what they're doing. I know it's a real question, it's not a hypothetical. I'm usually pretty facile and come back with the answer, boom. I had to sit there and mind my answer and think about this for a minute.

I said, "You know, let me say that I would hope you would rethink that. That you would not go to some other profession if this has been your passion." I said, "Because we've been there before. I said, "You're too young –" – and I'm actually too young [chuckles] – to have experienced the McCarthy era and the civil rights era.

A guy at the University of Georgia asked me today if I'd seen my surveillance report when I was applying to the University of Georgia. I said, "No, do you have a copy of it?" He said, "I'm going to send it to you immediately," because they don't even know who was spying on me and Hamilton and others. They found these surveillance reports in the papers of the late registrar, who was one of the plaintiffs in our case.

I said, "I don't know if I want to be in a bad mood." He said, "No. You could just laugh your head off at the things that they were surveilling in a serious way." I said, "We've been there before. We've been spied on. We've been had our phones tapped, civil rights movement people, we all know back then." I said, "We overcame and we were victorious." We didn't win everything but we won a lot.

I said, "It's going to change." I said, "Let me tell you one thing." I said, "Do this for me, don't get out." I said, "When you get your very first paycheck from your newspaper or your magazine or your TV station," I said, "don't spend it all on shoes."

[laughter]

**CHG:** I said, "Spend some on frivolous things that you – " I said, "Put a little bit aside as your safety net so that you never have to stay in any place where you have to compromise your principles or you have to do something that goes against what you believe in." I was telling a very good friend of mine who shall remain nameless as well as his institution, and he's not in the South. He was the president of a very prestigious big ten university but he comes from the South and he's a real Southern gentleman. I've never heard him even say, "Darn."

When I was telling that story to his wife in their kitchen, he was off doing something else and I'm not even sure what it was. When I finished telling the story, because I was so moved by this whole thing, he said, "I'll just use the alphabet." He said, "Oh we used to call that the FU money."

[laughter]

**CHG:** Well, that's a little bit more graphic than I put it to that student that I was stunned to hear it from him, but that's exactly what it is. You want to be able to walk away as I have had to do on occasion. The nice thing about being a barefoot girl from Georgia, you never get too far away from that that you can't go back to being a barefoot girl from Georgia. I don't even have a problem with that. Most of the time I don't have on shoes anyway.

[laughter]

**CHG:** That may sound a little bit frivolous, but I married a banker because I don't have a clue how to keep a checkbook balance. I like nice things and I love shoes and I don't have a problem with my status and my class or whatever. I don't have to live there. I could have half the shoes I have or I could live on all the shoes I have the rest of my life. It just may be that I have reached a point in my life where I can tell people to go – yourself.

I want these young people also to be prepared to do the same thing because we have to have a generation of conscious young people to follow in my footsteps and do better than I have done. Who may not have gone through what many of us went through in the movement, but who are still – Look at those kids at the University of Georgia who raised so much hell about the mural down there[10] that had "There goes the negro" on it under my picture.

While I didn't agree with them ultimately, I was so proud of them because it said to me that they are still confident, they're still – We like to down this generation. The last generation that did something likes to say, "You all ain't doing nothing." If they're not doing anything, whose fault is it? I was so happy to see these young people raising an issue, but I didn't put them down for what I thought was an incorrect position. I just praised them for being conscious. I saw that mural today and it is so beautiful. Their consciousness helped to make it better.

**PC:** To make it happen.

**CHG:** I would say to those young people, be conscious, stay in there, don't apologize for who you are or what you believe and find a good place. You talked about the establishment papers and they're going through a real hard time trying to find their identity now. They have been since the end of the Cold War. They're doing some things that are right. Why is it that some of us chose to work in mainstream media and not Black newspapers? I worked for one. We started one right here in Atlanta which is still going on. We need to be everywhere. We need to be in all those places.

I just did an amazing piece, I hope it's amazing, for *Essence* magazine on Ellen Johnson Sirleaf[11], the first Black woman African president in Liberia. I'm so excited. It's going to be in their October issue on powerful women of color. That just makes me feel real good to be able to make a first class contribution to *Essence*. It also makes me feel real good to be able to be our own PR and to be on those mainstream places because if they didn't have

10 "UGA to alter mural with slur," The Associated Press in the *Northwest Georgia News*, March 29, 2005.
11 Ellen Johnson Sirleaf (born 1938) served as the 24th president of Liberia from 2006 to 2018. Sirleaf was the first elected female head of state in Africa.

us, what would they have? They'd be back in 1960s and the '70s and they wouldn't know why.

**PC:** Exactly. I think that's a perfect note for us to move on into the book-signing phase of this program. I want to thank Charlayne for coming and talking with us. I want to thank all of you for coming out to talk with us.

[applause]

**PC:** Thank you.

**CHG:** Thank you.

# Sistahs on the Run

Ida B. Wells

Charlotte O'Neal

Mabel Williams

Kathleen Cleaver

Assata Shakur

*"Sistahs on the Run" originally aired on July 11, 2005, on The Women's Magazine on KPFA 94.1 FM in Berkeley, California, and later on* Some of Us Are Brave, *on August 11, 2005 on KPFK 90.1 FM in Los Angeles. Special thanks to Noelle Hanrahan, Ericka Bridgeman, Corinne Haskins, Lisa Dettmer and the Freedom Archives.*

**Thandisizwe Chimurenga:** Greetings and good afternoon. My name is Thandisizwe Chimurenga. Today on *Some of Us are Brave* we take a cursory look at the lives of several women intimately involved in the fight for human rights and self-determination of African people. From antebellum-era lynchings to modern-day police terror, these sistah warriors have used every means at their disposal to agitate and advocate for and to secure the rights of Black people and all human beings who are oppressed. A look at Ida B. Wells, Kathleen Cleaver,[12] Assata Shakur and others today on *Some of Us are Brave.*

[music]

On May 2, 2005, the New Jersey State Police with the assistance of the United States Federal Bureau of Investigation announced a one-million-dollar bounty for the arrest and return of Assata Shakur. A former member of the Black Panther Party for Self-Defense, Shakur was wrongfully convicted of killing a New Jersey State trooper on May 2, 1975, and sentenced to life. She was liberated from prison November 2, 1979, and now lives in revolutionary Cuba, where she has been given political asylum.

For every action, there is an equal and opposite reaction. In other words, repression breeds resistance. To quote a line from a poem by Assata Shakur,

---

12 Kathleen Neal Cleaver (born 1945) is an American law professor and activist, known for her involvement with the Black Power movement and the Black Panther Party. She married Eldridge Cleaver in 1967 and stayed married to him for for 20 years,

"There were Black people since the childhood of time who carried on a tradition of resistance."Resistance is not new and neither are the responses to it. Character assassination, discrediting, isolation, imprisonment and even death, but exile to be driven from one's home, one's family, ones people, in many instances, can be considered a social death far worse than the physical.

Today, we take a cursory look, and I stress that word, cursory, at the lives of several women intimately involved in resistance to the oppression and repression of African people. For this, their "crime of resistance," they have had to pay a heavy price: exile from their homes, their families, and their communities. In spite of this and other hardships, these women have continued to carry on the tradition of resistance.

[music]

**TC:** As an investigative journalist, Ida B. Wells' work documented the real motives behind lynchings, and in the process, the complicity of media in this terrorist activity. In this excerpt from her pamphlet *Lynch Law in Georgia*, she speaks of the April 1899 lynchings of Elijah Strickland and Sam Hose, which had been called for and carried in the *Atlanta Constitution* newspaper.

**Ida B. Wells:** During six weeks of the month of March and April just past, 12 colored men were lynched in Georgia. The reign of outlawry culminated in the torture and hanging of the colored preacher Elijah Strickland and the burning alive of Samuel Hose on Sunday, April 23, 1899. The real purpose of these savage demonstrations is to teach the Negro that in this house, he has no rights that the law will enforce. Samuel Hose was burned to teach the Negroes that no matter what a White man does to them, they must not resist.

**TC:** Wells elaborates further in her work *Lynching: Our National Crime* as read by elder Ruby Dee.

**Ruby Dee:** The lynching record of a quarter of a century merits the thoughtful study of the American people. It presents three salient facts. First, lynching is color-line murder. Second, crimes against women is the excuse, not the cause. Third, it is a national crime and requires a national remedy. Proof that lynching follows the color line is to be found in the statistics which have been kept for the past 25 years. During the few years preceding this period, and while frontier lynch law existed, the executions showed a majority of White victims.

Later, however, as law courts and authorized judiciary extended into the far West, lynch law rapidly abated, and its White victims became few and far between. Just as the lynch law regime came to a close in the West, a new mob movement started in the South. This was wholly political, its purpose being to suppress the colored vote by intimidation and murder. Thousands of assassins banded together under the names of Ku Klux Klan, Midnight Raiders, Knights of the Golden Circle, et cetera, and spread a reign of terror by beating, shooting, and killing colored people by the thousands.

In a few years, the purpose was accomplished and the Black vote was suppressed, but mob murder continued. From 1882, in which year 52 were lynched, down to the present, lynching has been along the color line. Mob murder increased yearly until, in 1892, more than 200 victims were lynched, and statistics show that 3,284 men, women, and children have been put to death in this quarter of a century.

During the last 10 years, from 1899 to 1908 inclusive, the number lynched was 959. Of this number, 102 were White while the colored victims numbered 857. No other nation, civilized or savage, burns its criminals. Only under the Stars and Stripes is the human holocaust possible. Twenty-eight human beings burned at the stake, one of them a woman and two of them children, is the awful indictment against American civilization, the gruesome tribute which the nation pays to the color line. Why is mob murder permitted by a Christian nation? What is the cause of this awful slaughter? The question is answered almost daily, always the same shameless falsehood that "Negroes are lynched to protect womanhood."

Standing before a Chautauqua assemblage, John Temple Graves,[1] once champion of lynching and apologist for lynchers, said, "The mob today stands as the most potential bulwark between the women of the South and such a carnival of crime as would infuriate the world and precipitate the annihilation of the Negro race." This is a never-varying answer of lynchers

---

1  John Temple Graves (1856-1925), an American newspaper editor who defended barring African-Americans from voting as well as lynching.

and their apologists. All know that this is untrue. The cowardly lyncher revels in murder, then seeks to shield himself from public execration by claiming devotion to women, but truth is mighty, and the lynching record discloses the hypocrisy of the lyncher, as well as his crime.

[music]

**TC:** From Georgia and Mississipi Goddam, we moved to North Carolina, where Mabel Williams and her husband Robert[2] were leaders in the Monroe Chapter of the NAACP, where they advocated and utilized armed self-defense against white supremacist terrorists. They founded *Radio Free Dixie*, a revolutionary radio news program, after they fled to Cuba.

**Mabel Williams:** We use the tactical demonstrations of non-violence. We picketed the swimming pool, we asked for one day in the swimming pool, if they could not build one in our community, "Well, just give us one day," and they said, "Oh, no, we can't do that." Rob said, "Why?" They said, "We'd have to wash out the pool after you used it." That's what spurred us to continue picketing for the right to swim in a tax-supported swimming pool.

We had a ten-part program that we presented to the city officials asking for basic human rights. They weren't about to budge because they knew they had the backing of the Klan and the state troopers and the federal government and everybody else. At one time, the Freedom Riders who were down in Alabama came in, asked if we would accept to have them come in and demonstrate in our hometown to help us. Actually, they wanted to prove that non-violence worked. Robert said, "Well, you can come in, and we will protect you as long as you're in our community, but I'm not going out there because they know that I am not going to allow anybody to spit in my face, or whatever, and get away and live."

[applause]

The Freedom Riders came into our community and supported us and they had tickets, and we had one white Freedom Rider that came from England. He was living in homes of some of our people and picketing along with us, but the officials were calling for support from the Klan and everybody else.

2 Robert Franklin Williams (1925-1996) and Mabel Ola Robinson Williams (1931-2014) were American civil rights defenders. After spending time in Cuba, they eventually returned to the U.S.

They were determined to crush our movement. Robert told them, he said, "Now, wait, let's not– I don't think you should demonstrate on Saturday or Sunday because that's when all these folks are going to be off work, and they're going to be getting their beer and stuff, and this is going to be pretty bad," but they chose to go ahead and demonstrate on Saturday and Sunday.

The city officials sprayed insecticide on the picketers while they were going around. James Forman[3] was there and he was on the picket line and when they got ready to leave, Robert had sent the groups of armed men in to bring them out because thousands of racists were surrounding the picketers and they had begun to shout at them, to kick them, spit on them, and assault them, and the police were on the side of the rioters. We were in our community, protecting our community, but waiting for them to come back, all hell had broken loose. People were really upset about what was happening to the young people who were on the demonstration line.

A white couple came into our community, and though Rob kept them from being killed, they said that they had been kidnapped. Then Rob got a telephone call saying, "You caused a lot of trouble, in 30 minutes you're going to be hanging from the Courthouse Square." He said, "Come on, get the children, we have to leave." We left thinking that we would go to New York, wait a while, let things cool off and then come on back home.

When we got to New York, there was an FBI bulletin saying Rob was armed and dangerous and schizophrenic and should be apprehended. Then at the end, it said he's traveling in the company of his family. We left Monroe thinking we would go back but he was on the "Ten Most Wanted" people list. His poster was tacked up in post offices all over. Lots of people have those posters now. I understand they couldn't stay in the post office because people would steal them for a souvenir.

[laughter]

Anyway, our family had to split up. This is one thing about our movement.

---

3 James Forman (1928-2005) was a prominent African-American leader in the civil rights movement. He was active in the Student Nonviolent Coordinating Committee (SNCC), the Black Panther Party, and the League of Revolutionary Black Workers. As the executive secretary of SNCC from 1961 to 1966, Forman played a significant role in the Freedom Rides, the Albany movement, the Birmingham campaign, and the Selma to Montgomery marches. After the 1960s, Forman spent the rest of his life organizing Black people around issues of social and economic equality

When we were in the South, we reached out all over the country and all over the world and created friends all over. Robert was a member of the Fair Play for Cuba Committee. He had traveled around speaking about the way the young boys in the "Kissing Case"[4] had been treated. We had friends all over. We had to break up as a family in New York. I didn't see my children again until after I got to Cuba, two boys, 9 and 11. I didn't see Rob again until I got to Cuba. We were able to survive through that network of friends that we had created all over, and eventually, end up in Cuba.

[applause]

[music]

**TC:** All power to the people, Black power to Black people, Brown power to Brown people, and so forth and so on. When Kathleen Cleaver came to the Black Panther Party after being in SNCC, the Student Non-Violent Coordinating Committee, she established herself in the party, as the communication secretary early in their development.

**Kathleen Cleaver:** A lot of stuff happened in the Bay area. To make a long story short, Huey Newton[5] was on trial for the shooting of an Oakland policeman and the wounding of another one. The very small local group that had been called the Black Panther Party for Self-Defense was in, basically, a state of collapse when I got here from California, and I was saying, "Well, you know, you want to get attention on this case, you should have demonstrations."

We started having demonstrations in front of the courthouse for the leader of the Black Panther Party and getting press. As people came out of jail and came back, the party built itself, again, around this case, around freeing Huey because we felt this issue was self-defense and the murder that we were subjected to was central to what was going on in the whole country as far as Black people were concerned.

---

4  "The Kissing Case" is the arrest, conviction and sentencing of two African-American boys in 1958 in Monroe, North Carolina. One boy was seven years old, the other nine. A white girl kissed each of them on the cheek and later told her mother, who accused the boys of rape. The boys were convicted of molestation and were released after three months.

5  Huey Newton (1942-1989) was an American activist and revolutionary who co-founded the Black Panther Party for Self Defense (BPP) in 1966 with Bobby Seale. The party was initially focused on armed self-defense against police brutality and oppression of Black people.

We could take it from there, organizing a movement to build a party around the ten-point platform and the basic principles of human rights and social justice, but the focus was on that trial. The trial was scheduled to start around the 14th or 15th of April 1968. On April 4, Martin Luther King was murdered in Memphis, where he had been speaking in support of a strike of the sanitation workers. Once he was murdered, the country changed. There was uprising starting in Memphis, going through the South, going through New York. Two hundred cities went up in flames. Washington DC was burning.

In the Bay Area, Bobby Seale[6] was actually in hiding because he had been getting threatening notes when he would go to court from the bailiff saying, "You come to court, we're going to kill you, nigger."

We didn't know whether it was really the bailiffs or was it somebody else and so Eldridge[7] had said, "Well, you should just lie low. Don't go to court till we figure out where they came from." There was a bench warrant out for him. Once King was killed, Charles Garry, the lawyer, said, "We have to – ." The Bay area was very tense. I think Garry got the bench warrant withdrawn and Bobby Seale and Garry and some other people were going around, requesting Black communities in the Bay area not to be destructive, and not killing. "Don't tear up your own community. Don't riot."

The Black Panther Party office in Berkeley, the headquarters, had been moved across the Oakland line. People were jamming the office asking for guns. They wanted to go out and start shooting. Two days later, there was an encounter between about fifty Oakland police and eight Black Panthers that ended up in a 90-minute gun battle. I don't think the police knew exactly who they were shooting until it ended. It stopped and it ended up they were shooting Eldridge Cleaver and Bobby Hutton.[8]

Bobby Hutton came out. They were surrendering, he came out with his

---

6  Bobby Seale (born 1936) is an American political activist and co-founder of the Black Panther Party. He became involved in political activism in the early 1960s, participating in protests against police brutality and discrimination against African-Americans. Under Seale's leadership, the party expanded its focus beyond armed self-defense to include community organizing and social programs.

7  Eldridge Cleaver (1935-1998) was an American writer and political activist who became an early leader of the Black Panther Party. Much later, he became a Mormon and a Republican.

8  Robert James Hutton (1950-1968) was the first recruit to join the Black Panther Party.

hands up and he was shot and killed, his body was riddled with bullets. Eldridge had been shot in the leg and couldn't stand up. He was trying to come out, and neighbors in that area had seen what was going on and they said, "Don't shoot. Don't shoot. Don't shoot." He was arrested, taken off to San Quentin. That was all in April, one weekend of April, the same weekend that King was killed.

Shortly after, Eldridge was released on a habeas corpus petition and in Solano County they said that the parole authorities had not proved that he had violated his parole. They let him out on bail and I can't remember now whether it was right before – I think it was right before that Robert Kennedy[9] was murdered in Los Angeles so this country was kinda off the hinges. Nobody knew what was going on. It was insane. It was crazy.

Eldridge was ordered to go back to prison. The habeas corpus thing was overturned. He was ordered to turn himself in, and he said he was afraid to go to San Quentin because if he went to San Quentin he'd be killed. That's where he'd come from so he wasn't going to go to – . In fact, he made a big speech and said "I didn't leave anything at San Quentin except half my soul and half my heart and I'm not going back there, I'm going somewhere else," and he disappeared. He eventually ended up in Cuba. I think on Christmas Day, 1968, he arrived in Cuba.

I tried to go to Cuba. I tried to join him. It wasn't easy. In fact, it never happened. I discovered after he left that I was pregnant. I wasn't run out of the country. I wanted to be with my husband and the only way – I mean, he wasn't coming back from there. [laughs]

I tried to go where he was. Now, the difficulty is that you're pregnant for a certain number of days. It's a very specific timeline here, and I kept trying to go and trying to go and trying to go, and it wasn't happening. I finally just picked up and went to France and called up Richard Wright's[10] widow Ellen Wright and said, "Help me. I want to get to Cuba," and I ended up

---

9  Robert F. Kennedy (1925-1968) was an American politician, lawyer, and brother of President John F. Kennedy. He served as the U.S. Attorney General from 1961 to 1964 and as a Senator from New York from 1965 until his assassination on June 6, 1968. He was known for his advocacy of civil rights, social justice and economic opportunity, and he worked closely with African-American leaders such as Martin Luther King Jr. to promote equal rights and desegregation.
10  Richard Wright (1908-1960) was an American author. He is best known for his novels Native Son and Black Boy, which are considered among the most important works of African-American literature of the 20th century. Wright travelled extensively and eventually died in Paris.

being told that I should meet Eldridge Cleaver in Algiers. I went to Algiers, and I met him there. We stayed for four years and had two children. [laughs] [music]

**TC:** Charlotte[11] and Pete O'Neal,[12] members of the Kansas City, Missouri chapter of the Black Panther Party for Self-Defense, have lived, worked, and organized primarily in East Africa since fleeing the United States in 1969 on bogus interstate gun charges. On the line with us now from Tanzania is Mama Charlotte O'Neal. How are you today, Mother?

**Charlotte O'Neal:** Good, very good. Greetings sister and greetings to everyone who is listening.

**TC:** Thank you so much for being here with us today. Can you tell us briefly your story?

**CO:** Yes. I joined the Party when I was 18 years old, fresh out of high school. I met brother Pete O'Neal, who was the founder and chair of the Kansas City chapter. Shortly after I joined, we lived and worked in Kansas City for a year before we left and ended up at Algiers. I'd like to point out that our community program was very, very strong. We had the first health clinic, the Bobby Hutton Health Clinic.

During that time, as you know, and as your listeners know, the COINTELPRO[13] program that the government had against the Party was going really strong. A lot of the leaders of the Party had been targeted. Brother Pete was one of those leaders who had been targeted and after he received that bogus gun charge, instead of him going to prison, we made the painful decision to leave. We actually planned to come back in two years. It was 20 years before I came back to America in 1990. Brother Pete has never gone back since 1970 when we left.

**TC:** That was a charge of carrying guns across a state line?

**CO:** A gun across a state line. That was a new charge, a new law that the government had made. I think that law came about maybe three weeks before he was charged. He had gone to the Senate to expose Chief Clarence

---

11  Charlotte Hill O'Neal (born 1951) is co-director of the United African Alliance Community Center (UAACC), founded in 1991 with the goal of empowering Black urban and rural youth in Tanzania.

12  Pete O'Neal (born 1940) was chairman of the Kansas City chapter of the Black Panther Party in the late 1960s. His life and exile in Tanzania have been the subject of a book and a movie.

13  See note on COINTELPRO on page 7.

Kelley.[14] He was doing some gun-running in those days and we had got the evidence that there was some gun-running going on. I'd like to point out, he became the head of the FBI later. Shortly after that, brother Pete was busted and he was given that charge of carrying a gun across a state line. A gun that he was never found with, a gun that he wasn't charged with doing a crime with. This was just one of the other ways that the government had to put the brothers and sisters in prison and throw away the key or kill them.

**TC:** You said it was a painful decision. You ended up staying 20 years before you came back. What led to the decision to come back? You can correct me if I'm wrong, you came back to visit. [chuckles]

**CO:** Yes, but not just to visit. In 1991, we formally started the United African Alliance Community Center, which brother Pete founded in the early '90s. This program targets at-risk youth, especially African-American youths, and tries to bring them here and show them a different way of life. We live in a village here and the African family is very, very strong here and we know that exposing these youths to this different way of being, to this different way of life, can help them to look at their lives in a positive way and to go back to their own communities and try to turn the youth around there.

Each time that I've gone back has been as a part of this program, spreading the word about this positive work that we are doing. Here at our center last year, we had 300 graduates. Right now we have more than 200 students. We're teaching them English, computers, health issues, HIV/AIDS, building construction, architecture, arts and crafts. All of the teachers are volunteers, youth themselves. This program has been an example, not only to Tanzanians, but to people all over the world. This work is informed by the work we were doing as members of the Black Panther Party. The spirit of the Party is continuing right here in East Africa.

**TC:** That's right, even exile has not stopped you from carrying on that tradition of resistance.

**CO:** If anything, we have become stronger.

**TC:** Mama Charlotte, can you tell us how we can get more information on the work that you're doing there?

14 Chief of the Kansas City Police Department in Kansas City, Missouri and the second Director of the Federal Bureau of Investigation

**CO:** Yes, we have a website. It's www.uaacc.net and I urge your listeners to go to that website and find out about the work and see what they can do in their own communities.

**TC:** Mama, give us that website address one more time.

**CO:** It's www.uaacc.net

**TC:** Mama Charlotte, I wish we could be online with you all day but we're going to have to do a couple of fund drives in order to make that a reality, but I do want to thank you for the little bit of time you've given us today. We're going to be calling you back in the future. Thank you so much for the work that you all are doing over there in Tanzania.

**CO:** Thank you, sister. Thank you all, power to the people, and I enjoyed talking to you.

**TC:** All right now, you take care.

**CO:** Thank you.

**Assata Shakur:** To be honest with you, I hate war in all its forms, physical, psychological, spiritual, emotional, environmental. I hate war.

[music]

I hate having to struggle. I honestly do because I wish I had been born into a world where it was unnecessary. This context of struggle and being a warrior and being a struggler has been forced on me by oppression, otherwise, I would be a sculptor, or a gardener, a carpenter. I would be free to be so much more.

[music]

I guess part of me or part of who I am and part of what I do is being a warrior, a reluctant warrior, a reluctant struggler, but I do it because I'm committed to life. We can't avoid it. We can't run away from it because to do that is to be cowards, to do that is to be subservient to devils, subservient to evil, and so that the only way to live on this planet with any human dignity at the moment is to struggle.

**TC:** A reluctant warrior speaking about why she continues to struggle. The name Assata means "She who struggles," but struggling does not always take the form of battle with the police.

**AS:** The question of sexism affects political work in many senses. For example, I joined the movement in the 1960s. I participated in different organizations, and since I was new and young and didn't know anything I basically was happy being a gopher[15] because you can learn a lot being a gopher. I didn't want to spend the rest of my life as a gopher, and there came a point when I began to resent people thinking that it was my biological destiny to be a gopher. [chuckles]

That's where it started to get rough, and I began to see that the sisters were the most efficient people in almost all of the organizations that I worked for, were also the most silent people in all of the organizations that I worked with and for, and were also the most neglected, unlistened to group of people in all of the organizations that I worked with, and were also the most powerless people in all of the organizations that I worked with. The image of a leader was always male. When people would talk about leadership they'd say, "The leader, he – " you know? There was never any female counterpart of the leader. It's something that we all, as women, have to face. How do we make ourselves heard?

As I was telling some of you yesterday, you just could not be the human being that you were. I couldn't be who I was because I'm a little timid. Although there's this image but I am naturally timid, naturally shy to get in front of a group of people. The first time I had to do it, I thought I was just going to literally die right then and there because I had been socialized to be timid. It wasn't just that my personality was timid, but it was the way that I had been socialized.

Women weren't supposed to get up in front of crowds of women. That was not an image that came easily to you. That was not something that I was primed for so it was like, "Oh, my god." I had to overcome that. When you see strong women who hold strong positions in revolutionary struggles you know what they went through. They didn't go through what men went through. Men go through half of what women go through to become effective political leaders.

I think the first step towards changing something is to educate, and I think that the first people that we have to educate are ourselves. I think that we

---

15 'go for' – "go for this this, go for that" – a gopher holds a subordinate position in an organization

have to go through and identify the different things that, as political activists, women suffer, the different things that women in our community suffer, and to start addressing those things systematically so that we have an analysis. If you don't have an analysis of the problem it's very difficult to educate. The first thing for us to do is, I think, make an analysis of where we are and make some progress.

Sisters are much more aware, thank goodness, than we were ten, twenty years ago. We've got to start sharing that with each other, sharing that with younger sisters, writing about it, documenting what our struggle has been and then trying to take it to another level. I think one of the problems that we have is being unorganized. There area lot of ways that sisters can be organized. We can be organized in political organizations and I think that's very important, but I think it's a lot of survival organizing that we can do. We can get together in terms of child care collectives, whether it's in terms of healing collectives. About healing collectives, I've heard some very positive things about healing collectives and some very negative things that comes with the tell-all and touchy feeling and cry all day.

[laughter]

I'm not talking about that when I talk about healing collectives. I think it's important for us to get things that are in our systems out, and some of the pain out. I think that's useless unless we do something. Healing has to do with activity, otherwise what's the point? You heal to do what? To stay a victim? To damn your daughters to the same situation that you're in? If you're not actively doing something then I think that, in terms of changing reality, then the whole healing approach to things is fraudulent.

[music]

**TC:** You've been listening to *Sisters On The Run*. My name is Thandisizwe Chimurenga and before I sign off for today, I want to leave you with this resource list. *Crusade for Justice* is the autobiography of Ida B. Wells and is published by the University of Chicago Press. *Ida B. Wells: A Passion For Justice* is a 53-minute video documentary directed by William Greaves and available at williamgreaves.com.

*Self-Respect, Self-Defense, & Self-Determination* are audio and video projects chronicling the life and activities of Mabel and Robert Williams available from the Freedom Archives by calling 415-863-9977 or by checking freedomarchives.org. *Negroes with Guns* by Robert F. Williams is published by Wayne State University Press and *Radio Free Dixie* by Timothy Tyson is published by the University of North Carolina Press. Kathleen Cleaver is the co-author of *Liberation, Imagination, and the Black Panther Party* published by Routledge.

*A Panther in Africa*, a film by Aaron Matthews that tells the story of Pete and Charlotte O'Neal, was nationally broadcast on PBS last fall. The Hands Off Assata Campaign in conjunction with the National Conference of Black Lawyers and others is spearheading the effort to have the $1 million bounty on Assata dropped, and her name removed from the domestic terrorist index.

Check these websites for more information: assatashakur.org, and AfroCubaweb.com. Her autobiography *Assata* is published by Lawrence Hill & Company. My name is Thandisizwe Chimurenga and you've been listening to *Sistahs On The Run*.

# An African Traditional View on Abortion

*Fasina Falade is a Babalawo, a priest of Ifa, a highly philosophical and sophisticated system of spirituality and divination throughout West Afrika. He is the author of four books including* Ifa: The Keys to Its Understanding *and* Ijo Orunmila. *Judy Rosenthal is a Professor Emerita at the University of Michigan-Flint. These interviews aired on* Some of Us Are Brave *on January 24, 2008, in recognition of the anniversary of the U.S. Supreme Court's Roe v Wade decision.*

[Clip from the 2007 film *Silent Choices*, directed by Faith Pennick, the first documentary to examine abortion and birth control from the perspective of African Americans.]

**Thandisizwe Chimurenga:** In 2004 there was a major march in Washington DC called the March for Women's Lives. And it was designed to be a march bringing together the largest gathering of women in US history, to advocate and organize around the right of abortion. Women of color who joined that effort said that the issue is much larger than abortion and after strugglin' and tugglin', going back and forth ...it became known as the March for Women's Lives. And one of the reasons for that is because of that concept that we now call reproductive justice. It's described as the complete physical, mental, spiritual, political, social, environmental and economic wellbeing of women and girls, based on the full achievement and protection of women's, US women's human rights, excuse me.

In the beginning, we talked about the fact that Faith said the comment that she ran upon was pretty much a current throughout the Black community: that abortion is seen as a ... "a white woman's issue." According to reproductive justice, indigenous women and women of color, our issue is not solely that of abortion. We believe that it is important to fight equally not only for the right to have a child, we must fight as hard for that right as we fight for the right to not have a child. And also because we are women of color, we know that we have to, we have to fight for the right to parent the children, we already have. The right to have a child, the right not to have a child, and the right to parent the children we already have, as well as controlling our birthing options, such as midwifery.

Again, in the film, it talks about the fact that during the early part of the century, Black women were already controlling our fertility. That's really nothing new. We know how to manipulate, we know how to work with the Earth ... how to work with herbs, how to conceive a child how to not conceive a child, we already knew these types of things. Midwifery was one of those ways that we utilized healers to help in that effort. We all know, we should be aware by now, of the attack that midwifery has suffered in this country, not just among Black midwives. But reproductive justice takes all of these things into account. It also fights for the necessary enabling conditions to realize those rights. And all of this, of course, is in contrast to the singular focus on abortion by the prochoice movement.

What I wanted to do today was to look at this issue from an angle that is not always looked at. For example, what do we do traditionally, what do we say? What do we feel? What do we think? What do we do traditionally, around this issue, such as abortion? I decided to have a conversation with an elder of mine by the name of Fasina Falade. He is a Babalawo in the tradition known as Ifa, popularly known as the Yoruba religion. He began his travels to Nigeria back in 1986, and has been practicing in the Leimert Park and the Pico Rivera area spreading the teachings of Ifa, a highly philosophical tradition, since that time. I attended a lecture of his several years ago where he spoke on this subject, and it intrigued me so much I had to go back and speak with him again. So this is Babalawo, or Awo, Fasina Falade speaking around this issue and what our tradition says on it.

**Fasina Falade:** In our tradition, our tradition is continuation. And to make sure that the community is able to grow within itself. We have a society which we call Egbe. Egbe is a society that is based, that is surrounded with children. A child that's a leader in a community can be called Elegbe, because they have a responsibility and they have the authority to lead that community. Also, in the society of Egbe, you have what you call the Emere. And the Emere child is a child that has been molded but hasn't completely came into the world, or a miscarried child or a child that is not full term.

Then you also have the Abiku, and the Abiku is a child that comes to "taste the Earth" but passes [away] before their mother and father, because in our tradition it's very important that the child buries their parent and nurture their parents and prepare them for their departure home, as those parents prepared us to come into this existence in the world. And last we have what we call the Akuisan. In the Odu Otura Obara, it talks about the "unyet buried." Spirit is molded and gifted by Olodumare, God. And when we have an aborted child, we in this world take the responsibility as God to stop that spirit from coming. We do not have that responsibility. Akuisan is a child that has been aborted, especially in today's technological, or civilized society, that is socially accepted, which is not accepted traditionally. So, Akuisan is a child, a spirit that tried to come; it's been molded in the body of the woman but has been stopped by humans from coming into the world. That's called the Akuisan because the human has taken the responsibility of life and death.

Even if we abort that spirit or stop that spirit from coming physically, that spirit still exists spiritually. So, when you abort a child, that spirit is still around those parents and has to be given a proper burial, to allow that spirit to come back. And this is where you get the Babatundes and the Yeyetundes,[1] to allow that spirit to come back into another form. And this is something that we're not realizing here in this society, is that when you have an abortion there are still spirits around those parents. And compensation has to be given.

**TC:** So usually, when we talk about abortion in the United States, it's about a woman's right to choose, and a woman's body, and what a woman has to go through or experience or what she must do. What I'm hearing

---

1 Babatunde/Yeyetunde or Yetunde: "Father/Mother has come again", or, "has returned", in the Yoruba language.

you say is that if a woman aborts a child, that spirit must be appeased by the mother and the father of that child, is that correct?

**FF:** Correct. Because, yes, it is the woman's body, but it was a dual relationship that brought that spirit into being. So yes, the father also has a responsibility in that abortion, the mother and the father [have] to bury that child, and you have to create a place, you have to give that child a name, you have to give that child a year's worth of praise in order for the spirit to be appeased.

**TC:** Okay so it's not a thing of the sista, maybe the sista and the brutha go to the clinic get the abortion and then it's over with, is that what you're saying?

**FF:** Exactly. It's not over with when you have an abortion. Spirit never dies, all they have done is gotten and have eliminated the physicality of that spirit, as we call the Igba Iwa: the container of that spirit. You know, we are so physical. But it is the spirit that makes the physical move. Yes, it takes one year of appreciation of that spirit, to allow that spirit to come back because that spirit will come again. And if you notice, when you see and find women who have abortions, they have more than one. Because it's that same spirit trying to come back. Because those spirits select the parents, we are under the illusion that we are in control of those spirits. But all we are are just the gatekeepers for those spirits to come into the world to fulfill their destiny.

**TC:** Let me ask you, this Baba. Now you are a Babalawo in the Ifa tradition, which we know comes primarily from the Yoruba people of Nigeria of Western Africa. So what you're telling me today, that only applies to Black folks, descendants of African people, in terms of an aborted child and the mother and father?

**FF:** Spirit has no color. Spirit has no geographical location, so that applies to everybody. What applies is a law, a law of nature. When you do not fulfill the sacrifice, when you do not fulfill your duty, there's a consequence. So no matter who or where you are, there will be a consequence. Yes, it applies to everybody.

Akuisan is a lot different from the Abiku or the Emere. When you talk about Abiku you talk about SID [Sudden Infant Death] You talk about the child who comes and goes home, all these things are identified. But when you talk about the Akuisan, you're talking about humans who have taken upon themselves to do God's work. You're talking about humans who would take it upon themselves to deny the spirit from coming into this world to fulfill their destiny. Destiny is the key here. And if that child does not or that spirit does not come here and become a child, to fulfill it's destiny, you will have chaos and if you notice again, most of the people who have abortions have very chaotic lives.

**TC:** Let me ask you this then: this question of destiny and the child returning because it chose the parent, it wanted to come through that particular vessel, and the child was aborted. And you're saying that it'll keep on coming back. But in the interim, the mother and father have to appease that spirit. I'm wondering about the concept of sin, because you talk about the fact that these are human beings who have basically stepped in and said, "I will be God, I will determine whether or not this child comes or not." So the concept of sinning, of doing something that a person should not have done and suffering as a consequence because of that, are you saying that this naming of the child, this caring for the child as if they were physically here for one year, the word you actually used was "appeasement," that is meant to make everything "okay"?

**FF:** Yes, there is no concept of sin. That's a Euro concept. We call it Eewo – taboo. It is taboo not to allow destiny to fulfill itself. So there has to be a consequence, when we do something that's taboo, and we violate a natural law there's a consequence, and the consequences of the abortion is to have a chaotic state around you and to be prepared for that. Because this is guaranteed. It's a natural law.

**TC:** What you're saying is that the chaos, the consequence of this action, is basically Earthbound? It's it's what happens to us here, there's no hell fire? When I, if I've had eight, however, many abortions as a woman, and then when I die, I'm going to hell because of these abortions I've had, you're saying that that's a foreign concept?

**FF:** Definitely a foreign concept. There is no hell bound, there is no, no suffering and all that other kind of, no, there is none of that. You know, there's just consequences. Everything that we do has a consequence, you know, and we have to be responsible. But we as humans, don't want to accept responsibility. We want to blame someone else or we want to point the finger at something outside of themselves. But it's the consequences of what we do that brings the so called dilemmas in our life. The dilemmas are because we have not learned the lessons. We don't understand the path and we want to separate ourselves from our spirituality, yet, everyone has always said that they're trying to find their inner self. But when looking for the inner self, you're looking for truth. And in the world, people don't want to accept the truth. Because we have a responsibility to the [inaudible]. We have a responsibility to God just as Jesus did. We too are the child and children of God, we call ourselves Omo Odudua, and we have the role and responsibility and the duty to do God's work. And God's work is to continue itself. And if we abort, are we not cutting off the arm and the continuation of God itself? So, Akuisan is when humans take on that responsibility to stop God's work. Life is about regeneration and continual motion and continuing existence. And when we stop that is taboo. It is Eewo.

**TC:** ... we're talking about the issue of abortion in the African American community and looking at a couple of ways to look at it as Black women. My next guest who I wanted to speak with on this issue is Judy Rosenthal. She is Associate Professor of Anthropology at the University of Michigan in Flint, and she came to my attention several years ago because as a student of traditional African spirituality, I picked up a book, actually the book picked me up – I was walking past it in the aisle and it said Psssst! And I looked and I saw this book it said *Possession, Ecstasy and Law in Ewe Voodoo*. The Ewe people are located in the areas of Ghana, Togo, and in parts of Benin, very closely related to the Akan and the Yoruba people. And I was looking through her book and I saw so many wonderful things but in particular, I wanted to speak with Prof. Rosenthal today about this issue of abortion, and how, as African American women, as Black women, we can draw on some information that we may have forgotten about or might [no longer] be privy to ... Prof. Rosenthal, how're you doing today?

**Judy Rosenthal:** I'm well, thank you. And I'm honored to be with you.

**TC:** Now you are a Professor of Anthropology, you received your degree from, is that from Cornell?

**JR:** That's right.

**TC:** Okay. And I was reading in your book, and it talked about the fact that you were working with some African students who suggested you get a degree in Anthropology, is that correct?

**JR:** [Laughter] When I was in Paris, they all told me to go do this.

**TC:** Okay, and you did that and you went to Togo?

**JR:** I did.

**TC:** In 1985 and from 1985 to 1996 you were a student, a researcher and also what we call a devotee of Voodoo, is that correct?

**JR:** That's right and I went back the last time in '99.

**TC:** Okay, so we don't have a whole lot of time here on *Some of Us Are Brave*, I end up getting long-winded. Let me jump, let me cut to the chase as we say, I was reading in your book *Possession, Ecstasy and Law in Ewe Voodoo* and on page 191, I saw one of many things that caught my eye, and I wanted you to clarify it for me and also for our audience today. You say in here, "acts such as abortion, which are normally against Gorovodu law can be performed if the person in question has thought a great deal about the action, and talked to the Vodu or the deities about it before carrying it out. The person must pay for it, so to speak," and you're talking about paying for it financially. But could you explain to me what I just read?

**JR:** Well, abortion is not a light thing. It's a very heavy thing to do. Being pregnant is as well, bringing children into the world is as well. And a lot of women lose their children very early in, several days after they're born. And when there's a kind of pattern to that, it's often called Abiku, or [inaudible]. And what the women say is that that child didn't want to stay with us it wanted to go back but it will come again. And that's actually what priestesses have told me about abortion. They've said, if you must not at this moment, you cannot bring another child into the world because it would be so hard on you that you wouldn't be able to carry out your duties to the spirits, then you must go and pray and talk about it. And, and then go to a hospital and get it done properly, not do any of those fast things that women sometimes do without thinking because that can be very dangerous for everyone. And if you do that, and then you give the Spirits gifts, it will be all right and that child will come back.

**TC:** So then, as opposed to the western concept of "This is evil, this is immoral and it should not be done, it should be illegal, it should be outlawed i.e. Roe vs. Wade should be overturned," what you're saying is that based upon your study, in African tradition, it is possible?

**JR:** Oh, yes. Oh, yes. And actually the, the women, especially one in particular I'm thinking of who just called me yesterday, she told me that she had had an abortion. She also had, she gave birth to nine children. But she said that one time she was pregnant and her husband had left her. And she knew that she wouldn't be able to hold forth with her other children and bringing another one into the world. So she said, these were her words, "I went to the hospital, and they removed it. But I prayed to my spirit for a long time first." So yes, because women, not only new people are important to the spirits and to the world, and the community but women are. So women can't always do what their bodies are in the process of doing. Sometimes they have to take action and change destiny.

**TC:** Now I see where you state, in an explanation you cite the case of, you state that "a woman who is sure that her pregnancy will ruin her life may go ahead and abort in the hospital if she has thought carefully about it and ask the Gorovodu for permission beforehand. If she simply goes and drinks," you know, "a solution or other abortives without preparing herself, the Vodus will catch her, for this is very dangerous for the woman. If she aborts on the spur of the moment and doesn't go confess to the Vodus she will probably die. The Vodu are unhappy with her because she did not think about it and she did not talk to them about it. If she goes to the hospital, she will not risk her life and she will pay for it, which means she cannot do it suddenly or because a man is forcing her to."

**JR:** Exactly

**TC:** "She goes to the Vodu in advance and speaks about a problem, they will tell her what they want from her, she must go to them in the first place with sacrifices. When she does it this way. Only the [inaudible]" or priest, I interpret that to be the priest?

**JR:** Yes, [inaudible] is a praying priest. And actually, I was also told, after that book was already out, I was told by a man, a priest, that sometimes people have to go in and pray to the Vodus alone, even without another priest or, or a praying priest with them. And that anyone can do that, that the spirits will hear out anyone who is in trouble, and help them make decisions.

**TC:** I saw in the book elsewhere, I'm trying to find it now and of course I can't find it. But somewhere earlier in the book, you talk about the fact that you, and I'm not sure I don't remember the context of it but basically, you were saying how you believe in a woman's right to choose and when it came to the tradition, you were not going to make the promise that you would never help a woman who wanted to do something like this.

**JR:** Exactly.

**TC:** Let me, here on *Some of Us Are Brave*, we try to have honest dialogue. So I'm going to come at you with a very straightforward question. How much? Well, okay, that's not fair, because, all right, but basically, how much of this information, you know you're a white woman anthropologist, when it comes to African tradition most of it has been brought to us in terms of anthropologists – those looking from the outside as opposed to the worshipers of it. How much of this is folk in Africa telling you, a white woman outsider, what you wanted to hear?

**JR:** I think that there's always some of that happening. There, there always will be some people telling an anthropologist and not just a white one, but anyone, what they think that we want to hear. That's why we have to talk to so many people, and also live with people. I lived in villages for five years over there. And I also have African children. And so, and I had a lot of people telling me things in secret. And I would then have to ask them, I would say, "Can I put this in this book?" And sometimes they would say no. And sometimes they would say "Yes, but just don't put my name in it." And of course, I never did. So there's always the possibility that yes, that we'll be told what people think we want to hear and I was told many contradictory things. That's why I had to be so careful going back and forth about how I explain things in that book and in articles that I've published since then.

**TC:** And you said your last trip was not in 1999, was it?

**JR:** Yes, it was. It was in 1999. I haven't gone back since because of my poor health, but I'm still in contact with people, and as I said, one of the women with whom I spent the most time just called me yesterday with her cell phone from Lome.

**TC:** Lome, Togo. Prof. Judy Rosenthal is Professor of Anthropology at the University of Michigan Flint. She is the author of *Possession, Ecstasy* *and Law in Ewe Voodoo,* and that's put out by the University of Virginia Press. Prof. Rosenthal, I want to thank you so much for giving me this little bit of your time today. And we want to, we look forward to having you back for a much longer discussion in the future.

**TC:** Anytime you want. I'm very pleased to have been with you.

**JR:** Thank you so much. Thank you.

**TC:** Having an abortion is a very personal act for a woman, but it is an act that has ramifications personally, physically, emotionally, spiritually, and yes, collectively. We've heard today from two people, one a practitioner in the Yoruba tradition, and also an anthropologist, a student of the Voodoo which is very closely aligned with the Yoruba tradition. And they talked about the fact that depending upon how you look at it in those two traditions, abortion might be considered taboo, something that is not good for you to do but if you have to do it, these are the steps that you have to take.

We also heard in the beginning of our clip, the beginning of the hour in that film *Silent Choices,* the woman Angela speaking about the grief that accompanied her decision. Not so much grief for the child that was aborted, but grief about maybe some possibilities, some things that may have gone a different way. She talked about also the fact that it brought up emotions for her that she had not really dealt with in a long time.

I'm very concerned about the issue of shame and guilt, especially when you look at how it is used against women by the religious right and, you know, let's not be timid here let's call it what it is: it is a predominantly white, right, with an increasing sprinkle of Black minions.

So what I was hoping to do in the short time that I had today was to open up this dialogue and discussion and we'll continue to talk about it here on *Some of Us Are Brave* with people like Faith Pennick, with people like Dorothy Roberts, who we've had on before, and with others. This dialogue about how we, in the African-American community, deal with this issue. We know that abortion is legal, as they talked about in the film, as Dr. Dorothy Roberts, Billye Avery and other people talked about, we might not feel it's the right thing to do. But we still utilize it, because we understand that we have to, that is something that no Supreme Court decision is going to influence as far as I'm concerned. It is still something that we need to have, it is still a necessary law on the books, and yes, it is very much in danger. But at the same time, how do we in the Black community deal with this issue? Like so many other issues, it affects us differently, which is one of the reasons why we have SisterSong, Black Women for Wellness, California Black Women's Health Project, the National Black Women's Health Imperative, all of these organizations that deal with the issue of reproductive justice, and how it is more inclusive, and all of these other issues that impact us in such a way.

NOW before you run out of wherever you are hollering about "Thandi was on KPFK saying you can go get an abortion everything be okay!" Or "Thandi was up there sounding like Jerry Falwell!" That's not true. You know, call me for a copy of the show and you'll see that's not exactly what I was saying. What I'm saying is that as African American women in particular, as Black women, we cannot be boxed into that same dichotomy of "Is it a woman's right to choose?" "Should it be legal? Should it not be legal?"

We have always had to do what we need to do. And we will continue to do that.

# Art for Our Sake

# adrienne maree brown

*adrienne maree brown grows healing ideas in public through her multi-genre writing, her music and her podcasts. The author/editor of seven books, she is the founder of and current writer-in-residence at the Emergent Strategy Ideation Institute. This interview was conducted on January 27, 2016 in Venice, California.*

• • •

**Thandisizwe Chimurenga:** I'm speaking with adrienne maree brown. She's the co-editor of *Octavia's Brood: Social Justice Stories from ...*

**adrienne maree brown:** *Science Fiction Stories from Social Justice Movements.*

**TC:** *Science Fiction Stories from Social Justice Movements* ... Adrienne, can you give our audience – KPFK audience by now should know who Octavia Butler is. If they don't I feel sorry for them. Let's just pretend that everyone within our 100,000-watt signal area knows who Octavia Butler is. Tell us about *Octavia's Brood*. What does that mean?

**amb:** Beautiful. *Octavia's Brood* is an anthology of twenty stories and two essays. The concept is basically to put ourselves directly in the lineage of Octavia Butler. She was a Black science fiction writer. A lot of what she did was to look at what's happening in our times and how do we use science fiction as a bomb or a playground or imagination place to go and address those issues and come up with new solutions. New ways of being human, being in community, being Black, being female, being queer, being polyamorous, being all these different things that she was calling in.

In our collection, Walidah Imarisha is my co-editor, we basically were doing similar work, which was we both had a foot in the social justice world. Actually, all of our feet and our hands and everything was in the social justice world, but then our imaginations were most compelled by science fiction work that we were reading, and feeling like there's actually a strategic direction here and guidance and suggestion and inspiration to be had in that science fiction work. Then we came into conversation with each other and had this moment like, "Actually, all organizing is science fiction." That became the thesis of this book with the idea.

**TC:** Let me stop you for a minute. What do you mean by that? "All organizing is science fiction"? When you say something like that, that kind of rattles me.

**Amb:** Right. I want to rattle everybody with it because my belief is, or our belief is, that if – We're talking about we want a world with no poverty, no homelessness, where everyone has an education, there's no one in prison, there's no transphobia; queer people, trans people, everyone can be in their love and their families and their relationships and their bodies with pleasure and power, no fatphobia. All of these things. We've never seen that world. It doesn't exist. It's only in the future and the basis of our timed experience in this world. Everything we're talking about in the future, we're basically engaged in science fictional behavior. We're trying to write new narratives …

**TC:** You mean as community organizers and activists?

**amb:** Yes.

**TC:** What you're saying is the work that we do as community organizers and activists is actually science fiction?

**amb:** It's actually science fiction, so you're actually trying to bring new worlds into being with your everyday activities. This reframe was exciting to us because I think a lot of times as organizers, as activists, you can get really stuck in the trenches, in the reacting to the bad and feeling overwhelmed by the conditions, and forget that what drew you into the work and fundamentally what you're moving towards is a different future that you are co-creating, that you're carving out with your comrades. The idea that it's all science fiction, hopefully it gives people more spaciousness, more playfulness, and even a more radical bent.

It's like, "Oh, right. We're not just fighting to get whatever's politically possible right now. We're trying to rewrite the entire game. We want to change it all." On the scale or spectrum between reform and revolution, I always end up on whatever's the most radical side in terms of the kind of changes I want to see. I consider myself post-nationalist, I'm interested in polyamorous and multidimensional relationship and family. There's all these things, but I'm fundamentally interested in how do we look at our practices and say, "How do these practices align with my highest intentions and my greatest beliefs?"

For social justice movements, I think it's easy to say we believe and long for one thing but be practicing something very different that actually... I was saying this last night. We had this event at Eso Won Books. It was our first event, our first *Octavia's Brood* book event here. It came up for me. I was like, "You're either moving towards justice or away from it at all times. There's not really a neutral ground. You're either perpetuating the status quo paradigm of heteropatriarchy, capitalism, top-down hierarchical systems, punitive measures, backstabbing, and all that. You're either doing that or you're actually practicing something different. You're mindfully attending to being a different kind of human being."

**TC:** What if I don't know what to do yet and I just stand still?

**amb:** What if you don't know what to do yet and you just stand still? Give me more context. What does that look like for an organizer or for an organization?

**TC:** No, I wasn't talking about organizers, I was just talking about regular people. Like, "I don't know. What do you mean? I'm either moving toward it or ... But I'm a good person. What do you mean?"

**amb:** I find that most people who think that they're neutral or standing still, the default is to go for the easy and the familiar. Right now we live in a capitalist-imperialist society. Our easy and familiar is there's most likely going to be one or more wars happening with our tax dollars in our name that we have no control over and we can't stop. There's most likely going to be less than 5% of the population that has the majority of the resources and the rest of us are scrambling to get whatever else we can, and we most likely don't have equal access or equity amongst things. We're most likely competing with each other rather than collaborating for things.

These are just things we get socialized into, we don't have choice. Then I find when people say, "Oh, I really want this," my choice would be to collaborate. I wish I could. Then when we get into our own structures, we don't do that. We don't always practice that, even if we mean to. I'll tell you, I was an ED for ... Confessions of an Executive Director ... but I was an executive director once. I came into the position very much like, "I'm going to do everything totally different. No hierarchy, nothing." You get into it and it's like, "Oh, there's a status quo. There's a familiar structure here." The nonprofit industrial complex or whatever you want to call it.

Everything is set up for me to compete with everyone else who's doing similar work to me for a very small amount of money, and to be in an urgent condition for every decision I have to make so that I usually I'm not going to be able to make decisions that feel new or different or take a little bit more process to figure out. I'm just going to be able to make whatever's the easiest decision and have to be better than everyone else. That's not the condition under which I'm going to create a radical new society. That is a great condition for me to perpetuate the existing society, and I think that's not an accident.

That's what I mean. It's like there's not really a neutral, there's a "most familiar." That means that what we're trying to create is not going to feel familiar yet, we have to actually practice it. Writing science fiction and reading science fiction, I think they're practices. They can be spiritual practices. I think it's mindfulness practice to intentionally put yourself in the way of vision.

**TC:** Something else that you just said in terms of social justice activism organizing and utilizing science fiction. You said it gives us the "spaciousness" but also the "playfulness." What do you mean by the playfulness?

**amb:** I think we take ourselves so seriously. Some of that is good. There's serious things happening and there's trauma happening all the time, but I also think we're not humble enough. When I spend time around kids ... I have three siblings. Do you know this term niblings? Have you heard this yet?

**TC:** I've never heard that before in my life.

**amb:** Okay. I'm super excited to share this with you. My friend Tenuja who lives in Chicago and works with Sage Healing, an acupuncture center, she taught me this. It's basically your niblings are the children of your siblings. It's a gender-neutral term. It means that you're not saying your little girl, your little boy, whatever. It's just your nibling. You haven't determined all that stuff yet. We're not going to tell you which one ...

**TC:** What is that? Niece, nephew?

**amb:** Niece, nephew.

**TC:** Of the sibling ...

**amb:** Exactly.

**TC:** Are nibling?

**amb:** Are nibling. That's how you feel about them. All you want to do is just nibble on their cheeks or whatever. They're like the cutest thing ever. Niblings.

**TC:** My niblings are rather old now. [Laughter]

**amb:** It happens, they grow up. Actually, I will say this. I've been loving their growing up process. When they were younger, I was always wanting to freeze them. I was like, "Just stay a little baby with the little cute fat. I love this." As they get older, I'm like, "Oh no. You actually like me." You know what I'm saying? Like you have your own choices, you've been to school. You start to interact with more people, and against that spectrum of other humans you're deciding that I'm someone worth your time and attention. It's even better because I'm like, "I think you're everything," and you start to think, "I'm everything." I don't know, there's just something really sweet about the aging process.

Hanging out with them, I see that they'll really get stuck on an idea or something that they want to experiment with. Then they'll try it, and then they'll either like how it goes or they'll fail and they'll let it go, and they'll just move on to the next thing. The humility of being young, that beginner's mind, is a real gift because it means they're not like, "I'm right, and I've got to hold the line for this righteousness." It's like, "Well, I thought I wanted to be a dragon, but I put the outfit on and I'm not really feeling it. I think

I need to be a princess right now. That's what I'm going to do." [Laughter]

**TC:** Yes, I hear you, but really now, how do we translate that into right now today? You and I are sitting right here in Venice where the LAPD killed a brutha not that long ago, and the chief came out against his own officers and said, "Yes, this was not a good shoot and he probably should be prosecuted." We're sitting in a spot right now where gentrification has gone amok and people of color, poor people who are out here attempting to capitalize off of the tourists, just like these "businesses" are being run out, and Brendon Glenn[1] murdered. Dragon princess playfulness …

**amb:** Where does it fit in, right? I think all of that is true. I think that we've been dealing with these traumatic situations for such a long time. What we've done to respond to them, we do the same thing over and over again and it doesn't work. We have not been winning, and we have not been surviving. The idea of the playfulness, for me, is really to have a mindset of experimentation. How do we start to say when something's not working, letting it go quickly, and really being willing to try out new things? I think that's part of why Black Lives Matter has actually been so successful is because if you went by the book of what makes a successful campaign, they have either evolved or just straight jumped in a totally different direction on almost all of those things.

This concept of leaderfulness and saying it's not just going to be this top-down campaign where here's the only way you can do Black Lives Matter and that's it. Instead, they were like, "Black Lives Matter is this call." You have to be intersectional, and it's about Black body surviving. It's about our Black community surviving. There's been the call for Stop Killing Us, but Stop Killing Us fundamentally puts that power in someone else's hands. It says, "Please, when you decide to come around, can you stop killing us?" What I love about Black Lives Matter is it says, "We're not asking you for anything. We are asserting that our lives matter, we're going to act as if." Then communities can take that and interpret it in whatever way they feel.

We've seen a lot of different interpretations of that in this last year inspired by what popped off in Ferguson,[2] but then taking a different iteration in

1 Brendon Glenn (1984-2015) was a Black man shot dead by police in Los Angeles. Clifford Proctor, the policeman who shot him, was never charged.
2 See note on Ferguson on page 14.

Baltimore, a different iteration in the Bay Area, a different iteration in LA, a different iteration in Minnesota, a different iteration in Detroit. I love seeing the divergence of all these methods. To me, I see them all as these are all experiments, and then that's one movement. I would say Occupy[3] is something that came before that. It was a different movement and a different experimentation. I like both of them in terms of not coming out and being like, "Here's the four-point platform," or, "Here's the way everyone has to roll."

It's actually going to leave a lot of space for people to figure out in your locale, with your particular police department, in your particular community, your particular funding paradigm, and all those things, how are you going to assert that Black Lives Matter? What are the direct actions that are going to be relevant for your community? I think that that's building off of what happened. Minnesota is a great example where they did an occupation. It's a beautiful way of building off of what do we learn from Occupy, and then moving it through this Black Lives Matter moment.

What have we learned about how to make good use of allies and having multiracial community showing up for the work, and not just saying either, "White folks are getting on our nerves," or, "We'll put white folks in positions of power," but actually saying, "No, here's a role you can play. You can hold these particular signs. You can push your bodies in this particular kind of risk." There's just so much more creativity to it. There's a lot of love and there's a lot of care happening. All of that, to me, is in the spirit of, these are the experiments we're trying out. Actually, it works much better to call people to an action if you feed them. It works much better to do an occupation when you have a lot of people cycling in and out to take care of the administration and the logistics and the care, not just a few people burning themselves out. Those are things we learn through experimentation.

**TC:** Like everyone else, what's next? I want to know what's next for, I know the book is called *Octavia's Brood*, but I feel like you and Walidah are the mamas. Like the two daughters of Octavia, and now you've got all these children. You're facilitating this brood. What's happening next?

3  The Occupy movement began with Occupy Wall Street in Zuccotti Park, Lower Manhattan, on September 17, 2011. It aimed primarily to advance social and economic justice. By October 9, Occupy protests had taken place or were ongoing in over 951 cities across 82 countries, and in over 600 communities in the United States. By the end of 2011 authorities had cleared most of the major camps, with the last remaining sites evicted by February 2012.

**amb:** A lot of exciting things are happening. One is that we continue to be invited to lots of places to share about the book. We do artist talks and signing like we did at the bookstore here, but we also do this series of workshops. We do one that's collective science fiction writing, where we have people actually practice collaborative ideation. The way we articulate it, it's like one of the issues of our world right now is that there's all these individuals coming up with plans and competing with each other to see how do we assert this plan? That's what we have right now. How do we learn to collaborate together, to ideate together, and to work together to come up with new ideas?

The idea is that the more people who envision the world, the more people who will actually fit into that world. We do those workshops. We do one on sci-fi and direct action, which is super fun, where we take people into existing sci-fi worlds like *Lord of the Rings, Battlestar Galactica*. What have we done recently? *Wizard of Oz, Star Wars, Star Trek*, all these different places. We'll say like, "Who are the most marginalized people in this world? Let's develop a direct action and change the future of this world." Then people get to practice it in a low-stakes environment, and then debrief on so now how could you apply that to the local direct actions that you're actually working on? Just getting people out of the box, getting more creative.

Then Emergent Strategy Workshop, which is something that I'm working on. I have a book coming out this fall on Emergent Strategy. Just basically, how do we learn from the natural order, the natural operating systems of this world? How do our movements learn to be involved in biomimicry? Can our movements move like a flock of birds or school of fish, and be that organic and resilient and adaptive with each other? We're doing all these workshops with people, and the idea is that the book is a jumping-off point. It's not the end-all be-all.

We also have several of our writers who are being invited to write more, put into other anthologies, and other things. Then Walidah and I are in conversations now about what is the future for us because there's so many possibilities. The good problem we have is that we want to say yes to all of them. We're just trying to figure out like, "Well, what does this actually look like? What's sustainable?" Also, how do we keep growing this beyond just the two of us? We're observers of this phenomenon. We look back and we see that Octavia, Steven Barnes,[4] Samuel Delany,[5] Tananarive Due,[6] Nalo Hopkinson,[7] and all these other people have been doing this work. Now we're in this generation and we want to make sure that we can look around and see Daniel José Older[8] and all these other people, who are ... Nisi Shawl[9] and Bill Campbell,[10] and other people who are growing the field.

Then looking at the next generations, how do we create more space for even more folks to come through? Getting people to apply to Voices of Our Nation, and to Clarion and Clarion West, and get into positions where they get to write speculative fiction and get feedback and learn to do it. Those are some of the things that are coming up for us. It's an exciting year. 2016 is about to be poppin'. And Walidah has a book coming out this spring, *Angels with Dirty Faces*, about the work that she's been doing in the prison. Basically taking down the prison industrial complex. It's a good year. There's more and more and more coming. [Laughter]

**TC:** I want to ask you about something that you said last night. When you talked about the origins of the book you had the idea, "We're going to talk to these social justice activists and organizers." You gave them your pitch and they were like, "Nah, sorry. Talk to somebody else." You kept at it, and then after a while, you told them like, "Okay. Four months. Give us 10 pages." Then when the time came, you said that they were saying that they had all of these different characters, 50, 60, 80 pages. Tell me about that.

**amb:** It's exciting for us and hilarious for us, that we had several people come back. I will say that there are some of the people, they were like,

---

4  Steven Barnes (born 1952) is an American science fiction, fantasy, and mystery writer.
5  Samuel R.Delany (born 1942) is an American writer and literary critic. His work includes science fiction, memoir, criticism, and essays on science fiction, literature, sexuality, and society. After winning four Nebula awards and two Hugo Awards over the course of his career, Delany was inducted in 2002 into the Science Fiction and Fantasy Hall of Fame.
6  Tananarive Due (born 1966) is an American author and educator. She won the American Book Award for her novel *The Living Blood* and is also known as a film historian with expertise in Black horror. She is married to Steven Barnes.
7  Nalo Hopkinson (born 1960) is a Jamaican-born Canadian speculative fiction writer and editor. Her fiction often draws on Caribbean history and language, and its traditions of oral and written storytelling. In 2020, Hopkinson was named the 37th Damon Knight Grand Master.
8  Daniel José Older is an American fantasy and young adult fiction writer.
9  Nisi Shawl (born 1955) is an African-American writer, editor, and journalist best known as an author of science fiction and fantasy short stories.
10  Bill Campbell founded Rosarium Publishing in 2013 with the goal to bring diversity to publishing.

"I've written," or, "I've got something." As I've been traveling in the country this past year, I've met a ton of people who have a secret novel or a secret writing project, and they just needed a little encouragement or invitation to let it out, but then, yes, we definitely had writers who were like, "I did not know that I had this world inside me. I didn't know that these characters were walking with me." Some of them occurred to people in dreams, some of them came to people as they looked at their families.

Once you open the spigot it can be a fire hose of creativity that comes pouring out. You don't know what's going to happen. I think as long as people are scared, it's going to be like a drip, drip, drip, drip, or like, "Nothing will be there," but I'm like, "At least try." Now we have people who are building ... Autumn Brown,[11] Alisa Garcia Morgan ... all these folks, they have novels basically. We're trying to figure out how do we support them to get the funding and space and the other things that they need in order to be able to work on that.

The other thing I want to throw in is that when we did the sci-fi writing workshops the same thing happened. It's not just for the writers that are in the book. When people come to our workshops they, we have had so many people who come to us afterwards and are like, "I had no idea. I didn't know." One of our theories is that everyone has these worlds inside of them, but again, we're not to let it out.

**TC:** Not just a book but a world.

**amb:** World, right. I want to say that distinctly because the idea of a book, you're building a world or you're speaking about a world. I think this is one of the core distinctions for science fiction. It's like in fiction you're basically referring to the world as it is. In visionary fiction or science fiction or speculative fiction, you're saying like, "I'm taking these rules off of the world as it is and I want to create." You're basically building another one. Some alternate parallel other kind of world, and your world has different rules to it. Other folks have these worlds and each one is shaped by all of your experiences, and all of your dreams and your wishes and your longings, so we need all of that unleashed.

........................................

11 Autumn Brown co-hosts the podcast "How to Survive the End of the World" with her sister, adrienne maree brown.

The world we have now is just a collective vision that basically white men had a long time ago. That was like, "We're going to never let the sun set on our empire," and we're still basically playing off that same rulebook for what makes a good world or what's a successful world. If we want new visions then we have to look for different kinds of dreamers too. I'm really excited about the dreams of the Zapatistas and how they have been realizing their dreams. I'm really excited for the Black Power movement and the Black Panthers. What were they dreaming? What were their visions? What seeds got planted in that, that are still growing through us?

Everything doesn't look the same way as a success. I was saying this last night; that capitalism has us all skewed and messed up about what we think is a success. We're like, "Oh, it has to be a bestseller and everyone has to do it," and that's the only version. I'm like, "No. Who do you want to reach? Who do you want to be part of your community and your utopia, your dream? How do you engage those people and plant seeds and be in the iteration?" Instead of thinking about what's the outcome I want to get to, to me I'm like, "I don't want to reach an outcome. I never want to get to the end." I want to keep having questions and keep being in the solution process, and keep iterating and iterating and iterating and coming out with new things. I want to be part of that human evolution, and I want more people engaged actively in shaping change.

**TC:** Adrienne, for KPFK listeners who want more information on the book, want more information on you, what you are doing, how can they get that?

**amb:** Two places: facebook.com/octaviasbrood/ is everything about the book, how to reach us, how to book us, where we're going to be this year. We're going to be a lot of places this year. We were like tourists. We tried to finish the tour last June and we're still going. In terms of people still booking and want us to come places, it's hard to say no because it's such an exciting thing. Then for my work, if you want to learn more about emergent strategy, pleasure activism, other kinds of sci-fi, other kinds of facilitation, my website is adriennemareebrown.net. maree is spelled with two Es.

**TC:** adriennemareebrown.net.

**amb:** Yes.

**TC:** Twitter, Instagram, anything?

**amb:** Oh yes, I do those. [Laughter] Twitter is @adriennemaree, Instagram is adriennemareebrown. I make it so that anyone can follow those. Instagram is my favorite. That's the one I'm mostly on these days. Instagram I like because I feel it gives the visual snapshot. I get to see something, and there's something about the art of that. I feel like people are more driven to art in that space and less to ranting or whatever was happening there. That's where I am. [Laughter]

**TC:** Thank you so much for speaking with us today. Thank you for all that you do. We appreciate and love you.

**amb:** Thank you so much for all that you do. I've been following your work for a long time. It's just so exciting to get to be woven into your world, so thank you.

# Ava DuVernay

*Ava DuVernay is a multiple award-nominated and winning television and film producer and director. A member of the board of governors of the Academy of Motion Pictures Arts and Sciences, she is the first Black woman to win the directing award in the dramatic competition at the Sundance Film Festival, and she is the first Black woman to be nominated for a Golden Globe Award for Best Director, and the Academy Award for Best Picture. Aired August 28, 2010.*

• • •

**Thandisizwe Chimurenga:** She is an award-winning public relations professional but she's also an award-winning film directher that's D-I-R-E-C-T-H-E-R. Ava DuVernay of the DuVernay Agency and a bunch of other things that I know like Nommo at UCLA, the Good Life on Exposition and Crenshaw. How're you doing today?

**Ava DuVernay:** I'm doing well. You're naming all my lives.

**TC:** And Lynwood and who knows what?

[Laughter]

**AD:** Lynwood. Wow. Way back.

**TC:** Way back, way back.

**AD:** Yes, good to see you.

**TC:** Good to see you too.

**TC:** On Monday on August 30, you have a film appearing on BET called *My Mic Sounds Nice*. Now, going back, you started the DuVernay Agency as a means of providing publicity for Black films.

**AD:** That's right.

**TC:** You have got such an impressive roster of Black films that you have been the PR agency for. Then you said, "I'm going to do a film, and I'm going to do something that's close to my heart," and you came out with *This is The Life*, a story of West coast hip hop as experienced by young folks such as yourself back in the day –

**AD:** Back in the day.

**TC:** At the Good Life on Exposition and Crenshaw. A wonderful film, award-winning film. It just blew up, it went all over the place, and now you've got this other film coming out. This is also on hip hop, correct?

**AD:** Yes.

**TC:** Tell our audience about this film.

**AD:** Well, that was a nice little synopsis of what's been going on the past few years. But, yes, this documentary *My Mic Sounds Nice*, another hip hop documentary, I think is really important 30 years into hip hop as a genre, as a culture, as an art form to start doing some serious documentary analysis. I love the whole art form of the hip-hop documentary. The first doc was fun. I was looking to do something – a second one. One of the ideas was to do something about women in hip hop and then BET happened to come to me and asked if I was interested in developing something about women in hip hop. Since it was already on my list of things I wanted to do, definitely jumped at it. They approached because they were looking to bring in outside documentarians to BET to do a series of elevated docs on urban music culture, and so this is the first one. Yes, it's *My Mic Sounds Nice* and it airs on Monday.

**TC:** Okay. Now, I want to ask you about this whole process of filmmaking, but let's talk more in-depth about *My Mic Sounds Nice*. Now, I was reading some of the reviews of the film thus far, and 30 years in, we're talking about the fact that the appearance of female rappers seems to be declining. I'm not sure which award show it was. I lost track, but there is one of the major awards. I don't follow them the way I should. They even dropped the category of best female rap artist because the field has been so depleted. What is the story of female rappers? What is happening with the sisters in hip hop?

**AD:** The little award show you're talking about is the Grammys.

**TC:** Oh, that little thing?

**AD:** Yes, that little thing.

**TC:** Okay.

**AD:** Yes, in 2005 they dropped the category of best female rapper.

**TC:** Five years ago.

**AD:** Yes, completely with like very little fanfare and nobody cared. But at this point, you cannot win a Grammy for best female rap hiphop artist because it doesn't exist. That's coming from a time when in the early 1990s you had upwards of 45 women signed to major labels, touring, recording, making music videos, and now we're down to three women signed to major labels.

**TC:** From 45 to 3. Yes. The documentary looks at that trajectory and starting from the heyday, Mercedes Ladies back in '79 and Sha-Rock and Roxanne Shante. '79 was the year!

**AD:** Yeah yeah! All the way through the '80s and then into the golden era of the '90s when it was a big commercial success with Foxy, Kim, and Lauren Hill and Missy. There were so many women during that time, Conscious Daughters, Queen Pen, Ladybug Mecca. I mean it goes on to the 2000s in the first decade of the new century, there really have been a handful of women that have charted, that have been recording in a commercial way. So yeah, now we're down to three on major labels and it's definitely something to look at.

**TC:** Not trying to give any credence to conspiracy theories, but other than them saying that "Well, women rappers is not really lucrative," from 45 to 3 and women are not lucrative? Sisters ain't lucrative?

**AD:** Well, it's tough because you do have women that sold millions of albums. You have Lauryn Hill, you have Missy Elliott who's the most commercially successful female hip hop artist of all time. She sold millions and millions of albums.

**TC:** More successful than Queen?

**AD:** More successful than Queen Latifah, more successful than Lauryn Hill, Missy Elliott, in terms of, if we count success in terms of record sales. Lil Kim sold, Foxy Brown sold. Women have sold, but just not in the ratio that would sustain interest from the labels. In the late '90s, the whole industry started to collapse on itself and major corporations had to downsize, there weren't as many small labels, and so it's kind of the first to go are the female emcees. It's a male-dominated field. While the female emcees did sell some here and there, not in enough numbers to sustain signing and nurturing women artists in this genre.

**TC:** Tell me then, how are sisters faring with underground hip hop with independent labels?

**AD:** Well, I'm glad you asked because when you ask the first question you said, "It seems that women are appearing less." That's what it seems like because that's what the commercial entities are presenting to us. But there are amazing sisters on the underground scene, alternative music scenes. Music festivals like South by Southwest, they're touring, they're on iTunes, they're all over digital. We have a little section in our film dedicated to them. It's a very, very short documentary. BET only gave us an hour to get all this in. In an hour with commercials, it's really only 41 minutes to tell this whole history. But, yes, we dedicate as much time as we could to just naming some of the prominent women in the underground scenes all over the country.

There are dozens and dozens of women that are nice on the mic, that are doing it in a major way, they're just not on the radio right now. So the answer to the question of where are the female emcees, they're there. You just have to look for them a little more than on your radio dial, but they are still rhyming and they're just as talented.

**TC:** Can you give us some names?

**AD:** Oh my gosh. Well, in the film I wanted to make sure that along with the Missys and the Rah Diggas and the Eves, that we also interviewed some of these women. So we have Jean Grae who's phenomenal, Tye Phoenix, incredible, and Medusa. They kind of represent that contingent. But in the film, there's a woman named Invincible out of Detroit who's amazing,

Pri The Honeydark, just all over the country you've got women that are really dope, you know what I mean? And are not being heard in the ways that we remember our female MCs from the '90s. Music videos, touring, and radio, that doesn't exist anymore. If you love sisters on the mic you have to find them.

**TC:** Now let me get into some of this other stuff that I wanted to ask you about. You did *This Is The Life*.[1] I saw the little short you did called *Saturday Night Life*, which I enjoyed. That was about what? Five minutes?

**AD:** Thank you, yes, I think it's like five, six minutes.

**TC:** I said, "Okay." Now we've got *My Mic Sounds Nice* and also know that you're working on a film called *I Will Follow*,[2] which stars Beverly Todd, Omari Hardwick, Michole Briana White. I said, "Now, wait a minute." You've gone from public relations, then you did this one film, *This Is The Life*, because that was close to your heart. It's like, "No, wait a minute," are you merging into another lane now, you being a filmmaker now? Wait a minute, aren't you supposed to be the PR lady? What you're doing now?

**AD:** Right right. I just love film. I just love film, and I was around it so much as a publicist, and as a marketer. I would be on sets with all these amazing filmmakers and just think, "I want to do what he's doing." I just started to study. I didn't go to film school. I cobbled together a film school experience for myself, but the great thing is that I was working on so many high profile film sets. I was able to watch some of the great directors actually doing it in real-time, which was amazing.

**TC:** Okay. Now you done let that part out. You haven't been to film school?

**AD:** No. No.

**TC:** Now you're really out your lane now. What are you doing?! What are you doing?

**AD:** I know right? I don't know.

**TC:** You're not leaving nothing for nobody else. You're supposed to be in your lane. You done merged into somebody else's lane now. [Laughter]

---

1 *This Is The Life* is a documentary, released in 2008.
2 *I Will Follow* was released in September 2010. Ava DuVernay won Best Screenplay from the African-American Film Critics Association.

You're the PR sister, and you got how many films under your belt? How many films you dealing with now?

**AD:** How many films have I publicized?

**TC:** No, directing.

**AD:** Oh, directing. I think it's six now.

**TC:** Okay. See? You're doing too much.

**AD:** I think it's, yes, six.

**TC:** You're doing too much, Ava.

**AD:** I know, I love it.

[Laughter]

**TC:** But you're doing it so well though.

**AD:** Thanks, sis. Thank you.

**TC:** So we've got *I Will Follow*. Tell us about that film.

**AD:** Yes. *I Will Follow* – I shot *This Is The Life* which is the hip hop documentary on LA hip hop that I made. I self-distributed that because I do marketing work with the studios and work on distribution, I knew how to do it and I find that part really fun. So I said, "Well, let me just do it for myself." Instead of selling the rights and getting a little DVD deal, I just did it on my own. I made a little money from it and I put that into *I Will Follow* along with an investor who basically was an in-kind investor. He had cameras, he had equipment, and he let me use that, plus my little money and we made *I Will Follow*. We shot it in November. The lead is Salli Richardson-Whitfield. You'll know her from *I Am Legend* and *Antwone Fisher*. A lot of people remember her from *Posse*, now she's on this incredible show on Sci-Fi network called *Eureka*, that's a big cult favorite. She's incredible. She's in this great film called *Black Dynamite* that was at Sundance last year. She's really an underrated actor. Omari Hardwick and Michole Briana White, who's amazing, and Beverly Todd and Tracie Thoms. It's a really great cast. I've got that and then I also have the Essence Music Festival. I did a two-hour documentary on the Essence Music Festival that airs tonight.

**TC:** Okay see I didn't know about that one. Tell us about that.

**AD:** Yes. That airs tonight. That premieres tonight on TV One. *Essence* magazine and Time, Inc. asked me to do a documentary about the Essence Music Festival. I didn't know that it was the largest African-American gathering in the country, annual gathering. It's a three-day mega-concert fest that happens in New Orleans every year. Upwards of 300,000 of our folks congregate together, they descend on New Orleans, and they just party for three days. It's really beautiful. I did this two-hour concert documentary. It's Alicia Keys, and Janet Jackson, and Earth, Wind & Fire, and Trey Songz, and Raphael Saadiq, and Jill Scott, and Mary. It's awesome. I shot that this summer.

**TC:** Okay, okay, okay. Hold up. That's airing tonight.

**AD:** That's airing tonight on TV One.

**TC:** We've got, that you've got a film on the Essence Music Festival.

**AD:** That's Saturday.

**TC:** You've got *My Mic Sounds Nic*e coming up Monday.

**AD:** That's Monday. *This Is the Life* re-airs on the movie channel on Sunday.

**TC:** *This Is the Life*

**AD:** So Saturday, Sunday, Monday.

**TC:** This is just the Ava DuVernay weekend.

[Laughter]

**TC:** You've got *I Will Follow*, which is scheduled to come out next year.

**AD:** Come out next year. We're premiering as a closing night selection of the Urbanworld Film Festival in September in New York.

**TC:** With all of these major actors in this film: Salli Richardson, Beverly Todd, Omari Hardwick?

**AD:** Yes.

**TC:** You ain't been to film school?

**AD:** No. Unfortunately, not.

**TC:** You got these major players in your films. You got major play on these – How're you doing all of this? You said now, going back, *This Is the Life*, you funded that yourself.

**AD:** Yes.

**TC:** You didn't go in the hole. It actually made some money and you parlayed that into ... How're you doing all of this?

**AD:** I don't know.

[Laughter]

**TC:** You don't have any idea?

**AD:** No.

**TC:** You can't help our audience out? Give us a little ... what kind of mojo are you working, sista?

**AD:** I think life in the universe is letting this all happen. And um ...

**TC:** Letting?

**AD:** Yes! Because I really for a long time had wanted to do this and forces were against me. It wasn't the time I guess, and I didn't realize it at that moment. But I've been wanting to make films for a while and tried to do it the traditional way, try to package, try to add, attach actors, try to go to the studios, try to beg people for money at the studios, "Please, green light my piece." Then finally when I started to just say, "You know what? I'm going to do what I can do and it might be small and it might not look as polished but it's going to be from the heart. I'm going to use what I do know how to do." I know how to do some publicity, I know how to market something. I'm going to do the best I can. I'm not going to say that, "Because I didn't go to film school, I can't do this." I'm not going to say, "Because I don't have a lot of money, I can't do this." I'm not going to say, "Because I don't have an agent, I can't do this. I can do this. I can tell my stories and it's going to be done as best I can." When I had that realization, that's just like everything started to fall into place.

**TC:** Wow. Now that's an incredible story in and of itself. You didn't worry about what you didn't have you worked what you did have.

**AD:** Right. But for a long time, I worried about what I didn't have. I felt insecure about not going to film school. I felt insecure, "Oh, I'm a publicist. What are people going to say?" Or, "Is anyone going to think that a publicist can make a movie? Does anyone care about the kids at the Good Life like I do? Does anyone care about women in hip-hop like I do?

Does anyone want to see this little film that I made with Salli and Omari, and those guys in this super small film about just a day in the life of a Black woman?" Not a lot happens. It's just a sister going through her day. I like it. "Will, other people like it? I don't know, but at this point, I don't care." It took me a while to get over that hump and once you make that mental shift I think things, mighty forces come to your aid.

**TC:** Wow. Make a mental shift and the universe opens up. The planets do align.

**AD:** Yes, amen.

**TC:** Wow. Ava DuVernay, if people want to keep up with you and all the wonderful things that you are doing, how can they do that?

**AD:** Well, I'm a big Facebooker as you know, Thandi. [Laughter] I'm on Facebook and all the films are on Facebook. You can put in *I Will Follow* in Facebook and our page will pop up and you can follow everything that's going on. You can put in *This Is the Life*. You can put in *My Mic Sounds Nice*. I'm also on Twitter, @AVADVA.[3]

**TC:** @AVADVA on Twitter, okay.

**AD:** The DVA is not for diva, it's for DuVernay Agency, even though people want to make it about diva, but no. I'm just a nice gal from Lynwood. That's all.

**TC:** You are just so professional, and so humble, and so beautiful, and so wonderful, and so gracious, and so powerful. That's what I think of when I think of diva.

**AD:** Oh, okay.

**TC:** That's what I think of. You do stuff with class. You talk about you ain't been to film school, you got films out here. You winning awards. I know people have been in film school and ain't done a film yet. They could have YouTube'd something by now, they ain't done nothing yet. You got films out here winning awards.

[Laughter]

**AD:** Funny.

**TC:** To me, that's a diva. If that ain't a diva, I don't know what it is.

---

3 The Twitter account @AVADVA is now obsolete. Ava DuVernay can be found now at @AVA

**AD:** Okay. I need to change my thoughts about diva then. Maybe I need to look it up. All right.

**TC:** Thank you so much for gracing this mic on *Some of Us Are Brave* today. We appreciate you.

**AD:** Thandi, I love *Some of Us Are Brave! Some of Us Are Brave* is dope. It's incredible. First of all, just the name. Years ago, I asked you what that meant and you put me up on game and if people that are listening to the show don't know, you need to Google and figure it out.

[Laughter]

**TC:** Check it out.

**AD:** Check it. It's a beautiful show and thank you for always supporting me.

**TC:** Thank you. Thank you so much, Ava DuVernay. Not only will I follow, I will holla.

**AD:** All right. Holla.

**TC:** Holla.

[Laughter]

# Carol Maillard

*Recorded December 7, 2003, at the Wilshire-Ebell Theatre in Los Angeles prior to* Sweet Honey in the Rock'*s performance on their 30th anniversary tour. This would also be the last tour of retiring founding member Bernice Johnson Reagon. Carol Maillard, a founding member of* Sweet Honey in the Rock, *is also an accomplished actress who has performed in film, television, cabaret and on stage.*

• • •

**Thandisizwe Chimurenga:** There are just so many different things I want to ask about. But one thing in particular ... I've heard *Sweet Honey in the Rock* often referred to as a woman, why is that?

**Carol Maillard:** I think that's something that started to come about when people were dealing with the name *Sweet Honey in the Rock* and the idea of what the properties of honey are. And the idea that honey is ...when it is warm, it's flowing, it's sweet, it's malleable, it's easy, you know, and very luscious, and when it is left out in the cold it can be very, you know, stone like the rock. you know like rigid and, you know, uncared about and so, I think, little by little, "Well, you know that's pretty much Black women." You know the feelings around Black women, you know we're very loving and very sweet, luscious, you know, entities on this planet and you know when not cared for not ... or left out in the cold or allowed to just like harden then there is that you know portion of us that is, you know, very strong and solid. And I think that's where that came from, *Sweet Honey in the Rock*, yeah.

**TC:** That was wonderful. I have never heard that explanation before, but I knew exactly what you were talking about. I noticed on the email you said that you were the interview contact for December.

**CM:** Yes.

**TC:** Obviously that rotates?

**CM:** It rotates, yeah. There are three of us who do interviews and then … Well actually there are four of us, but we start with one person at the beginning of our season and then each person takes two months. So, I am doing interviews for December and January.

**TC:** Now, why is that?

**CM:** We rotate because it's easier. I think it's easier that way. One person is responsible for doing media for two months, I think if there were more of us who were actually doing it we might, you know, break it down to a month. You know everybody would take a month. But if you have like everybody is doing media, and a lot of requests are coming in, things can kind of get like really scattered. You don't want one person overburdened more in one month than another. So, this is your month, this is your month, blam, do that. The next two months will probably be Ysaye. Ysaye Barnwell will do the next two months and then we'll just keep rotating like that.

**TC:** And *Sweet Honey in The Rock* in its history has had many members come through, return, some move on or what have you. Is that part of the structure? Has that been intentional to rotate, to have people come and go and for the group to continue after Dr. Reagon leaves? Is it the passing on of the torch of leadership or – ?

**CM:** No no no it's not, no. *Sweet Honey in the Rock* comes out of a theater company in Washington DC that was started to give African-Americans an opportunity to be in a professional theater setting, and to learn all of the skills and acting talents and, you know, how to produce your own plays and in that way we learned a lot of things. We learned how to use our voices, how to use our bodies, how to create characters, how to make costumes. The whole nine yards, you know, of theater.

And one of the things that happened was out of the vocal workshop that Bernice was running, the music that she was teaching us as our vocal director was like … it was just like amazing. We did children's songs, we did everything. But with *Sweet Honey in the Rock*, after we had several incarnations, men and women, and all sopranos and, you know, you just had all these kind of different configurations of people who kept coming back and forth to rehearsal. When the final group manifested we had three actresses and we had Bernice who was our vocal instructor.

So, you know, if you're an actress – which I'm an actress – you wanna work, you wanna be in the theater, you wanna do things, you wanna sing too but you also want to do your craft in other ways. So, people would come and go. I was the first one to have to take a break because I was doing a show at the Kennedy Center with the D.C. Black Repertory Company.

And two people who were in the vocal workshop, Rosie Lee Hooks, who is the director of Cultural Affairs here in Los Angeles, and another woman, Ayodele Harrington, who now works with a senator in New York City for special projects, special advocacy for children. They came in when I was gone. And Bernice started to realize that everybody was going. You know, if it's Black women, if it's people who are working trying to do their craft, people are gonna come and go, people are gonna come and go and the workshop gave her a way to always be able to train singers and then filter them into *Sweet Honey in the Rock* as they needed once we started working more.

At one point we did go outside of the workshop and held auditions and there were several women that came in. Evelyn Harris came in through an audition. Pat Johnson came in through an audition. Yasmeen Williams, she was a part of the theater company, the Black Repertory Theater Company and in the voice workshops. So, and Dianaruthe Wharton was our piano player when we used to work with a piano player in the very beginnings of *Sweet Honey in the Rock*.

So, you gotta live, you gotta eat, you gotta breathe, things happen, you gotta pay your bills. So, if *Sweet Honey in the Rock* can help you in any way in that area then you like kind of, you know what I mean, you go for it and we always have subs. You know we started to initiate ... Sweet Honey came up with the idea of having someone who can come in at the last minute, a former member of Sweet Honey. Someone that may be auditioned at another point who didn't make it into the group.

And so that we ... Sweet Honey would always exist and there are women, just amazing women and some men who have actually said, "If you all wanna go with men, you know, I'll learn my parts and come on in and sing with you all." But there's always people who wanna see Sweet Honey live and thrive and survive and continue, and they would do whatever it is that they can do, just ... I would say not even just women, just people who wanna make sure that there is a Sweet Honey for the world.

**TC:** And that ... that leads into the question but I wanted to hear the answer from you, of course: why is *Sweet Honey in the Rock*? Why is it here?

**CM:** Oh. I think there is a need in the world. Because while I was in New York pursuing my acting career and working a lot and [sigh] people wanted Sweet Honey, people needed Sweet Honey. There's a need for the group in the world and I think any time the group got to a point where they thought, well maybe we oughta, you know like, fold it up or I'm tired. I don't ...You know, every time we would get to that point, I think the audiences and the need for the music and the healing and the thought processes that go into the music I think all of those things, the universe calls Sweet Honey to continue to be in existence and, those of us who will remain after Bernice moves on to do, you know, other more incredible and amazing things with her talent and her intellect. We're gonna, you know, keep rolling. We've got a lot ... there's still a lot more to say, a lot more to do, a lot more to sing about. We have two amazing women that are coming in, you know, to participate in *Sweet Honey in the Rock* after Bernice's last concert in February.

**TC:** Okay. Now sitting in there watching all the goings on, I was like, "Wow, that's a lot of stuff going on."

**CM:** Yes, it is.

**TC:** How come you all just can't get up and sing? That's a lot.

**CM:** Well, this is not just getting up and sing. When we were here at Liberty Hill we just got up and sang. When we were in Burlington, Vermont we just get up and sing, you know, but there's a documentary on *Sweet Honey in the Rock*.[1] I found a producer about five, six years ago, Stanley Nelson. He's an amazing, wonderful, brilliant filmmaker documentarian. This milieu of live concert performance is something that is really new for him,

---

1 *Sweet Honey in the Rock: Raise Your Voice* aired June 29, 2005.

it's new for Sweet Honey In The Rock to be followed this closely for the last ten months of our 30th anniversary year.

It just worked out that he came on board right when we were getting ready to embark on this anniversary year and then we found out Bernice wanted to retire from actively performing and singing with the group. So, it's all, you know, grace, God's grace and it happened at a great time. So what they're doing today is just like this maja mega production going on and hopefully, you know, this will be a beautiful part of the documentary. They want the concert to be just a gorgeous, beautiful event and that's what they've tried to create with this production, yeah.

**TC:** And I'm sure that it will be, but I was just wondering in terms of, I understand there's a technical aspect, but also what other preparation does Sweet Honey engage in before they do a concert or do a performance?

**CM:** I can't say that Sweet Honey has any. We don't have rituals and we don't have things that we do to, you know, gear ourselves up. Everybody finds the place inside themselves that they need to go to be able to do the work. We travel and sing on the same day that's what ... the way we work. And it is challenging. We did an amazing concert last time. I know I keep saying amazing but it's been an amazing year. But we had a slamming concert last night at Berkeley.

We did our collaboration, it's called "Evening Song" and, it's a show that we do with Toshi Reagon who is Bernice's daughter, who I met when she was just eight, nine years old. And she has a rock band. So, when audiences see us you know we've got men on the stage, we've got white folks on the stage, we got Rock on the stage, we've got the guitar, you know, and we're dancing and moving about so we did that last night and we got up this morning and we got on a plane and we're here. So people are in their rooms doing what they need to do to be ready. So, we hope to have a marvelous experience with Liberty Hill tonight. And hopefully, they will have us back again next year.

**TC:** Oh I'm quite sure they will and we will be back and so many other women will and men here in Los Angeles who love you, will be back. But if you could tell me, as I said this is for a Black woman's radio program, here in Los Angeles. We're new. We're attempting to give voice to Black women, the various aspects of our lives and experiences that we share. In addition to this beautiful gift that you're gonna be giving us tonight, what else would you like to say to Black women, in particular, I know you speak to everyone, but what can you say to Black women here in LA?

[Laughter]

**CM:** Oh my goodness. That's like really ... that's a really big question. There's a lot of things, you know, I think the most important thing is to understand who you are on the inside first. To be a friend to yourself. To nurture your own spirit and to find ways to not only take care of yourself but find ways to give the blessings, and the grace, and the power, and the beauty that God has so blessed us with. To really find ways to, you know, stretch it out and share it to the world. Because you can't help nobody else until you know how to really help yourself, and you can't save the world on an E, you know on E. So you have to continually replenish and love yourself and love, you know, love your other sister friends and just really I think embrace who you are, embrace your God-self and let your light shine.

**TC:** Okay. Well, I know that you're busy and I know you only had a few minutes so I wanna thank you for this time you have given me.

**CM:** Oh, Thandi, thank you for your patience, you know, helping me figure out how to do this. So imma dash on in there, y'all buy them CDs and be looking for that video, looking for that film next year! Because the film is gonna be great! It's gonna be really great.

**TC:** Definitely ... But thank you oh so much for your time.

**CM:** You're welcome.

# Euzhan Palcy

*Born in Martinique, Euzhan Palcy is a film director, writer and producer. The first Black female director to be produced by a major Hollywood studio (MGM), her most notable films include* Sugar Cane Alley, A Dry White Season *and* Aimé Césaire: A Voice for History. *Recorded August 17, 2009, in Los Angeles, California.*

• • •

**Thandisizwe Chimurenga:** This is Thandisizwe Chimurenga. I am running the streets currently at the Downtown LA Film Festival at the Downtown Independent. I'm sitting with Euzhan Palcy who is here tonight, screening her film on Aimé Césaire.[2] How are you doing?

**Euzhan Palcy:** I'm doing well, thank you.

**TC:** Thank you so much for giving me this opportunity. I want to start by saying how much I love your work, and so many people I know who love your work starting with *La rue Cases-Nègres, Sugar Cane Alley,*[3] which was such a wonderful film, and then progressing to, of course, *A Dry White Season.*[4] With *A Dry White Season*, you were the first Black woman to direct a film for a major film studio. Of course, for English speaking audiences, that was our first introduction to you. Most of your work has

---

2 Aimé Césaire (1913-2008) was, like Euzhan Palcy, born in Martinique. Poet, playwright, and politician, Césaire was a key figure in the struggle for political and cultural independence for Martinique and other French-speaking Caribbean countries. Martinique is still a territory of France.

3 *Rue Cases-Nègres, Sugar Cane Alley* was released in 1983.

4 *A Dry White Season* was released in 1989.

been in French, is that correct? Most African-Americans are not familiar with French-speaking culture, would not know your body of work. For example, the film tonight, this is a three-parter on Aimé Césaire that was first done in 1994. You talked about the fact that you left Martinique at the age of 17 to go to France. How in the world did that happen? Seventeen years old and going to Paris, France?

**EP:** Yes, because when you have a passion and you want to study and the entity that can give you that knowledge that you need to fulfill your dream is outside of your country so you go. I didn't go just like that. Of course, my parents supported me and I went to a students' house. I didn't have friends in Paris. I didn't know anybody until I went there and I made friends there because I met other girls like me who left Martinique or Guadeloupe, the Caribbean, to come to study and we became friends.

**TC:** Which brings me back to my question. You knew no one there, you were 17, but you were determined to go to Paris?

**EP:** Absolutely.

**TC:** Now you knew Aimé Césaire there in Martinique because he was the mayor of the town. You talked about his influence on you prior to your leaving to go to France. I believe that you became a poet at the age of ten because of Aimé Césaire?

**EP:** Yes, because I loved his poetry and I used to listen to the words, even if sometime I couldn't understand the full sense of the word because he was a genius. He was a genius. Just to give you another picture, when he was doing his electoral campaign, he would have many, many old people, male and female from the countryside. They would come wherever he would be talking. They would come with their little stool, they would sit on it and just to listen to everything. The African-American churches, when they say, "Yes, father said to us –" If sometimes they wouldn't understand all the words that he would say, but they would feel what was behind the words. They would still get it. It was amazing, and that's what he – He opened our minds, he helped us to breathe and to think, and to be proud of ourselves. That's a major thing for all Black people in the world. Not only all Black people, but all people who have been mistreated by history. Black or Asian, Arab, whatever.

**TC:** He was international.

**EP:** He was international. He was a humanist.

**TC:** Understanding his development on you as a young child and you decided to go to Paris, France, how is it that you came to believe that film was your destiny?

**EP:** I always loved film. My sister, she loved dancing. She loved reading and dancing, but I always loved painting and film and music. I was writing little songs and stuff like that as well. I would go to the theatres very often and I would see the movies coming from the States, from friends, and from Europe, and at home, I was the only one with that passion. I knew immediately, knew that that's what I wanted to do for one reason, because I was fascinated by the screen, by being in a theater, and then have that screen, darkness, and then the light coming. It was a magical thing. It was fantastic for me, that one thing. Also, what really made me decide to be a filmmaker was the fact that I couldn't understand why we were absent. Black people were absolutely absent on the screen. We were not there. If we were there, it was in some American film that would go to the Caribbean and we would see one Black person or two Black people, but in parts that were very degrading, not nice. Always, as a child, I couldn't understand why. I was thinking maybe because we never –. We should do it. We should just do it. Of course, when you are a child, you see that everything is easy.

[laughter]

**EP:** I said, "I'm going to do that because I can write." When I came across that book *Sugar Cane Alley*, I knew at that precise moment that that was it. That would be my first film.

**TC:** That was going to be your first film.

**EP:** Absolutely, I knew it in my heart, in my flesh, that would – Yes.

**TC:** We talked tonight about your film on Aimé Césaire is available through California Newsreel. *La rue Cases-Nègres, Sugar Cane Alley* is also available out there in the world?

**EP:** It was in here. I think that for the moment, the deal is over. We are in negotiation with another distributor to have a release of the film in the theatre, a new release, and to put together a wonderful DVD collection for *Sugar Cane Alley.*

**TC:** That would be so wonderful. Can you give us an estimated timeframe on how that might work?

**EP:** I think that we will need a year to do that.

**TC:** About a year?

**TC:** Yes.

**TC:** I know that I will be one of several who will be anxiously awaiting that on DVD. Other than that, do you have any other projects coming up that we can look forward to?

**EP:** Well, recently I did a movie called *The Dissident Journeys*,[1] that means a veteran's journey during the Second World War. That means it's about young kids, girls, and boys adolescent, when de Gaulle asked French people to come to help save France because France capitulated under the Germans' pressure. All these many kids from Martinique and Guadeloupe, they left to go to meet de Gaulle, to help, but the story is about how they did it. It was incredible and what happened afterwards.

That movie is 88 minutes filmed and I'm working right now on the bonuses and I'm working on the DVD collector for that too. In the meantime, I'm working on another project, a feature film. The script is ready. We have the cast, we are looking for some money to book the budget to do the film. It's a movie called *Midnight's Last Ride*,[2] shot in New Mexico with Ellen Burstyn and Sam Shepard, and everybody is there. What I love about that story, it's something about illiteracy.

**TC:** Illiteracy?

**EP:** Yes.

**TC:** Okay, Euzhan Palcy, thank you so much for your time. Thank you, thank you, thank you.

**EP:** Thank you to you too, for interviewing me. It's a great honor as well, because I know your work.

**TC:** You're very welcome. Thank you.

**EP:** Okay. Bye-bye.

---

1 *The Dissident Journeys (Parcours de dissidents)* was aired in 2006.
2 *Midnight's Last Ride* has not yet been released.

# Evelyn C. White on Alice Walker

*Evelyn C. White is the author of* Alice Walker: A Life; Chain, Chain, Change: For Black Women in Abusive Relationships; *editor of the Black women's health book* Speaking for Ourselves; *and a co-author of the photography book* The African-Americans. *Her writing has been anthologized widely and has appeared in numerous publications. The following presentation at the African-American Museum and Library at Oakland (AAMLO) was recorded February 16, 2005.*

• • •

**Evelyn White:** Welcome to all of you. This is my second time in this library. I think it is a very beautiful space and I encourage you all to learn a little bit about the history of the library here, if you are so inclined. I would like to thank the Oakland Public Library for inviting me and especially Maureen Aliya, a librarian at my neighborhood branch, the Piedmont Library right there. Like Maureen, and perhaps some of you, I have been suffering for a bit with this flu thing that has been going around. So, I am not at my full capacity, but I am here. I am very happy to be here in service of the ancestors.

Yes, this book is finished. It is rather an amazement to me that it is. I was looking just earlier today at the letter that Alice wrote for me almost exactly a decade ago. I am going to ask my beloved friend Elaine Lee, one of the first people I met when I moved to the Bay area in 1986 to begin reporting for the *San Francisco Chronicle*... I am going to ask Elaine if she will come up here and read this letter, because we all help each other out.

**Elaine Lee:**

*Alice Walker. Sent February 15, 1995.*

*Dear Evelyn,*

*This is to inform you in writing that I have authorized you to write a biography of my life. That I will assist you in every way possible. That I will make myself and my files and my records available to you as needed and as possible. I understand you will need to interview family members, colleagues, friends, etc. I will do everything in my power to make sure each and every person is apprised of my support of this project. Perhaps this letter might be used in that regard.*

*Yours sincerely,*

*Alice Walker*

[Applause]

**EW:** Thank you, Elaine. Again, the date of the letter is February 15, 1995. Alice, born February 9, 1944, celebrated her sixty-first birthday last Wednesday. A week ago today. She had a few people over. She lives here in the East Bay. It was a wonderful gathering, as gatherings with Alice tend to be. She didn't ask for us to bring any gifts other than a story about a gift that we had received and that we understood to be a gift. When it was my time to talk, I chatted some about the incredible gift she had given me to let me be in her life for a decade to give me complete and total access to herself, her records, her life. To never once say to me... You have to understand the contract for this book was signed in 1995 and the book was to be delivered on June 1, 1999. The book was not... With the assumption, understanding more or less, that the book would be published in the year 2000. So, the book was essentially four or five years late and not published until this past October. Not once during that entire time did Alice Walker ever say to me, "When is the book going to be finished? What are you doing still lurking around my life?"

[Laughs]

"Aren't you finished yet? What is your problem? Can't you get it together? I am tired of seeing you everywhere I go."

[Laughs]

As I said at the gathering a week ago, Alice's prevailing message to me throughout the journey was "How can I help you?" It is a gift that will remain with me for my entire life. It showed me what is possible in terms of support. There are many artists and writers, I know, in this audience and we talk about the lack of economic support for our work. We talk about the lack of understanding in American culture of what artists and writers do and what our contributions can be. But, it is almost always couched in the economic. The lack of the financial support, the political support, the cultural support. To have had the emotional and spiritual support of many people. Many out here. I had your emotional, spiritual, practical support; which I am eternally grateful for. But, it is another thing to be the subject of the book. The person, meaning Alice, that I basically was just there for a decade. So, it was an incredible gift and I am very happy that the book is finished.

Because we are approaching Academy Awards time, I believe in a couple of weeks, I thought I would read a bit about the movie and how the novel, which as many of you know, in 1983 won the Pulitzer Prize, making Alice the second Black woman to win the Pulitzer Prize. The first was the magnificent Gwendolyn Brooks[1] who won the Pulitzer in 1950 for her 1949 collection of poems *Annie Allen*. It was thirty years before another Black woman won what is considered the most prestigious prize in Arts and Letters in this country, the Pulitzer for *The Color Purple*. The novel was made into a film. I believe the film opened in December of 1985. So, I am going to read you a little bit about the background of the film.

To set the stage, basically, Alice... This won't surprise any of you who are aware of Alice. Alice wasn't necessarily interested in Hollywood or a Hollywood movie. She was very interested in having her mother have some understanding of *The Color Purple* and what it was about. Alice's mother had had a stroke. Alice is the youngest of eight children born in very impoverished circumstances in rural Georgia. Her mother, Minnie Lou Walker, had a stroke shortly after *The Color Purple* was published and was never able to read more than a few pages of the book. Alice said to me and others that her primary interest in a film was to give her mother

---

1 Gwendolyn Brooks (1917-2000) was an American poet, author, and teacher. She was the first African American to receive the Pulitzer Prize. Her poetry often delved into the complexities of urban life, racial injustice, and the pursuit of equality. She also wrote several novels and children's books.

an opportunity to understand the story of *The Color Purple*, which is, in part, based on Alice's paternal grandparents and part of her maternal grandparents and forbears, also.

She wanted her mother to understand this story. Her mother, who had never been able to read the novel. That is the main reason that she agreed to the film. It wasn't because Steven Spielberg[2] and Quincy Jones[3] came knocking. Though, in the absence of Quincy Jones, it is pretty clear that the movie probably never would have been made. It was because Quincy Jones was involved and Alice greatly respected the music that he had done for *Roots*, the television series, that she agreed to the film. But, the primary reason was so her mother could understand the story. I will begin reading with that background.

"Illness prevented Mrs. Walker from reading more than a few pages of *The Color Purple*. Her 'decline,' meant the stroke that she had in the late 1970s or early 1980s. "Her decline had catapulted Alice, who named the character Nettie in honor of her maternal grandmother, into a wrenching despair, but she kept her anguish concealed from the public eye." Alice was very much in the public eye after she won the Pulitzer Prize for *The Color Purple*. This is a quote from Alice: "From the moment I realized my mother would never again be the woman I knew, something fell inside of me."

Alice later wrote of her life beyond the shimmer of the Pulitzer Prize: "There was a strong green cord connecting me to this great, simple seeming, but complicated woman, who was herself rooted in the earth. I felt this cord weakening, becoming a thread. There was not a day that I didn't not feel the emptiness left by my mother's absence. Particularly, as she gradually lost the ability to talk beyond a slurred reading, which true to her spirit, she slurred cheerfully." Alice hoped the movie would help her mother recapture memories, reimagined on the palette of art of her

---

2  Steven Spielberg (born 1946) is an acclaimed American filmmaker, producer, and screenwriter.who has received three Academy Awards for Best Director and the Presidential Medal of Freedom. He is known for his philanthropic efforts and has been actively involved in various charitable causes, including those related to education, health, and human rights.

3  Quincy Jones (born 1933) is an American musician, composer, record producer, and arranger. Among many other projects, he produced Michael Jackson's landmark album "Thriller" (1982), which became the best-selling album of all time, and he has released his own albums as a solo artist, winning 28 Grammy awards. He has also been an advocate for social justice.

early life as a young Black woman in Putnam County. Which is the rural area where Alice grew up in Georgia. Although Mr. Walker had passed on, Alice envisioned a film that would likewise ennoble his spirit, which she put forth with poignant touches in the character Harpo. You remember the character Harpo in the book or the movie is based, on part, on Alice's father, Willie Lee Walker, who had died in 1973.

And, of course, there was the language: vibrancy, rhythm, poetry, and flair. As Alice had written to John Theron, the editor of *The Color Purple*, she was certain that a well-cast adaptation of *The Color Purple* would reconnect moviegoers of all hues to the language of their hearts. "I loved the way my mother taught, which was always fresh, honest, straight as an arrow," Alice mused, describing the rich folk language many of her critics had rejected as insulting to Black people. In the movie, she could hear her voice and know that it was authentic, sturdy, and strong. As it happened, it was a voice that grabbed the attention of an actress later cast in a lead role in *Moonsong,* the decoy title used by Spielberg to avert the masses now wild to appear in the first major Black film to be released by Hollywood in years.

Now, we are talking the mid-1980s now. There had been very few major Black films. It is twenty years ago now, so we can find it is difficult to remember. They used the decoy title *Moonsong* because they knew if they said *The Color Purple* that everybody would descend upon Hollywood to try to be cast in this film. So, they used this decoy *Moonsong.* As it happened, it was a voice that grabbed the attention of an actress later cast in a lead role of *Moonsong.*

Born Karen Johnson in New York City, the actress exhibited early talent, performing in community arts workshops. The divorced mother of a young daughter, Johnson moved to California in the mid-1970s where she joined local theatre troupes and honed comedy routines infused with satire. To pay the bills she took odd jobs: bricklayer, cosmetologist for a funeral parlor. When there was no work to be found, Johnson signed up for welfare. In 1984, after an acclaimed one-woman show about Black comic Jackie Moms Mabley, the actress now rising with an adopted stage name opened in "Whoopi Goldberg: Direct from Broadway."

It was a name fated for stardom, but before she achieved international celebrity, Goldberg was driving near her Berkeley home when, enthralled by a voice on the car radio, she pulled to the side of the road. It was Alice Walker reading from *The Color Purple*. Goldberg remembered, "What I heard was so moving, I just stopped and listened. When the program ended, I drove right to a bookstore and bought the novel. I wrote her a letter begging for a part if a movie was ever made. I was ready to play the dust on the floor, the lint on a sweater, the grease in a skillet, anything!" More reserved in tune, Goldberg's dispatch read in part:

> *Dear Alice Walker,*
>
> *I would like to begin by telling you that I think* The Color Purple *is amazing. I have just read it to my daughter. My mom just received it. Again, it is wonderful! I called your publisher to ask about the movie. Well, the name "Whoopi Goldberg" sounds like a joke and I don't think they realized I was not a crank caller. If you think I fit any of the folks in your book, perhaps you would let me know whom I should contact about auditioning. I don't know what else to say, except thank you for your time.*

Already familiar with Goldberg's work, Alice alerted Spielberg and casting director Reuben Cannon, who after a screen test knew they had found in the driven, dreadlocked actress, the perfect Celie. "I was beyond the beyond," Goldberg recalled. One of the premier casting directors in the industry, Cannon called on his credentials, shrewd eye, and international ties with actors. "As a Black man, I had to outwork everybody," is what Reuben Cannon said to me. So, he had to call on his international ties with actors as he continued to contract the best talent for the ensemble performance that would be *The Color Purple*. For example, originally from the Virgin Islands, Deserita Jackson, who played young Celie, wowed Cannon at an open casting he held at a Los Angeles high school. "There were at least three hundred girls there," Jackson recalled.

With his film career on the ascent in the early 1980s, Danny Glover, who had starred in *Places in the Heart, Witness,* and *Silverado,* "had scant competition for the role of Mister," Cannon said. Ghana native Akosua Busia had arrived in Hollywood determined to make her mark "either in a Spielberg movie or on *The Tonight Show with Johnny Carson*," she said. A bus rider, Busia splurged on a taxi after learning, while shopping, that she had been cast as Nettie. Her agent had tracked her down. Willard

Pew, primarily a television actor who had been mostly in *Hill Street Blues*, endured five nerve-wracking screen tests before he landed the role of Harpo. "I blacked out for a minute," he said describing his elation.

Besting singers Chaka Khan,[4] Patty LaBelle,[5] and Phyllis Hyman,[6] licensed realtor Margaret Avery[7] won the part of Shug, but only after the much-desired Tina Turner[8] declined. Then, in Los Angeles to record *We are the World*, the star-studded Africa famine relief extravaganza produced by Quincy Jones, Turner had agreed to a meeting about the film. Jones recalled, "Everybody was all excited, thinking we would have our first choice for Shug. But when we started to talk, Tina said, 'Forget *The Color Purple*.' After twenty years of abuse, she said the only role she wanted to play was Indiana Jones."

[Laughs]

By contrast, the woman cast as Sophia felt destined to play the feisty character who went tit-for-tat with Harpo. Born January 29, 1954 in Mississippi, Oprah Gail Winfrey braved a life of poverty and childhood molestation to emerge in her thirties as a widely-hailed television personality. In the early 1980s, Winfrey arrived in Chicago where, in a few months, ratings for her local program surpassed that of the silver-haired talk show king Phil Donahue.[9] Winfrey said she bought *The Color Purple* after reading an early review and became obsessed with the novel, buying copies by the dozens and handing them out like holy water to friends. "I was gone with the book," she remembered. "I always had several copies on

---

4 Chaka Khan (born 1953), better known as Chaka Khan, is an American singer. Her career has spanned more than five decades. Khan has won ten Grammy Awards and has sold an estimated 70 million records worldwide.
5 Patti LaBelle (born 1944) is an American R&B singer and actress. In a career that has spanned seven decades, she has sold more than 50 million records worldwide. LaBelle has been inducted into the Grammy Hall of Fame, the Hollywood Walk of Fame, the Black Music & Entertainment Walk of Fame, and the Apollo Theater Hall of Fame.
6 Phyllis Hyman (1949-1995) was an American singer, songwriter, and actress best known for her music during the late 1970s through the early 1990s. Hyman also performed on Broadway in the musical *Sophisticated Ladies* based on the music of Duke Ellington.
7 Margaret Avery (born 1944) is an American actress and singer best known for her performance as Shug Avery in *The Color Purple* for which she was nominated for an Academy Award for Best Actress in a Supporting Role.
8 Tina Turner (1939-2023) was an American-born singer. Known as the "Queen of Rock 'n' Roll", she rose to prominence as the lead singer of the Ike & Tina Turner Revue before launching a successful career as a solo performer. As of May 2023, Turner had reportedly sold around 100 to 150 million records worldwide, becoming one of the best-selling recording artists of all time. She was the first Black artist and first woman to be on the cover of Rolling Stone.
9 Phil Donahue (born 1935) is an American media personality, writer, film producer and the creator and host of *The Phil Donahue Show*. The show had a 29-year run on national television that began in Dayton, Ohio, in 1967 and ended in New York City in 1996.

me. For two years, I steered every conversation toward *The Color Purple*. If there was a movie, I knew in my heart that I would be in it." With her talk show drawing an unprecedented millions of viewers and advertising revenues, Winfrey was in negotiations for national syndication. We forget that *Oprah* wasn't always a national show. It was only in Chicago in the early eighties.

So, Winfrey was in negotiations for national syndication when she received a call from Cannon – the casting director – about the upcoming movie *Moonsong*. By chance, Quincy Jones had been in Chicago and seen Winfrey on television. Taken by her downhome style, he stopped in his tracks and peered at the screen. "It just slapped me in the face that I was staring at Sophia," he remembered. "I didn't know if Oprah could act or not, but I immediately called Reuben. He arranged an audition." Certain though she was about her movie future, Winfrey had never performed on film, but her lack of acting experience didn't deter her from pursuing her dream. "They were using this fake title, but it didn't fool me," Winfrey recalled with a laugh. "I told Reuben, 'I know these people. This ain't no *Moonsong*. This is *The Color Purple*.' Sophia is married to Harpo. The name Harpo is Oprah spelled backwards. This is my destiny."

Well, Alfre Woodard[10] felt the same. Indeed, Winfrey's heart sank upon learning that her competition was the accomplished Oklahoma-born actress who had garnered a 1983 Oscar nomination for her role as Geechee in *Cross Creek*. If you haven't seen it, please see *Cross Creek* starring Alfre Woodard. "When Reuben told me that Alfre had also auditioned for Sophie, I knew I would never get the part," Winfrey said. "I mean, how could I beat Alfre? So, to free myself, I prayed to Jesus and asked to be released from the desire to be in *The Color Purple*, that way I could get on with my life."

Winfrey began her detox while at a "fat farm" – her words – in Wisconsin, having made a public bet with entertainer Joan Rivers[11] to shed fifteen pounds. Joan Rivers had been substituting for Johnny Carson on *The Tonight Show*. Oprah had come on and Joan Rivers and her typical style

---

10 Alfre Woodard (born 1952) is an American actress. She has received various accolades, including four Emmy Awards, a Golden Globe Award, and three Screen Actors Guild Awards, as well as nominations for an Academy Award and two Grammy Awards. She is also known for her work as a political activist and producer.

11 Joan Rivers (1933-2014) was a comedian, actress, producer, writer and TV host. She was noted for her blunt, often controversial comedic persona. She was the first woman to host a late night network TV talk show.

had been teasing Oprah about being fat and made a bet with Oprah that she couldn't lose fifteen pounds. So, Oprah had taken on this bet and she was to come back after she had lost the fifteen pounds. "I really needed to lose fifty-five," she shrugged. This is in an interview I had with Oprah. She just finished an exercise session when she received a phone call from Cannon admonishing here to abandon her weightloss regimen. "Ruben said that Steven wanted me for Sophia and I needed to stay the same size," Winfrey happily remembered. "Girl, I packed up and went directly to Dairy Queen!"

[Laughs]

Alright, I am going to skip ahead a bit to the Oscar situation.

The sense of triumph that had infused the cast and crew in the making of *The Color Purple* was not shared by the voting members of the Academy of Motion Picture Arts and Sciences, who deemed the film unworthy of a single Oscar. Blanked, *The Color Purple* joined ranks with *The Turning Point* as the only films to ever garner eleven nominations and no wins. Reuben Cannon said it was excruciating to sit through the evening – and this would be in February or March 1986, so, about twenty years ago – excruciating to hear *The Color Purple* announced in nearly every category, only to have no one ascend to the stage to receive an award. "After a while, it became laughable," remembered Cannon, who escorted Oprah Winfrey to the festivities.

"The dislike of Steven was obvious. Everyone understood that the backlash was about him. I was disappointed for the film, but not for myself, because the whole experience had been a marvelous dream," added Winfrey, who lost the Oscar to Angelica Huston, who was in *Prizzi's Honor*. "I had on the tightest dress of my life. So, even if they had called my name, I wouldn't have been able to get up out of the seat. I was just happy to go home and cut the dress off my body!"

[Laughs]

Peter Guber, who was one of the producers of the film, was privy to the inner machinations of Hollywood power brokers. You have to understand, at this point, Steven Spielberg was known as the boy wonder who made *E.T.* and those alien films. There were a lot of people that didn't think that he was being serious enough. Then, of course, there had been all the controversy about *The Color Purple* with Black folks picketing it. So, many felt that they were taking it out on Spielberg. Like Cannon, he agreed that the Academy was sending Spielberg a message that he yet had dues to pay. A message they aimed to temper by honoring him the next year with the Irving G. Thalberg Memorial Award for creative producers.

Guber was certain that Spielberg would have preferred an Oscar, which for all his blockbuster clout, the director had never received. So, when Spielberg directed *The Color Purple*, he had not yet received an Oscar. Instead, *Out of Africa* dominated the evening, winning seven Oscars including those for best picture, best director, and best musical score. Ironically, Lionel Richie, who had helped compose "Ms. Celie's Blues (Sister)," a song in *The Color Purple,* won the Oscar for best song for another tune, "Say You, Say Me" from the film *White Knights.*

"As the person who also bought the movie rights to *Out of Africa*, I can tell you that *The Color Purple* was a much more daring and audacious film," Guber declared. Steven brought the white light of celebrity in getting the movie made and became a lightning rod of liability when it was released. *The Color Purple* deserved Oscars, but for whatever reasons, the Academy deduced that it wasn't Steven's time. Never one to hold her tongue, Whoopi Goldberg said that Oscar prospects for *The Color Purple* were damaged by critics who diverted attention from the film's artistic merits with a "pissy" political fight.

"The Hollywood NAACP cost us every one of the Academy Awards," insisted Goldberg, bested by Geraldine Page for *The Trip to Bountiful.* "They killed the chances for me, Oprah, Margaret Avery, Quincy, everybody. I truly believe that." And Blacks in Hollywood paid the price for years to come, because after all the hell that was raised the studios didn't want to do any more Black movies for fear of the picket lines and boycotts.

While sympathetic to the frustration of the cast and crew, Alice said she considered the Academy snub of *The Color Purple* a blessing that preserved the purity of intention with which the film was made. The way she saw it, everyone from Spielberg to the impish Black child in the movie who warned Harpo, "It is gon' rain on your head!" Remember that little boy who said, "It is gon' rain on your head!"?

Alice thought that everyone deserved more than an Oscar for "their loving radiance as a healing balm for our communities and the world." This is a quote from Alice, "Because we had so many nominations, I thought someone on the jury understood the impetus of the movie, which was love," Alice explained. "But, when I realized that they had understanding, but no courage, I lost interest in winning. We were freed from the corruption that prizes often bring." But the experience brought other benefits. Ever the curious artist, Alice said she was grateful for the adventure of attending the Academy Awards show. The naysayers protesting the movie – "*The Color Purple* destroys the color Black," read a placard – only added to the stockpile of fabric for her future writing.

I want you all to be thinking about this if you are watching the Oscars in the next couple of weeks. "It was a lot less sophisticated up close than it appears on television," she remembered. "With people outside on bleachers yelling and screaming, it was like entering a high school gym. I had never crossed a picket line before," she continued. "I never thought that I would, but I wasn't going to let my people either in the movie or the book go into such hostile territory alone. My characters had gotten me from New York to San Francisco. Now really, how could I leave them amidst bleacher seats in Beverly Hills?"

Thank you.

[Applause]

# Julie Dash on St. Clair Bourne

*Filmmaker St. Clair Bourne, whose many works included biopics on Paul Robeson[12] and John Henrik Clark,[13] passed away on December 16, 2007 in New York City. In Los Angeles members of BAD-West, the Black Association of Documentary Filmmakers – West, gathered at a memorial for Bourne in the Leimert Park area. Julie Dash, whose* Daughters of the Dust *was the first full-length film directed by an African-American woman to obtain general theatrical release in the United States in 1991 and was named to the Library of Congress' National Film Registry, was asked to comment for the KPFK Evening News.*

• • •

**Julie:** I do what I do, and I do it the way I do it because of St. Clair Bourne. I started working for him and the Chamba brothers in 1971. I was a film student, and a student at City College in New York, and I was one of his production assistants. And I was coming out of the Queensbridge housing projects, and exposed to a whole different way of thinking, doing, performing, basically a scholarship in excellence. And I've tried to continue that in my own life and career, but it's pretty much all due to St. Clair Bourne and the efforts of the Chamba brothers, and just, you know, the zeitgeist of the time, the spirit of the time. You know, everyone was trying to advance the culture, advance the race, advance the notion of documentary film, what it could be, what it ought to be, and I was glad to be a part of that. And we'll all miss him very much, and we're all deeply in shock, but he was definitely cut from a different mold. And a great loss, a great loss.

----

12 See note on page 30
13 John Henrik Clarke (1915-1998) was an African-American historian, professor, and pioneer in the creation of Pan-African and Africana studies and professional institutions in academia starting in the late 1960s.

# Sharon L Graine on
# Mary Ellen (Mammy) Pleasant

*Playwright Sharon L. Graine founded the Playhouse Theatre Players in 1993. The company has put on a number of performances throughout Southern California including* My Name Is Eartha, But You May Call Me Miss Kitty!; Dorothy and Otto, The Dorothy Dandridge Affair; A Salute to Ella Fitzgerald; Sammy Davis Jr. & Friends *and* A Tribute to Michael Jackson. *Her website is sharonlgraine.com. Aired January 13, 2010*

• • •

**Thandisizwe Chimurenga:** *She has been called everything from a blackmailer to the mother of civil rights. She has been described as tall, dark and thin, short, fair and full, with one blue and one brown eye. Photos that were taken of her are claimed to be a Hawaiian Queen, who had her picture taken at the same time and in the same studio as Mary Ellen Pleasant. However, most agree that she was a formidable presence, even though there is no real agreement as to where she was born, or who her parents were; and if she was born as a free slave, or born into slavery. Of one thing we can be certain, Mary Ellen Pleasant has made an impressive mark on African-American history.*

This is from the opening of "House on the Hill: The Mammy Pleasant Story," that was written by Sharon L. Graine, the founder of Playhouse Theatre Players, which unfortunately closed its doors at the end of 2009. Mary Pleasant, also known as Mammy Pleasant, passed away

January 10, 1904. In studio with me now is Sharon L. Graine to talk about this woman. Thank you so much for coming in to speak with *Some Of Us Are Brave* today.

**Sharon L. Graine:** Thank you, and thank you for inviting me. I'm doing great because it was raining this morning, and now the sun is out. It's always great when the sun is out in Los Angeles.

**TC:** Absolutely. So, "House on the Hill: The Mammy Pleasant Story," this is a play that you wrote and directed and starred in, is that correct?

**SLG:** Correct.

**TC:** And it premiered at the Playhouse Theatre Players and had a very long run. What is it about Mammy Pleasant's story that made you decide that she needed to be brought to life in a play?

**SLG:** Dr. Mayme A. Clayton,[1] who founded the Mayme Clayton Library Museum and had the Black American Film Festival for a number of years, she's my godmother. And I was writing a number of other plays and doing a number of other plays. And Mayme gave me this book called "Mammy Pleasant's Partner." And she said this woman amassed $30 million in the early 1800s. Now, in a night ...

**TC:** I'm sorry did you say $30?

**SLG:** $30 million. See, that's that was my reaction, you should see her [your] face, and so...

**TC:** Thirty million.

**SLG:** $30 million. And so I kept setting the book aside. And then one morning, I got up and I'm thinking "I've had this theater. I'm writing all of these plays. I'm a, you know, fairly intelligent Black African-American woman; slavery is over; I've not been on a plantation, and I don't have $30 million: you need to pick up the book." So, I picked up the book and started reading it because I wanted to know how a woman before slavery had stopped, had done this. And so finally, I started reading about it. And the more I read about it, honestly I'm getting ready to write two other segments of it, because this woman had such a colorful history. And I know we have a short period of time, so I'm going to be giving you capsulated

---

1 Mayme Clayton (1923-2006). Mother of noted African American artist Avery Clayton (1947-2009).

versions of this woman ... is called the Mother of Civil Rights in the state of California because she wasn't responsible for Black people being able to intermingle on a bus; she was responsible for Black people being able to ride on a bus in the state of California. She was also instrumental in helping John Brown.[2] So for those of you who remember your history, John Brown, here's a little song they sang, you know, "lies a-mouldering in the grave", John Brown was ... an abolitionist trying to help slaves in the early 1800s.

And he went to Canada. And he had put together this whole army that he thought was going to help free the slaves. And Mary Ellen Pleasant joined him in Canada and bought four pieces of property so he could gather and have all these meetings. But after they finished talking to him, they were trying to explain to him he was planning on taking all the territory east of the Allegheny Mountains and thinking that if he had guns, all the slaves would leave the plantation and run and follow him. And Mary Ellen was trying to say: you don't understand, these slaves are used to being held down on plantations. They're not going to do that without leadership. So they found out that the authorities were looking for him. So Mary Ellen fled south, her husband who was helping went back west and John Brown decided to go ahead and move. Now she had come with $1,500 to give to him and $500 collected from the freed slaves in San Francisco but she decided to wait and she wrote him a little note saying, "When the axe falls at the root of the tree, I'll send you money and help," but at the time she just thought it was not the right move to make, and obviously it wasn't.

**TC:** But she did provide some land?

**SLG:** She provided four pieces of property for him to meet up there, she did end up giving him some money for him to try to buy guns in the start of battle. She even ...

**TC:** Wait wait ... Mammy Pleasant was gun runnin' ?!

**SLG:** Hey ... she gave him ... I mean, let me put it this way ...

2 John Brown (1800-1859) was an American abolitionist leader. Brown first gained attention when he led anti-slavery volunteers during the Bleeding Kansas Crisis of the late 1850s, a state-level civil war over whether Kansas would enter the Union as a slave state or a free state. He was eventually captured and executed for the failed incitement of a slave rebellion preceding the American Civil War.

**TC:** I know Harriet [Tubman][3] was trying to get one of them guns, but the guns were provided by another Black woman?!

**SLG:** You know the opening that you read, what's very interesting about that opening 'cause I'm getting ready to tell you, that has to do with John Brown; she was described as "very light and fair," but this is my opinion: after reading all of the information, when I was much younger and you're looking at me right now you see that I'm a mid complexion person, I'm tall. My eyes are very light but I was born with blond hair and blue eyes. And as I got older, I got darker in complexion. I do honestly believe, and one of the books said, that's what happened to her, because when she decided to run south and everybody was looking for them after this whole John Brown thing, she pretended she was a jockey and she rolled through all the plantations and a lot of slaves you know ... we know each other; other people may be mixed up when they look at one of us ...

**TC:** I'm trying not to laugh on the mic. I'm sorry.

**SLG:** But we got to know each other. So those slaves, and I don't care how light she is, I know. So they all would gather around [Laughter]

**TC:** [Laughter] Aww Lawd

**SLG:** And to hear this, to see this Black jockey, and she would tell them about this "uprising" that was going to happen. But of course they were still looking for her in the north and so she had to flee. The story of Mary Ellen ... I can only say this ... is when the movie finally does come out, Mary Ellen was also considered a voodoo queen. Um, some people ...

**TC:** Okay ... okay ... okay ... okay ... now ...

**SLG:** [Laughter]

**TC:** We stirring up problems on the bus. We riling up the slaves. We giving money to a "notorious and unsavory character" such as a John but now you done threw the voodoo I got to leave the building. I got to go. What do you what do you mean voodoo?

**SLG:** And I hope that most of us are still reading about people like John Brown in our history classes and and, for all of your listeners that are

---

3 See note on Harriet Tubman on page 10.

saying no, no, CJ Walker[4] was the first millionaire. CJ Walker's the first millionaire you heard of. CJ Walker was about five years old when Mary Ellen Pleasant made her money. Now when she had to flee to the south, and there's so much about this woman's story that we cannot do in half an hour and I do plan on doing the play sometime in April or May so if you will invite me back, we can talk a little more.

**TC:** Definitely, most definitely.

**SLG:** I can only give you cursory stuff right now. But I know the voodoo thing is a little interesting. And I have a whole voodoo scene in my play.

**TC:** Wait a moment, I just want to backtrack real quick. I should have backtracked earlier, when you say she was a jockey, exactly, what do you mean by that?

**SLG:** Riding horses, and she pretended that she was a jockey, you know, when they came out to see this first Black jockey rider, okay? And so she could gather them around where obviously the white folks wouldn't bother, you know, and she could go ahead and spread the news. You know, a lot of ways of communicating back then was through gospels and a whole bunch of other things. I don't want to mislead the listeners. So in the early 1800s, and the late 1800s you had many people, Blacks that were going to college, light-complected Blacks that had you know, that got freed earlier. This is one woman's plight, who gave her life trying to free slaves, trying to make sure she bought property for them and put it in their names. So this is a different kind of story.

**TC:** Okay.

**SLG:** How did she come up with this knowledge? Well, when she was traded off of the plantation where she was born in Augusta, Georgia, she went to live with a family because Ellen and Mr. Williams – she would always call them Ellen and Mr. Williams – and her name was Mary. But she took her middle name Ellen from this woman who helped raise her who loved her. But her husband was very jealous of her. So they sent her to Nantucket. And in Nantucket, there were a bunch of abolitionists. Nantucket had these whole areas of Blacks that had their own stores and all

4 C.J. Walker (1867-1919) was an African-American entrepreneur, philanthropist, and political and social activist. She is recorded as the first female self-made millionaire in America in the Guinness Book of World Records.

of that. And even though she wasn't taught to read or write, she could add up anything in the store and put it in her head. She watched everything. So when the woman who owned the store died she went to Boston, and in her mind she's building the business of what she wants to do. But when she had to flee through the South a woman by the name of Marie Laveau took her in. Now Marie Laveau was a voodoo queen.

**TC:** In New Orleans

**SLG:** In New Orleans. And she specialized in trading secrets and freeing slaves and buying up businesses. And Mary started to understand how that trading in secrets started to work in the freeing of the slaves. So now let's skip to San Francisco and California.

**TC:** Let's just jump

**SLG:** Let's just jump to this million dollars. These millions of dollars she amassed, okay? She got off the boat ...

[In the voice of Mammy Pleasant]: *"I got off that boat in 1852. Walkin' through the crowd not knowin' nobody. I had $15,000 in my pocket. I went straight away, bought myself a laundry. Invested in another one. Bought myself some of that land traveled by the San Jose stagecoach so I could build a building suited for travelers and the rich. I learned a lot between the island of Nantucket and them in New Orleans. And I was putting it in the works right then, and right there."*

**SLG:** So she where'd she get this $15,000 from? Well, Miss Mary Ellen had married a gentleman by the name of James Smith who was Cuban who looked white. And he had a plantation in Virginia and when they were in Boston they would be helping free slaves under the underground. Well, he died, she sold the plantation, and that put some money in her pocket. When she started building boarding houses, all the rich men would come in San Francisco and stay in those boarding houses. And she would serve them just like she didn't know. But she taught all the people who worked for her to "listen carefully." So when she got into a relationship with a businessman, and they got to be business partners, she would tell him what stock to buy and what stock to sell.

**TC:** Hmmm.

[In the voice of Mammy Pleasant]: *"I'd find out and sell it before them white people even got into the 'do'."*

**SLG:** And so she started amassing this money.

**TC:** So okay, so we fast forward to 2009-2010, what they call "insider trading", what we know is the hookup, right? She had the hookup, okay okay.

**SLG:** [Laughter] And then she also does other things like, you know, she had this big mansion built, and in the basement of her mansion she had a room put in there for her ceremonies. And she'd have these voodoo ceremonies. And, you know, the same thing is working. It's like those of us who believe in prayer and the spirit. We also just happen to believe in a great deal of retribution. So there are certain things that we don't do. But you know, you have to figure for a Black woman in that day and age to make the kind of money she did in the kind of real estate she did. There were things that she had to do that would not be done now. Nobody's going to accept anybody that obviously looks Black coming in to buy some real estate. It's not going to happen. So she found ways around all of these things, which I think were completely brilliant. She made one mistake and I didn't put this in the play. And I think we all should know who Mary Ellen Pleasant is because she also made it possible for us to testify in court.

The one thing Mammy Pleasant did that was a part of her downfall was a court case, and then an invitation to a party. William Sharon was a senator and he was buying up all the property banks and everything and her partner Thomas Bell – I think she kind of loved he was a Scottish man – was, he was kind of a well, I hate to say it this way, but maybe a wimp? And so she would tell him what to do. But when he came to her and said, "You know, Sharon is buying up all the property and if I wasn't vice president of the bank, we'd be in ruins." So she had a nice voodoo session. And she said,

[In the voice of Mammy Pleasant]: *"Bring me Sarah out there. Now Sarah I want you to go to Sharon and I want you to sleep in his bed."*

**SLG:** And so she ended up, Sharon and Sarah had a long relationship. He tried to leave her, Mary Ellen Pleasant sued for alimony blah, blah, blah. But Sharon was so rich that he could keep the battle up longer than she could. And it was using up her money, but she was doing that to weaken his position in real estate. But her complete demise came from, and all of us need to acknowledge this and listen to this because I've written I think in the last six years, maybe 23 plays. And when people ask me about them, and I honestly believe this sincerely to my heart, "I'm the instrument God is the tool," God is the one that drives this. Sometimes we as the instruments of whatever happens to us, or recognition or whatever it is, start to believe a certain press about ourselves, and our egos start to get in the way, and as wonderful a person as I think she was, and as conniving as she was, I think her downfall was to receive an invitation to a party.

And she got these invitations from these wealthy rich men all the time, because they never wanted to slight her but she always had the good sense not to go. But this time, she got dressed up, very sexy, and walked in the front door of the white folks' house, and the wives and everybody else lost their mind. And that was the kind of the beginning of the end. Besides the fact she was no longer cute and all that and new people were coming into San Francisco, businesses were being held differently. A lot of people were trying to sue her. She was written about over 100 times in the San Francisco paper more than anybody else. Now you're talking about a Black woman. So she ended up living with a doctor friend of hers and dying in poverty. However, she had a ranch in Santa Barbara, and the house is still there. When I did a play, this woman came down from Oregon who was part of the family of a young lady that she had bought property for and married her business partner. And she owns so, so very many things. Finally, they put a gravestone on her grave in 1999. And the one thing she wanted it to say was "she was a friend of John Brown's." And I think finally they put that on her grave.

**TC:** Where is she buried?

**SLG:** In San Francisco ... in Napa Valley. She died January 10, 1904 in Napa, and the headlines read when she died, "Mysterious Old Negro Woman at 89 Ends a Life of Schemes and Varied Fortune." That's not what you would have read in the headlines of the Black press. That's what you read in the headlines of the white press.

**TC:** What would we have read about Mammy, what would we have read about Mary Ellen Pleasant in the Black press?

**SLG:** Mary Ellen Pleasant, the founder of civil rights, an abolitionist, a person who helped free slaves. We lost her today at age 89. January 10, 1904.

**TC:** That sounds about right. That's about par for the course, the differences in opinion on this wonderful woman. Now, please tell me, you say April or May possibly you will be doing another run of "House on the Hill: Mammy Pleasant's Story"?

**SLG:** Yes, what I'm going to have to end up doing, because I'm going back over all of my material now. She had such relationships with all of the people that she knew, there's so much to tell that I'm breaking it down ... the play is called "House on the Hill: The Mammy Pleasant Story"; now it will be "House on the Hill: Mary Ellen and William." William was her confidant, the man that worked in her house. He was a Black man that she bought a home for that would oversee [her] property. Mary Ellen also had a daughter. She also had a number of relationships. There was a lot about Mary Ellen Pleasant, and so I'm going to start breaking some of this down before I finish the screenplay.

**TC:** And the screenplay, we'll be waiting on that also. Sharon L. Graine: playwright, actress, all around Renaissance Woman, thank you so much for joining us today on *Some of Us Are Brave*.

**SLG:** Thank you so much for having me.

# Shirley Jo Finney

*Shirley Jo Finney was "an actor's director who created safe spaces and environments for writers, actors and the creative team to produce inspired storytelling." Finney, who passed away on October 10, 2023 after a short bout with cancer, was best known for the shows Lou Grant, Hill St. Blues and Amen, and her portrayal of Olympic gold medalist Wilma Rudolph opposite Denzel Washington in the film Wilma. Her website is shirleyjofinney.com. Aired on April 9, 2010.*

• • •

**Thandisizwe Chimurenga:** You're listening to *Some of Us Are Brave: a Black Woman's Radio Program* here on KPFK 90.7 FM in Los Angeles. And I'm in the studio now with Shirley Jo Finney. Shirley Jo Finney is an actor and a director and also a playwright. She is an award-winning director and actress and why are you looking at me like you've just now heard that?

**Shirley Jo Finney:** Because I'm not a playwright.

**TC:** Oh producer! I saw something where you did a play and you produced the play. But you're not the playwright?

**SJF:** I'm not the playwright of this particular play. But I work with writers, part of my career has been developing new works, so that's probably what you were ...

**TC:** Okay, so that's probably why you looking at me like "who she talking about?"

**SJF:** Don't be lying out here because somebody will see and go "why she lying on the radio?"

[Laughter]

**TC:** I'm so sorry. I apologize to you and to any listener I have offended calling you a playwright.

[Laughter]

**TC:** Shirley Jo Finney. Thank you for being on *Some of Us Are Brave* today. How are you doing?

**SJF:** I am wonderful! I am breathing, I'm alive. All is good. All is good in life.

**TC:** You are currently directing a play in – is it West Hollywood or Hollywood?

**SJF:** We'll call it West Hollywood.

**TC:** Okay. And it's called *Stick Fly*, And we're going to talk about that in a moment but I want to talk about some of your other works also, since you're not a playwright and we don't want nobody writing us up calling us up talking about that stuff. But you have directed several plays, you've got several things under your belt. I want to ask you about a couple of them though, *Gee's Bend*? Now this is about the women quilters in Alabama. A play has been made about them. Tell me about that.

**SJF:** *Gee's Bend* was developed in 2007. It was based on the women quilters of Gee's Bend in Alabama. And they are now in the Smithsonian Institute. And they had a tour of their quilts and as you know, historically, for us, it's like, quilting in Africa was always about telling a story. And we brought that over and Gee's Bend has retained that part of our oral history, and people kind of all of a sudden discovered ... you know, we use quilting, you know, our grandmothers quilted, and we use that as a necessity to survive. We took and recycled – like people are recycling now – we recycled old clothes and we never ... we as a tribe, always recycled and used scraps for other things. And so the mainstream world found out about these quilts that we used to sell for $10 or they were on our beds. I know every, every Christmas I received a quilt from my grandmother, you know, and that went on our beds. But then when the world decided "Oh my God look at these quilts," and all of a sudden they became famous and the women in their 80s or 90s all of a sudden were rediscovered. And they were just rediscovered every 20 years and so [Laughter] so now this has become an art form. For us, as women in this tribe, we've used this as a survival tool, and now it becomes an art form. And it's great for these ladies because not only are they recognized, they're being compensated for it, and so it's a good play.

**TC:** So this is a play about the women quilters of Gee's Bend, Alabama. They've got what they call a quilting cooperative. And they have a quilting, I believe a "quilting bee" every year. And so now their works are in the Smithsonian.

**SJF:** Yes, exactly. And then, about two years ago, their quilts did a national tour in different parts of the United States to get exposure.

**TC:** Okay, so now who came up with the idea for a play and how did you get involved?

**SJF:** The Alabama Shakespeare Festival has a special festival that features southern writers. And it was developed there. I was not part of that development, I came on board about a year after that, after she had her first two plays produced and then I directed it at ...

**TC:** You said "she"?

**SJF:** The playwright.

**TC:** Okay, the playwright whose name escapes me at the moment ... Elyzabeth Gregory Wilder ...

**SJF:** I directed it at the Cleveland Playhouse.

**TC:** Okay, so that's *Gee's Bend*. You're also involved, real quick, we're going to get to *Stick Fly* but I wanted to get in get into this real quick: you're involved with *For Colored Girls Who Have ... Considered* not *Committed* yet, we're trying to keep them from committing; Lawd they're going to be calling up this show ...

**SJF:** I know! You're telling me I'm a playwright, now I'm saying all Black women are committing suicide ...

[Laughter]

**TC:** *For Colored Girls Who Have Considered Suicide / When the Rainbow Is Enuf,* Ntozake Shange's wonderful play. I believe it's 25 years old now?

**SJF:** It's close to 30 years old, yes.

**TC:** Now this production –

**SJF:** I'm going to direct in the fall in New York, it's a revival starring India. Arie.[1]

**TC:** Tell me about that.

**SJF:** It's real exciting. India.Arie agreed to be a part of this because she's been stepping out and exploring other facets of who she is. She is a storyteller, you know, and we felt that Ntozake Shange,[2] being a poet of her time, and India.Arie speaks as a musical poet, and we thought it was a good fit. And so I was asked to come on board as the director of the revival, the "re-envision revival" of *For Colored Girls Who Have Considered Suicide / When the Rainbow Is Enuf.* Hinton Battle is the choreographer

**TC:** And this production is produced by Whoopi Goldberg?

**SJF:** Yes

**TC:** Wow

**SJF:** Yeah, exactly, exactly. Because she also said that *Colored Girls*, like millions of women of color, affected our lives because it was the first kind of oral history depicting our psychological or emotional or spiritual journey as women, and Whoopi said this particular play helped change her life

**TC:** ... and affected a generation of women.

**SJF:** Absolutely. And one of the things that was so beautiful about the Dream Team and Victor Walker, who's the producer, he felt, because it's almost 30 years old that, you know, when it was announced that mothers are now bringing their daughters or grandmothers are bringing the granddaughters.

**TC:** To see this play.

**SJF:** So it is one of those things where it becomes and part of the concept of that is bringing, it's a ritual, a modern day ritual, you know, bringing the women into circle to celebrate and having these women, a rite of passage for the young women. So that's so exciting.

**TC:** Generational, definitely.

---

1 india.arie (born 1975), is an American singer and songwriter. Her debut album, *Acoustic Soul*, was released in 2001, and she has since released six more studio albums.

2 Ntozake Shange (1948-2018) was an American playwright, poet, and novelist. Shange was best known for her play *For Colored Girls Who Have Considered Suicide / When the Rainbow Is Enuf*, which premiered in 1976 and became a landmark work in African-American and feminist literature. Shange was also an activist and advocate for social justice, particularly for women and people of color.

**SJF:** Absolutely

**TC:** She grown up. She's 30 years old now. Close to 30 years old. She a grown woman.

**SJF:** She a grown woman.

**TC:** Wonderful, wonderful. So let's talk about *Stick Fly* real quickly. I've been hearing so much about this play. And I knew you were going to be the director. And Michole Briana White is one of the people it's like, okay, but I keep, it's just something about that name. I'm like, "what in the world could they possibly be talking about?" It's called *Stick Fly*.

**SJF:** Now that's real interesting.

**TC:** Please tell our audience what this play is, tell me what this play is about!

**SJF:** First I'm going to tell you what this 12-year-old girl who came to the play last night said, okay? Out of the mouths of babes. "It's not that deep." I said, my friend Erin, I said okay, I want your daughter to tell me what she thinks this play's about. And so Erin calls me up this morning, she said, "She says the play is about people getting stuck; people who are stuck in their lives." And I went simple, I got it, I'm going on the radio today, and I'm going to tell the simple … explanation and so yes, it is about how we get stuck in our perceptions about our world, about the individuals about our place in our lives. And so it takes place on a weekend, about an African-American family, upper middle class African-American family who summers on Martha's Vineyard. And in four days how this family unravels.

**TC:** Just in four days.

**SJF:** it took four days.

**TC:** And they came apart.

**SJF:** And they came apart. And the themes are about gender, race, class, betrayals and family secrets. And you can imagine.

**TC:** Yes, I can. I'd rather not. [Laughter] So tell us who else is starring in this play?

**SJF:** Well, okay, it's Chris Butler and … Chris is known to LA audiences, I directed a play about two years ago called *Yellowman* at the Fountain Theatre.

**TC:** Which you got an award for.

**SJF:** I got multiple awards for yes, and the actors got multiple awards for, so he's starring in this and he's a fabulous actor, and he also was on Broadway in *100 Degrees in the Shade* starring with Audrey McDonald, a musical, and Avery Clyde, Tinashe Kajese, again, another actress LA audiences would know her from the Athol Fugard[3] piece that was also done at the Fountain Theatre ... and Terrell Tilford, John Wesley, Michole Briana White who the LA audiences probably have seen in the latest August Wilson[4] piece that was done at the new Ebony Repertory Theater that starred Glynn Turman and this cast is phenomenal. And one of the things it's done, it's at the Matrix Theater.

**TC:** Now that's on?

**SJF:** That is on ...7637 Melrose. And the response, we've had eight performances and previews. And the response is like, someone said, "I don't know I've never seen this caliber of work in Los Angeles," and people are responding to it because Lydia Diamond[5] is a 38-year-old woman who writes, she's lyrical in her language, and she writes what she knows, and I call this the underserved story, because usually our stories are either rural, or urban. And we don't tackle contemporary. There's very few African-American voices talking about the middle class, upper middle class plight, unless you get them in novels,. The only one, you know, going to Ivy League schools and what that means being the "only raisin in the oatmeal."

[Laughter]

**TC:** The "fly in the ointment "

**SJF:** The "fly in the ointment," and having to navigate. You know it's, I think it was really interesting, because I think of the advent of the last two

3 Athol Fugard (born 1932) is a South African playwright, director, and actor. Fugard is best known for his plays that explore the effects of apartheid and racism in South Africa. Fugard often collaborated with Black South African actors, and his plays were banned in South Africa during apartheid for their criticism of the government's policies.

4 August Wilson (1945-2005) was an acclaimed African-American playwright. He is best known for his "Pittsburgh Cycle," a series of ten plays that explore the lives of African-Americans in the 20th century. Wilson was the recipient of numerous awards and honors for his work, including two Pulitzer Prizes for Drama and a Tony Award for Best Play.

5 Lydia R. Diamond (born 1969) is an American playwright and professor. Among her most popular plays are *The Bluest Eye* (2007), an adaptation of Toni Morrison's novel; *Stick Fly* (2008); *Harriet Jacobs* (2011); and *Smart People* (2016).

years of Barack Obama is people, the mainstream America, it opened a portal you know, because we then had to combat the American wound, and this demographic that people didn't have to confront. And so, *Stick Fly* confronts that and is the first portal that you can see what happens in our homes. What are the classics when you go classic music? Well in our show, classic music is Miles Davis.[6] Classic music is Stevie Wonder.[7] Classic music is India.Arie, classic music is Aretha Franklin.[8] So we have classics that they're generational that are in our family. And so when you come into the show, you know you may have a Daddy you know and he may put on some Miles "Some Kind of Blue," and then the little girl is hip hoppin' to Lil Mama,[9] you know, and then you got Stevie Wonder that they're partying to. So it is the living, the laughing, the dying and crying of us today, what we do in a generational family.

**TC:** Now is that what drew you to the play?

**SJF:** Yes, because this is my story, okay? My family was the first family to integrate a neighborhood in northern California. I was the only one going into junior high schools and high schools. I was the first person to get a graduate degree an MFA, first woman of color, UCLA graduate program. So, as a Black female director in regional theater across this country, some of the regional theaters I have gone into in this country, I was often the first woman of color that had even stepped into many of those. So having to confront, navigate, that terrain of being the "pioneer."

Also how, there's one of the scenes that Taylor, that Michole Briana White plays, she talks about having to teach "Cultural Dynamics 101" ever since she was in the third grade, about people wanting to know who you are, you know? It's, you know, in this country it's about like, I call it it's like being bi-cultural that we as people of color have had to know, the mainstream

---

6   Miles Davis (1926-1991) was an American jazz trumpeter, bandleader, and composer who is widely considered one of the most influential musicians of the 20th century. He was known for his distinctive trumpet playing style, which was characterized by a muted, introspective sound.

7   Stevie Wonder (born 1950) is an American singer, songwriter, and multi-instrumentalist. He first gained fame as a child prodigy, signing to Motown Records at the age of 11. He has also been a prominent activist in the civil rights movement..

8   Aretha Franklin (1942-2018) was an American singer, songwriter, and pianist She also became an icon of the civil rights movement, performing at Martin Luther King Jr.'s funeral and using her music to address issues of race and social justice.

9   Niatia Jessica Kirkland (born 1989), better known by her stage name Lil Mama, is an American rapper, singer, actress and television presenter from New York.

America. I know your world and I know my world. But mainstream America has never had to really confront and know anyone's until recently. And so I call it being bicultural, bilingual, I know your language. And so that's part of the dynamic that's happening in this play also. But the transcendancy is regardless of what the theme is in the play, it is really about family, and perceptions of family, and in family relationships, about communicating. So the discussion in the play is about all those things. But ultimately, it's about the family dynamic. Like I said, one of the things is gender, race, class. The other one is absentee fathers. You can have a father in the house and be absentee. And then you can have that father who isn't there but the emotional dynamic, the emotional wound is just the same. So that is the thing that transcends everything that's being talked about.

**TC:** Absentee father and he's standing right there. Wow.

**SJF:** Yes.

**TC:** Absentee fathers, and they're right there. They're supposed to be right there. But they're really not.

**SJF:** Absolutely.

**TC:** Wow. So that's part of what we can expect?

**SJF:** Absolutely. Absolutely. And people come out of there saying, "Oh my goodness." I felt like when I had done, I had directed this play two years ago, 2007 at the McCarter Theatre in Princeton, and that was a 750-seat theater. And, the Matrix is a smaller theater, and the dynamic is you feel like you're right there in the living room. So when people leave out, they're talking about "Oh, my God, I felt like I was part of the conversation." It was so real, you know, they identified with each of the characters; are so clearly delineated. You know it's not ... she doesn't have you side with this one or you side with that one. That's the beauty of her, the dynamic of her writing.

**TC:** Lydia Diamond?

**SJF:** Lydia Diamond. It's everybody's voice. You know, Daddy goes off talking about well, you know, "you show me a man that hasn't made mistakes," right? And then one of his sons goes, "Well, Daddy, it doesn't make it all right." Then you have someone saying, "I was raised with a single mother. And even though I climbed the ladder, I will never be accepted in Jack and Jill[10] because I'm a single mother." So Jack and Jill is up in there.

**TC:** I'm going to leave that one alone.

**SJF:** Okay? You know? And what happens when you have an African-American family who has African-American help to maintain the house?

**TC:** Oh, y'all going there?

**SJF:** Oh, we're really going there.

**TC:** Y'all is up in that one.

**SJF:** No ... y'all? It's Lydia!

[Laughter]

**TC:** Well, yeah, when I heard about Martha's Vineyard,[11] I was like, "Oh, here we go." So yeah, okay.

**SJF:** And Martha's Vineyard, and that's the other thing – Martha's Vineyard has such a major history, people don't know that. African-Americans can be sighted there from the 1700s, when they annexed Oak Bluffs, but this family doesn't live ... Oak Bluffs, as you know, is the part of Martha's Vineyard where the African-Americans live with the cottage homes, etc. But this family lives in like Edgartown. So ... they up on the hill.

**TC:** Ooh

**SJF:** Yeah.

**TC:** Looking down?

**SJF:** No, they go there

**TC:** They're just looking around.

**SJF:** They're just looking around. Right, exactly.

**TC:** *Stick Fly* is playing at the Matrix Theater on Melrose.

Shirley Jo Finney, you've also taught at Southwest College and you taught at Terminal Island and Actor's Workshop, when was this?

---

10 Jack and Jill of America is a leadership organization formed in 1938 by African-American mothers to bring together children in a social and cultural environment.

11 Martha's Vineyard is an island in the northeastern United States, located south of Cape Cod in Dukes County, Massachusetts, known for being a popular, affluent summer colony.

**SJF:** I taught at ...

**TC:** I know you taught everywhere

**SJF:** I've taught everywhere; and presently I'm teaching in the film department-cinema department at USC. But I taught at Southwest College 30 years ago. So it was a long time ago.

**TC:** And when was your class at Terminal Island?

**SJF:** Again, that was about 30 some odd years ago, back in the day.

**TC:** Nothing recently, no actor's workshops

**SJF:** Haven't gone to prison yet.

[Laughter]

**SJF:** Haven't gone back to prison

**TC:** Okay, I'm going to leave that one alone too. But you're currently at USC.

**SJF:** Yes.

**TC:** You've done also film directing, television, you've directed episodes of *Moesha*[12]

**SJF:** Yes

**TC:** And as an actress are we going to be seeing your lovely face anytime soon?

**SJF:** I don't think so. No, I like telling stories. I think my part of my mission, the acting, was my way into storytelling because I'm an actor's director. And I work with writers knowing how to get to the heart of the story. I like directing and found that, a long time ago, I didn't have to act to feel fulfilled. I had to create, and the directing fulfills that part where I'm a collaborator with designers, and everything leads to the process of telling the story. And that just fulfills me and that's where my soul is at this moment.

**TC:** Okay. Shirley Jo Finney, it has been wonderful having you today. Thank you so much for being on *Some of Us Are Brave*. We greatly appreciate you.

**SJF:** I greatly appreciate being here. Truly truly.

**TC:** *Stick Fly*, playing until they tell it to leave. Thank you again so much!

---

12 *Moesha* was an American TV sitcom that aired on UPN from 1996 to May 14 2001. The series stars R&B singer Brandy Norwood as Moesha Denise Mitchell, an African-American teenager living with her upper middle class family in Los Angeles.

# Sonia Sanchez

*Sonia Sanchez – poet, playwright, activist, scholar – is one of the most important writers of the Black Arts Movement. Winner of the 2021 Dorothy and Lillian Gish Prize – a $250,000 lifetime achievement honor given to "a highly accomplished artist from any discipline who has pushed the boundaries of an art form, contributed to social change, and paved the way for the next generation" – she is the author of more than 20 books, and has lectured all across the United States and has traveled extensively, reading her poetry in Africa, Cuba, England, the Caribbean, Australia, Europe, Nicaragua, the People's Republic of China, Norway, and Canada. This interview took place on April 26, 2010 in Century City, California.*

• • •

**Thandisizwe Chimurenga:** I'm just so thankful for this opportunity!

**Sonia Sanchez:** Oh, my sister, thank you.

**TC:** I greatly appreciate you. I remember the first time I saw you, you came and spoke at a UCLA Black Student Alliance banquet.

**SS:** Oh, my goodness.

**TC:** And then a couple of years ago, I saw you in San Francisco with Marvin X at the University of Poetry.

**SS:** That's right, that's right, when he had invited us all out.

**TC:** That was a wonderful gathering, I don't know if he still does that?

**SS:** I don't know if he does or not, to be frank, but it was great because I saw like Emory [Douglas].[1] I hadn't seen brother Emory in years! You know he had done the cover for my first book *Home Coming,* and then when some problems came up with the Black Panther Party about what they call – it was a big uproar – about what they call "cultural nationalists," and [Eldridge] Cleaver was the head and he said "No," so he called me and said "I can't do the cover for your second book, Sonia." So I saw him when they put out a big book of his artwork, and he came to Philadelphia and he said simply, "I apologize," and I said "No, my brother, you were in a movement, and when people made a statement of what could be, hey, you had to go along with it." But I truly understood it. I said, I just love your artwork so very much, so everything is cool, you know." Right?

**TC:** Right! Again, let me say thank you for your example, thank you for your work. I know you didn't think that you were consciously doing an example, you were just doing what a woman ... what a sista should be doing, but its such an inspiring example.

**SS:** Well, I thank you.

**TC:** I have a sister friend who is just, "Sonia Sanchez is here?! Let me at her!" Because she talks about the fact that, you and Nikki [Giovanni][2] and Maya [Angelou][3] are not, she doesn't feel that you've been honored the way you should be, and your poetry, your writing has been such a lifeline for so many people but for Black women in particular.

**SS:** Thank you.

**TC:** I'm sitting here speaking with Sonia Sanchez who is a professor, an author and a poet. She is a Sista and worker in the struggle for Black peoples' human rights and human rights in general for so many years who's done such wonderful work. She's the author of numerous books, her most recent book is *Morning Haiku,* and I wanted to ask you about

---

1 Emory Douglas (born 1943) is an American graphic artist. He was a member of the Black Panther Party from 1967 until the Party disbanded in the 1980s.[

2 Nikki Giovanni (born 1943) is an American poet, writer, and activist. She is known for her powerful and socially conscious poetry, which often addresses issues of race, gender, and social justice. In addition to her writing, Giovanni has been an active voice in the civil rights and feminist movements.

3 Maya Angelou (1928-2014) was an American poet, memoirist, and civil rights activist. Her most famous work is *I Know Why the Caged Bird Sings,* a memoir that details her childhood experiences of racism and trauma. She worked with Dr. Martin Luther King Jr. and other prominent activists in the 1960s and served as a UNICEF ambassador in the 1990s.

this most recent work. It's like you're returning to your roots, is that safe to say?

**SS:** Well ... yes. When I was in university doing grad work I studied with a woman named Luz Bogan at NYU. And in many of my books I've included haiku. I decided to do a whole book of haiku, at this particular time, most especially because of what the haiku talks about: it talks about beauty and non beauty, ya know? It talks about those things that are good and bad. It makes us see things immediately and we see the beauty of things, but also at the same time the beauty disappears very fast like the sunset, ya know? Or the dawn. But it still is retained within us. So what I'm trying to say with the haiku, most especially in teaching it to young people, is that if you can see the beauty in a flower and a butterfly; if you can see the beauty of a woman going to work pulling her three-year old behind saying "C'mon, c'mon I'm late, I got to get to work," that's a haiku. That beauty, then you can take that beauty inside yourself and feel the beauty of nature and human beings at the same time, and if you can feel the beauty of a human being then you can also at some point begin to see yourself as beautiful which means you will not want to destroy yourself or anyone else.

It is that kind of thing that I am aiming to do, asking people to develop what I call a "haiku mind," a "haiku life," a life with no greed attached to it, a life that says simply "there is beauty in everything, and there are things that are ugly too, but our mission here in life is to always lean towards the beauty, the beautiful part of our lives and to control that which is ugly in our lives because you know, none of us is Jesus at all, and so we have to always fight against those things that are not correct in ourselves." So this is what I am doing with the haiku, bringing the short form that will resonate, that you can walk with it, you can say it you can breathe it, you can breathe this form, this form will tell you sometimes how to breathe, and if you know how to breathe well, also, you will stay alive.

We don't know how to breath quite often, ya know? And so therefore we're not always living at the height, so the haiku takes about the same amount of time it takes to take a breath. Like,

*Let me wear the day*
*well so when it reaches you*
*you will enjoy it*

And then you breathe. Whatever. It is that breath that is so important for me when one sees the haiku.

**TC:** Thank you for that. I greatly appreciate that and your talking about the beauty in all things, because I want to ask you, you're considered to be one of the main pillars of what we know as the Black Arts Movement (BAM)

**SS:** Right

**TC:** And the BAM was said to be that creative, cultural arm of the Black Power Movement

**SS:** Exactly

**TC:** So why was it, why is it necessary to have a poetry, a literature, a dance an arts movement that complements Black Power? When we think about Black Power ... its guns, its self-defense, its self-determination, its fighting back; why is it even necessary to have an arts, an aesthetic to complement that?

**SS:** Well, ya know, the first time I got up on a stage and said "I am a Black poet," somebody booed in the audience [chuckles] which told you a great deal about what was going on but even to this day, a lot of poets don't really think that Black poets are good poets because "they're always," as someone said, "writing about that Black stuff." Isn't that amazing?

Whereas, when you look at their poetry, they're writing about white stuff, ya know? Period, ya know? But that's never said at all. And its not that we're writing about Black stuff, what we did is that we put the Black man and woman on a world stage. We had been removed from the world stage; we put the Afrikan back on the world stage and said, "Look, we are a part of this stage, we are a real 'we,' and here," and I think probably that's what many people did not like. Once you can do that, then we're saying simply we are human beings. We are these human beings who do exist because, we had been taken off the human stage, the world stage that said we had not only power, but also we were people who were human. We're not all funny, funny people and we're not all horrible, horrible people.

So what poetry did was simply a complement to Black Power, and people are saying self-determination and we're saying yes self-determination in poetry. Look at this, we're saying I am Black, I am a Black woman. I do the following: I am this human being, I am writing about children, I am writing about my family, I'm writing about the big family, I'm writing about Africa, I'm writing about everything that at some point can teach people what this is truly all about. And the Black Power Movement was about talking about finally answering the question the way that we tried to answer the question with our poetry, and that is what does it mean to be human? Because it is very obvious that we were in a country with people who were not acting as human beings should have acted, right?

And so what we were talking about then, answering that question what does it mean to be human, and someone said to me in an interview, "but why this form the haiku?" And I said simply: the haiku is a fascinating form in that I think that this form speaks to the heart of us. It's like how sometimes you see things and you listen to something and then you get to the heart of the symphony, the heart of the jazz piece, the heart of the poem. The haiku is the heart of the poem. When you say it and you read it, then you hear the real beat of the heartbeat, that heartbeat that keeps you alive. And so what I've tried to do with this is to teach a lot of young people is that the haiku is the heartbeat, it is the heartbeat of the poem and if you embrace it, if you say it, whatever, then you will learn really truly what a heartbeat means. And then you will not want to in any way kill another human being who has that heartbeat.

So I do exercises with young people, I make them face each other, and I take my right hand and I put it on my partner's heart, and my partner takes his or her right hand and puts it on my heart, then I take my left hand and put my hand over his or her hand, and the same thing happens. And then I say to the class, to the group, "Stop. Quiet now. Let's listen to each other's heartbeat." And we listen to each other's heartbeat and a miracle happens in that classroom or that auditorium or wherever we are. Once young people listen to each others heartbeat, my dear sister, they don't want to hurt someone, they don't want to curse someone out, because what they're doing is they're hearing another human being, and we never take the time to listen to each other's heartbeat, do you know what I'm saying? And you listen to that heartbeat, and it's a constant, and that heartbeat goes around the room, and that's an amazing moment. And then when you drop your hands, people stop and look at each other, you know?

And they turn and they look at you, you know? Up there, the teacher, the professor, and then there's a different feeling now in that classroom, that's important that we began to ask each other to listen to each other's heartbeat. And the haiku helps us hear the heartbeat of each one. The haiku that I recited, was one that I had done in Beijing. When I got up to climb the Great Wall of China. It was a Monday morning. So I called home to my children when they were really little little. And I said, "Hi, It's mommy. I'm calling from Beijing – at that time Peking – China. I can't talk long." And they said, "Did you get the sword? Did you get the hat?" And I said, "Yeah, yeah. But I just want to say, you know, hello, on Monday morning." Then all of a sudden, they stop their little two-year-old chat and said, "Aunt Sarah Aunt Sarah ... It's Sunday but mommy says is Monday." So, it was so hard to explain that to two-year-olds so I wrote a haiku for them later on, but said, "Let me wear the day well, so when it reaches you, you will enjoy it." If I learned how to wear the day while obviously in Beijing, by the time they got the haiku in New York City, right? They would have to wear the day well, and that evening, at the University of Beijing, I read that haiku and one of the officials stood up and said "Ah Professor Sanchez, if we here in the East, learn how to wear our days well, by the time you get the day, you will be obliged to wear it well, and then perhaps we will have peace."

**TC:** In other words they got it.

**SS:** They got it. And this is what is at the core of the haiku – is to bring some peace to this thing called poetry, this thing called life, this thing called eyes and heartbeat. Our young people need a little peace, you know, they are so inundated with noise from the idiot box, the television noise, noise from the radio, noise from the music you know, and you, if you walk and talk and noise, then you never hear your own heartbeat or the heartbeat of anyone else. If you walk and talk with so much noise, you see, you know, you don't see what is human out there. So we're saying, I'm saying I'm going to quiet it down just a little bit for you. And once we listen to each other's heartbeat, we'll survive better than how the country wants us to not survive in a sense.

**TC:** Thank you so much for that. Thank you. Thank you.

**SS:** You are more than welcome my dear sister.

**TC:** We were informed recently that sister Carolyn Rodgers[4] made her transition. And I wanted to ask you about Lucille Clifton[5] and Carolyn Rodgers. I just wanted to get your thoughts on these two women.

**SS:** My dear sister you know, I was in Michigan, I think at Ann Arbor, when I got the news that Lucille Clifton died in February. And I was on the road, and was able to make it to her memorial. And then I was at home and I got a call that Sister Ai,[6] you know, the sister who writes the name A-I and she pronounced it "I", she died from breast cancer at the early age of 63. And then I was in Chicago in, I want to say February or March, at the DuSable Museum? For the Freedom Sisters exhibit; I brought that down for you to see, the Freedom Sisters exhibit. And I was asked if it was okay if sister Carolyn Rodgers and sister Angela Jackson read with us? And another young poet who was in Chicago, I said, that'd be fine. I haven't read with them in a long time. And so I saw Carolyn, for the last time then, and we exchanged telephone numbers, and she was frail. But you know, even though she was frail at the time, we didn't expect her to die. But you know, we're talking about those three women, great poets, women poets or African-American women poets, women who taught us about our womanhood; women who taught us about the world; women who made a line that we would lean back on and laugh, you know, and say, "That's right, girl, you got it," you know, whatever. So it is indeed a loss. And so finally, you just stop and say, "Okay, enough is enough. That's three African-American women poets. Let's stop, you know, at this point in the year 2010." Right? But they were wonderful poets, and they will be greatly missed, my dear sister.

**TC:** I was in Chicago at the end of March, and I was unable to get to the DuSable. But I heard about the exhibit. I wanted to see it. But I'm at least glad I did get the chance to meet some members of Ida B. Wells Barnett's family and I got the opportunity to stand in front of her gravesite.

**SS:** Wonderful.

4 Carolyn Rodgers (1940-2010) was a Chicago-based poet who was associated with the Black Arts Movement, attending writing workshops led by Gwendolyn Brooks and through the Organization of Black American Culture. She co-founded Third World Press in 1967 with Haki Madhubuti, Johari Amini, and Roschell Rich.

5 Lucille Clifton (1936-2010), author of numerous books for adults and children, was a poet, writer, educator, state of Maryland Poet Laureate and a two-time finalist for the Pulitzer Prize for poetry.

6 Ai (1947-2010), was born Florence Anthony and legally changed her name to Ai which means "love" in Japanese. She was the author of eight collections and was a National Book Award for Poetry winner as well as an American Book Award winner.

**TC:** So I was able to do that. I'm sorry I did not get to see the exhibit. But you've been doing a lot. You've been moving around a lot

**SS:** Yeah, I've been with that Freedom Sisters exhibit. You can have that if you'd like it.

**TC:** You're giving that to me?!

**SS:** This is where we were in Dallas. And these are the local ones. Sister Pamela who worked for Ford is the one who had the idea for this whole idea of Freedom Sisters. So there are 20 African-American women ...

**TC:** Right. I heard about this last year when it left Sacramento

**SS:** And of course, they were, they selected twenty, fifteen had made their transition. And there were five who were still kicking. Dr. Height[7] was one of the five still kicking. And so you know, I'll be going down to her funeral, you know, soon as I get back, back East.

**TC:** I know Kathleen Cleaver[8] is one

**SS:** Yes, and sister Myrlie Evers[9] is another one. Charlayne Hunter-Gault and myself, we're the four last ones kicking. And it was quite an honor. In fact, my sister, when I was called there from Cincinnati, and asked about this, I said, "My dear sister, what an honor, I said, but I can give you the names of about 100 other Black women who could be there." And they listened very carefully. They said, "Well, one, we wanted a writer, and secondly, we chose you, do you want it?" And I said, "Well, yes, I am, I am very humbled by this." And so I did, it was very, very good, because you meet all these school children who come in, and you get a chance to talk to them. And I talked to them about myself as a writer, but other people as writers also too, so I can spread the word about all the other writers who are writing out there, you know, sister Maya, sister Toni, Sister Carol and sister Lucille, sister Nikki, you know, all of these, sister Alice, all of these women who are working. June Jordan, all these people who have been working and have passed away, but celebrate these women writers who are an amazing group of women who have what I call "Stir It Up Literature in

---

7 Dorothy Height (1912-2010) was an African-American civil rights and women's rights activist. Height is credited as the first leader in the civil rights movement to recognize inequality for women and African-Americans as problems that should be considered as a whole. She was the president of the National Council of Negro Women for 40 years.

8 See note on Kathleen Cleaver, page 105

9 Myrlie Evers (born 1933), civil rights activist, is the widow of fellow activist Medgar Evers (1925-1963). He was assassinated by the Klu Klux Klan outside his home in Jackson, Mississippi.

America," has made American literature live, come alive, and say "indeed, you know, I am here," right? These African-American women are here and will be here for a very, very long time. And looka here.

So yeah, it is an honor to be a part of this Freedom Sisters exhibit. I've been on the road for this because we've been in Cincinnati. We've been in Sacramento, Chicago, went to the Birmingham Civil Rights Museum and the Memphis Civil Rights Museum. Sister Myrlie Evers and I stood on the balcony where Martin [Luther King] was assassinated. And then she was walking through this great exhibit and she came face to face with her husband's big picture. And we just stood there holding each other. And then we passed by Malcolm on one side, and there was my poem to Malcolm there on the side. So it was, it was just amazing. It's been an amazing experience.

And most amazing, because looking at having a chance to talk to these sisters who are still kicking, and looking at Dr. Height also to, coming out every day, dressed beautifully, would have beautiful hats. And also, just as sharp as she could be. I mean, that brain was sharply sharp, if someone said something, and sometimes she would close her eyes and you think she'd happen to be sleeping. And then someone would say something, my dear sister, and she opened her eyes, and "No, that's not quite right," you know, she would correct them! And also to be down there at her place at the inauguration week, went down there, and we all stayed at her, in her building, stayed overnight, and got up the next day for the inauguration. So it was just wonderful. She was a great, great woman. So I'm so glad they're giving her a lying in state, a ceremony with her Delta sisters, and at a Baptist church, and then the next day, the third day, the National Cathedral.

And you know we don't get this with women. You know what I mean? So, when I read that, I mean, Yay, you know, this is the deal. So yes, I'm very happy. But you know, I've been on the road with this new book *Morning Haiku*. And, you know, Beacon Press is just an amazing press, when I just say you know, this is what I want to do.

**TC:** So you're traveling with the Freedom Sisters exhibit, and with your newest book, *Morning Haiku*. Are you going to be slowing down anytime soon?

[Laughter]

**SS:** Well, you know in August, Duke University will bring out my collection of plays, because, you know, I was a playwright coming out of the Black Power Movement, the Black Arts Movement rather, and, and so they are bringing it out in August. So I'll be also moving around, you know, doing some things, you know, with that. With the sister who edited that collection, and Erica Cosby illustrated my children's books, so I've just really been doing a whole lot of stuff. And, and that is so good.

**TC:** So in other words, the answer's no, you're not slowing down anytime soon!

**SS:** No! You know, you got ... Dr. Height ... look ... Dr. Height, she died and she was 98 years of age, my dear sister, right? And that woman was moving up until the time that she went into the hospital, right? So I think that's what keeps us all alive and sane and healthy. That movement that we do, always knowing that you're doing things with our people you know, and for our people and bringing knowledge also too at the same time. So that's the beauty of that.

**TC:** And that's just one of the many beauties that you represent. Thank you so much, Sonia Sanchez, for your time.

**SS:** Thank you! Thank you! Appreciate that!

# S. Pearl Sharp, Ruby Dee and Nora Davis Day

S. Pearl Sharp                          Ruby Dee

*S. Pearl Sharp is many things: artivist, author/writer, filmmaker, actor, literary editor, creativity coach, and broadcast producer and host. Ruby Dee[1] was known as an actress, poet, playwright, screenwriter, journalist, and civil rights activist. She was nominated for and won numerous awards for her work on screen, including an Academy Award for Best Supporting Actress, winner of the Screen Actors Guild Award for Female Actor in a Supporting Role, a Grammy, Emmy, Obie and Drama Desk award. She was also a National Medal of Arts, Kennedy Center Honors and Screen Actors Guild Life Achievement Award recipient. She worked frequently with her husband of 57 years, Ossie Davis.[2] Nora Davis Day, daughter of Ossie and Ruby, is an educator and philanthropist. "The Ruby and The Pearl," in a conversation about love, aired on April 12, 2007.*

• • •

I'm S. Pearl Sharp and today we'll spend the hour talking about love with our most cherished Queen Mother, actress and author Ruby Dee and her daughter Nora Davis Day.

---

1 Ruby Dee (1922-2014) was an American actress, poet, playwright, and activist. She was known for her roles in *A Raisin in the Sun, Do the Right Thing*, and *American Gangster*. Dee was also a civil rights activist, working alongside her husband, actor Ossie Davis. She was awarded the National Medal of Arts and the Kennedy Center Honors for her contributions to the arts.

2 Ossie Davis (1917-2005) was an American actor, playwright, and activist. He was known for his roles in *Do the Right Thing, The Cardinal*, and *Grumpy Old Men*. Davis was also a prominent civil rights activist and worked alongside his wife in the struggle for equality. Ossie Davis delivered the eulogy for Malcolm X.

Ruby Dee blew into Hollywood like a swirling Santa Ana. In just four days, she filmed a guest star role for the TV series CSI, did several book signing events with a newly published collection of her husband's speeches and essays, and received a Grammy nomination for the spoken word recording of *Ruby and Ossie Davis: A Joint Autobiography.* Ruby, Nora and I sat down to talk on February 12, 2007. Sit back and dip into the wisdom of the one and only Miss Ruby Dee.

**S. Pearl Sharp:** I want to talk about with you, especially about love.

**Ruby Dee:** Love, oh my.

**SPS:** About the love of your art, love of community, personal love. And for the starting point, one of the things that I love most about you and Ossie is that you had this great talent and skill and you could awe us with it, but you always connected it, you always used it to enlighten the community, to protect the community to educate them to defend that kind of love. People seem to be hesitant to go there.

**RD:** When I think about love, I think about it mostly as an aspiration. And I think why it's been so hard to achieve. It was like democracy, you know, love is something we're still reaching for. And, and we're making some progress. And we see great examples of it among peoples, among people we know. But that is still an aspiration. It hasn't yet clicked in the sense of our everyday lives. When I think of love, I think of it as an emotion that goes way beyond yourself and translates and into something much more universal than we than we were accustomed to, to practice it because I'm thinking the personal love spirals into something that transcends itself into a wider, wider area. So that because people can't possibly live in a society where where they kill each other, or anybody goes hungry, where children are homeless, and families are homeless, you understand, and there's war ...

**SPS:** But yet we do that.

**RD:** We're evolving. We have a notion. And we're living around the edges of the notion of love. And we see some shining examples of it, what we think is love you know? It is it's a notion rather than the realization.

**SPS:** What is it in us that says, "We love and yet we still do have homelessness? We still do have murder, we still do have people doing without, abandoned children"? What do you think is that other thing in us, that keeps us from loving completely?

**RD:** There's something about having things that keeps us from realizing, completely, this phenomenon of love. Love doesn't take your life and my life to make your life. Love is seeking attributes of my life that come to me, that fulfill something about you. You see an emptiness and a need and a longing is something that compels you to want to help fulfill it. That's simplistic in the sense it's an ultimate God-driven impulse, you know? We're still reaching to understand that. It's a striving towards the realization that comes to me of your purpose on life, as it is in my power to help with that, and if we're fortunate enough, seeing beyond our own wants and needs to the spiritual, universal needs of other people. There's something about it that is all tied in with other people. It's something that defies specific definitions. It's like the air we breathe. It's like, a heartbeat. It's a life force thing.

We're thinking "thy kingdom come, thy will be done." Thy kingdom come." We've mistaken something we've, we've missheard. It was thinking, "thy thingdom come," you know? And that's a mistaken notion that's blocking up our path. It's like going through the wilderness in a forest and chopping down the trees, and destroying everything and thinking that's going to help us see, get towards the light that we get out of our lostness, find our way. And it's it is doing just the opposite. It's hampering our way, hampering our journey to the sea, or to the heavens, but we continue to hammer and hammer away in the direction that doesn't lead us to the light.

**SPS:** "Thy thingdom come," I like that.

**RD:** What's happening in our world, now, are we really thinking that all the things we own, the gouging of the earth and the seeking of wealth for wealth's sake is what is will bring us fulfillment and satisfaction? But there are creatures in our midst now who are trying to show us one of the components is knowing that nothing that you own can bring you joy, and can bring you happiness, nothing, you don't own anything that doesn't own you, that things are a form of enslavement. You know?

**PS:** Let me share this with you. My film is called *The Healing Passage: Voices From The Water*. And when I was working on it, I went to a healing passage.

**RD:** Healing passage.

**SPS:** And its cultural artists, Tom Feelings,[3] Isaye Barnwell from *Sweet Honey in the Rock*. Some of the other artists, they're looking at the residuals from slavery, the present day residuals. So I had the film channeled, actually had some channelers, who channeled the film because I wanted to make sure I was doing the right thing. The message I got back was that the Ancestors were very upset with us because we were putting so much emphasis on the pain and the loss and the hurt, and not on the love that existed in that time that existed in our people. And I just wanted to share that with you and see if you had any thoughts on it. We don't include the love that might have existed among our people. When we talk about slavery, when we look back at that.

**RD:** I can see what that that perspective would, would be a dam against love; if you're looking at it like looking at the hole in the donut and not the donut. If you're going to be satisfied in any way, you really have to put aside that which you do not want and concentrate on that which is most desirable, that you can achieve for yourself and others despite all appearances, so you give your advertising space to those things that you then have to be realized in order to achieve a wholeness of spirit. And body and soul for yourself and other people.

So in terms of slavery, there were such notable examples among slaves, of self-sacrifice, of moving towards the light, towards the divine promise, we don't hear those stories. There was a selflessness amongst slaves that we don't talk about. I think some of the things that are with us, even today, particularly in terms of Black women who sacrificed so much so that their children could live, and could go to school. And I've seen examples in my life of people who, with the only joy they had, was in seeing that their efforts, and the things they did enabled somebody else, to, to enable their children and their husbands to move forward. They say, "Here's my back, here's my shoulder." And the thing about that, so wonderful, in that process, the back and the shoulder, gets stronger, it has the energy that emanates, is filled with the kind of status spiritual satisfaction you want to send. When you see the results of people who have families and communities and worlds. And people don't call it sacrifice. It's just something we have

......................................

3 Tom Feelings (1933-2003) was an artist, cartoonist, children's book illustrator, author, teacher, and activist. He focused on the African-American experience in his work. His most famous book is *The Middle Passage: White Ships/Black Cargo.*

to do. A lot of slavery was tied up in that kind of sacrifice, though. We don't hear about that.

We hear about, we do hear about the the cruelty and the lack, and the selfishness ... because it's so devastating. And its impact in the general society. But when they, when the general society decides that one way to achieve love is, is in all instances, to practice it, no matter what it is, it is all tied up and forgiveness is tied up in being able to envision a wholeness in yourself, to affirm your wholeness, and to see it in other people, is light recognizing light. It's light recognizing light, it's not a study of darkness, this business of love, and coming into an appreciation of each other's virtues. Love is a determined effort to open the doors to other people's virtues, as well as your own. It has to do the mirror recognition. Recognition of the divine spark in in every living creature, you know, and you recognize it because you feel it. A roomful of laughing people will make you laugh, you understand, at something like that. So you say well, how do I bring laughter here? So not only so that those people can laugh, but there's hope I can also have.

**SPS:** Ruby Dee and Ossie Davis met in the theater world in New York City in the 1940s. They became true partners, working together in the theater in films and traveling the world with concert readings of the work of Black writers. They have always been vocal and present to support civil rights and human rights issues. They produced a radio series for three years, several plays, a PBS television series and three talented children. When Ossie passed in 2005, they had been married for 56 years.

You and Ossie, I'm sure you know, were our number one couple, our King and Queen couple. And you didn't have any decision about how that was our choice.

[laughter]

**RD:** Yes yes yes

**SPS:** But you and Ossie were role models for many people. And would you share with me a little bit about love in that situation, not the young love when you first met, but the kind that carries you through all the years that you were together?

**RD:** It is, again, is the aspiration towards it, you think you're in love. We think we're in love, I think, at some point in our lives, we try to describe that feeling. But after you've been together a number of years, and lived in the world a number of years, you discover something that may be called love. If, for instance, even the most backward person in the world is born, that we might consider backward or lacking in something, is born with that an absolute source of completion in terms of what the entity was put here for in the first place. It's something like that, that I think happens between people who want the best for your children, your family, and you would even lay down your life for that completion, to get that person on the road to the recognizing of that center, that divine spark within themselves. Some is easily available and in some people we recognize it, and they can recognize it in themselves. And other people, love leads us to help them find it, but also in marriage I've glimpsed it.

**SPS:** Wait, all of those years that you were married, you just glimpsed it?

**RD:** I think you have moments of absolutely knowing it. But to glimpse it is like a universal, great miracle. Just to glimpse it in its moment. You know, it's like you can look, look through the sky and see everything, you can see everything in the universe in a moment. When you when you glimpse love, glimpse it, I think that that's an enormous gift. Because when you glimpse it, you have to know it – it doesn't land on you and bounce off. It is an attribute that you have to absorb. It changes you, I think.

**SPS:** If you claim it it changes you.

**RD:** It claims you.

**SPS:** To talk about mother-daughter love, so many of my friends when their daughters became teenagers it was like all hell broke out and there were these, these kind of mother-daughter wars that took place. And then after five or seven or nine years, they would come back together. I don't know if you two went through that? But just talk to me a little bit about that relationship, which I don't think Black women talk enough about, coming together, learning together growing together, evolving together.

**Nora Davis Day:** Well, first of all, I have to speak as one of my mother's daughters, I do have a sister. My sister and I have shared sisterhood and daughterhood, together. One of the things I always felt was that my mother was always honest with us. And also, I felt, I guess, I have to back up and say that one of the greatest gifts that my mother and father gave to us was each other. As a family, and we always had an extended family of grandmothers and grandfathers and cousins and uncles and aunts. And so we weren't alone in our relationship always.

Also, keep in mind that we didn't have a family that was traditional in terms of nine to five and always there. Whenever work came that they could afford to take, they took it. And by that I mean, they didn't leave us, many times when opportunity presented itself, especially mom. So one thing I could rely upon my mother was honesty. She always taught us the truth of things, the truth of love, the truth of what you can expect in a relationship, the truth of honoring other women. She always said, "If you can't say anything nice about someone, better not to say anything at all," and certainly in the business that they're in, you know, which is always full of gossip, she taught us to be supportive of each other as women. So I don't remember going through tremendous storms. And first of all [laughs], I grew up in a disciplined household, you didn't flare up so much. They didn't ask you, they told you, and you didn't do too much asking why. These days, my daughter and other young women say, you tell them something and they say "Why?" We didn't have that "Why?" It was like, "Oh, yes, ma'am." When your mother called you, you were there before she closed her mouth. It wasn't about "What?" from a distance, you know.

So she gave us a true sense of discipline, of hard work. I remember people coming to the house and saying, "[gasp] Your mother's Ruby Dee and she vacuums?!" Not only does she vacuum, she has us vacuum, and taught us the value of hard work, knowing that our generation was going to have to experience it in exactly the same way that hers did.

**SPS:** You said something very important, "honoring other women," that she taught you about honoring other women. Let's talk a little bit more about that.

**NDD:** Well, honoring other women in the context of honoring other people. But she was such a good example of a woman, I think, not just honest, but honorable, they're different, you know, those are two different things. And she taught us to look for the best and call for the best in other people. There's so much that I could say, it's just that she's been a good example, sometimes a personal example, because she's our mother, and sometimes a broader example because of the position that she and Dad occupied in the world.

**SPS:** Ruby, when you were first facing motherhood, was it scary?

**RD:** Oh, yes, I think it's scary to become a mother. You go through something very physical when you become responsible for another person's life. And it's not the same as just being responsible for yourself. And we have to learn a lot as women, because I think women need much more recognition of our importance in this world and to our families. And so there were many things to consider as we grew up. And as I'm thinking now too, one of the things I'm thinking is that when children are very small, our children don't tell us what to do. And also, you're not friends right away, your mother is not necessarily your friend. In the beginning, she's your mother. And mother means in a sense, there's a little bit of dictatorship going on there. Because we aren't equals at all [chuckles]. I am older, I am wiser, and I can't wait for your opinion, if you're about to put your hand in the fire I got to snatch you away. And I've got to make give you an order and expect you to follow it. And so there's that.

And so life has these balances. And you have to know that if you're in trouble, that you're supposed to be able to go to your parents, you're supposed to have some refuge and so forth. I'd like to see those equations strengthened a little bit. I think it would give our children a greater sense of security. And then also mothers would know when it's time to not be the dictator, when children begin to have judgment. And I began thinking that the world has to study the role of women much, much more. They have to work too hard, that the women I think need a sense of finding out who they are and enjoying life. And I think they should have a vacation. I think they should have some control over their financial affairs. This may not be always be true, because they are in charge of the family these days. But I think mothers and fathers should be in charge together. Love would see to that.

**SPS:** And I look at the young women today, I fear our young women are making decisions and making choices, presenting themselves in ways that I'm saying, if they just understood their history or if they just loved themselves more, if they just knew that divine spark. Are you seeing that or do you see something else in our young ladies?

**RD:** I see it, and I feel as if each one of us is reaching out to find the current that turns on the light, but we don't know always how to get there.

**SPS:** I call them the hoochie mamas, the sisters that are seen on the videos, basically undressed, kind of doing sexual acts, and they're very proud of themselves in most cases, that they feel that their bodies are beautiful, that they're representing themselves in a certain way. But sometimes I look at that and I say, "There was a price paid by our ancestors, for you to be able to do this." And I just wonder if, I sometimes feel like if they had more self-love, if they had that spark that you talked about, that center, that they might make some other decisions. Not everybody agrees with me. So I'm interested in how you see them.

**RD:** There's the anti-love forces, you understand, the grip of the world, I'm for doing battle to encourage the struggle towards love, but it's a dangerous one for those who come out of the dark, and live in the dark, who haven't yet understood, who haven't turned on the light in themselves, that alone helped others to find that spark in their lives. But they're dangerous and they're powerful. But I don't think they're as powerful as the forces of love. They just seem to be. Going all kinds of ways to get to love, even war is some mistaken representation of what brings us, what brings us joy, and happiness. And what brings that to other people, to people that they really love. How do we find the lark in our spirits singing? And so it's all tied up with looking outside ourselves, for the motor that keeps us running, but that spark for the center. In life, this phrase, like "The kingdom of God is within you," the kingdom of whatever religion, you know, God, Yahweh, Jehovah, is within you. Each of us comes with that center, each of us comes with that God center. And we, we, each of us comes with a flash of God, we are Gods, you know, at the core of us.

**SPS:** Talk a little bit more about war as a misrepresentation.

**RD:** War is a mistaken journey toward the kind of fulfillment that comes with the divine spark that lights the path of ourselves. We think it's in things, but it's ludicrous, it's like somebody getting buried in their Lamborghini, you know? [chuckles] It's like a dying wish, it's like there's nothing more. This is what's idiotic, or nonsensical or ridiculous. A consummation of blessings, to have everything, you know, having everything is possible, but not in the ways we presently envision, and especially when having everything means that somebody else has to go without, it sort of becomes the antithesis of the need to recognize the God path, the divine spark in each of us, for any of that to make sense.

It's like the monkey putting his hand in the jar to get the nuts that are in this bottle. And he puts his hand in the jar, and he grabs all the nuts, and because he's going to enjoy the feast. But then when he goes to withdraw the nuts, he can't get his hand out of the jar. So this is what we, as human beings do, in terms of seeking fulfillments in our lives, somebody might have to fall into an abyss. We keep struggling toward becoming the link in the chain toward making it to the better side of our nature. We haven't realized that quite yet. And we see examples of everywhere we go, we see it in our own families. We see it in our own communities. We see it among people we know who really care about the human condition, about the world, about animals, so that I want for you the best that you can be, your fulfillment gives me joy.

**SPS:** In their highest power your highest power, your Higher Ground.

**RD:** Your higher ground gives me fulfillment. And only then am I able to reach mine. So that question about willingness – we've got a job to do because I think that we women need to participate much more in worldly affairs and we need to come together because around children and marriage and husbands and war we need to take a strong stand. And I think that we can help to strengthen the love quotient in our societies. If we come together on the subject how do we love each other? I think we could stop wars. I think we're a powerful entity. We just have to find out how we do it. Maybe internet or maybe something ...

**SPS:** It's a good moment for me to ask you, if you would read one of my favorite poems that you wrote

**RD:** Which one is that?

**SPS:** "I Am Somebody"

**RD:** "I Am Somebody." This is this is something that expresses a struggle for what I believe love is, I see it. I see the capacity to love in some very famous people, I see it sometimes in the poorest of the poor, those with little or nothing. But you can see it, you see it and know it immediately. Something happens inside you. It's physical, it's spiritual, it's a hair-raising kind of thing, you know, that translates. So, I guess

*I I I*
*Oh Yes oh yes*
*I I I*
*I say I say I*
*Oh I'm I say I am*
*I am somebody*
*I am somebody*

I got this the idea listening to Jesse Jackson,[4] because we're constantly exploring this path of love, like, we will help other people to express and get over the chasms in the deep pits, in our own thinking and own relationships. And there's always somebody that becomes a match to the light that is on, on the subject of yourself.

**SPS:** And it took us a long time to be able to say I am somebody not connected to white people and trying to prove ourselves, just to know that we are

**RD:** We are somebody. Yes. And we as Black people certainly understand coming through slavery. It's been because out of necessity. We were in a position at the bottom where we could see, the bottom of the social and political and economic structure in a nation. We had to find something else that carried us through, that made us survive. In that sense, you can say that survive is a good, good term. But there's this aliveness. And because, in some of these things, I'm sure we've all felt, we've seen people unjustly treated, and we make an effort to redress the grievance, we join with other people to free somebody, we join with other people to relieve hunger and anxiety, and poverty. And we join together in our best selves to do that, and this is from the same dish as man, woman, personal love, when we get there in a relationship, and when you see it in other people, you can rejoice because you share it.

When you yourself are incredibly fulfilled in some way, it's hard to believe that other people can feel the same way. It's like ecstasy, you know, how can every creature on earth know ecstasy? But every creature does, from

---

4 Jesse Jackson (born 1941) is an American civil rights leader, Baptist minister, and politician. Jackson first rose to national prominence in the 1960s as a close aide to Martin Luther King Jr. He has also been involved in international humanitarian and peace efforts.

puppies and dogs and mosquitoes, or else we wouldn't even be here, and you recognize the fact when you relieve hunger, or unhappiness or fear, especially fear. And there's such a joy in it. When you see people satisfied and fulfilled and you come together in the moment where you may have been part of the fulfillment. And you can even love yourself and you know

*I. I. I say I am. I say I am somebody.*
*Somebody because – because you – you make me--somebody,*
*Because – because you are part of*
*Because you – you share the – the Somebodiness of me.*

*When you laugh, you make my lips a part of laughter.*
*When you cry, tension pulls me from inside.*
*When you are hungry, my food turns to poison, makes me burst*
*Bony fingers clutch my tongue when I--when I know your thirst*
*Because you are part of – because you – you share the*
*The Somebodiness of me.*

*When I see your precious blood out of place, your bones exposed in death –*
*My blood chills and stops as I try to – try to – give you breath.*
*I must keep you from all – all fear and danger –*
*I must woo your peace of mind –*
*Help you – help you find joy –*
*Help you – help you find release*
*Because you are part of – because you – you share the*
*the Somebodiness of me.*

*I cannot own that which you cannot also possess.*
*Your crime is mine, and from now on I'll confess*
*Because you are part of – because you share the*
*the Somebodiness of me.*

*You – you – you are at the other end of the steel spring of hate,*
*So I cannot hate.*
*When you know my love – my love will warm you –*
*Cleansing, deep*
*So, let me – let me take your hand. Let me touch your fingers,*
*Feel your face. Know your heartbeat and all – all your doubts erase*
*Because you are part of – because you – you share the*
*the Somebodiness of me.*

**RD:** We will fulfill in and throw each other on so many levels. You know? It's like picking up a phone and calling somebody, is the thing is not complete until you reach that person, the circuit is not complete until you somehow make the connection. A person with a depraved mind, it's the elements of love that have been thwarted in some way, but they're capable of, we're capable of, caring about each other. That same person that murders, I believe, has it too. It's something that's, we wouldn't be human, if we didn't have it in some part of us. I think that's what education is all about, is wooing the good spots in us. But every now and then it comes, the understanding of love comes through like a light from heaven, or like a light from some ethereal source. And if we're lucky, we will have experienced something like that.

**SPS:** That's when we can make change when we can change, transcend, transform, transformation...

**RD:** Transformation, yes. But love is a kind of energy too that can fall on you like stardust or something like that is something but very, very real. This business of love, and when,the essence of it lands on you, you're a transformed person. You know, and it opens you to be beyond yourself, it opens you up to be each other, we can be each other. I'm still working on it.

**RD:** If you had to pick one word, to describe the bond that you have with each other, what would it be?

**NDD:** After you, mom

**RD:** That describes a profound understanding and deep respect that that would govern a good relationship between mothers and daughters. And I suppose the same thing applies to fathers and sons. And but I think, there's something about mothers, because you really are working for the people that you bring into this world, I would say, a profound understanding,

**NDD:** As I think about one word that would describe the relationship or the way that I feel about my mother, and you know, we all have ups and downs and ins and outs and life changes and all of that. But I think the one word that I would describe would be indestructible.

**SPS:** Thank you so much, my sisters. I'm really honored Thank you.

Isaye Marie Barnwell of *Sweet Honey in the Rock* wrote these lyrics as a mantra in the wake of the bombings here in September 2001.

*I don't have the answers to your questions.*
*I don't have the answers to your prayers.*
*But I know this is a moment of transcendence,*
*  if only we will take the time to care.*
*Let us let us rise in love.*
*Let us rise in love*
*when the universe is polarized by hatred,*
*when we ourselves have been baptized in fear*
*when some of us are paralyzed in principle,*
*when there is anger in the falling of each tear.*
*Let us let us rise in love. Let us rise in love*

*Some Of Us Are Brave* is a Black women's radio collective. Thanks for joining us today. We hope it nourished you. Big thanks to my production team engineers Mark Maxwell, Jee and Thandi Chimurenga, to EmmaLin Two Productions and again to Jee our always Smooth Board Operator today. I'm S. Pearl. Every day, rise in Love.

# Ellene Miles and Tina Mabry

*Ellene Miles is an award-winning public relations and marketing specialist. Currently the Senior Vice President of Global Intersectional Marketing at Sony Pictures Entertainment/Motion Picture Group, she has worked in partnership with virtually every major studio in Hollywood for more than 20 years. Tina Mabry is an award-winning film director, producer and writer.* Mississippi Damned, *her directorial debut, won top awards at numerous film festivals throughout the U.S. Aired January 29, 2011.*

• • •

**Ellene Miles:** I am Ellene Miles, your host, and we are in conversation with writer, director, and all-around filmmaker, Miss Tina Mabry. Her feature directorial debut is *Mississippi Damned*, it will be running on Showtime throughout February, as part of their Black History Month programming – today, on *Some of Us are Brave.*

Tina is a graduate of USC School of Cinema and Television, and was named among the 25 New Faces of Independent Film in *Filmmaker* magazine, in July 2009. She was recognized by *Out* Magazine as one of the most inspirational and outstanding people of 2009. She was featured in *The Advocate* magazine as part of their Top 40 Under 40 – which features top 40 individuals who are raising the bar in their respective fields. Recently Tina has been named as a James Baldwin Fellow in Media by United States Artists – a national grantmaking and artists' advocacy organization. Tina, welcome to *Some of Us Are Brave.*

**Tina Mabry:** Thanks for having me.

**EM:** Tell us a little bit about your new film, which is your feature directorial debut, *Mississippi Damned*.

**TM:** Well, *Mississippi Damned* is a true story and it's based on my life. It follows three Black kids in rural Mississippi and how they each individually struggle to get out of their dysfunctional situation with their families, so we're talking about molestation, alcoholism, abuse, and it's about how do you break a cycle when you have no examples to follow? So, it was important to me to try to have a story that would echo some of the things that I had occur in my life, but at the same time have a message about trying to move beyond what your immediate situation is – to try to get something better even though you don't know anything else.

**EM:** Where are you from?

**TM:** I'm from Tupelo, Mississippi, the birthplace of Elvis Presley, I'm afraid that's our claim to fame. [Laughter] that's all we pretty much have as far as people know our town. But we set the film in Herford County, Miss. – which is a completely fictional place (laugh). But we wanted something that would somehow capture the essence of where I grew up – in a small, rural town.

**EM:** How long have you been in southern California?

**TM:** Ooh, god, I moved to Los Angeles, about 10 years ago. So, I'm still a southerner, I'm not letting that go, but, I've definitely been away from home for a while.

**EM:** And would you say it was quite a culture shock to come to a big town like this?

**TM:** Oh, yeah (laughs) it was completely a whole 'nother kind of beast to tackle. The one thing I guess I do miss about being in the South is kind of the personal relationships and the – just the kind of coziness that we have in the South. And I guess our lil southern drawls that we have – I kind of miss that. But the thing is, you know, I wanted to be a filmmaker, and I didn't see anyone making films in Mississippi at that time. And so I knew I either needed to go to New York or Los Angeles to fulfill that dream, and USC was my top choice, the film school – so, thankfully I got accepted, that helped – (chuckle) but I moved out here before I got my acceptance letter. And I've been here ever since.

**EM:** One of the recurring themes in your film, that I picked up on, is escapism. You in your personal life wanted to get out of your small town, and also in the film, the character of Kari is really trying to get out of town. Tell us a little bit about her character and who plays her.

**TM:** Kari, we have two different time periods in the film. It starts in 1986 and then picks up in 1998. For the young Kari, we have Kali Russell playing her. And for the adult, Tessa Thompson, who was just in *For Colored Girls*. Her character is based on me, in a way, which is always difficult to kind of craft a character, after yourself, but, she's basically just a caregiver, you know, in her family. She takes care of everyone, but rarely takes care of herself. And while she has a dream to move out of her situation and to use education as that vehicle to do it, she's hesitant to go, because of her family situation and feeling remorse, if she gets out of a situation that is dire. And to leave her family behind in that, to try to do something more, I mean, it's a difficult decision for her to make.

**EM:** Was it difficult to expose this to your family? I mean, you made a film about your own life and there's some pretty – you know – heady topics that are explored in the film, was that difficult to share with them?

**TM:** Oh, it was definitely difficult. Always, people ask me, you know, "Has your family seen the film?" That's the main question. And I'm like, "Yeah, I took it to 'em at Christmas. You know, that cheery time of year? [Laughter] When you want to show this kind of movie, the deep drama?" But, my family knew, they knew I was writing the screenplay, when I was doing it, so it was never a secret. But, I was a little bit scared to show 'em the final product. I guess, one, you really want people to enjoy your work, but then, two, you know I didn't know how they would take it, seeing some of the images and reliving some of the incidents.

But, the thing is, we watched it, we had some moments where we cried. Lord knows we laughed. And it was hard to watch certain things that we had gotten over. But at the same time they felt at the end that it was very true, it was honest, and that was the way that we were. And they were really happy with the final product of it. And my sister, who's based on the character of Lee, played by Chastity Hammet, she said she felt like a mirror was held to her face for the first time. She really couldn't understand, at the age of 17 or 18, why she was in that situation. And looking back on it, and especially from another person's point of view, she understood why she didn't have certain choices and why she was stuck in Mississippi, tryin' to be an out lesbian in a small town.

**EM:** Not easy to do, I would imagine [Laughter]

**TM:** No, not at all [Laughter].

**EM:** One of the other issues in the film obviously is pretty glaring, and that is child molestation. I think in the Black community it's one of our overall dirty little secrets. Was that particular aspect of the film more difficult than other parts to film?

**TM:** The actual production was a little bit difficult. In the 1986 scenes we're dealing with two young actors, and I'm very very protective (laughs) of all my actors, so I wanted to make sure that they were comfortable with it. And we had talked to their parents, during the casting process, and I'd explain how the cinematographer was going to shoot it, that we had all of that mapped out – but in the midst of actually shooting that scene, we realized, you really couldn't tell, you know, if she was being molested or not. And I'm not going to put my actor, actress in a very wrong situation. I don't want her to get molested for real. So, I, we ended up having to change a couple of things, to maybe still get the point of the scene, but we had to adjust it. And it took us a long time. And, kind of, bless his heart, the young actor playing Sammy, Malcolm David Kelly, he was so nervous during the scene, his lavalier mic, you could hear his heart beating through it. So, we couldn't use that track (laughs) in the sound cutting of the film. But he played it perfectly on screen, and seemed very calm, cool, and collected, but you know that lavalier was letting us know, he was really nervous. And I guess I was nervous, too.

**EM:** What are some of the joys and some of the perils of independent filmmaking?

**TM:** Oh, god, I can go on for days, I guess. The joys of it is that you really get a chance to tell, I think, very human stories. You don't have to worry about the commercial appeal, where a lot of times, films kind of hold back, they sugar-coat a lot of things, so you get a chance to hit issues that aren't prevalently talked about. You tell it like it is. But the problem is, at the same time, you're not mainstream, so how do you get it to the public? And that's the problem that a lot of independent filmmakers face. And so you know you gotta find a way to distribute your film, get it to your audience, and at the moment we're all struggling to get that to happen.

**EM:** And who would you describe as your ideal audience for this film? Who do you want this film to reach?

**TM:** It's hard to pin down a certain audience for it, because we definitely see a variety of people become attracted to it. And I think that's the beauty of the film, it's very universal, has a lot of universal elements in it that people can relate to. I often describe it as the kind of film you know where the secrets you sweep under the rug, things we don't talk about but you don't have to look any further than just across the street to see it happening. And so it's something that transcends race and gender and sexual orientation, and I think that's something that attracts people to it.

**EM:** Absolutely. You are kind of an inspiration, I'm sure, to quite a few young filmmakers out there. What inspires you each day to kind of get up and tell the stories that you want to tell?

**TM:** The thing that really inspires me is that if I don't tell it, who will? As I grew up I watched a lot of films, in my little small town, cause we didn't have a lot of stuff to do. But I never saw a lot of films that represented me. Or my people, where I was from, my community. And so I waited for a long period of time for an artist to emerge and do that – then I realized as I got older, "Let me do it." And so I think it's important for us to all tell our stories and to have a voice. And I come from a rather impoverished community, and I'm speaking for the disenfranchised. So for me it's important to let us have a voice, and film is the vehicle in which we can do it.

**EM:** As a woman and a Black woman, do you find that those kind of ups and downs are more difficult than other filmmakers encounter? In the business?

**TM:** You know I don't know – I think it's hard, at the moment, for everybody, given the state of independent film and how the economy is. So I know it's definitely difficult for a lot of people. I think anytime you can look in mainstream, you don't see a lot of African-American female directors getting a shot at having a lot of movies. I mean, we got Kasi

Lemmons and she's had what? Three films theatrically released. That's a phenomenal director and she's only had three? Something is wrong with the system, you have to admit that – that a woman who's as talented as that has only been able to have three films theatrically released, and she's got the highest number.

**EM:** Three films, and few and far between. You know, there's many years between her releases. Gina Prince-Bythewood[1] is another one who's an amazing filmmaker, but again you know you wait long periods of time for this stuff to come out and you wonder what are the holdups and hangups, and you wonder if it's a matter of gender and class and race. Wondering if you have kinda run into that wall, through the process – this is your first feature. I'm sure you would like a long career making films. But what is your next step towards that?

**TM:** I just want to keep making movies. The best thing that we can do is to get some kind of return on the movies that we make so we can make the next one and that's the important thing, to keep it going. Because you finally get one film made and now you're out of money and the audiences aren't investing in your next project. And it somehow dies. So, as audience members, we have to realize that in order to see art that represents us, we must support it. And it's great to emotionally support it, you have to, but sometimes we have to also put our dollars behind it.

When you see the mainstream looking at independent cinema, they feel like the audience isn't there – they are looking purely at the dollar return. And it's a financial business for them and I can't [laughs] say that that's wrong, for them to look at that, but that's what they're looking at to see what the demand is. And there's nothing more disheartening than hearing studio executives tell you that Black people don't watch dramas. I grew up on dramas, I love dramas and I'm pretty good at making dramas, I got a lot of drama to tell [laughter] and I know a lot of African-American people who do like watching drama, but the reason they say that is because of the box office figures, and they don't feel that people come out enough to see those movies. But I think there's a little bit more to that, it depends on

---

1 Gina Prince-Bythewood (born 1969) is an American film director and screenwriter. She became the first Black woman to direct a major comic-book film, *The Old Guard* (2020). She earned nominations for Best Director at the Critics' Choice Movie Awards and the British Academy Film Awards for *The Woman King* (2022).

how you market it to your target audience, and what section of the Black community are you going for, cause we're not all just one together.

**EM:** And we're not all Tyler Perry[2] fans. I think there can be room for many more directors to tell stories, I think, it seems as if one person gets their foot in the door, i.e., a Tyler Perry, and then they just say, "OK, we've got the Black audience with him, that's all we need." But there's so many other stories to tell, as you have been saying. We're gonna get into another clip from *Mississippi Damned*, this one is really addressing one of the core issues in the Black community, which is the power of denial.

• • •

**EM:** What was it like working with Tonea Stewart[3] and Jossie Harris Thacker?[4]

**TM:** It was phenomenal. I worked with Jossie on my short thesis film, *Brooklyn's Bridge to Jordan*. So we had a relationship already when I asked her to come aboard the project. And with Miss Tonea, as I affectionately call her, it was so funny, because we're in the same sorority, and when I was an undergrad she came to speak at the university, and I went up to her afterwards, I introduced myself, and this was before I was going to make the transition to do film, but she struck me, listening to her words and where she came from, and how she got to be where she was, so it was a dream come true to get a chance to direct the woman who is one of the women who changed my life. The direction of that. And the funny part is she remembered me.

**EM:** You mentioned *Brooklyn's Bridge to Jordan*, and that's one of the films I wanted to talk about as well. Your powerful short film that I saw some years ago at the Pan-African Film Festival – I was blown away, it really stuck with me. And that short is actually a special feature on the *Mississippi Damned* DVD. Can you talk about *Brooklyn's Bridge to Jordan*?

2 Tyler Perry (born 1969) is an American actor, filmmaker, and playwright. He is the creator and performer of Mabel "Madea" Simmons, a tough elderly woman, and also portrays her brother Joe Simmons and her nephew Brian Simmons.
3 Tonea Stewart (born 1947) is an American actress and university professor. She is the former dean of the College of Visual and Performing Arts of Alabama State University in Montgomery, Alabama. She did not act full time until her retirement from teaching in 2019.
4 Jossie Harris Thacker (born 1970) is an American actress, acting coach and writer.

**TM:** *Brooklyn's Bridge to Jordan* is a short film about a mother who loses her life partner in a car accident, and has to rebuild the relationship with the couple's estranged son. We take a look in this film, politically, at the lack of visitation rights afforded to gay and lesbian couples. We made the film six years ago, and thankfully now that's something that's being rectified. But more importantly than the political aspect, the film delves into a mother and a son, so something that goes beyond just being a gay story. It has a very deep human element to it, which I think a lot of people connected to. And it did well on the festival circuit, did well on television run, so I'm really happy that we're able to share it, finally, on DVD with *Mississippi Damned* so people can take a look at it.

**EM:** That's pretty awesome. What role do you think sexual orientation plays in your films and in your work?

**TM:** It's always gonna be an element in there because that's who I am. As a lesbian woman, I definitely want to have characters that represent me to some extent. But there are certain issues, too, that I want to talk about, as a lesbian. So you see it like in *Brooklyn's Bridge to Jordan*, talking about visitation rights, you see it in *Mississippi Damned*, talking about the homophobia within the Black community. The Black southern community, to get even more specific. So it's something that's gonna keep going in my work. And I do have a lesbian character in *County Line* coming up. So I don't see myself doing a movie without having some kind of lesbian character, 'cause I want to see us definitely represented.

**EM:** That's interesting, so how is this lesbian character portrayed in *Mississippi Damned*?

**TM:** It's based on my sister, she's an alienated, secluded lesbian woman growing up in the 1980s, trying to be out, and my sister had such strength to try to do that. And I think she downplays that a lot. We talk about it now and she's like, "You know, I really wasn't that much, I had to go through kinda go through hell and back, but hey," and I'm like "No, you know, you made it a lot easier for me." I didn't come out until I moved to California, so I wasn't in my parents' home, and when I did come out, my parents didn't make much of a fuss about it. There's a ten-year age difference between us. She laid the path for me, and she took the cross on her back for me, and I can't thank her enough for that, and at the same time I feel guilty that I didn't have to go through the same thing, you know what I mean? It's – I just hate that she had to go through it alone.

When she was going through it I was seven – she was 17 – and I was trying to be there for her, but how much can you be there for someone at that young age? But she was by herself, and I think you see that a lot, it really does translate onscreen, with the character of Lee. Behind the scenes, Chastity pulled herself away from the cast, to keep trying to have that same feeling, so she never felt a part of the family. And so she even did that when we weren't on set shooting, so – which I still, I wanted her to come in and have fun with us, cause Lord knows we had a good time off [laughs] you know, off the set.

**EM:** Right.

**TM:** But she wanted to bring that and have that feeling and keep that feeling going, even when we weren't shooting, so I commend her as an actress for having the kind of dedication to do that kind of part.

**EM:** I was gonna say, that's quite amazing. Now, do you ever feel kind of a trepidation or a hesitation with regard to injecting that story line into your films?

**TM:** No, I don't. I would feel upset if I didn't. To leave it out, that would seem wrong. So I never have any hesitation of telling things that I think are true, or neglected, to kind of shine light on those things. Because if you don't, no one's gonna know about it and you also, like I said earlier, you feel like your voice is stifled. You feel like somehow you don't count. And everybody should be counted.

**EM:** Absolutely. What is the next project you're working on, and what's it about?

TM: The next project, I'm taking a little bit of a departure [laughs] from *Mississippi Damned*, and I'm doing a crime drama. It's called *County Line*.

**EM:** OK

**TM:** And it's about a small town southern sheriff who has a secret drug alliance with his family friend. And his son becomes addicted to the very drugs he's allowed to infiltrate his county. And so it's more the "sins of the father fall upon the son" kind of a film. But even though it has a crime drama plot to it, it's definitely still a character-driven story, really focused on the relationships between a father and a son, and the cycles that go on with that as well, so I'm really excited about that.

**EM:** We are here on *Some of Us Are Brave*, having a discussion about sexuality, and denial, and all the things that make up amazing stories in the tapestry of African-American life. There's never just one story, there's always so many. And I'm really happy that you're here and that you are on the scene to continue making stories that we all can relate to.

**TM:** I thank you for inviting me, it's been wonderful.

**EM:** I'd like to thank Tina for coming on board.

# Paula Kelly and Wren Brown

*Paula Kelly, Emmy-nominated actress, dancer, choreographer and singer, died February 8, 2020 at the age of 77. Kelly came out of retirement in 2009 to join the cast of the Ebony Repertory Theatre's production of* Crowns *by Regina Taylor at L.A.'s Nate Holden Performing Arts Center.*

*Wren Brown, descended from three generations of performers, founded the Ebony Repertory Theatre in 2007, the first and only African-American professional (Actors' Equity) theatre company in Los Angeles, and serves as its producing artistic director. Aired May 7, 2009*

• • •

**Thandisizwe Chimurenga:** This is *Some of Us Are Brave: a Black Woman's Radio Program* here on KPFK 90.7. FM Los Angeles, 98.7 FM Santa Barbara, and I am so gassed right now, I am just so cheesy. My cheeks are beginning to hurt from smiling so much. I have in the studio with me Paula Kelly and Wren Brown. And y'all just, just, if you just could just see how much I'm smiling right now. It's really embarrassing. I need to stop it. How are y'all doing today?

**Paula Kelly:** We smiling as much as you are.

**Wren Brown:** We are absolutely smiling just as much as you are.

**PK:** Same way you do.

**WB:** Thank you so much for having us here today.

**TC:** Thank you all so much for coming. I just ... first of all, I'm happy to have you all here because this is like really cool. And when I found out that *Crowns* was coming to LA I was like, "Oh, I'm so there. I'm so there." I saw it in 2005 in the Bay Area. And I was so like, "Oh my god!" This is a wonderful play. It's a hilarious play. It's a beautiful play. And I was waiting for it to come again so that I can tell people about it. And now it is coming. It is here. It's opening May 8 at the Nate Holden Performing Arts Theater, which is the home of the Ebony Repertory Theatre, of which you are a co-founder along with Israel Hicks.[1]

**WB:** Yes, that's correct.

**TC:** And Paula Kelly, who ... and you know, you know, I know how actors hate to be stereotyped. I know they do. But every time I hear that name, I think of "Leggy Peggy."[2]

[Laughter]

**TC:** I can't help it. And you've done so much in your career. I'm not trying to be disrespectful.

**PK:** Ohh, you know ...

**TC:** I mean, I think of "Dahomey Queen"[3] and you know so many people love *Spook Who Sat By The Door* and your performance. But you know, just so many different characters come to mind.

**PK:** All those things bring back such rich memories. I cannot tell you how much I was blessed to have worked with Sidney Poitier,[4] Ivan Dixon,[5] who

1 Israel Hicks (1943-2010) was an American theatre director who was best known for his stagings of the entire series of plays by August Wilson about the African-American experience in the U.S. during and following the Great Migration.

2 Paula Kelly's character in the 1974 film *Uptown Saturday Night*.

3 Paula Kelly's character in the 1973 film *The Spook Who Sat By The Door*.

4 Sidney Poitier (1927-2022) was a Bahamian-American actor, director, and diplomat. He became the first Black person to win an Academy Award for Best Actor for his role in the 1963 film *Lilies of the Field*. Later in life, Poitier served as a diplomat, as the Bahamian ambassador to Japan and UNESCO. He was an influential figure in breaking down racial barriers in Hollywood and beyond.

5 Ivan Dixon (1931-2008) was an American actor, director, and producer. He is best known for his role as Staff Sergeant James "Kinch" Kinchloe in the 1960s television series *Hogan's Heroes*. Dixon was also a prominent civil rights activist, and he participated in the March on Washington in 1963. He later went on to co-found the Negro Ensemble Company, a theater company dedicated to promoting the work of Black playwrights and actors.

directed *Spook*, Robert Wise,[6] Bob Fosse.[7] I have been blessed and touched by some of the most entirely gifted, committed people. And I mean, slave drivers as well. [Laughter] And they taught you lessons that you don't forget. You don't forget. And it's hard to think about yourself and what you have done or things that you, other people connect with you. You know, sometimes I look back and say did I do that? Was that me?

**TC:** Your career is so your career is so much more than Leggy Peggy. I just can't help it. But you studied dance at Juilliard?

**PK:** Yes, under Martha Graham.[8]

**TC:** You've been on Broadway. We know you from television. We know you from films, you've just been all over the place. [Laughter] And you, Wren Brown. If people see you they're like "I know that brother! I know that brother's face!" You're one of them folks, "I know you!" But you grew up right there in the neighborhood. And you came back to the neighborhood. Now that's something we don't always see.

**WB:** Well, I have to tell you one thing. I was literally born and raised ninety yards from where the Nate Holden Performing Arts Center is. If I have any terra firma in the world, that is my terra firma. Every qualitative experience I've ever had in my life took place on those surrounding streets. My siblings, my friends, my barber, the pharmacist, the cleaners, the supermarket...

**TC:** That's your home,

**WB:** It's home

**TC:** It's your home.

**WB:** Literally walk past where the Nate Holden Performing Arts Center is every day to go to grammar school, to go to middle school, and to play with my friends, so to be home there now in a role of cultural leadership

6 Robert Wise (1914-2005) was an American film director and producer. He began his career in the film industry as an editor, then went on to direct films as diverse as *The Day the Earth Stood Still*, *West Side Story*, and *The Sound of Music*. Wise won four Academy Awards over the course of his career, including two for Best Director.

7 Bob Fosse (1927-1987) was an American dancer, choreographer, director, and actor. He is best known for a style of choreography characterized by its sensual and provocative movements. Fosse's most famous works include the stage musical *Chicago*, the film *Cabaret*, and the semi-autobiographical film *All That Jazz*, for which he won an Academy Award for Best Director. Fosse also won eight Tony Awards for his work on Broadway.

8 Martha Graham (1894-1991) was an American dancer and choreographer who is often referred to as the mother of modern dance. She founded the Martha Graham Dance Company in 1926 and went on to create more than 180 works over the course of her career.

means the world to me and it's a great joy for me to be aligned with this august woman called Paula Kelly. As you stated, she for me, is one of our great great heroines just not within the parameters of the art, but within the parameters of all that I find good and worthy. So I'm just thankful.

**PK:** Well all I have to say is, it's bigger than "thank you." It's a blessing. And it teaches me lessons on receivership and receiving, because we think of giving and giving and giving, you know, when we perform and when we present ourselves, "Is it worthy to put before an audience? Is it worthy to bring to people?" But when you get it back, there's no bigger honor than to be remembered and take into someone's memory for their own personal tapestry, if you will. There's nothing bigger than that for someone to say, "I'm going to keep that memory for me." That's the gift. That's the biggest gift you can have.

**TC:** Okay, well, both of you, again, have done so much memorable work. You, Wren, have been nominated for an NAACP Image Award. You've been nominated, Paula, for an Emmy Award. You have also been a producer in your career you produced or was it co-produced? *Boesman and Lena*.

**WB:** Yes, with Danny Glover[9] and Angela Bassett.[10]

**TC:** That wonderful film. Regarding Azania/South Africa

**WB:** That's exactly right.

**TC:** You have let's see you, you've done Shakespeare.

**WB:** Yes.

**TC:** So many Black actors are champing at the bit to do Shakespeare, you have that in your repertoire. You've worked with Whoopi Goldberg ... *Waiting to Exhale*.

**WB:** Yes.

**TC:** Even *Biker Boys*. You've got a film coming out I believe it's called *Midnight Clear*, is that correct?

**WB:** *Midnight Clear* has already come out but the film I do have coming

---

9 Danny Glover (born 1946) is an American actor, film director, and political activist. He has received numerous accolades and nominations for his acting work over several decades and has also been outspoken on political issues.

10 Angela Bassett (born 1958) is an American actress. She had her breakthrough portraying singer Tina Turner in the biopic *What's Love Got to Do with It* (1993).

out is called *Stand* with Tavis Smiley,[11] Dr. Cornel West,[12] Dr. Michael Eric Dyson,[13] Dick Gregory,[14] Dr. Eddie Glaude,[15] and many others.

**TC:** And I believe that's going to be part of the BAD-West, Black Association of Documentary, filmmakers day of "Black Docs," which is coming up?

**WB:** That's exactly right.

**TC:** So yes, you've done so much. And now you've come back. Let's talk about that for a moment. Now my geography is off so I need you to help me a little bit. The Ebony Repertory Theatre, which is in the Nate Holden Performing Arts Center, is that on the site of the old Ebony Showcase Theatre, or is it near there?

**WB:** That's exactly right. The Nate Holden Performing Arts Center is absolutely on the site where, for over 40 years, the Ebony Showcase Theatre was.

**TC:** Now the Ebony Showcase Theatre, founded by Nick and Edna Stewart; Nick Stewart was the character of Lightnin' in *Amos 'N Andy* which you know, some people find hilarious some people find offensive. Nick's particular character whose nickname was Lightnin', he was actually rather slow. And he took a lot of heat for that character. But he also took that salary he made in Hollywood as that character and poured it into the Ebony Showcase Theatre, to have a place in the community where people could come and not only see talent, but also get the opportunity to explore their talents. And the theater is no longer there. Nate Holden Performing Arts Theater is now there, and you are the resident theater there now. So you're continuing in that legacy?

**WB:** Absolutely. And I want to tell you that as a very small child, the first marquee that I ever saw in my life was that of the Ebony Showcase Theatre.

11  Tavis Smiley (born 1964) is an American talk show host and author.
12  Cornel West (born 1953) is an American philosopher, political activist, social critic, actor, and public intellectual. During his career, he has held professorships and fellowships at Harvard University, Yale University, Union Theological Seminary, Princeton University, Dartmouth College, Pepperdine University, and the University of Paris. From 2010 through 2013, West co-hosted a radio program, Smiley and West, with Tavis Smiley.
13  Michael Eric Dyson (born 1958) is an American academic, author, ordained minister, and radio host.
14  Dick Gregory (1932-2017) was an American comedian, civil rights leader, business owner and entrepreneur and vegetarian activist. Gregory became popular among the African-American communities in the southern United States with his "no-holds-barred" sets, poking fun at the bigotry and racism in the United States. Gregory was at the forefront of political activism in the 1960s, when he protested the Vietnam War and racial injustice.
15  Eddie S. Glaude Jr. (born 1968) is an American academic. He is theChair of the Center for African American Studies and the Chair of the Department of African American Studies at Princeton University.

So when it came time for me to found my company, I founded it based on seeing that marquee and wanting to honor that tradition, because that was a tradition where I got a chance to see Abbey Lincoln[16] come to that theater and work. I got a chance to see ...

**PK:** *Pig in a Poke.*

**WB:** That's exactly right. To see so many of the great artists who were not just appearing in film and television, but were in my neighborhood in real life. James Edwards[17] had worked there. Of course, in 1949, he starred in *Home of the Brave*, but it was just an extraordinary opportunity. John Amos[18] before, you know, *Good Times* was famous, he was there and Michael Warren[19] and so many others. Juanita Moore [20]...

**PK:** Dorothy Dandridge.[21]

**WB:** Dorothy Dandridge

**PK:** The director that directed her in *Carmen*, he actually ...

**WB:** Otto Preminger.[22]

**PK:** Otto Preminger actually contributed money to keep the theater going. I went through the Ebony Showcase Theatre. *Once in a Wifetime*, it brought me in to direct that I mean, everyone has their fingers, they had their fingers on everybody.

**TC:** Everybody's got a story.

............................................

16 Abbey Lincoln (1930-2010) was an American jazz vocalist, songwriter, and actress. She began her career as a nightclub singer in the 1950s and went on to release a number of critically acclaimed albums throughout the 1960s and 1970s. Later in life, Lincoln focused more on her acting career and received critical acclaim for her performances in films such as *Mo' Better Blues* and *The Talented Mr. Ripley.*

17 James Edwards (1918-1970) was an American films and television actor. His most famous role was as Private Peter Moss in the 1949 film *Home of the Brave*, in which he portrayed a Black soldier experiencing racial prejudice while serving in the South Pacific during World War II, and later played many roles on TV in the 1960s.

18 John Amos (born 1939) is an American actor known for his role as James Evans Sr. on the television series *Good Times*. Besides many other TV roles, Amos starred in the miniseries *Roots* as the adult Kunta Kinte.

19 Michael Warren (born 1946) is a retired actor who played a major role on the series *Hill Street Blues* (1981-1987) and made many guest appearances on other television series.

20 Juanita Moore (1914-1914) was an African-American actress whose most notable role was that of Annie, whose light-skinned daughter attempted to deny her roots by passing for white in the 1959 remake of *Imitation of Life*, for which Moore received a best supporting actress Oscar nomination.

21 Dorothy Dandridge (1922-1965) was an American actress, singer and dancer. She was the first African-American film star to be nominated for the Academy Award for best actress, and in 1959, she was nominated for a Golden Globe sward for *Porgy and Bess*.

22 Otto Preminger (1905-1986) was an Austrian-American film director, producer, and actor. He began his career in the film industry in Europe and later moved to the United States, where he directed a number of highly influential and controversial films.

**PK:** Yes.

**WB:** And I just want to share with you very briefly the generational history, Mr. Stewart and my paternal grandfather, Troy Brown; my grandfather, both of my grandfather's worked in vaudeville and they both worked in blackface at points in their careers, but they were together in *Swinging in a Dream* on Broadway in 1939. My grandfather, Troy Brown Senior, and Nick Stewart. So Mr. Stewart knew me every single day of my life until his demise, but he knew my grandfather and had worked with him. My grandfather played Snout in that jazz version of *Midsummer Night's Dream* with Louis Armstrong and Benny Goodman and many others. So there was a long and rich history and, particularly, that site is so creative because in 1924, it was the site of the Rimpau Theatre, which was a silent movie house, and then it became the Metro Theatre, and of course, the Ebony Showcase was founded in 1950 elsewhere, but took over that building in 1965 until the early 1990s. So it's a rich theatrical legacy there.

**TC:** A lot of good energy.

**WB:** Absolutely

**TC:** On that corner.

**PK:** Absolutely. A lot of history.

**TC:** A lot of history. And we need to have you back to talk about that history because I know your grandfather told you some stories.

**WB:** Well ...

**TC:** I know some folk told you some stories.

**WB:** Oh, absolutely. I am, I have been a repository of the elders of my community, and certainly within my family. As I said, both of my grandfather's worked in blackface, and both of my grandmother's were Cotton Club dancers. And so I come out of a history that way.

**TC:** You're doing what you're supposed to be doing.

**WB:** Yes, it's in my blood and in my DNA, yes it is.

**TC:** It's your destiny. Right, right. Most definitely.

**PK:** No one can do it better than he can because he is he infuses us all with this energy that you feel right here and now, one hundred percent top to bottom.

**TC:** So with this energy, coupled with the energy of *Crowns*, I want to be there opening night!

**PK:** Yes!

**TC:** Man! Okay, let's talk about *Crowns*, let's talk about this real quick. The Ebony Showcase Theater is producing *Crowns*, in conjunction with the Pasadena Playhouse. Is this a usual type of thing? Or is, are the playhouses supposedly in competition with one another? How did this come about?

**WB:** Well, I don't believe in competition, I believe in companionship. And I will tell you that this is unique. I don't know that it's terribly unusual, but it's unique. And Sheldon Epps, who was the Artistic Director of the Pasadena Playhouse, before he took over as the AD there, I was in his first play that he directed there in early 1990s, and so we've had a relationship from that time, the early '90s forward. He was taught as a sophomore at Carnegie Mellon by our artistic director Israel Hicks, in the early 1970s. So there's this wonderfully rich triangulated history between we three, and Sheldon, their season there at Pasadena is in celebration of women, and its "Women: the Heart and Soul of Theater." And in early December, Sheldon phoned and said, "Wren, I would really like for you all to consider allowing us to join you to present this in both houses." That's where the rarity is. We just saw a co-production between Def West and Center Theater Group with *Pippin*, but it didn't play the Def West Theatre, it just played at the Mark Taper Forum. So this is unique and unusual in that it's playing both houses. We were the company who had announced it first and we have the rights, and so it starts at our house, beginning in previews May 5, and then it goes starting July 10, at the Pasadena Playhouse. So it's a case of real reciprocity.

**TC:** Now, the Pasadena Playhouse most recently was home to a performance of Leslie Uggams[23] in the show based on a version of Lena Horne's[24] life and it broke records?

---

23 Leslie Uggams (born 1943) is an American actress and singer. Uggams is recognized for portraying Kizzy Reynolds in the television miniseries *Roots* (1977), earning Golden Globe and Emmy Award nominations for her performance. Later in her career, Uggams received renewed notice for her role in the *Deadpool* movies.

24 Lena Horne (1917-2010) was an American dancer, actress, singer, and civil rights activist. Horne's career spanned more than 70 years with roles in film, television, and theatre. Horne advocated for human rights and took part in the March on Washington in August 1963. She continued recording and performing sporadically into the 1990s, retreating from the public eye in 2000.

**WB:** Broke box office records

**TC:** Box office records

**WB:** Absolutely

**TC:** I believe it may even have been the highest grossing in recent history, if not in their entire history.

**WB:** Absolutely.

**TC:** So ... you all have, I didn't know, you all had this history together. So that explains this co-production. So let's talk about this production of *Crowns*. How is it that the Ebony Repertory Theater's decision on staging *Crowns* came to be in your purview, can you tell me about that?

**WB:** Well, through my friendship with the playwright, the brilliant Regina Taylor. Regina came to see our inaugural production, which was August Wilson's *Two Trains Running* in October of 2008. She has known, reputationally, and has worked with, Israel Hicks who I consider a master at what he does.

**PK:** Amen.

**WB:** Regina found the work we were doing very worthy. She knew that it was well entrusted directorially to Israel, and so that's how it came about. And she said, "Yes, I would love that you would do it and afford to make its Los Angeles premiere, because as wildly successful as *Crowns* has been all over the country, it has never played in Los Angeles." It played at the San Diego Repertory Theatre, but never in Los Angeles proper. So we consider ourselves tremendously fortunate to be able to present the Los Angeles premiere and co-production with the Pasadena Playhouse

**TC:** And it was the most produced musical of 2006.

**WB:** And it has actually done that a few years.

**TC:** Y'all got enough seats over there?

[Laughter]

**WB:** Yes, I hope that we absolutely can't sell another one. I want that to be the case.

**PK:** I just wanted to just confirm, this is the first Equity contract endeavor for the Ebony Repertory Theatre too, which also makes it important for me, as a standing union house.

**TC:** Now what does that mean in terms of equity?

**WB:** Equity is the professional union for working theatre actors. And we are the first African-American Equity theatre in the history of Los Angeles. We produced our inaugural production under that banner, and *Crowns* now the second of our first season. And we're very proud of that because my grandfather, my maternal grandfather, used to say to me, "Amateurs get trophies and pros get paid." And it's vitally important that you honor people who are professional with professionalism. And people will work for lesser salaries if they know that you are encouraging through dignity, integrity and grace, a disposition that they can embrace. But being there working at a professional standard, contributing to the pension and health, and the welfare of people's lives is vitally important to us. So Paula, thank you very much for that confirmation.

**PK:** Absolutely, because it's important. Lots of us work for nothing. Gladly, gladly, work for nothing. Just want to be a part of something.

**TC:** We're witness to that, the work that you all do for free for the love of it, for the love of community for the love of acting, in various ways, we're witness to that.

**PK:** Yes, this combination, as Wren says, gives us dignity, pension, insurance, welfare, we can survive beyond that. We're going to do it anyway. We're gonna do it, and wait till you see and hear our cast.

**TC:** So now the cast members of *Crowns* that is going to be playing there, you're playing the part of Mother Shaw. Mother Shaw is the grandmother, she's not the wife of the pastor?

**PK:** No

**TC:** She's the grandmother ... I remember, of course, the grandmother but also remember the pastor's wife, for some reason she stands out in my mind.

**PK:** Got to! And She's played brilliantly by Ann Weldon.

**TC:** Vanessa Bell Calloway is also going to be in this production. She's playing the part of Jeanette.

**WB:** Yes. Dawnn Lewis was originally cast as Jeanette, but she needed to bow out, and it has been our great good fortune that a consummate professional, Vanessa Bell Calloway, has come in as if she'd been with us since day one. I mean it has been seamless. And so I just want to really celebrate that extraordinary wife and mother and artist that is Vanessa Bell Calloway.

**TC:** And Suzanne Douglas?

**WB:** Luminous.

**PK:** Luminous, brilliant. I believe she left New Jersey, to make this journey with us, from New Jersey, for this length of time. And I'm telling you she's going to be a light in the theater, a light, just a total light for all of us in the cast, as well as the audience.

**TC:** Now Suzanne has played in *The Parenthood, The Inkwell, Tap, Jason's Lyric, How Stella Got Her Groove Back.* She's also starred on *The Cosby Show,* and *The Parkers.* Vanessa Bell Calloway, of course we remember her from *Biker Boys* and *Coming to America.* Ann Weldon, *Death and Texas,* I'm not familiar with that. The festival hit *I'm Through With White Girls,* definitely not familiar with that one. She also starred in *Roots.* Tell me about Ann Weldon.

**WB:** Ann Weldon is an extraordinary artist. She's the sister to Maxine Weldon, a wonderful singer, and sister to the wonderful actor Charles Weldon.

**TC:** I'm familiar with Charles. I believe Maxine was in concert or is about to be in concert somewhere in Watts

**WB:** But Ann Weldon was the first African-American leading lady, as a part of a repertory theatre company, at the American Conservatory Theatre in San Francisco under Bill Ball. She played Broadway during those seasons. *Time* magazine did a wonderful exposé on Ann in her capacity as leading lady at ACT in the late 1960s and early 70s. She's a trooper of the first order and a lady. She's elegant, she's brilliant, and ...

**PK:** Funny

**WB:** Funny. Oh Ann is funny.

**PK:** A glorious voice, a glorious voice, but she's playing the preacher's wife. And you'll ...

**TC:** I'll see why

**PK:** You'll say amen

**TC:** I'll say 'amen' when I see her. Angela Wildflower Polk is playing the part of Yolanda, Yolanda is the young woman who comes down south in the production. Tell me about Angela.

**PK:** Angela has one of the most, how can I say it? Angelically soulful voices I've ever heard. It comes out of nowhere. It's pristine, it's effortless, and she has the face and the attitude to prove it, to bring it all to fruition. She is a one hundred percent package and someone to really, really watch.

**WB:** I have to just echo that, she is what we would call the newbie in terms and she's the youngin'

**PK:** She don't seem like it

**WB:** But I tell you, she has wisdom. Her artistry is so rich and so deep. She's so completely present in all the work that she does. We're very, very proud to be a part of this work with Angela Wildflower Polk from Kansas City, Kansas.

**TC:** Sharon Catherine Blanks?

**PK:** Well, I gotta say this. Sharon is related to me as a cousin, okay? And we always bring this up. I remember Sharon from when she was three years old. She's Johnny Brown's[25] daughter, if you remember Johnny Brown, comedian, entertainer.

**TC:** Bookman from *Good Times*.

**WB:** That's exactly right.

[Laughter]

**TC:** These are my references I can't help it.

**PK:** Sharon can tell you a thousand stories in in two minutes.

[Laughter]

**PK:** She is a light in the cast, but wait until she's a light on stage as a human being. She's a new parent, and she's worked very, very hard with in the aspect of foster care and all of that she's thrilled for all that. She's a light in

---

25 Johnny Brown (1937-2022) was an American actor and singer. He was most famous for his role as building superintendent Nathan Bookman on the 1970s CBS sitcom Good Times. Brown portrayed Bookman until the series was cancelled in 1979.

the cast, but she plays, in one section she plays, she plays the part of Velma. But in one section she transforms into a character called Mrs. Mary who just loves to sing. And when she sings "His Eye Is On The Sparrow" there's not going to be a dry eye or, or a silent voice, in the house.

**TC:** Wow.

**PK:** Just period that's all I can say.

**WB:** That's right.

**TC:** And rounding out we've got of course Clinton Derricks-Carroll. He was in the production that I saw in the Bay Area. He's back again. I don't, you know, I get this thing, 'Do I want to tell the audience or do I not want to tell them?' But he's playing different parts. His name is "Man." One of the parts he plays is of the pastor. When that pastor got up there and did the duck walk in full robe

[Laughter]

**TC:** That Chuck Berry[26] duck walk I almost fell out of my chair. I said "What is he doing on stage doing the duck walk?" But that's the pastor for you. But at any rate, Clinton Derricks-Carroll who's rounding out this cast, ain't no slouch up in here obviously. Y'all not, y'all not playing y'all serious!

**WB:** Well, we're very serious. Clinton Derricks-Carroll is a consummate artist. He's so soulful, and rich, and so present, you know what I mean? And he's generous. He's so generous

**PK:** And genuine

**WB:** Yes.

**PK:** Genuine and kind and compassionate. Compassionate, he gives all, all the time. I remember Clinton, and Cleavant, when we were doing the *Black Alice,* a version of *Black Alice in Wonderland* with Vinnette Carroll[27] who adopted Clinton and Cleavant, as her sons, hence the last name Carroll.

---

26  Chuck Berry (1926-2017) was an American guitarist, singer, and songwriter who is often referred to as one of the pioneers of rock and roll music. His duck walk, a style of dancing in which the performer squats low and shuffles across the stage while keeping their upper body relatively upright, became a feature of his stage performances.

27  Vinnette Carroll (1922-2002) was a playwright, stage director, actress and the first African American woman to direct on Broadway.

**TC:** This is *Your Arms Ain't Too Short to Box With God.*

**PK:** There you go. And *Don't Bother Me I Can't Cope.*

**TC:** I'm actually not telling my age, I am younger than I look

[Laughter]

**WB:** That's right.

**PK:** But he's perfect as the part of "Man" because there's a piece of him that all of us can relate to and he can relate to all of us, which is rare, rare in one male you know, one male figure he played, and that's a part of Regina's gift too.

**TC:** This is Regina Taylor's *Crowns*: "Yolanda, a woman full of attitude, is proud to be from Brooklyn, New York. After her brother is shot and killed she is sent to stay with her grandmother in South Carolina. Reluctant at first, Yolanda accompanies her grandmother Mother Shaw," that's you Paula, "to church where she joins a strong spiritual and proud circle of women. Each has a lot to say about history, family, and hats. These ladies tell their stories as we travel back and forth in time, from the tobacco fields to the picket lines of the Civil Rights Movement, from a funeral to a baptism. And it is from these women and in these places that Yolanda learns not only what 'hattitude' is all about, but of ancient rituals, rich tradition and where she fits in." This is *Crowns,* which Regina Taylor adapted into a play from the book *Crowns,* about a photography book about Black women and their [church] hats. It is playing at the Ebony Repertory Theater, which is housed in the Nate Holden Performing Arts Theater.

I can't wait. I'm gon' be up in there. I love this presentation. I love what you all are doing. I want to be able to support you in any way possible. Thank you oh so much for coming here today. Is there anything else you want our listening audience to know?

**PK:** Don't forget Mother's Day, if you can get in, or any other day.

**WB:** That's exactly right. But you know, I'm just reminded as we leave; I was raised by women. My mother, my grandmother and great-grandmother raised me. So I have a particular affinity for the matriarchal line in my experience. But I'm reminded of that brilliant lyric by the genius

Dianne Reeves.[28] She says, *I am an endangered species / but I sing no victim songs / I'm a woman and an artist / And I know where my voice belongs.*

**TC:** Don't get me started up in here!

**WB:** So that's what I, when think about these ladies? When I think about the brilliance of Regina Taylor? I think about all of these ladies discovering and knowing where their voices belong.

**TC:** Wren Brown, Paula Kelly, thank you all so ... I can't thank you enough. I wish I could devote the whole show to y'all, but you know, there's so many haters out there. I wish I could devote the whole show to y'all. Thank you so much for coming down here.

**PK:** Thank you Thandi

**WB:** Thank you for having us.

**TC:** Thank you, and we will see you at the Ebony Repertory Theater.

**WB:** Thank you.

**PK:** Come on down.

---

28  Dianne Reeves (born 1956) is an American jazz singer. She has won five Grammy awards.

# About The Author

Thandisizwe Chimurenga is an award-winning freelance journalist based in Los Angeles, CA. She is a former Assistant Editor of the LA-Watts *Times* newspaper and a former reporter and co-anchor for Free Speech Radio News and the KPFK Evening News (Pacifica). She has been a commentator for *Hard Knock Radio,* a daily public affairs show for the Hip-Hop generation heard on KPFA Radio (Pacifica-Berkeley) and has been recognized as a "Champion of National News Reporting" by the San Francisco *BayView* Newspaper, Block Report Radio and the County of San Francisco, as well as New America Media for "Outstanding Reporting on Health and Health Care."

A writer and creator or co-creator of grassroots community media (newspapers, cable TV, radio) for over 20 years, she co-founded *Some of Us Are Brave: A Black Women's Radio Program* with others in 2003.

Her activism has ranged from electoral organizing; anti-police terror work; freedom for political prisoners and prisoners of war; to organizing against violence against women. Her first book, *No Doubt: The Murder(s) of Oscar Grant,* was independently published in 2014.

She is currently the host of *Rootwork: Getting Down to the Roots,* a show of analysis, news and interviews airing on KPFK and the Black Power Media platform.

www.ingramcontent.com/pod-product-compliance
Ingram Content Group UK Ltd.
Pitfield, Milton Keynes, MK11 3LW, UK
UKHW020919100625
6320UKWH00022B/411